COOL

As soon as he closed the door behind Dylan Hart, Alex headed for Kat's bedroom, checking his Colt .45 semi-automatic pistol. He had to get her out of the apartment and someplace safe.

It was going to take him years to forgive himself for losing her at the Botanic Gardens—if he ever forgave himself. He'd gone soft, gotten too used to never having to protect her from anything more than a bad news rock-and-roll boyfriend or the other shoppers at a Neiman-Marcus shoe sale.

But tonight. *Christ.* Tonight had been insane.

It was nothing short of a miracle that Hawkins and Hart had given her up and left.

At least that's what he thought until he entered her bedroom, saw the open window, and instantly knew he was screwed. A soft curse left his mouth as he raced for the window. One look down into the alley proved he was too late.

Damn, oh, damn. He turned and ran for the door. When he reached the street, all he could do was stand there and swear. The chop-shop boys had aced him again. Dylan Hart, Hawkins, Katya—all of them were gone.

ALSO BY TARA JANZEN

Crazy Hot

CRAZY COOL

Tara
Janzen

A DELL BOOK

CRAZY COOL
A Dell Book / November 2005

Published by
Bantam Dell
A Division of Random House, Inc.
New York, New York

This is a work of fiction. Names, characters, places, and incidents
either are the product of the author's imagination or are used
fictitiously. Any resemblance to actual persons, living or dead,
events, or locales is entirely coincidental.

All rights reserved
Copyright © 2005 by Tara Janzen
Cover design by Lynn Andreozzi

Dell is a registered trademark of Random House, Inc., and the
colophon is a trademark of Random House, Inc.

ISBN 0-553-58611-4

Printed in the United States of America
Published simultaneously in Canada

www.bantamdell.com

OPM   10 9 8 7 6 5 4

AUTHOR'S NOTE

Anyone familiar with the beautiful city of Denver, Colorado, will notice that I changed a few things to suit the story. Most notably, I took Steele Street and turned it into an alley in lower downtown, a restored historical neighborhood in the heart of Denver known as LoDo. Also, I would like to thank Nigel for sharing his encyclopedic knowledge of muscle cars—there was no question too obscure, no answer that didn't tell me more than I'd asked. A special thanks to Stan for taking me under the hood and letting me get a little grease on my hands. Any mistakes in the book are mine ... in other words, if one of these cars "splits a gut" it's because I didn't take my mechanics' advice!

CRAZY
COOL

PROLOGUE

Washington, D.C.

GENERAL BUCK GRANT, commanding officer of an outlaw team of black ops warriors known as Special Defense Force (SDF), stared down at the orders in his hand and swore under his breath. He'd been in this man's army for thirty years and seen plenty of bureaucratic nonsense come down the pike, but this took the friggin' cake. What in the hell, he wondered, was going on over at the Pentagon?

He threw the sheaf of papers down on his desk and sank deeper into his chair. Then he swore again. Politics, that's what was going on, bad politics. Nothing else could have gotten two of his SDF operators assigned to a low-level security detail for a friggin' art auction.

It didn't make any sense, especially given his team's current situation, which was going from bad to worse on the hour, every hour. He picked up the papers again, scanned the page, and yes, there it was, at the bottom, "... art auction benefit at the Denver Botanical Gardens."

Unbelievable. The brass wanted him to pull his men off a top priority mission in Colombia, South America, to do guard duty at a garden party? Davies must be out of his ever-lovin' mind to have let this get by him, but there it was, in black and white.

UNITED STATES DEPARTMENT OF DEFENSE

Office of the Honorable William J. Davies,

Assistant Secretary of Defense for Special Operations and Low-Intensity Conflict.

To: General Richard "Buck" Grant
Re: Special Defense Force (SDF)
Mission: Security Detail, Denver, Colorado

Buck,

Don't kill the messenger. I don't dream this crap up. I just expedite it. Your men have been requested for a security detail in Denver, specifically Christian Hawkins and Dylan Hart—so find them and get their butts on a plane to Denver. The CIA pulled out of northern Colombia last night. The Marines you somehow shanghaied into helping your team have also been ordered out. The mission is over, Buck, by order of the secretary of defense, and from what I can see of the scoreboard, you lost:

- **Creed Rivera**—taken hostage by the National Revolutionary Forces (NRF), a narco-guerrilla group terrorizing northern Colombia; presumed dead (Rpt. 32A.91M)

- J.T. Chronopolous—taken hostage by the NRF,
  presumed dead (Rpt. 32A.92M)

That still leaves three SDF operators running loose in
the jungle:

- Dylan Hart
- Christian Hawkins
- Peter "Kid Chaos" Chronopolous

They failed to negotiate a release, and we've run out of
time for a rescue, which leaves us with damage control
and to salvage what we can, like the lives of the men still
down there, before even more crap hits the fan.

I know your guys don't play well with others, but SDF
operators have pensions, too, Buck, unless they go
AWOL and end up with Unauthorized Absence (UA)
on their records. Don't let that happen. Bring them in.
Let them do themselves and the secretary of defense a
favor: Hart and Hawkins, August 29, suits and ties,
armed and dangerous, seven P.M., security detail for an
art auction benefit at the Denver Botanical Gardens.

You do this for me, Buck, and I'll see what I can do to
get your boys set loose on the NRF bastards who killed
Creed Rivera and J.T. Chronopolous. They were both
fine soldiers.

Buck tossed the papers back on the desk. Davies was
missing some facts. As of yesterday, Dylan was already
back in Denver. He had negotiated one release, and
Creed was only half dead. Report 32A.91M was wrong.
Buck was praying 32A.92M was wrong as well.

He checked his calendar—August 27. He had two days to get Hawkins out of Colombia and into a suit and tie. Then, when this garden party was over, SDF was going back, and they were going to be taking names the hard way.

CHAPTER

1

Two days later

TWENTY BUCKS says the guy in the Armani suit is hired muscle."

Hired muscle? Katya Dekker looked up from her auction catalog.

"Where?" She glanced around the outdoor amphitheater, her brow furrowing. She knew what her secretary, Alex Zheng, meant. She knew exactly what he meant, and she could only think of one reason for there to be any "hired muscle" at an art auction: *her.*

The thought only deepened her scowl.

She followed Alex's gaze across the delicately lit nighttime grounds of the Denver Botanic Gardens, searching through the crowd and the two dozen canopied tropical huts that had been erected for the dining comfort of the evening's guests. She found the "hired muscle" on the edge of a group of people next to the caterer's tent.

He was good, discreet, but she could spot a security

detail at a hundred yards—and he had "high-priced bodyguard" written all over him, very high priced.

"What do you think of the suit?" Alex said. "I almost bought that one myself."

"No way, babe. Too structured. Too conservative," she told him, her gaze going over the man in the distance. There was nothing particularly remarkable about him, other than his choirboy looks, his shock of silky brown hair, and the alertness of his every move—the dead give-away. He was quartering the gardens with his gaze, looking for God only knew what. Fund-raising art auctions hosted by the Denver Botanic Gardens were not hotbeds of intrigue.

"Not with my blue silk shirt," Alex countered. "So you don't know him?"

"No," she said, trying to keep her jaw from clenching, trying to hold back the first, faint teasing of the headache she felt coming on. Even for August, the day had been unconscionably hot, and for Denver unbelievably humid, and the night wasn't setting up to be much better—especially now.

A bodyguard. Dammit. She knew who was behind this, just like she knew this wasn't the sort of event that required a bodyguard. Bottles of French wine and magnums of French champagne were being opened by bartenders in tuxedos. White-boxed dinners tied with forest green bows were being delivered to the tables by waiters in tails. Every female patron at the art auction had been given an orchid wrist corsage upon arrival, and each man sported a boutonniere of exotic rain forest leaves and a bit of liana—even the choirboy. Tonight's auction was for the Amazon River Basin Coalition and in honor of the

Botanic Gardens' new orchid pavilion. Alex had designed the boutonnieres, his contribution, and they were nothing short of fabulous, very masculine, very primal. They would speak to the Rain Forest God in every man, and to his wallet, according to Alex, who had impeccable taste and instincts—two of the many reasons he was Katya's right-hand man.

His six years with the Los Angeles Police Department were another.

"What about the other man?" he asked. "Next to the Jaguar Gate."

Two bodyguards?

"My mother wouldn't dare," she muttered, biting back a curse and turning toward the Jaguar Gate, a multi-columned, elaborately constructed plywood and papier-mâché portico serving as a grand entryway into the party.

There was only one man standing beneath the fierce black cat bridging the last pair of palm tree posts, and he turned away just as she looked at him. All she saw was his back and the champagne flute in his hand as he disappeared into the trees, but that was enough to make the hair on her nape rise in sudden, unexpected awareness.

She hadn't known the first guy, but this one . . .

After a couple of seconds, she let out her breath in a soft rush and told herself to get a grip. Of course she didn't know him. Maybe it was the cut of the stranger's dark hair, longer than most of the men's at the exclusive and rather elegantly conservative soirée, that had sparked her fleeting instant of recognition. Maybe it was his height, or the way he carried himself, or maybe it had been nothing at all.

She'd been wrong before in her life, an inordinate number of times actually, especially about men.

"Your mother would dare anything she thought she could get away with." Alex belied her statement with a short laugh. "As a matter of fact, her latest pork-barreling in Congress was a consummate dare to every budget-watcher in Washington."

Katya cast her secretary an annoyed glance. He did not look like someone who read the *Los Angeles Times* and the *Wall Street Journal* every single morning of his life—but he did, religiously, usually while drinking a double espresso and wearing his autographed Lakers jersey, which he'd had his tailor integrate into a cinnabar-colored silk robe. His hair was short, jet black, expertly cut, bleached gold on the tips, and moussed to artistic perfection. He had beautiful Asian/American features, a black belt in tae kwon do, and a boyfriend he'd left in L.A. His suit *was* Armani, his shoes Chinese red, his shirt snowy white and worn open at the throat with a loosely knotted Prada tie.

She didn't know how she was going to keep him with her in Denver, Colorado, or what she was going to do without him when he'd had enough of the former cow town and hightailed it back to Los Angeles.

"That's going to cost you a mocha latte," she said. Growing up in Denver as Senator Marilyn Dekker's daughter, Katya had lived, breathed, and eaten politics every day of her life. As an adult, she didn't touch the stuff. She voted. End of story. That, however, did not dissuade Alex from keeping her informed of every maternal political detail he gleaned out of the newspapers or saw on CNN—and every bit of unwanted news cost him a latte.

"And I'm still up on you by seven for winning the point spread on the Lakers game. The last time you got a mocha latte out of me was before the last Ice Age."

True, but he didn't have to rub it in.

"Mr. Armani Suit and his friend probably don't have anything to do with me. Let's just ignore them, and maybe they'll go away," she suggested, glancing back at her catalog. She did not want to deal with unwanted bodyguards. Not tonight or any other night. "Our painting is up first. Maybe we should go check and make sure it's still in one piece."

Katya's newest addition to her art dealership business, the Toussi Gallery of Denver, had donated a large, beautiful floral painting by Oleg Henri to the auction. The staff at the Botanic Gardens had picked it up two days ago. It only made sense to go check on the painting before it went up for bid.

But Alex was like a dog with a bone.

"Sorry, luv. You're the only one here worthy of high-caliber security. My guess is your mother sicced the two freelancers on you. Though God knows why, unless she knows something we don't," he said, his tone of voice suggesting she give him her undivided attention until they figured this out. "I guess we could ask her Sunday morning."

"No, we couldn't," Kat was quick to say. Her mother was kicking off her campaign with a brief stop in Denver on Sunday, but there had been no plans for them to get together. Marilyn was too busy—thank God. Stifling a sigh, Katya looked up at him again. "My mother is paranoid."

"About everything," he agreed, tracking the choirboy bodyguard with his gaze. "But this . . . I think this is about your youthful transgressions."

He *would* bring that up, she thought, feeling the headache start to win.

"Who was it you said you ran into tonight?"

"Ted Garraty," she said flatly, hating the turn of the conversation. "But I didn't exactly run into him. As a matter of fact, I made a point of *not* running into him."

She'd gone to school with Ted at Wellon Academy in Denver. They hadn't been friends, but Wellon was small, very exclusive, and she and her date had ended up in the same crowd with Ted and his friends on prom night thirteen years ago—a night that had changed her life forever.

"Well, your mother obviously got ahold of the guest list and didn't like it."

Katya rolled her eyes in his direction. "I don't need a bodyguard to protect me from Ted Garraty, let alone two bodyguards."

But on that long-ago prom night, she had needed someone to protect her from Ted and his group of drunken friends.

Her gaze slid to the Jaguar Gate, but just for an instant before she forced her attention back to the catalog. Just about every gallery in Denver had donated something to the auction, but the Oleg Henri was a true signature piece, and she expected its sale to help launch her into the Denver art world—not that her name wasn't already about as high profile as it got in the Mile High City.

And with that unpleasant thought, she finally did give

in to another sigh. God, what an odd night. Seeing Ted had been nothing short of a ten on her weird-o-meter, and the visceral reaction she'd had to the second bodyguard had red-lined the weird-o-meter and hit an easy number one on her Don't Go There, Girlfriend list.

Bodyguards, dammit.

She'd known that returning to her hometown, the location of her "youthful transgressions," had held the inherent risk of zealous parental meddling, but she truly hadn't expected her mother to jump in with both feet at her first event. Marilyn had left her well enough alone in Los Angeles, barring a couple of embarrassing intrusions into her personal life over the last several years. Professionally, though, her mother had been strictly hands off.

But then it was here in Denver, not Los Angeles, that she had been associated with a high-profile, high-society, front-page, scandal-ridden murder of another senator's son. That sort of thing was bound to stir up even the most latent parental instincts, and Marilyn's had been pretty darn latent while Katya had been growing up—at least until Jonathan Traynor III had shown up dead in a back alley in lower downtown, a neighborhood known as LoDo, with a bullet through his brain, heroin in his veins, her phone number written on the back of his hand, and a bloodstained piece of her prom dress stuffed in his pocket.

Of its own accord, her gaze shifted back toward the gate again, and this time she let it linger.

No, she assured herself. The man who'd disappeared beneath the trees couldn't possibly be who she'd thought. A teenage car thief who had been sentenced to life imprisonment for Jonathan Traynor's murder thirteen years ago couldn't possibly be wandering around the Botanic Gardens wearing a suit and drinking French champagne. He'd been pardoned after two years in prison, justice had finally been served, but this would still be the last place he would show up, right? The last place he would ever be invited.

But for a moment, just a moment, her heart had raced and she'd remembered how it had been on another hot summer night in Denver. She'd been eighteen, a little crazy, a lot in love, and scared senseless by the intensity of living so far out on the edge she wasn't sure she'd ever get back to familiar ground. The boy had been a year older, the wild boy, the bad boy, the street thief who had saved her. That boy, the boy she'd loved, would never have murdered Jonathan, but he'd been convicted of the crime, and she'd sat by helplessly and watched it happen.

The trial had been a travesty, her silence a betrayal she still hated herself for, and deep in her heart, she knew he had to hate her for it, too.

HAWKINS drained his glass of champagne, wished it were Scotch, and took a breath.

Kat Dekker.

Son of a bitch.

His luck couldn't possibly be running that bad—except "Bad Luck" was Katya Dekker's middle name. Hell, it was her first name—Bad Luck Dekker.

He hadn't believed General Grant had called him back from South America for a frickin' garden party to begin with—her being here just made it all that much worse, all that much more unbelievable.

He'd left Kid, and he shouldn't have, not the way everything had gone to hell. Dylan had been driving a hard bargain with the NRF for the release of two SDF operators who had been ambushed and taken hostage two months ago, J.T. Chronopolous and Creed Rivera. But on the designated day of the release, the NRF had brought only one man, Creed Rivera, saying J.T. was too ill to be moved from the mountain camp where he and Creed had been held.

All the more reason to let him go, Dylan had insisted, but the commander had been adamant. The second prisoner would be released within a few days' time.

Dylan had immediately left Colombia to take Creed home, and Hawkins had stayed with Kid.

Geezus, Creed had been messed up, beaten to within an inch of his life and drugged to the point of unconsciousness. It had been hard to see him like that, and his condition had just made everyone that much jumpier about J.T.—especially Kid.

Early this morning, they'd received a message that J.T. was dead, that he hadn't survived the journey out of the mountains. They'd heard those rumors before, about both J.T. and Creed, but Hawkins had a real bad feeling about today's message—that it was true. The final part of the message, that the rebels would deliver J.T.'s body to the village of Rosalia in northern Colombia tonight, had made it seem even more real—and Hawkins wasn't there to be with Kid, because some asshole somewhere in Washington, D.C., had decided he should be here, eating foie gras and drinking champagne and providing additional security for a bunch of "very important people."

That's what Grant's orders had said anyway, but Hawkins would be damned if either he or Dylan had been able to find any VIPs on the local police's priority list or in the rest of the crowd of upper-class Denverites. Unlike what the policemen they were working with tonight thought, having a big fat stock portfolio or owning a company that supported the Denver Police Department's Benevolence Fund wasn't enough to get a person ranked as Very Important—not by SDF standards. For that designation, a political connection was needed, and the only politically connected person he'd seen all night was Katya Dekker, walking out on the auction stage.

He glanced over his shoulder, still not quite believing it was her.

But it was.

This couldn't be good. It couldn't possibly be good. The orders for tonight had come down directly from General Grant, but now Hawkins wanted to know just exactly who had made the special request.

No way in hell should he have ended up at a garden party, let alone one that included Katya Dekker.

With her connections she should have been at the top of the cops' list, or at least in their top ten. She was at the top of his list, all right, his "avoid at all costs" list.

Dragging his hand back through his hair, he looked at his empty glass again, then back to Kat.

Son of a bitch.

She hadn't changed. She still looked like trouble with

a capital T—wild blond hair, sea green eyes, clothes so expensive it used to make his teeth hurt, all of it wrapped around a small bombshell package set to explode. That was Kat Dekker, one big bang for the buck, big enough to blow a man's life to hell.

Maybe this was all one huge coincidence, the two of them showing up at the same place at the same time, but he doubted it. She certainly couldn't have been the one to get him and Dylan called back from South America. She didn't have that kind of power, and she sure as hell hadn't bothered herself anytime in the last thirteen years to look him up. She especially hadn't bothered herself when he'd been arrested and thrown in jail, when he'd needed her the most.

Swearing again, he started across the lawn, skirting a string of canopied platforms decked out like jungle huts and working his way closer to the caterer's tent and Dylan, who was also working this cakewalk.

Hell. If this was a coincidence, it was one of the worst badass mojo coincidences he'd ever heard about. She was obviously part of the art auction, helping some guys move a painting, hanging around down by the stage, which was all decked out with fake palm trees and twisted vines, like a rain forest. She belonged here.

He didn't.

Dylan looked over and caught his gaze as he neared the caterer's tent.

"You saw our problem?" Dylan asked, the coldness of his gaze telegraphing his mood—royally pissed off verging on ballistic. Everyone's emotions were scraped raw from the likelihood of J.T.'s death, but for Dylan it was worse: He was the boss. J.T. and Creed had been his responsibility.

"Yes." Problem was a good way to put it.

"Do you think she's the reason we're here?"

Hawkins hated to think so. He *really* hated to think so.

"She wasn't named in our orders," he said, trying to convince himself as much as Dylan, who knew the orders as well as he did.

"She's the highest-ranking civilian here," Dylan said, his glacial gray gaze going to the woman on the amphitheater stage and giving her a cool once-over. "She hasn't changed at all."

Without wanting to, Hawkins found himself looking at her again.

"No. She's changed." He'd been wrong earlier, real wrong, the way he'd always been about her. She'd changed. Plenty. She wasn't scared, alone, and eighteen anymore. She wasn't the prom queen or the poor little rich girl tonight—two acts she'd had down pat—and she wasn't naked in bed with him. She'd been most of those things, most of the time, that whole crazy month they'd spent together.

Then the earth had opened up and swallowed him whole. He'd spent two years in the state penitentiary, thanks to Katya Dekker and her crowd of too-rich, too-fast, too-frickin'-dumb-to-stay-out-of-trouble friends.

And thanks to her mother, the mighty Marilyn Dekker. What a piece of work that woman was. Christian had been steamrolled, hog-tied, and locked up before he'd even known what had hit him.

"She wasn't on the cops' list, and none of these guys seem to appreciate who she is, so maybe we better keep an eye on her. I'm going to put in a call to General Grant, in case there's something else going on here and this isn't as simple as it was supposed to be," Dylan said.

Hawkins slanted him a dry look. "There is nothing simple about you and me being at a friggin' garden party."

Dylan conceded the point with a grim smile.

Geezus, what a mess. Hawkins looked back at Katya Dekker and felt something cold harden in his chest. She'd cost him. Loving her had cost him.

If it hadn't been for Dylan and his Seventeenth Street lawyer working their asses off to get the case reopened, Hawkins knew he might still be in prison. What had clinched his pardon was the deathbed confession of a downtown vagrant named Manny Waite. In and of itself, the confession might not have been enough. Manny had been a lush whose grip on reality had been tenuous at best, but with one helluva lawyer and Dylan pushing hard to get him a pardon on one end, and poor old Manny giving it up on the other, Hawkins had been set free.

He'd been tough when he'd gone in, but not as tough as he'd thought, and not tough enough, not at nineteen years old. By the time he got out at twenty-one, he *had* killed a man, and his whole world had changed—all thanks to Katya Dekker.

Down on the stage, the auctioneer stepped up to the podium as Katya finished directing the placement of the first painting. The piece was at least six by eight feet of bright, oversize flower petals in a thickly ornate gilt frame. He recognized it as an Oleg Henri, nothing he'd want in his own collection, but a beautiful piece and one sure to appreciate in value once the artist became better known.

The irony of the night wasn't lost on him. Thirteen years ago, he wouldn't have gotten within a hundred yards of a place selling an Oleg Henri or any piece of collectible art. Thirteen years ago, no one would have let him. Back then, he'd looked exactly like what he was, a street kid on the take and one of the most successful car thieves to ever give the Denver cops a run for their money. Dylan had always had a way of looking innocent no matter what crime he was committing, but Hawkins knew he and the rest of the guys at the chop shop on Steele Street had always looked like trouble.

Just the way this damn garden party looked like trouble. Either he needed a Scotch, or he needed to be back on a plane to Colombia. What he didn't need was to be hanging around an art auction with a bunch of socialites—like Katya Dekker.

His gaze followed her as she crossed the amphitheater stage and went down the steps. There had to be a bounty on the dress she was wearing: a little black nothing, slit to the hip. With her mane of blond hair, her golden tan, and a pair of spike heels, she should have looked cheap.

But she didn't. She looked sleek and expensive. A California wet dream come true. Barbie with an attitude.

She had a tattoo, which, oddly enough, unnerved him. She hadn't had a tattoo at eighteen. It wasn't discreetly hidden on a hip or an ankle, or twined around her navel, and it wasn't a butterfly, or a rose, or a unicorn. Nothing sweetly banal for Kat; she'd decorated herself with a shooting star at the top of her arm, just below the curve of her shoulder.

Kee-rist. He shook his head. Kat Dekker was back in town.

He looked back out over the rest of the crowd, then heard Dylan swear softly next to him.

"I'll be a sonuvabitch."

"What?" he asked.

In answer, Dylan lifted his chin toward the last cabana. Hawkins followed the gesture, and what he saw sent a cold chill pumping through his veins.

"Garraty," he said. "Ted Garraty."

The fat boy who had testified against him at the murder trial had turned into an even fatter man, but Hawkins instantly recognized him. Garraty was talking on a cell phone, walking away from the cabana toward the caterer's tent.

"Yeah," Dylan confirmed. "This party is really starting to suck."

"Or get weirdly interesting," Hawkins said, not taking his eyes off Garraty as the man got closer and closer. He was completely absorbed in his conversation, his face flushed, his expression angry as he toiled up the slight incline, heading away from the rest of the crowd.

Hawkins didn't want a thing to do with Katya Dekker, but he wouldn't mind having a few minutes alone with Ted Garraty. No, siree, he wouldn't mind that at all.

"You keep your eye on Ms. Dekker," Dylan said. "I'll see what Garraty is up to."

The hell he would, Hawkins thought. "No, I'll take Garra—" he started to protest, but Dylan cut him off.

"We are *not* here to kick ass and take names. We're

here to protect these people, not spook them into next week."

Hawkins didn't give a damn if Garraty spooked. As a matter of fact, he'd like to spook the hell out of the guy, give him a real heart attack, but Dylan was right, and if Garraty was up to something, Dylan could find out what it was as well as he could. Then he could spend his time making sure Katya Dekker didn't sneak up on him, which he could guarantee would give *him* a heart attack. Even at forty yards, she was too damn close for him to take an easy breath—a fact he definitely wasn't going to be analyzing anytime soon.

CHAPTER

2

KATYA WAS FROZEN in the shadows on the west side of the stage, her gaze riveted by the two men standing and talking just outside the caterer's tent. Her chest was tight; she could hardly catch her breath.

Oh, God. Her heart was pounding.

That *was* Christian Hawkins, and every mistake she'd ever made in her life was roaring up behind her and threatening to take her down.

Hired muscle? God help her—Alex didn't know the half of it. Christian Hawkins had saved her life once, and he'd saved her virtue, and for the wildest month of her life, he'd taken her for his own. Not even thirteen years was enough to disguise the lean angles of his face, the coal black silk of his hair, or the midnight eyes that had promised her heaven—and delivered.

And not even thirteen years was enough to assuage her guilt, or her doubts, or the way she'd felt about him. Her pulse was racing with an awful mixture of shock and wariness, and a truly horrible excitement at just seeing him again.

She must be crazy.

Marilyn. Oh, sweet Jesus, her mother couldn't have any idea who she'd hired. This was insane—and with that thought, Katya's headache won, hands down, with a flash of pain.

Suddenly, her decision to expand her business by buying a gallery in her hometown was looking extremely shortsighted. What in the world had she been thinking? Toussi's was right smack dab in the middle of LoDo, only a few blocks from the alley where Jonathan Traynor had been found murdered.

Alex had warned her to have her stars read before she rearranged her whole life, and now she wished she had. Something this cataclysmic must have been splashed all over her personal cosmos like a supernova.

Had Hawkins seen her? she wondered, and then could have kicked herself for being stupid. Of course he'd seen her. She'd been up on the stage for the last fifteen minutes. Everybody in the whole damn garden must have seen her.

So what was she going to do?

Get Alex. Yes, that was right. She needed to find Alex, who had disappeared God only knew where, and tell him he'd been absolutely right: Her mother's paranoia was extremely well-founded, but her meddling, as usual, had only made things worse.

Much, much worse.

The bidding on the Oleg Henri was still going on. She could hear the auctioneer's voice behind her on the stage, cool, calm, and collected—the way she would be, she swore, in just a minute. She just needed a minute to adjust, to catch her breath and breathe her way through the pain ricocheting between her temples.

If Hawkins had seen her, what must he be thinking? Maybe he hadn't recognized her. She'd changed a lot since she was eighteen. Or maybe seeing her didn't make any difference to him one way or the other, because from where she was standing, it was clear he was not having the same heart-palpitating reaction she was having.

Which made her wonder if she and Alex had read the situation all wrong. Maybe her mother hadn't hired him—but if Marilyn hadn't, who had? Maybe he and the other man weren't there to protect her.

What if he'd come for revenge?

The alarming thought took hold for all of half a second. Then she told herself to calm down and get a grip. He deserved better of her. He always had. No one took revenge for idiocy—and that had been her biggest crime against him, being a weak-willed coward who, no matter how hard she'd tried, hadn't been able to make her voice heard over the hue and cry for his conviction.

Katya had never doubted that her mother and Senator Jon Traynor II, Big Jon, had both come down hard and heavy on the judge in the case—Marilyn for a quick resolution that did not involve her daughter, and Big Jon for swift and terrible justice. That his son had been revealed as a drug addict had drawn a lot of attention to his failure as a father, and he'd been hell-bent on finding someone else to blame. Christian Hawkins, a street kid with no visible means of support, no family, and a record had been all too easy to put away.

And then he'd been pardoned. Two years in prison for a crime he hadn't committed—he had to be angry about that. Very angry.

The Prom King Murder, as the media had dubbed the whole horrible affair, was thirteen years old, with poor Jonathan long dead and buried, but the prom queen from that fateful, awful year was still alive and well.

Though, so help her God, she'd been a lot better before she'd seen Hawkins.

The boy she'd known would never have hurt her, but he'd had those two awful years in prison since then, and—

She never got a chance to finish the thought. The explosion that rocked the stage knocked her down with a blast of heat and noise and sparks, throwing her hard onto the lawn.

HAWKINS and Dylan reacted instantly, running toward the amphitheater, while everyone else in the gardens was either scrambling to get away, or frozen by shock where they stood. Hawkins headed straight to where he'd last seen Katya and found her just a few steps from the stage. He dropped to his knees, with Dylan right behind him. A quick check proved she had a pulse.

High above them, another explosion ripped the sky. He threw himself over her body and looked up. The rocket that had exploded out of one of the palm trees on the side of the stage had set the tree on fire and burst into a cloud of showering, shimmering sparks that hung in the air. In the next second, another rocket exploded out of another palm tree, starting another fire and shooting into the sky.

Fucking fireworks? he thought, watching colorful streamers and sparks explode out of the second rocket.

"Get her out of here," Dylan said. "And yes, that's an order." He rose to his feet and took off at a run.

Neatly done, Hawkins thought grimly. He couldn't remember the last time Dylan had pulled rank, and he couldn't help but think that if he'd been thinking even a split second faster than his boss, he could be the one racing across the gardens, drawing his gun, figuring out what the hell was going on while fireworks exploded out of the scenery.

But Dylan had beaten him to the punch, and now he was stuck with Bad Luck Dekker.

"Alex . . . what . . . oh, wh-what in the hell? I—" Panic and exasperation edged her voice as he did a quick patdown. She slapped at his hand and a grin flitted across his mouth. She could talk and move, and didn't have any broken bones. They were good to go.

Another rocket exploded with a concussive boom, and she curled up beneath him, putting both of her hands over her ears.

Geezus, the whole place was coming apart.

When she tried to roll over and push herself up, Hawkins didn't let her. He held her down for another second, covering her until he finished a quick scan of the gardens.

"Please . . . stop. No—" Her voice ran out on a breath, and she went a little limp.

Beneath the fireworks display, pandemonium had taken over the party. The lights in the trees and on the huts had gone out, plunging the gardens into darkness. People were running everywhere, women screaming, men shouting, as one by one the forest of palms rimming the stage exploded and draped the night sky and the gardens in showers of hot, colorful sparks. *Boom. Boom. Boom.* The explosions kept coming, faster and closer together. Nobody was in charge of the situation yet, but he could see the cops here and there, doing their best to keep people from trampling each other.

Deciding the coast was nominally clear of shooters looking for a target, and having no intention of hanging around for the grand finale, Hawkins dragged Katya to her feet and did a quick assessment of her ability to run: not so good—she was swaying, and she looked a little stunned. So he scooped her into his arms and was gratified to feel her molding herself to him. She wrapped one arm around his neck and used the other to cover her ear as she buried her head against his jacket. He could have moved faster by throwing her over his shoulders in a fireman's carry, but just because he didn't see any shooters didn't mean they weren't out there, and in his arms, she was a smaller target.

And she was small. He'd forgotten how small. In his memories, she'd more than held her own with him, but carrying her, he had to wonder how.

Showers of sparks fell all around them. One of the canopies on a jungle hut caught fire and caused a whole new set of screams, and Hawkins figured it would only take one more semidisaster for the whole place to go up in sheer, unadulterated panic. By the time they reached the parking lot, a few dozen people were following in their wake. The elegant garden party had definitely gone and turned into an out-and-out rout.

In a sea of SUVs, Mercedeses, and BMWs, he didn't have any trouble finding his car. Roxanne was the only Sublime Green 1971 Dodge Challenger R/T in the lot, probably in the whole damn state, the only cruise missile packing a 426-cubic-inch Hemi and a set of Hooker headers under the hood. She was pure American muscle from her rubber to the pair of wide black stripes racing over her body from her nose to her tail, and he would have bet her pink slip that she was the only thing in the lot that could do a quarter mile in under twelve seconds.

Holding Katya tightly to his side, he let her feet drop to the ground as he jimmied his key into Roxanne's passenger door lock.

"My head," she moaned into the front of his jacket, her hand cradling her forehead. She was slumped against him.

He gave her a quick once-over and didn't see any blood or scrapes.

"You're okay," he said, and hoped to hell it was true.

Regardless, he had her in the car, strapped into her seat, and was dropping himself behind Roxanne's steering wheel in under thirty seconds—well ahead of the pack.

As a getaway, this one was looking good. Dylan was still out there somewhere, but Dylan could take care of himself, and in far more dangerous situations.

If he was worried about anybody, it was still Kid, waiting it out in Colombia, waiting for J.T.'s body to come out of the jungle. Hawkins should never have left him. Never.

Shit. He fired up the 426 Hemi, and Roxanne roared to life, shaking like a wet bitch and growling deep in her throat.

Well, he had left Kid, following orders, and he'd ended up here with Katya Dekker, and sure as hell, enough bad crap had come down that he'd ended up saving her— again.

Hell. He slid Roxanne into first gear and power-shifted his way up to a rubber-burning launch out of the parking lot onto York Street. By the time he hit fourth, the Botanic Gardens were no more than a faintly lit memory in Roxanne's rearview, and they were cruising for the freeway at forty over the limit, punching lights and leaving a trail of smoke.

CHAPTER 3

KATYA DIDN'T KNOW which was her most serious problem: the utter depth of her own stupidity, the number of G-forces pushing her back into the bucket seat of the rocket she was riding, or Christian Hawkins. It looked pretty much like a toss-up to her. Any of the three could prove to be lethal.

Her pulse was racing like a freight train.

It was the car that had cleared her brain, the sound of it, the feel of it. She'd lived her whole life gliding along the world's roads in her mother's Cadillacs, her father's Town Cars, her own little Mercedes when she'd hit sixteen, and a never-ending series of boyfriends' Beemers, Hondas, and SUVs. But at eighteen she'd tasted power, the bone-shaking, body-trembling, pulse-pounding power of more cubic inches than any sane underwriter would insure. The night Hawkins had pulled her out of the middle of a drunken fraternity-boy brawl in LoDo, he'd taken her home in the kind of car that put the bad in badass. "Get in the car, princess" had been his first words to her, spoken as he'd stood between her and the unruly group of young men who only minutes before she had called her friends—before they'd decided the night's game would be to see who could get a piece of Katya's prom dress, before the game had degenerated into getting a piece of Katya, before Jonathan had pulled out a knife to cut off a piece of pink tulle and, in his drunken clumsiness, cut her.

It had been incredibly stupid to get in a strange boy's car that night, a fact she'd been too hurt and frightened to assimilate until he'd gotten in with her and started the engine. She'd never been in a car that came to life in every metallic molecule all at once, growling and shaking, and she hadn't been in one since—until tonight.

She'd thought it was Alex covering her as she lay facedown on the lawn, stunned by the first explosion. She'd thought it was Alex who'd lifted her into his arms. Her secretary was buff beyond a doubt, but not much bigger than she was, a fact that had come into play when, partway across the garden, she'd come around enough to realize Alex seemed taller than usual, and bigger, and that the body she was cradled against went beyond merely buff into the "ripped" or "cut" category.

But oh, no, that hadn't been a big enough clue for her. With the fireworks exploding and sparks raining down, with her head breaking and her heart pounding, she'd taken the coward's way out and clung to the strongest, closest thing she could find.

She was good at hiding from the truth, and the lion who'd pranced his way down the yellow brick road to Oz had nothing on her in the cowardly department. She'd tried being brave once, thirteen years ago to be exact, and her mother had systematically badgered and argued and screamed and all but beaten the inclination out of her.

So there it was, the sad truth. Her one chance to build a little character had ended in failure.

Too bad, because it sure looked like she could use a little character in her current situation. Her party-girl résumé was hardly likely to reassure Christian Hawkins that any sacrifices he'd made on her behalf had been well worth the effort.

Christian Hawkins. Her gaze went to where he gripped the steering wheel. The back of his hand was broad, powerful looking, the veins prominent beneath his skin—but it was the tattoo that extended just beyond the snow-white cuff of his dress shirt that held her attention, the dark curve of ink, the merest hint of what snaked up his arm and lay beneath the rest of his shirt. No one who had ever seen him naked would ever forget. No one who had seen him naked would ever, ever mistake him for another.

Christian Hawkins. Oh, God. It took every ounce of strength she had not to just bury her head in her hands and burst into tears.

HAWKINS looked over at his passenger, and his mouth tightened. She looked like hell, her hair all wild and tangled, her face smudged with dirt and grass stains, and the slit in her little black dress split to halfway up her rib cage. He could see her underwear. One tiny black satin strap arching over the smooth curve of her hip. Unfuckingbelievable. He'd worked through his anger at her years ago. The only thing he felt for her now was complete and utter indifference.

And yet she was making him sweat.

Given how much she paid for her clothes, he would have thought they would hold up a little better. But that wasn't the worst of it. He could handle underwear, even hers—and he resented like hell that he had to specifically notate hers. The worst of it was the look on her face. He knew women, and he knew Bad Luck was on the verge of crying, which was the last thing he needed.

"I'm taking you to Doc," he said, keeping his gaze firmly on the street ahead. "He'll check you over, make sure you don't have a concussion or anything."

Silence met his announcement, a long silence so deep he could almost hear her pulling herself together. *Come on*, he silently encouraged her. *You can do it. Don't cry on me, Dekker. Not tonight.*

"I—I don't have a concussion. I have a headache."

Good, he thought. She'd done it. Composed herself and saved them both from a messy, emotional scene.

"I'm sure Doc will have something for it." Doc had everything, including, at one time, too much gin thinning his blood and a shade too many narcotics fogging his brain, which was why his medical license had been revoked twenty years ago.

He heard her swear softly, and looking over, saw her lower her head into her hands.

"Déjà vu." The words whispered from her mouth on a weary sigh.

Well, hell. Some things didn't change, he could have told her, and Doc was one of them. It was true: Thirteen years ago, Doc's was the first place he'd taken her—

though he'd offered the police station as an alternative. The local precinct certainly hadn't been his favorite place, but if she'd wanted to press charges, he'd have been willing to back her up. Of course, they would have first had to ditch the car he'd been driving, a stolen Chevy Malibu—very recently stolen, a 1969 SS 396 with three-deuce carburetion, and without a doubt the hottest Chevelle he'd ever driven.

She'd chosen Doc's, and the former surgeon had put a few stitches in her arm and offered her a dizzying array of pharmaceuticals to stave off the pain. To his surprise, the pretty little prom princess hadn't had a clue what she was looking at, so Hawkins had grabbed a couple of Percodans and shelled out fifty bucks for the call.

"He's cleaned up his act since then." Clean and sober, Doc Blake now ran the neighborhood AA meetings, but he was still open for his unofficial late-night business, especially for the street kids.

The sound she made from behind her hands was indecipherable, but came damn close to sounding like a very unprincesslike snort.

Fine. She could think what she wanted, but he was calling the shots.

"Y-you can just take me home," she said after another long moment, lifting her head up on a steadying breath and dragging one hand back through her hair. "Please. I'll call my own doctor from there."

Please. He liked the sound of that. He liked it a lot, but her request was impossible.

"I'm sorry. I may be able to take you home later, but I'm afraid first it's going to be Doc's."

He felt more than saw her turn in her seat and level her gaze at him.

"May be able to take me home later?" she repeated. "Are you kidnapping me?"

Ah, he thought. There it was, the regally cool tone of voice only a prep-school girl and senator's daughter could pull off.

"It's not exactly kidnapping. There won't be a ransom note, but we need to make sure you're safe, and we won't be able to do that until we figure out who blew up all those palm trees while you were standing under them."

Her answer was another long bout of dead silence, which he didn't for a second misinterpret as acceptance.

"Y-you think somebody was trying to hurt me?" she finally said, her voice a shade too breathless to continue qualifying as regally cool, a degree too hesitant to maintain even the illusion of icy calm. Dammit. "And who's 'w-we'? Do you mean the man you were talking with at the party?"

"Don't panic, Ms. Dekker," he said calmly, and took his advice for himself. "I work for the Department of Defense, and we don't know that anybody was trying to hurt you. That's what we're going to try and find out." She was just a job tonight, just a job in a black satin thong.

O-kay. He shifted in his seat.

"If you want to give your mother a call, I'll give you a number in Washington where she can verify that my partner and I were at the Gardens tonight under the authority of the DOD. My only request is that you don't give her my name, at least not yet. It'll be up to my partner to decide how much she needs to know." He tried to sound as reassuring as possible. He wanted the full ice-princess package here tonight. He needed the ice-princess package. That was the picture of her he'd nurtured all those months in prison, because what had nearly driven him insane were the memories of her heat—hot mouth, hot love, hot temper.

And all of it was the last thing he wanted to be thinking about.

"Department of Defense?" she finally said. "*Our* Department of Defense? You're kidding, right?"

Her confidence in him was downright heartwarming.

"No." He wasn't kidding, dammit. He'd turned out just fine, no thanks to her. Was that so damn hard to believe?

She mulled his answer over for an annoyingly long time.

"So my mother didn't hire you to be my bodyguard tonight?"

Good God, no. "I think I'm the last person your mother would hire for any reason, but especially for watching over you." He hoped Dylan got in touch with Grant soon and figured this mess out.

"H-how can she verify, if I don't tell her your name?" she finally asked.

Good question, but he didn't like the sound of the voice asking it. She was going to lose it, if he didn't get her calmed down.

"I'll give her a code and route her through someone she knows," he said. "She has more than a few friends at DOD." It was Marilyn Dekker's *only* redeeming quality. She was an all-American, blue-blooded hawk from the top of her no-nonsense, dirt-brown pageboy haircut to her black patent leather pumps. Every time he saw her, he wondered where Kat had come from. That the blond bombshell and Mrs. G.I. Joe shared a genetic base was hard to imagine. Marilyn Dekker was built like a linebacker, one square block on top of another, and Kat had more curves than a cyclone.

"No." The word came out dangerously breathless, yet damnably insistent. "I don't think so."

"No?" He shot her a quick glance. "What do you mean, no?"

"No, I'm not . . . n-not going to call my mother."

Perfect. She wasn't going to call her mother, but she was going to hyperventilate herself into a dead faint. He could hear her over there on the other side of the car, each breath coming faster than the last, each one shallower than the one before. So much for the ice-princess package. She was going into full meltdown mode.

"Take a deep breath," he advised. "Please." *For my sake*.

"I . . . I—" Her voice caught in her throat.

Ah, hell. She wasn't going to make it. Easing down on the brake, he quickly slid Roxanne down through her gears and pulled over.

"Put your head down."

"C-can't."

Okay, that was his fault. He'd buckled her in using Roxanne's three-point harness. Moving fast and sure, he reached over and undid the seat belt with one hand, then put his palm over her nose and mouth as he gently pushed her head toward her knees.

The last thing he wanted was for her to faint, but this . . . this was crazy. He was in a car with Katya Dekker, and she was holding on to him like her life depended on it—one hand gripping his wrist, the other cupped around his hand. And she was breathing on him like a package deal of bolt-on boost, fast and cool on the inhale, warm on the exhale.

A small, tearing sound drew his gaze downward, and he watched in calm disbelief as her dress slowly ripped another two inches, maybe three. She was going to come out of it in about two more seconds, with him practically on top of her.

There was a lesson in here somewhere, he was sure. Or maybe he'd offended some ancient, pre-Columbian god while he'd been in South America—because this was a test.

"Breathe," he reminded her when she stopped for a couple of seconds.

She did, and this time kept going, sounding like she was starting to get the hang of it. In. Out. In. Out. Going slower, getting steadier.

Hell. He turned his face into his shoulder and looked over her head out the passenger-door window.

Katya Dekker. He didn't deserve this.

He didn't have any room for her anywhere in his life. No room for regrets, or anger, or memories. No room for anything. She didn't exist for him. That's the way he'd arranged things. That's the way he liked things.

But for someone who didn't exist, she was taking up a helluva lot of room in his car.

CHAPTER 4

"HOW ABOUT SOMETHING for panic attacks?" Hawkins asked Doc Blake. "She just about hyperventilated herself into a coma on the way over."

Doc peered up at him over the rims of his bifocals, turning from his shelves of neatly organized and labeled drugs. Hawkins knew he got them from a couple of ER doctors over at Denver General who figured any help Doc Blake could give out was better than some fool kid dying on the street because of an overdose or an infection.

"Maybe if you quit scowling at her, she won't be so nervous."

Scowling? He wasn't scowling at her, or if he was, it was for his own self-protection.

"She's—" *What in the hell?* he wondered, leaning a little to the side to better see into the examining room. Doc had left the door open, and Kat was standing next to the exam table doing...what? His gaze dropped down the length of her body, then ran back up right along with his pulse. Four-inch heels did amazing things for her legs, especially in the oddly twisted, hipshot stance she'd taken, trying to safety-pin her dress together over her hip.

Geezus.

He forced his gaze back to Doc. "She's the...uh—" His mind went blank. All he could think was that even dressed she looked half naked.

"I know who she is." Doc came to his rescue with a jaundiced lift of one bushy, white eyebrow. "But maybe you need a reminder."

His gaze slid back to the examining room. Yeah, maybe he did.

"There were people lobbying for the death penalty for the way that Traynor boy died," Doc reminded him.

Yeah. It had been ugly. Real ugly.

And Bad Luck Dekker was beautiful—if a guy went for that whole long-blond-hair, green-eyed look.

Right.

She'd finally gotten the pin in place and was smoothing her dress down. It was absurd, of course. She needed about a hundred safety pins to really do the job.

"Lots of people seemed to come up dead that summer," Doc continued. "The Traynor boy, Lost Harold, and the floater they fished out of the South Platte River."

Lost Harold was a wino who had keeled over with a massive seizure down by Union Station. Being kind of a reclusive-type wino, it had been three days before he was found in the jumble of cardboard boxes he'd been calling home. The floater was a woman, Hawkins remembered, a young woman, and she'd been in the water a long time before some hapless jogger had seen her body caught up in a tangle of trees.

"My record's clean, Doc," he said, returning his attention to the portly older man. "I didn't kill the Traynor kid."

"Somebody did," Doc said flatly. "And a lot of people thought Manny Waite's confession was just a little too pat for an alcoholic who'd been living on the street for twenty years and hadn't managed a coherent sentence in ten."

Hawkins got his point. As grateful as he'd been for Manny the Mooch's confession, he'd had a hard time picturing the old buzzard getting up enough gumption to murder anyone. According to Manny, he hadn't acted alone, which had made his story a whole lot more plausible, but the pusher Manny had fingered as Traynor's other killer had never been found—and since Manny had died of cancer shortly after, probably never would be.

A couple of years after Hawkins had been released, when he and Dylan had accumulated a little pull through their government work, they'd made some inquiries, trying to get ahold of the investigation, but by then the case had been sealed tighter than a Colfax Avenue street-boy's—

Well, it had been sealed pretty damn tight.

"She bought Suzi Toussi's gallery down on Seventeenth," Doc offered. "It was in all the papers about a month ago, Senator Dekker's daughter coming back to Denver."

Well, hell, Hawkins thought. *This really is old home week.*

He knew Suzi Toussi. He'd bought a number of pieces

from Toussi's over the years, paintings and sculpture. The gallery was just a few blocks from Steele Street in LoDo, and it was where Quinn Younger's new sister-in-law, Nikki McKinney, was having her first big showing tomorrow night. Dylan had bought a few paintings through Suzi's gallery, too.

But Dylan hadn't dated her.

Hawkins had—up until the night the two of them had accidentally run into Creed in a Larimer Square bar. Suzi had taken one look at SDF's jungle boy, and Hawkins had been history. Suzi was nice, a lot of fun, but he couldn't say he'd missed her, or that Creed had done him anything but a favor by taking her off his hands.

Katya Dekker did not fall in the same easy come, easy go category. She'd been stolen from him, and he'd felt the loss every day he'd been in prison, and for way too many days after he got out.

"I haven't been in town much lately," Hawkins said, filing Doc's information away, though he was sure Dylan was already checking out the Toussi connection by now. Katya must have donated a painting to the art auction, probably the Oleg Henri, since that's the one she'd been helping move.

"The gallery's just two blocks from where they found the Traynor boy's body."

Something in Doc's tone made Hawkins narrow his gaze. "Are you saying you think she did it?"

"Somebody did," the older man repeated. "Somebody besides Manny the Mooch and maybe a drug dealer nobody else in LoDo ever saw."

Maybe, Hawkins silently agreed. It wasn't like he hadn't thought the same thing a thousand times, but whoever the other killer was, it had not been the prom queen.

He slid his gaze back to the examining room. She'd been sound asleep when he'd left her in bed that night, absolutely worn out. The loving had been crazy between them, so very hot. It had haunted him, the things they'd done—and he'd had two long years in lockdown to go over every last detail.

Fuck, he swore to himself, then had to fight back a wry curve of a grin. Yeah, they'd done that, too. Their last night together was the night he'd taught her the difference between all the sweet love they'd shared and just how far he could really take her.

They'd ended up in the bottom of the shower with her melting against him and crying, and him holding her and praying he hadn't given himself a freaking heart attack at nineteen. She'd been so beautiful, lying between his legs, naked in his arms, the water pouring down on them, her lashes wet and spiky against her cheeks, her breath coming soft and fast against his chest, her skin flushed. Holding her, he'd known he could go to the very edge of the universe and not see a more beautiful sight—and he'd given her his heart.

Bad, bad, Bad Luck Dekker. She'd been the end of him, but she hadn't killed Jonathan Traynor, not alone, and not in cahoots with Manny the Mooch.

"It wasn't her, Doc," he said, believing in her innocence as much as his own. Whoever had put a bullet in Traynor's brain had also shot him up with a load of smack big enough to stop his heart. The gun had never been found, but the needle had been lying in the alley with the boy, without a fingerprint on it.

Hawkins knew that under the right circumstances, anybody was capable of murder, but Katya Dekker hadn't put a gun to her ex-boyfriend's head, and she hadn't stuck a needle in his vein, not with enough premeditated cunning to clean her prints off the syringe. As for Manny the Mooch, he couldn't have premeditated a late-night leak, let alone a murder.

"Watch yourself. That's all I'm saying."

Fair enough. "How much longer?" he asked, nodding toward the examination room.

Doc glanced back to where Katya was working on her dress with another safety pin, and a big grin split his face. "Twenty minutes," he said, heading back toward the room. "Maybe half an hour."

Hawkins stopped the old man with a heavy hand on his shoulder. Now he was scowling, without a doubt.

"Five minutes," he said in warning when Doc turned and looked up at him. "And keep the door open."

He let the old man go and pulled his cell phone out of the inside left pocket of his suit coat. The right side was where he kept his Glock 9mm in a shoulder holster.

He punched in a number and put the phone to his ear, keeping his eye on the doc and Katya.

"Yeah," Dylan answered on the second ring.

"It's Hawkins. What's going on?"

"Fireworks. The shells were planted in the fake palm trees. Electronic detonators. The auctioneer is a little scraped up, but mobile. Some of the paintings are torched. The place is crawling with Denver cops, and the lovely Lieutenant Loretta Bradley is in charge. I'm sure she'll give us a full report when she's finished. That's the good news."

"And the bad news?" The way the night had gone down so far, there had to be bad news.

"They found a corpse in the cottonwoods. Double-tapped between the eyes, a clean hit."

Hawkins let that nasty piece of information sink in for a couple of seconds, then took a deep breath. *Holy shit.* "Anybody we know?"

"Not yet." Dylan's voice came over the phone. "It spun him around a bit, blew off the back of his head, and he landed in some bushes. I have to give the cops credit for getting the area cordoned off and for keeping everybody out of it until homicide gets here. We'll know pretty soon."

He knew what Dylan wasn't saying. He was thinking the same damn thing.

"It couldn't possibly be Ted Garraty, right?"

"The odds are four hundred to one. Four hundred and fifty-five to one if we include the caterers and auction staff."

Shit. He'd wanted Lotto odds on that one.

"Who's the Asian guy who was talking with Ms. Dekker?" Pure professionalism all the way—that's the way he was going to deal with her. She'd be Ms. Dekker to him until he handed her off to Dylan, or until hell froze over—whichever came first.

"His name is Alex Zheng, and he's rabid about losing her, but I gave him the secret handshake, and he's going to hold off calling in the Marines or the senator for about another thirty seconds. If you don't give her back by then, he's going to do his worst."

Hawkins wasn't too worried about the guy's worst anything. "Tell him to call Gunny Howzer at Quantico. If it's gotta be Marines, that's who I'd want coming after me if I'd been snatched and grabbed."

"Zheng spent six years with L.A.'s finest, before coming on board with Katya Dekker five years ago."

"If he's her bodyguard, she needs a new one." It was a flat statement of truth.

"According to him, he's her secretary, but I wouldn't be surprised to find Senator Dekker's phone number tattooed on his butt."

Neither would Hawkins.

"So are we giving her back?" He didn't like the idea, which surprised the hell out of him, but it was the logical thing to do. With that kind of connection, Katya didn't need him.

"Probably," Dylan said, but with the same hesitation in his voice that Hawkins felt.

"Okay. Tell Zheng we're hell and gone from the Botanic Gardens, but if he wants his girl back, he can meet us at her place."

There was a slight pause. "Yeah, well, it seems her place is his place, and he already suggested you meet us there. They live in a loft above the Toussi Gallery on Seventeenth."

Well, that made everything just about fucking perfect.

Hawkins took another deep breath and asked himself again why he'd quit smoking. He was on day three, which was two more days than he'd made it the last time he'd quit.

"We'll be leaving Doc's in a couple of minutes." He shifted his attention back inside the examining room and couldn't help himself—his gaze went over her from the top of her streaked blond hair to the tips of her pink polished toes.

Of course she had a boyfriend. She probably had a dozen.

"You want some advice?" Dylan's voice came back at him.

"No."

"Don't make any stops," Dylan told him anyway.

A brief grin flickered across Hawkins's mouth.

"Right." He hit the disconnect button and slipped the phone back in his inside pocket. What could Dylan possibly be worried about? That he might tape her to a lamppost on East Colfax and take the highest bid? Or dump her in a bad part of town and hope she made it out in one piece?

Well, he had news for the boss. He'd matured way beyond such petty revenge. Way beyond. He was a civilized guy, a member of an elite, hand-picked United States force used solely at the discretion of a two-star general who reported directly to the secretary of defense. In the years since prison, he'd cruised his way through dozens of embassy and consulate parties from Washington, D.C., to Riyadh. He'd gone through a receiving line once in Houston and come face-to-face with Marilyn Dekker. Without so much as a blink of his eye, he'd introduced himself as Niles Hahn, a name guaranteed to slip even the most determined minds, shaken her hand, and moved on.

Or maybe Dylan was afraid he'd try to hustle Bad Luck into Roxanne's backseat and jump her bones.

Well, he'd matured way beyond that, too. Way beyond—no matter how much of her dress was falling off.

His business now was getting her to Toussi's, dumping her back on her boyfriend, and then calling General Grant and finding out what in the hell was going on, so he could get the hell back on a plane to Colombia.

He was going to start by questioning her about what had happened at the Gardens, find out if she knew anything. He'd go easy on her, though. If Dylan wanted to get tough with her, that was Dylan's call. Hawkins just didn't want her falling apart on his watch. That's what had gotten him into trouble at nineteen—into trouble and into her bed—holding her together when she'd fallen apart. He'd had a reputation even back then for being damn near invincible, but she'd broken him with one soft, shuddering sigh, looking up at him with her green eyes swimming in tears.

He'd never in his life seen anything like her, and he sure as hell had never held anything like her. The girls he'd known, well, they'd been different. Some sweet, some not, some good, some real bad, but no out-and-out fluff balls. That's what had caught his attention in the first place.

He'd been cruising in the 350 Malibu that Sparky Klimaszewski had asked him to pick up out in the suburbs. He'd cased the car for a week, then on Friday night had J.T. take him out to Lakewood and drop him off. After they'd boosted the car, J.T. had gone straight back to Sparky's, but the 350 was hot, and Hawkins had driven it around LoDo a bit. Going by the old chop shop on Steele Street where they'd all gotten busted two years earlier had been a spur-of-the-moment decision. The shop had been shut down tight, with bits of police tape still hanging off the doors and a big FOR RENT sign posted in the window. Four blocks down from the shop was where he'd noticed a fight going on in the parking lot at Seventeenth and Wazee.

Normally, he would have kept on driving. But he'd caught sight of something bright in the middle of all those guys pushing and shoving each other around in the parking lot. A moment later, a girl had broken free from the crowd, running like a track star and making for the street. She'd been wearing the most amazing dress, yards and yards of shimmering pink and white material, the skirts fisted in her hands, her back bare except for two tiny straps running from the front, her hair bright blond, a look of sheer terror on her face.

Hawkins had jammed the Malibu into reverse so fast the shifter had almost come off in his hand. The engine had screamed as he'd buried the gas pedal in the floorboards and taken off backward to pick her up, or at least give the assholes chasing her something to think about so she could make her getaway. A couple of the guys must have actually been track stars, though, because before the girl even got close to the street, they'd headed her off and run her into the alley.

Fuck, he'd thought, his heart racing. They were going to gang-bang Tinkerbell.

He'd kept going, tires squealing and smoking, running the Malibu the wrong way on a one-way street. He knew where the alley emptied out, and in seconds he was there, throwing the Chevy into Park and jumping out of the car. A cloud of smoke had billowed over him, and he remembered thinking Sparky was going to have his ass for running the tires off the car.

He'd caught the girl almost instantly upon entering the

alley. Either she hadn't seen him or she hadn't had the sense to avoid him, because she'd run right into his arms—and stayed there, clinging to him.

It wasn't exactly what he'd expected her to do, but he didn't second-guess his luck.

"Get in the car, princess," he'd said fast and low, putting her behind him.

It wasn't until she stepped away that he realized his hand was wet where he'd been holding her—wet with her blood.

Things changed for him then. It was a shift inside himself, a subtle but profound shift from pulse-pounding excitement fueled by fear into utter, no-way-am-I-going-to-die-here calm.

There were eight guys in the alley with him, but three of them must have already decided they didn't have the stomach for more trouble and were heading back out the other end. That left five—all of them wearing tuxedos, Hawkins had noted somewhere in the back of his mind—and two of those were backing off, too.

That left three.

"Who cut her?" he asked, and watched as two sets of eyes landed on a dark-haired kid who looked like he'd gotten into something a little more mind-altering than his daddy's liquor cabinet. When Hawkins checked, the stoner, indeed, was holding a knife in his hand.

Hawkins had a knife in his hand, too, but he didn't think the other guys knew it—not yet.

And they might have pushed him into using it, if he hadn't heard a car door shut behind him. The fairy princess had actually gotten into his car. It surprised him—and suddenly there was no contest about where he wanted to be and what he needed to do. Slicing the bow ties and cummerbunds off the bad boys in the alley would have to wait.

"Touch her again, and there won't be enough of you left to put in a box." The words were fair warning in his book. Then it had occurred to him that any one of those penguin-suited guys could be packing a piece and might be wired enough to use it.

So he'd backed toward the car, keeping them all in sight, not realizing he'd just prophesied his own doom. Later, in prison, he'd had plenty of time to mull those words over in his mind, the sheer hubris of them. Yeah, sure, he'd been so fucking tough.

Tough enough that when one of the boys had come after him, Hawkins *had* cut him, just a little, a lightning-quick slash up his chest, enough to cut his shirt, just enough to draw a little blood and seal his fate.

The boy had fallen back into the arms of his stoned friend and the third boy, and Hawkins had leaped into the car with Tinkerbell and taken off for the wildest ride of his life.

CHAPTER
5

ROXANNE.

Katya blew out a short breath and glanced sideways, then looked over her shoulder, checking out the backseat. She was sitting alone in the car, while Doc Blake and Hawkins stood in the alley, talking in a pool of light cast by a street lamp and the clinic's open door.

Hawkins had named his set of wheels, and he called her Roxanne.

The name fit.

She was a Roxanne. Big, green, and mean, hot under the hood, and all pitch-black leather on the inside.

"How's Roxanne?" Doc had asked him, after they'd finished up in the examination room.

"Running low elevens," Hawkins had answered. "Skeeter ported and polished her heads, and we've got damn near perfect flow. We're going to blow Quinn's new Camaro off the track, if he and Regan ever come back from their honeymoon."

Ah, Katya had thought. They were talking about the car, the rocket he'd launched out of the Botanic Gardens parking lot.

The Botanic Gardens, where her beautiful Oleg Henri was probably in ruins. *Who in the world would blow up a charity art auction*, she wondered, *and with fireworks of all things*? Some neo-Nazi, antienvironment, orchid-hating group of radicals who'd decided to move onto the world stage by destroying botanical art?

It didn't make sense. No matter how many times she'd asked herself the same questions in the last half hour, she wasn't even close to coming up with an answer.

She didn't know if her insurance would cover an act of environmental terrorism. If it had been negligence on the part of the Botanic Gardens, some mistake with the fireworks, she and the other gallery owners could sue. She certainly hadn't been told or warned about a fireworks display—not that she thought suing the Botanic Gardens would be good for business. In fact, the whole thing was one big public-relations disaster.

God, she hoped no one had been hurt. That's what bothered her the most. There had been a lot of people milling about the stage area, though none as close as she had been, and she hadn't been seriously hurt. A little singed in spots, and scraped up, but not really hurt.

She needed to call Alex and make sure he was okay, but she hadn't seen a phone in the back rooms at Doc's, and her cell phone was still in her purse back at the Gardens.

Hawkins had a phone. She'd seen him using it while Doc cleaned her face, and as soon as he got in the car, she was going to ask to borrow it.

He'd said he was working for the Department of Defense, not her mother, but she couldn't shake the feeling that somehow her mother had made a horrible mistake and accidentally hired Christian Hawkins as a bodyguard, and then by some horrible coincidence, he'd been forced to leap into action—which, admittedly, he'd done very well.

Exceptionally well. She'd barely landed on the ground before he'd been on top of her, shielding her from danger—which seemed to be his specialty.

Of course, if she remembered correctly, her specialty was ruining his life.

Swearing softly under her breath, she brought her hand up to cover her face.

She was in trouble. Oh, man, was she in trouble, but she wasn't going to give in to panic. Later, she could panic, but not while she was sitting in his car.

Lowering her hand, she took a deep breath and another look around. The alley where he'd parked emptied out on Seventeenth Street. Her gallery was on Seventeenth Street in LoDo, a couple of miles west, just up from Union Station, which didn't mean diddly-squat, because she wasn't going to leap out of the car and escape, bust out, make a break for it. If it had been anyone but Hawkins, she might have walked away, but she wasn't going to walk away from him. She couldn't.

What she was going to do was apologize to him, so help her God, and try to ease the weight of her guilt a little, before it crushed her where it had lain so heavy on her chest for thirteen years. Apologies were kind of her forte, her trump card, her secret way out of all sorts of sticky social situations, and she'd never been in a stickier social situation or owed anyone an apology more than she owed him. Getting the words out could only help her breathe a little easier here tonight. Then, when they got to her gallery, she would thank him at the door, lock herself inside, and just give herself over to panic while she waited for Alex.

She was *not* putting herself in his custody and just disappearing with him, no matter who he worked for or how many paintings had gone up in flames and fireworks. She and Hawkins had disappeared together once before, for a month in a two-room suite at the Brown Palace Hotel, living on room service, sleeping late, and partying even later. He'd shown her places in Denver she'd never known existed.

It had been the wildest time of her life. She still daydreamed about it sometimes, about him, though she was pretty sure tonight's events were going to blow those fond moments of idle introspection straight to hell. He'd been a great fantasy, all hormones and heartbreak, and she'd been so crazy in love with him. Insane, really, her mother had been so kind to point out. Unbelievably, irresponsibly insane to throw her whole life away, right into the gutter, the *very gutter*, by taking up with a street thug. It was more than her mother could bear—and this from a woman who bore the weight of the Free World on her shoulders every single day of her life, a woman who was *proud* to do so, a woman who had fought long and hard for the *privilege* of bearing the weight of the Free World.

Pride. Now there was a word. Didn't Katya have even an ounce of pride? A shred? Hadn't she learned anything from her parents? Especially her mother?

Well, yes, she had, but it was all kind of hard to put into words. So she'd bitten her tongue and weathered the awful storm, and been sent to Paris—as far away from Denver and drug murders and car thieves as her mother could get her.

And now she was back, right smack dab in the middle of a full-blown disaster, the whole damn night about as bad as it could get.

Her gaze inadvertently went to the two men in the alley, and she swore softly under her breath, reconsidering her last thought. The night could easily get worse—much worse.

Hawkins hadn't changed, not nearly enough to suit her. It was all too easy to look at him and still see the nineteen-year-old avenging angel who had appeared from out of nowhere and saved her. Except now he was an avenging angel in an expensively tailored suit with an unnerving quietness about him—a beautiful angel, his face more angles than curves, his silky dark hair brushing the collar of his shirt. He was broader through the shoulders than he'd been as a teenager, possibly taller, still lean, but more solid.

She'd felt safe in his arms, but then she'd always felt safe in his arms, from the very first time he'd held her until the last—which was as far as she needed to go with that train of thought. He was a stranger now, and she didn't need her mother to tell her that's exactly what he should remain.

Still, she was as curious about him as she'd ever been.

She should ask Alex to do a background check on him. Sometimes her secretary amazed her with the kind of connections he'd forged as an L.A. cop. Alex could find out all about Christian Hawkins, if she wanted him to—unearth his secrets and his sins and hand them all over to her in a sealed manila envelope.

It wouldn't be the first time she'd had somebody dig through his life. Of course, Alex was bound to do a better job than the private investigator she'd hired years ago, who'd taken a whole lot of her money to tell her Christian Hawkins still lived in Denver and sold cars for a living.

At the time, she'd just opened her new gallery in L.A. and felt like she'd finally left her past behind, overcome it and gotten on with her life—and she'd needed to know he'd done the same. He'd already been pardoned, but she'd needed to know he was okay. The information the investigator had come up with had fit, so she'd paid the price and let it go.

But he was no car salesman.

Light from the doorway spilled over his face, contouring his features with shadows, the square angle of his jaw, harder than she remembered, the straight dark lines of his brows, the seriousness of his gaze—and the world's most amazing mouth. Or so it had seemed thirteen years ago, when she'd been very young and naive.

It had taken him less than a week in the Brown Palace to change the naive part.

God, what she hadn't known.

A blush stole up her cheeks, and she had to admit that besides being half scared, half guilt-ridden, and half worried sick about what had happened at the Gardens, she should probably be at least half embarrassed to see him again.

Yes, that was a lovely mix: fear, guilt, worry, and mortification.

She watched him step off Doc's back stoop and head toward the car, and thanked God she wasn't eighteen years old anymore.

He slid in behind the steering wheel and glanced in her direction.

"How's your headache?" he asked.

"Better. Thank you."

"Doc said he gave you aspirin."

"Two, and an ibuprofen." Oh, this was perfect, so polite. She could do polite all night long. It was right up there with apologies on her list of social survival skills.

"He's gotten pretty conservative in his old age. If you'd like something stronger, I'll get it for you."

"No. Thank you. I'm fine." And she was fine, practically. Her headache had eased half a degree from wretched, and she'd gotten her panic down from a wailing screech to a low, manageable hum. Christian Hawkins was polite, and she was fine, and everything was perfect except for whatever the hell had happened at the art auction, and the fact that for some reason two men possibly—or improbably—from the Department of Defense had been at the party, and one of them—unbelievably—was a car thief she'd once been in love with, who had gone to prison for the murder of her ex-boyfriend.

"Great. I'm glad you're feeling better," he said.

Well, gee. It didn't get any more polite than that.

Taking another deep, calming breath, she readied herself to say something sincerely remorseful, something tinged with years of hard-won wisdom about the regretful failings of youth—and, so help her God, she would have gotten it all out, if he hadn't started his monster muscle car and forced a quick shift in her priorities. She grabbed for the door with one hand and the seat with her other and held on for dear life.

HAWKINS slanted her another glance and noticed her white-knuckled grip on the door handle. He didn't blame her for it. They'd had a wild ride from the Botanic Gardens—not that he had any regrets. Given Dylan's news, they hadn't moved any faster than necessary.

"I talked with my partner while you were with Doc, and he cleared me for taking you home. He and your secretary are going to meet us at the gallery." That should make her feel safer, knowing she was only minutes away from a reunion with her dweeb boyfriend.

"Alex is all right, then?" She turned sideways in her seat, a concerned look on her face. "He wasn't hurt?"

"He's fine, very worried about you."

Relief instantly softened her features, though she didn't loosen her grip on the car. "He's the world's worst worrier, such a fussbudget. Of course, that's what makes him great at his job."

Fussbudget? That didn't sound like a boyfriend. It sounded like a roommate.

"Did you tell him I was okay?" she asked.

"My partner did," he assured her. A roommate as gay as he dressed, he decided, giving her a discreet once-over. No sane straight man could share her bathroom on a platonic basis—and that was pure experience speaking. Living with her for a month in the Brown Palace had been his own personal, excellent adventure into the never-never land of girls and girl stuff. He'd loved all of it: silk demibras hanging from the towel rack, hand-washed underwear, eight kinds of lotion, necklaces draped over the mirror, a perfume for every mood, sex in the shower, the whole sensory experience intensified by the warm humidity and small space of the bathroom. The only place he'd liked better was the bed with the window open and a summer night breeze blowing over their bare skin.

Admittedly, he'd had kind of a one-track mind at nineteen, but he didn't now, and all his other tracks were telling him to get off that one track—get off it, and stay off it.

He cleared his throat. "Only one person was injured at the Gardens." It wasn't exactly a lie. Dead was about as injured as a person could get.

"Who?"

"I don't have a name yet," he said, sliding Roxanne into reverse. "Did you know anybody at the auction?"

"A few people. It was a society event, and I . . ." Her voice trailed off, but, yeah, he knew why she would know a few people in the Denver Social Register. More than a few.

"Who was there that you knew?"

She thought for a second, but just a second. "Well, you, of course."

Of course, he silently repeated, and wondered why her inclusion of him among people she would admit to knowing gave him even a hint of satisfaction.

"And Vickie Martin," she continued. "We were debs together. She was there with her third husband, whom I hadn't met before, and Brenda Kaplan was there, and her mother, Mary Anne Parfitt, and Ted Garra—"

Her voice came to a dead stop.

"Garraty," he finished for her. So she'd seen him, too. Ted Garraty had been one of the boys in the alley that night. Their names had all come out at his trial, all the rich boys with no manners who hadn't done an hour's worth of time for terrorizing their little prom queen. There had been no charges pressed against the Wellon Academy boys, not a single one—but when Jonathan Traynor had shown up dead in that back alley, every one of those bastards had pointed their finger at him and declared him a murderer. "Did you talk with him?"

"N-no," she said, her face suddenly pale. "I was avoiding him, but you, me, and Ted all in the same place—that seems a . . . a little odd, doesn't it?"

Yeah. And seeming odder all the time—and if the stiff turned out to be Garraty, he probably wasn't going to be getting back to South America anytime soon, which didn't do a damn thing to improve his mood.

He had pulled his cell phone out of his pocket to punch in Dylan's number when it rang.

"Hawkins," he answered, putting the phone to his ear with one hand and throwing Roxanne up into neutral with the other.

"Okay. It's bad," Dylan said.

"Garraty." He knew it. He knew it down to his bones.

"Yeah. Garraty," Dylan said. "And he had a piece of stained cloth in one of his pockets, and I'm not talking a handkerchief. The cops bagged it up as an unidentified textile, but when I looked it over, it reminded me a helluva lot of that piece of bloody prom dress they found in Jonathan Traynor's pocket—pink and kind of gauzy."

Everything inside Hawkins froze for one god-awful split second. Then he swore.

"That's what I thought you'd say," Dylan said.

Hawkins shifted his attention out the window and reached up to loosen his tie. Unfuckingbelievable. Another Prom King boy had been murdered.

Whatever was going on, Hawkins had a bad feeling he was in it up to his ass and getting set up for another fall.

"You check your horoscope lately?" Dylan asked.

Hawkins let out a short laugh. This was way beyond a bad horoscope.

"I don't think it was me who got this all stirred up."

"How long has Katya Dekker been back in Denver?" Dylan asked, reading his mind.

"A month. Long enough for somebody to decide they had some unfinished business." That was his take on it.

"That's what I was afraid of," Dylan said, then paused for a second before continuing. "We've got to make some quick decisions here."

Yeah, Hawkins knew it.

"Our orders were just for the party, and the party is over," Dylan continued. "Which means I'm free to go back to South America, right now, tonight—or I can stay and work with you on this, let Kid and the Marines finish up in Colombia."

"I work fine alone, and you know it," Hawkins said after a long pause. He didn't like being within a million miles of this mess, but Dylan was right. He couldn't just walk away from it. Not now. But he didn't like Dylan going back to Colombia without him. With Creed in the hospital, he was the best jungle fighter SDF had left.

"Okay. I've got a call in to General Grant, and he's going to go up the ladder on this one to see who made the initial request to have us work the party. He'll contact you when he's got something," Dylan said. "I can be wheels-up to Colombia in three hours on a transport out of Peterson. I'll give the NRF rebels one more day, and if they haven't released J.T.'s body by then, we'll go back in after them."

"No." Hawkins sat up a little straighter. "That's no good."

"I'd call in an air strike, if I could," Dylan said, "but I don't think the U.S. ambassador would back me on that. The oil companies probably would. They'd love to blow the leftist bastards to hell, but even though they own half the Colombian army, they don't run it."

"Our boy isn't a hundred percent." Hell, Kid might not be fifty percent by now. Or even ten, and he'd be running on bloodlust, not brains, which was a good way to get killed. He was young and tough and the best shooter SDF had, but they were bringing his brother home in a body bag—if the rebel forces would just give him up.

Hawkins needed to be in Colombia. He didn't want Kid and Dylan going up against the rebels without him, especially with the Marines who had been down there ordered out. God, the mission was so far off the books, there wouldn't be anybody there to back them up after the Marines left—and they would leave.

SDF operators were expendable. That was the whole point of their existence, but nobody could afford to have the Corps associated with a black ops mission where things had gone wrong.

"Maybe you should wait for me. This thing at the Gardens with Bad Luck, give me two days and—"

"Bad Luck?" Dylan interrupted on a short laugh. "Please, tell me you're not calling her that to her face."

Hell. He just had, but that was beside the point.

"I could be in Colombia by Sunday night."

"And Katya Dekker?" Dylan asked. "She's in this up to her neck."

"Simple. If we don't have a suspect in our sights by Sunday morning, we turn everything we've got over to Lieutenant Bradley. I'll have a little talk with Alex Zheng and put him and"—he paused for half a second—"Ms. Dekker on a plane to Washington, D.C."

"Send her back to Mommy?" Dylan asked.

Basically, yes.

"Yes," he said.

"I'm sure the senator would make one helluva bodyguard."

"Definitely up to the job," Hawkins said. "Darth Vader in Chanel wouldn't have anything on her."

"Well, that's a fascinating visual there—and amazingly accurate." Dylan's voice came back at him over the phone. "But I think you're being overly optimistic about Sunday morning. You're going to have to trust me and the Marines on this one, Superman."

Superman. Right. Hawkins wished to hell he *was* Superman.

"You know I'll bring Kid home," Dylan continued.

"Yeah." He dragged a hand back through his hair. "I

never should have left him, though, not for this, no matter who was handing out orders."

"We left a full squad of Marines with him—he's not exactly alone. And if we don't follow direct orders, you and I end up in Leavenworth with a rap sheet a mile long. You know it as well as I do."

Yeah, he knew it. The chain of command for SDF was short, but it was as ironclad as that of any branch of the military, and saying "No, thank you" was not an option without serious repercussions.

"I'm going to talk with Lieutenant Bradley before we leave. Give me half an hour. I'll stop at the gallery with Zheng on my way to Steele Street and let you know what she's got, and you can take it from there. Do you want me to call in Skeeter?"

"No." That was a no-brainer. Hawkins could interview a LoDo art dealer and her gay secretary without Skeeter backing him up. His only doubt was whether he could do it without a cigarette. He didn't think so, not tonight, and not this art dealer. Besides, moral support wasn't really Skeeter's strong point. Fooling around with Kid's electrical gizmos, spray paint, and combustion engines was Skeeter's strong point.

What Dylan really wanted to know was whether he could handle Katya Dekker on his own. She'd broken him once, and no other person alive could say the same.

"I'll check in with you when I catch up with Kid," Dylan said. "We should be back in Denver by tomorrow night."

Hawkins didn't like the plan, but he didn't have to like it—and despite everything, this might be the chance they hadn't thought they'd ever get: a chance to find out who really had killed Jonathan Traynor III.

"If you end up flying out of Panama City in that rat trap of a Cessna Miguel Romero calls a plane, be sure and check the duct tape on the passenger-side door before you take off," he said.

"Right." Dylan let out another short, mirthless laugh and hung up.

Hawkins looked at the phone for a second before closing it and slipping it back inside his suit jacket. Well, hell. Despite possibly being handed the opportunity of a lifetime to clear his name for good, everything had worked out just exactly the opposite of what he'd been hoping for—the exact opposite.

Perfect.

"Darth Vader?" his nemesis repeated from across the front seat of the car. "In Chanel?"

He wasn't going to respond to that. No way.

Instead, he let out a breath, careful to make sure it didn't sound too long-suffering and fed up, careful to keep his gaze focused straight ahead. He was stuck with Bad Luck, up close and personal, for at least two days. Probably longer, if he was completely honest with himself, and he couldn't afford to be anything less than completely honest with himself, not with a thirteen-year-old murder, an hour-old murder, and Katya Dekker all dished up on his plate and practically sitting in his lap—and J.T.'s death weighing on his soul.

Mama Guadalupe's—that's where he needed to go to find Mickey Montana, and Mickey was the guy he needed to find. An undercover cop whose loyalties were as slippery as two eels in heat, Mickey had been working

LoDo a long time, long enough to have been around during the Prom King murder. Luckily for Hawkins, Mickey's favorite hangout just also happened to be the only place in town where they sold his brand of cigarettes.

He reached for the gearshift and slid it back into reverse. A quick stop, a little chat, a pack of Faros—just one pack, he swore—and then he and Alex and Katya could all sit down at the gallery and take this thing apart— which should prove to be damned interesting.

He'd never had a chance to talk to her after his arrest, never seen her again after his conviction. In all those hours he and Dylan and Mickey had spent going over the case, trying to figure out who could have set him up for the Traynor murder and why, she'd been the missing piece. She was the only thing he'd ever had that anyone else would have wanted, the only thing worth committing murder over—and somebody had done just that. Not Manny the Mooch, not some drug pusher no one had ever been able to find—but somebody who'd wanted Kat for himself. That's what he'd always figured.

And after thirteen years, he was finally going to get his chance to nail the bastard. Coming up for air to double-tap Ted Garraty was going to be the murderer's final and fatal error.

Twisting to the side to look over his shoulder, he braced his hand on the back of the passenger seat and released Roxanne's clutch. The Challenger roared back down the alley. At Seventeenth, he braked hard, looked behind him, and, when the traffic broke, gunned the motor and shot across the street to the alley on the other side, heading south.

He noticed the way she froze in her seat, noticed the startled look of fear on her face, but did his best not to pay it too much mind, because it wasn't her startled fear that was threatening him at the moment.

It was her dress, with the two tiny, ineffectual safety pins, and the curve of her breast he was trying so hard not to see, and it was the way she smelled, part female, part perfume, part pure Kat.

Roxanne was never going to be the same, not after a night with Bad Luck. Hell. He was never going to be the same.

Is Garraty dead?"

"I never miss, Birdy. You know that," the big man said, closing the French doors behind him. The house was a mansion, old brick and old money and a couple of servants who didn't ask questions about the comings and goings of guests.

"What about the rifle?"

"The Remington?"

Had there been another gun besides the Remington? Another gun besides the rifle he'd paid five thousand dollars for some underpaid grunt at the Marine base in Quantico, Virginia, to steal off the firing range? The rifle he'd had this reject Army Ranger drive all the way across the country so he could use it to kill another idiot in Denver?

"I left it on the roof, just like you said."

Perfect. The police would find it, and find Christian Hawkins's fingerprints all over it. This time when the street scum went down, he was going to stay down.

Birdy's employer had waited years for justice to be served again, and it was Birdy who was going to give it to him—again.

"And the fireworks?"

"They kept everyone distracted."

A stroke of genius. A dramatic stroke to be sure, but everything about the Prom King Murder had been dramatic, a media circus full of spectacle. Birdy had wanted to recreate that atmosphere, to savor it, and besides, he liked a little drama, if it was of his own making.

"How about your part of it? How'd that go?" the ex-Ranger asked.

Perfectly, of course. Birdy always executed his own plans perfectly.

"Katya Dekker needs better locks on her doors," Birdy said drolly.

CHAPTER 6

Rosalia, Colombia

IT WAS HOT, a hundred fucking degrees even at midnight.

Kid Chaos watched the last drop of condensation roll down his beer bottle onto his hand. Eight empty shot glasses were lined up in a neat curve on the other side of the beer, flanking a fifth of the local firewater, real rotgut cane whiskey. The bartender called it *aguardiente*. Kid called it novocaine, but the only damn thing it was numbing was his hunger. He hadn't eaten in two days, not since Hawkins had left, and he hadn't stopped drinking since the Marines had been extracted late this morning.

It was stupid, not eating, but every time he tried to eat, he threw up. The only thing he could keep down was beer and rotgut.

The Marines had offered to go UA for him, Unauthorized Absence, so he wouldn't have to stick the god-awful waiting out alone, but he'd turned them down.

They'd had their asses on the line for him and J.T. for three weeks, long enough for a mission that had gone bad, and actually, it was easier being alone—easier to get drunk, easier not to talk.

And the waiting was over now. It had ended about oh-seven-hundred that morning.

Lifting the fifth, he tilted it and ran it over the top of the shot glasses, filling them all. Eight was his lucky number. He didn't know why. He'd been eight when his mother had finally left for good. In eighth grade when he'd crashed his brother's motorcycle and broken his collarbone. Eighteen when he'd joined the Marines.

Setting the bottle aside, he picked up one of the shot glasses and downed the whiskey. *Geezus Kee-rist.* He sucked in his breath and gave his head one hard shake, waiting for the fire to go out or work its way into the empty pit that was his gut.

How in the hell, he wondered, was he living on this stuff? Or maybe he wasn't living on it. Maybe it was killing him, and that's why it felt so bad.

A movement in the corner of the room made him go still, except for the finger he tightened around the trigger of his M249 SAW, the big motherfucking machine gun cradled in his lap.

The drunk at the far table gave him a woozy look, then dropped his head back down in a puddle of spilled booze and passed out all over again.

Kid eased up on the trigger. He and the drunk were the only two people left in the shack that passed as a cantina in Rosalia, Colombia, a collection of hovels and huts a couple of kilometers from the infamous Caño Limón pipeline. Everyone else had cleared out at oh-two-hundred, at exactly the same time a beat-up old pickup had roared through town and made a real quick delivery, dropping a long box off the bed without bothering to stop.

It was just as well that they hadn't stopped. The SAW put out seven hundred rounds a minute, enough to have stopped them and their truck permanently.

He reached for the next shot, lifted it to his mouth, and knocked it back with hardly a shiver. The second one always went down easier. By the time he hit the fourth, they'd be sliding down like twelve-year-old Scotch.

And yeah, it was killing him. He could tell, because he felt like he was dying. Dying from the inside out without a mark on him, which was more than the rebels had granted his brother.

J.T. had been marked hard. Cut. Beaten. Mutilated.

Kid had looked.

He lifted the next shot in line and downed it in one swallow.

Oh, yeah, he'd just had to know if it was really J.T. in the box. So he'd looked.

His fingers curled around the fourth glass. He downed the shot and squeezed his eyes shut on a gasp as an excruciating wave of pain clamped down hard on his stomach, riding him. Sweat broke out on his brow and upper lip. Jesus save him, he didn't want to be sick again. He didn't have anything left to throw up.

Rigid with pain, he endured, until slowly, inch by inch, the pain eased off. The nausea passed, and he slipped back into simple, abject misery. Misery unlike anything he'd ever known. Misery outside his comprehension.

God, he felt so fuckin' awful. If the whiskey didn't kill him, the sheer, utter awfulness of how he felt might do the trick. How did people survive this kind of pain? He could hardly breathe.

J.T.'s body had been desecrated—invincible, bigger-than-life J.T. Just being his little brother had given Kid enough street cred to overcome his natural geekdom. It hadn't really mattered that he'd been too good at math and way too interested in computers. J.T.'s reputation on the street had been big enough to cover both of them, even though Kid had never spent a day on the street in his life. J.T. had made damn sure of that.

The fifth shot went down without a hitch. He didn't have a choice but to endure from one minute to the next. Devil dogs didn't give up, and he was a devil dog to the core, a devil dog with mayhem in mind. Murder and mayhem. He was trained in the art of killing. He had a warrior's soul, and the men who had killed his brother were going to die. Creed would want to be part of the mission—if he lived. Hawkins was who Kid needed back with him right now. Superman. Dylan was a diplomat, a con man, the brains of Steele Street and SDF. Hawkins was just the man of steel.

He and Hawkins could take the motherfuckers out. He'd be back out there already, if it wasn't for J.T.

He didn't have to look at the box on the floor to know it was there. The box weighed on him. It held him in his chair, at his post, no matter how tired he got, no matter how drunk. He wasn't leaving J.T. alone, not for a minute.

And he *was* drunk. So drunk, he hurt. So drunk, he'd practically paralyzed himself.

Not that it mattered. All he wanted was to get J.T. home. He'd made his radio call to Miguel for a pickup. He'd been less successful making contact with Steele Street, but he could call from Panama City once Miguel dropped him off. It would just be a matter of hours then, not days, until he had J.T. home.

Home . . . for one minute, he let his mind dwell on the word and what it meant. He'd met a girl his last night in Denver—met her, saved her life, made love to her, and fallen in love. A wild girl, an artist who painted naked men. Nikki McKinney. After the first week here, slogging through the jungle, it had all started to seem like a dream, those hours with Nikki. The hell of it was, he was afraid it might be seeming that way to her, too. A guy couldn't make a phone call in the middle of a covert op. God, she'd been a virgin when they'd made love, and he'd up and left her in the middle of the night—and he'd done nothing but want her ever since.

She was so beautiful, just thinking about her was enough to make him ache.

He reached for the next shot glass, then stopped when he heard the sound of an engine approaching. He rose silently to his feet. It wasn't a plane engine. It was a truck.

He was drunk all right, but there was a part of his brain that was lucid, and it was in complete control as he slipped across the bar to the door. The night was pitch-black, and Rosalia was quiet, except for the approaching vehicle.

A flash of light to his right brought his head around.

Headlights were cutting through the trees, following the curve of the road leading into the village. There was no way to know who was coming, friend or enemy, so Kid waited, his body angled close to the door frame, the SAW ready.

The vehicle's speed was a bad sign. It wasn't slowing down. When somebody opened fire before the truck even completed the last turn into the two-bit town, Kid automatically dove out the door and off the side of the porch. The thatched building was no protection from bullets.

He hit the ground hard and rolling as a fusillade of automatic gunfire cracked and spat from the back of the truck in one long continuous burst, all of it aimed at the cantina. The flames of homemade incendiary grenades followed, arcs of flame flying through the air and landing with the crash of gasoline-filled soft-drink bottles— Molotov cocktails, South American style.

His finger had tightened on the trigger, and the SAW was blazing in his hands. The fight was over in seconds, the truck careening out of Rosalia.

Shit.

His mind was clear now, crystal clear, the blood and adrenaline pumping through his veins, his heart pounding. Flat on his belly, staying absolutely still, he stared at the two lumps lying in the road, waiting to see if one of them moved. Off to his side, the cantina had gone up in a whoosh of flames, the thatch catching fire like tinder and engulfing the whole building in seconds.

He wasn't moving to save the drunk, who probably hadn't survived the hundreds of rounds of automatic-weapon fire that had gone into the cantina—and he wasn't moving to retrieve J.T.'s body. Hell, no. It was way too late to save his brother. He was going to let the fire be what it was: a funeral pyre.

He took a breath, forcing himself to concentrate. The rush of instant fear and instant instinct was over, and the rotgut was flowing back into his brain. He took another breath and waited.

They might come back.

Hell, they *would* come back. He was getting the picture loud and clear. No more gringos were going to leave Rosalia alive, if the NRF rebels had their way.

For two long minutes, Kid continued to lie absolutely still, hidden in the undergrowth of the jungle. Heat from the fire bellowed up with a slight breeze, nearly scorching him on one side, but he could take the heat. Bottles snapped and exploded inside, their contents adding fuel to the flames.

One by one, the residents of the village appeared from out of the darkness, fearful, whispering. No attempt was made to save the cantina. It was already gone.

When neither of the men in the road moved, he carefully got to his feet, swaying slightly. A throbbing pain at the side of his head brought his hand up to check it out. His fingers came away smeared with blood.

Measuring every step, he pulled his sidearm from the holster on his hip and started forward. They looked dead, but Kid had been trained well, trained not to take chances. And it was training, rote and religious, that made him fire a single round into each man's head.

He stood there in the middle of the muddy track, his

chest heaving, his heart breaking. Behind him, flames lit the night sky. J.T. was gone, completely gone. His warrior spirit purified in the flames of one last battle.

It was over. Everything was over.

Kid checked his watch. Dawn was only a few hours away. If he survived the rest of the night, Miguel would come and pick him up at dawn—and then he could go home. Home to Nikki.

All he had to do was survive the rest of the night.

WELL, *Hawkins's driving hasn't changed at all,* Katya thought. Most people slowed down as they grew up. Most people at least braked for red lights, and most people used the forward gears just a wee bit more than reverse.

Hawkins didn't seem to care about any of that. In truth, she wouldn't have been surprised if he'd driven the car sideways.

But they were stopped now, somewhere in the warren-like urban landscape of the west side, with downtown all lit up to the east, and she was grateful, so grateful to be parked outside the sleaziest-looking place she'd ever seen. Mama Guadalupe's gave new meaning to the term "hole in the wall," and she couldn't wait to get inside and call a cab to take her home.

If he wanted to disappear for a couple of days, that was fine by her. But he was doing it alone. She didn't care what he was doing with the Department of Defense; if her mother wasn't involved, it didn't have anything to do with her.

Yes, it was a strange coincidence about her and him

and Ted all being at the Botanic Gardens for an art auction, but in that group, Christian Hawkins was the odd man out. She was an art dealer, and Ted Garraty was a rich man who patronized the arts, especially when Denver society was involved.

She'd pulled herself together at Doc's. She'd done some thinking, and if she could just get out of this beast of a car, she was sure she could keep herself together very well without Christian Hawkins's help.

She reached for the door handle, then stopped.

On second thought, maybe she should just ask to borrow his cell phone. The windows on the club were boarded up behind iron bars. The door was a slab of industrial-strength steel. Rainbow-colored graffiti covered the outside walls, relieved only by the pit marks, or possibly bullet holes, in the dirty beige stucco. A vacant lot with two junked cars and an overturned Dumpster bordered the club to the north.

He'd taken her to nicer places at nineteen. The club didn't look like anyplace a government guy would hang out, unless he was a Force Recon Marine looking to work off a little excess energy in a bar brawl.

No, she decided, looking over at him. His hair was way too long for a Marine, and his manners were too crude—and that was saying a lot.

Bad Luck. That's what he'd called her, what he'd probably been calling her for the last thirteen years—and she wasn't even going to touch his "Darth Vader in Chanel" comment.

She should definitely ask to borrow his cell phone, but she wasn't speaking to him, which left her in a bit of a bind.

"This will only take a minute," he said, getting out of the car.

Was he going to leave her in the car? In this neighborhood?

She went for her seat belt with one hand and the door handle again with the other, but he beat her to it, coming around the front of the car and opening the door for her.

Avoiding his presence, his very existence, to the best of her ability, she got out of the low-slung bucket seat and pulled her dress down as best she could—which wasn't very good.

"Here," he said, slipping out of his suit jacket. "Put this on."

Her eyes immediately fastened on what the jacket had been concealing. He was wearing a gun. The dark straps of a shoulder harness slid down his arms as he shrugged out of it and casually released both the gun and a couple of extra magazines. The harness and the magazines went back in the car, the gun went into his left pants pocket, which absolutely ruined the line of his slacks.

A gun. None of the guys she'd ever met from the Department of Defense had carried guns. They'd all been paper pushers. A smart girl would call her mother, if she ever found herself in this much trouble, and she was plenty smart—but she'd be damned if she called *her* mother.

"No, thank you," she said in a voice that said he could go to hell and take his jacket with him.

Hawkins grinned. He'd take her angry any day. It beat the hell out of taking her scared—and oh, yeah, he'd done that once, the very first time, made love to her when she'd been frightened. He'd been seeing her for a week, coming over to the Brown Palace, having lunch and dinner with her, sometimes showing up for breakfast, sometimes taking her out, wondering what kind of strange gig he'd landed in—a beautiful girl who lived alone in the fanciest hotel in Denver, with unlimited room service and some sort of power over the manager, who seemed to be at her beck and call. He hadn't asked a lot of questions, because he hadn't wanted to answer a lot of questions. Street rat, car thief, these were hardly the things he'd wanted her to know—so he'd just gone with the moment, falling crazy in love with a girl he knew he could never have. Then one night she'd taken a phone call in the suite, and it had come out who she was, Senator Marilyn Dekker's daughter.

He distinctly remembered his blood instantly running cold. Jet-set playgirl princess he could have handled. Senator's daughter had sounded like the perfect way to get busted, and his first thought had been to get the hell out of there and never come back. She'd known it, too, and that night, she simply hadn't let him leave, not that it had taken much to keep him. A few kisses, her soft hands on him, everything she'd already given him that week would have been enough to hold him at her side, but that night she'd given him more, and he'd taken it all. He'd taken her, and she'd taken him, blowing his mind in the process and sleeping like a baby the whole rest of the night.

He hadn't slept a wink. He'd lain there, wide-eyed, wondering what in the hell had happened and waiting for the cops to bust down the door and throw his ass in jail for nailing a senator's daughter. Eventually, they had. He'd been convicted of murder, but he'd always known his true crime had been sleeping with an American princess.

"It's just for a minute, just long enough for me to grab a pack of cigarettes without you starting a riot."

She shot him a look of exasperation. "I'm hardly likely to start a riot."

"You already have, babe." He let the words sit there between them, let them sink in, let them give her a little warning about where he was coming from. No, he didn't like her, and he didn't like the situation they were in, but neither had his memory short-circuited. He remembered plenty, and her dress wasn't helping matters.

He held the jacket up again. This time she took it.

She wasted no time in rolling up his sleeves and pushing them up her arms, instantly transforming his he-man suit jacket into part of her bad-girl ensemble. As the coup de grâce, she slipped both of her hands inside the collar and freed her hair, sending it sliding down the back and over the side of his coat.

Thank God Mama Guadalupe's sold Faros, because he definitely needed a cigarette.

At the back door, he pressed a palm-sized call button and in seconds, a small panel in the door slid open. Two eyes peered out of the hole.

"¿Que?" came a voice to go with the eyes. A rectangle of light spilled through the darkened doorway, accompanied by a cacophony of noise and the smell of food.

"*Es Cristo,*" Hawkins said, bending down so the person on the other side of the door could see his face.

"*¡Cristo!*" came a glad cry, before the panel was slammed closed. He heard the sound of locks being opened, and within seconds, the door swung out, revealing a scene of chaos: Mama Guádalupe's kitchen.

CHAPTER 7

KATYA HESITATED at the door, taken aback by the wall of heat and steam that came pouring over the threshold. Hawkins put his hand on the small of her back and pushed her forward. The temperature inside the kitchen had to be close to a hundred degrees. A dozen waiters, busboys, dishwashers, and what-have-you, along with a dozen cooks, were all talking at once, chattering, yelling, all moving in the confined space. Dishes clattered, people shouted out orders, food sizzled and steamed—incredible food, Mexican food. They weren't five steps inside the door before someone shoved a plateful in her hands.

Behind her, she noticed Hawkins was already eating. With the subtlest of body English, he kept her moving forward, while listening intently to the wizened old doorkeeper give him a rundown of complaints in rapid-fire Spanish. Katya understood the old man's tone of voice far more than she understood his words, and it sounded like Hawkins was being implored to right a thousand wrongs.

"*Sí, sí, qué asco,*" he agreed, interjecting other appropriate nods and condolences between bites. By the time they hit the doors into the dining room, he'd finished a fajita and half an ice-cold beer, and the old man was smiling, beaming.

"*Gracias, Superhombre. Gracias.*" The old man nodded and took Hawkins's empty plate before shooing them out the door into the equally chaotic, but more dimly lit and far more upscale dining room.

Superman? What was that all about? she wondered, startled by the name, by hearing someone else call him that. She knew just enough Spanish to order lunch, and the old man had called him Superman.

She didn't have time to ask why, though she was pretty sure it wasn't for the same reason *she* had called him by that name. The doors no sooner closed behind them than someone else called out.

"Cristo!"

"Daniel." He lifted a hand in greeting as his other arm came around her waist, his body English suddenly far less subtle as he guided her over to the far end of the bar, as far out of the melee as they could get.

Mama Guadalupe's was packed to the rafters with a boisterous crowd of Denverites, young and old, eating Santa Fe gourmet and listening to a bluesy jazz quartet. In the bar area, people were dancing where they stood, and the waiters all looked like they'd been hired out of a Latin boy escort service—especially Daniel, who had followed them over to the bar.

God, he couldn't have been twenty-one on his best

day, and he was simply beautiful. Silky black hair and a fifty-dollar haircut, flashing dark eyes and a blinding smile, honey-colored skin and a lean, muscular build.

"Cristo, ¿qué pasa? What's happening, hombre?" Daniel's questions were for Hawkins, but his gaze was on her, making it clear he was angling for an introduction. To top it off, he'd taken her plate and set it on the bar, produced a set of napkin-wrapped silverware from out of the apron tied around his waist, and signaled the bartender for a glass of water, all in the course of greeting Hawkins.

Katya couldn't help herself. She was charmed. He was adorable, practically jailbait but adorable, and in about two more seconds she was going to ask him to call her a cab.

"I'm looking for Mickey Montana. Is he in tonight?" Hawkins asked.

She could feel him standing close behind her, where she'd sat down on a bar stool, and amazingly, found she didn't mind, not with Daniel's adorably predatory gaze giving her a once-over—twice. She was also glad she'd taken Hawkins's coat.

"Mickey's always in on Friday night, since he broke his leg," Daniel said, shifting his attention to Hawkins.

"Broke his leg?" Hawkins repeated.

"Sí. At the Cataclysm Club three weeks ago. There was a band, una banda muy mala, and a little rumble in the alley. Mickito, he fell off the dock and broke his leg. So now he's in every night, but especially on Fridays."

Well, that made perfect sense—almost.

"I'll be back in a minute," Hawkins said to her, leaning in closer. "Rick."

She looked up and saw him offer the bartender a five-dollar bill over the bar. Without a word, the bartender reached under the bar and slid a pack of cigarettes back over to him.

"No toques," he said above her, and she glanced up in time to see the very cool, very steady gaze he was leveling at Daniel.

"Sí, señor." The boy's smile disappeared, but only until Hawkins walked away. Then it returned in full dazzle. "I'm Daniel," he said, extending his hand.

"Katya." She took his hand in hers, felt its warm strength. "What did he just say?"

"Superman, he tells me 'Don't touch,' but—" His smile grew even broader as he gave their hands a quick glance. "We're touching, no? Would you like a margarita or *una cerveza*? It's on the house. Everything's on the house for Cristo."

"Why is that?" she wondered aloud, gently retrieving her hand.

"This is Mama Guadalupe's *restaurante*, and many, many years ago, Cristo and his *amigos*, Quinn and Creed, they saved Mama Guadalupe's life," Daniel explained.

She was beginning to detect a pattern here. No wonder they called him Superman. She also remembered Christian's two friends. She'd repossessed a car with Hawkins and Creed Rivera one night, an experience as close to sneaking up in the middle of the night and stealing something as she'd ever had. It had been both exciting and terrifying, and something she still couldn't believe she'd actually done. The other guy, Quinn Younger, she'd met one early morning when Christian had taken her to a chop shop on the north side of Denver, in an industrial area known as Commerce City. Quinn had been in the middle of dismantling a Honda Civic and none too happy about it. Hawkins had explained that they'd all gone clean, or at least tried to go clean—but sometimes old friends got into trouble and old debts came due, especially, it seemed, if the old friend was a guy named Sparky Klimaszewski. The next time she'd seen Quinn had been on a full-page photo spread in *People* magazine, his shirt unbuttoned, his pants unzipped, and a smile on his face that had made all kinds of promises. Unbelievably, the chop shop hood had become an all-American hero, an F-16 pilot shot down over some war-torn country who had lived to tell the tale and become one of *People* magazine's Most Beautiful People.

"The margaritas are very, *muy* good," Daniel continued, his smile both teasing and encouraging her. "Rick is *famoso* in all of Denver for his margaritas, and for *mis amigos*, he uses only the finest *ingredientes*, only the freshest limes."

"Then I'll have a margarita, thank you," she said, just to be agreeable. It was the polite thing to do.

"Ah, you won't regret it," he assured her, and signaled the bartender.

She doubted if she would, as she had no intention of actually drinking it. What she intended to do was go home, on her own, and lock the door. To further that end, she gave Daniel a warm smile.

"Could you call me a cab, please? Christian might be a while"—she hoped—"and I don't really want to be waiting around very long."

"Absolutamente." Daniel grinned.

She watched him leave and felt some relief at having finally taken back a little control.

In retrospect, all that had really happened was a few fireworks going off—too close to the amphitheater, that was for darn sure, but still, it had only been fireworks. The biggest amount of damage had probably been to the paintings that had been on the stage. Alex, she knew, would have the complete lowdown on the Oleg Henri, and they would have to decide what to do if it was irreparably damaged—whether to write it off as a business loss, or whether it would still be considered a charitable contribution.

The margarita arrived with a smile from the bartender, and to be polite, she took a small sip. Her hand shook just the tiniest bit, and a corner of her mouth twitched in a brief smile.

Okay, she admitted it, she'd panicked, too. But there had been explosions, and fire, and people screaming, and she had been knocked senseless, and then Christian had come, and he'd been all over her—but she wasn't going to think about that. Not now. Not ever.

She took another sip of the margarita, looking over the top of the salt-rimmed glass for Daniel. He was flirting with the hostess at the front desk, who was hanging up the phone.

Wonderful. If all went well, the cab would get here before Christian, and at least she'd be saved the awkwardness of a confrontation.

She still needed to apologize to him—that went without saying. But he was in Denver, and she was in Denver, and she could arrange something a little more formal, a little more dignified than an apology with her wearing a ripped dress on a night that had gone to hell in a hand-basket.

She took a bit bigger swallow of the margarita. It was everything Daniel had promised, and it was helping. Her hands weren't shaking anymore.

Maybe an invitation to the gallery? She and Alex were launching a new artist at Toussi's tomorrow night, a brilliant young local woman named Nikki McKinney. Suzi Toussi, the woman she and Alex had bought the gallery from, had been watching McKinney for years and had begun arrangements for the show months ago. It would be the perfect opportunity to smooth things over with Hawkins, a lovely gallery setting, lots of other people around, and her looking her best, doing what she did best.

He'd obviously done well for himself. He had a government job that paid him well enough to buy very expensive clothes. She didn't need to look inside the jacket she was wearing for a label. She could tell by the way the jacket fit, the feel of the cloth, and the fine detailing that the jacket had been handmade by a tailor.

He'd definitely done well for himself, but so had she, and against odds nearly as awful as his—maybe even more awful.

A memory shuddered through her, but she shoved it away and took another drink.

They'd both survived their past, and that was something to celebrate.

She would need his address for the invitation. She slipped her hand in his pocket while she took another drink, hoping to find a business card.

Her fingers immediately encountered something solid,

made out of metal—and full of bullets. Another magazine for his gun, she realized, gingerly removing her hand.

She switched her margarita to her other hand, took a drink, checked the other pocket, and found money. Glancing down, she pulled the bills partway out and fanned them with her thumb.

Goodness sakes. He had over five hundred dollars of pocket money in his pocket.

Guns and large amounts of cash only brought one thing to mind, and it wasn't the Department of Defense.

Thinking she had better stop before she found God only knew what else, she set her drink on the bar and asked Rick for a pen and some paper. She would jot Christian a quick, polite note, inviting him to the gallery and leaving her phone number. Then tomorrow night, she could find a quiet moment to tell him how sorry she'd been—how sorry she still was—for what had happened. If he didn't call, she at least knew she could track him down through Mama Guadalupe.

While she waited for the pen and paper to arrive, she took one more sip of Rick's rightfully famous margarita.

HAWKINS threaded his way back through the crowded bar, his gaze searching for and finding her right where he'd left her. Great. He relaxed a fraction of an inch. His meeting with Mickey Montana had taken longer than he'd expected. Come to find out, Mickey hadn't exactly fallen off the loading dock at the Cataclysm Club. He'd been pushed from behind. Right in front of a tractor-trailer that had been rolling up to unload. It was enough to make a guy think, and as much as Mickey didn't want to think his cover had been blown, it wasn't looking good, so he was spending some time laying low at Mama Guadalupe's. Mickey had given him a name, though: Ray Carper. It was a name and a man Hawkins hadn't thought about in years. Ray had been a pigeon for the cops when Jonathan Traynor III was murdered. LoDo was his beat, and with all the dead bodies that summer, he'd had a busy season.

Ray had gotten a little fixated on the Traynor murder and, in between drinking binges and bouts of schizophrenic paranoia, he'd spent his time trying to piece together a grandiose conspiracy theory that included all the murders and half the city council. Knowing Ray and his history better than most of them wanted to, the cops hadn't paid the guy much mind. Dylan had talked to him a number of times during the trial and had wanted him as a witness for the defense, despite his difficulty in keeping his stories straight. So had Mickey, but they'd been overruled by Hawkins's court-appointed lawyer. The last Hawkins remembered seeing Ray was in a flophouse on Blake Street before all the flophouses on Blake Street had been turned into upscale condos.

By then, he'd been released from prison, and Ray's story about a bunch of guys in tuxedos and a girl in a pretty dress had mirrored his own story of the night he'd saved Katya, except in Ray's version, the girl had died— so no, Hawkins hadn't thought publicly promoting Ray's story would do him much good. He'd always known he'd been railroaded into taking the fall for Traynor's murder, but when it came to putting Ray Carper on the witness stand, he figured his lawyer had probably made the best decision.

But now Ted Garraty had been murdered, and Mickey had thought of Ray, and Hawkins had to wonder if they'd all missed something in Ray's drunken ramblings. And then there was that piece of material they'd found in Garraty's pocket—which just set Hawkins's teeth a little harder on edge. If someone wanted to fuck with him, he'd prefer they did it face-to-face and left Katya out of it.

He lost sight of her for a second as a waiter carrying a large tray of food passed between them, and when he saw her again, a little warning bell went off in his brain.

She wasn't moving, not at all. She was staring straight ahead, her gaze narrowed, her face flushed, her body positioned on the barstool with all the precision of someone who knew she was in danger of falling off.

He looked down at the bar in front of her, and sure enough, her hand was still wrapped around the evidence: an empty margarita glass. One of Rick's empty margarita glasses, the condensation rolling down the side and making a little slough of the salt.

Daniel's ass was grass. Rick's margaritas had a way of blindsiding a person, especially if Daniel had ordered her a house special.

Great. Now he not only had Bad Luck on his hands, he had Drunken Bad Luck, which sounded like an ancient Chinese curse to him. As a matter of fact, he was pretty sure it *was* an ancient Chinese curse.

"Hey, babe," he said, leaning on the bar and putting himself in her line of vision. At this point, he knew she was going to be real careful about moving her head too fast, if at all.

"Hey." Her voice was kind of weak, kind of soft, as if she didn't want anything accidentally ricocheting around inside and bouncing off her skull.

"You okay?"

"I-I was fine . . . and then . . . and then I wasn't."

Yeah, just like that. One minute a person was fine, and in the next second, wham, they'd been coldcocked from the inside out, thanks to the *mezcal* from across the border that put the "special" in Rick's "house special" margaritas.

"I thought I'd take you home now."

She made the monumental effort to shift her gaze and make eye contact. "Roxanne again?" She didn't sound too thrilled by the idea.

"I'll drive like your grandmother," he promised. "You won't feel a thing." Easy enough for him to say. She wasn't feeling a thing now. "Come on. Let's go."

He carefully moved the glass out of her hand, not realizing it was the only thing holding her up until she started sliding off the stool. He caught her in his arms. Probably not his smartest move, but he was willing to give her a chance to find her feet.

It took a long time.

A very long time, in which she just lay there against him, all curves and heat, her face pressed into the middle of his chest, her breath getting his shirt wet.

Just part of the job, he told himself, staying calm, keeping cool, despite the fact that her hands had moved to his waist and were fisted into his shirt and holding on to him like she was never going to let him go.

Yeah, despite all that, he was cool. Getting a little turned on, but staying cool. Because the truth was, she wasn't coming on to him. This was one of those "any port in a storm" situations, and he was a big enough boy to understand the difference. Plus, he reminded himself, this kind of discomfort in her presence was nothing new.

But that was all in the past and would have stayed there, he was sure, if she hadn't gone and done the damnedest thing. Still clinging, still plastered against him, she tilted her head back, sending a long fall of golden hair sliding over his suit jacket, and she looked at him, caught his gaze with her own, and slam-dunked him for the score. If his timing had been even a fraction of a second better, he could have averted his eyes and been fine. But he hadn't, and he wasn't.

She was locked onto him like a tractor beam, and he couldn't look away. His body grew very still. His pulse picked up speed. Warning bells, big loud ones, started going off all over in his brain—"Danger, danger, Will Robinson!"—and he still didn't move. Oh, no, not him. That would have been too easy. He went the hard way, letting his gaze slide slowly over her face, letting his awareness of her body seep past his barriers, letting the first rush of arousal run amuck.

His hands tightened around her arms where he held her. Hell, he didn't need this, he told himself, not for a minute, but God, she was beautiful, and she was in his arms, all warm and lovely and drunk, with sea-green eyes and a mouth that had been his undoing from the first moment he'd ever kissed her.

Kiss . . . her lips parted as if she'd read his mind, and his brain started shutting down, all his energy focusing on her. There'd been a time when he would have given everything he had just to kiss her again. A time when he would have given his last days of freedom, if she would only come and see him, come and make love with him, come and make him . . . make him . . .

He'd been one badass heartbroken boy, and here she was, practically his for the taking, no money down, no freedom lost.

He was so tempted—and might have followed through on it except for the slight tremor that went through her body. His gaze instantly narrowed. As promising as a little trembling sometimes was with a woman, he instinctively knew this was not one of those times. Then she went and proved him right. Tears suddenly filled her eyes, and in the next second she was crumbling, starting to cry.

Ah, hell, he thought, it was déjà vu all over again.

"I'm sorry, Christian." Her voice was barely a whisper, her words a little muddled and filled with remorse. He knew exactly what she was sorry for, and frankly, it was the last damn thing he wanted to talk about with her. The last thing he needed tonight or any other night was a sobbing confession designed to ease her guilt and make him feel like shit, but he was going to get one. He could feel it coming in the tightening of her hands in his shirt, in the way she was pressing herself against him, making sure she had his undivided attention.

She did.

"When you were . . . I wanted to—and then I missed you," she started on a hiccupped sob. "I tried, but the whole mess was . . . and then I was in Paris, and—"

Well, this was priceless, Bad Luck and hiccups, and what she'd said was just swell. She'd gone to Paris, and he'd gone to the penitentiary.

"—and I couldn't get in touch with you, and the money, and the letters I sent—"

That was interesting. He'd never gotten any letters, and he sure as hell had never gotten any money.

"All back. All of it—and Margot . . . Margot told me about the cigarettes, so I really, really wanted you to have the cigarettes. So no one would . . . oh, God, Hawkins, I am so sorry."

Well, now she was starting to hit nerves, and fuck Margot, whoever the hell she was. He could just imagine what the girl had told Bad Luck he could buy with cigarettes. You couldn't buy a goddamn thing with cigarettes, not on the inside, not anything that counted.

"Y-you shouldn't have ever even," she said, not making much sense, but he understood her.

"I-I told them it wasn't you. Not you." She gave him a little shake, as if he were the one who needed convincing, and he was convinced, of her sincerity if nothing else. She looked miserable, beautiful but miserable, the tip of her nose turning pink, her lashes getting all stuck together with tears. "All the other boys. I told them, the knife, everything, about the knife and Jonathan, and how you saved me."

And the boys had told the cops about his threat— instant Kiss of Death, but he didn't hold it against her. He'd told the cops the same thing.

"I told my mother, too, how you'd saved me, b-but she didn't care. She was so . . . so—"

And this was the part he really didn't want to hear, the part about Linebacker Dekker, and how she'd thrown her weight around because she'd been so . . . so—pissed off, he figured. Shocked. Stunned. Outraged. The list was probably endless.

No, he didn't want to hear it, but he didn't stop it, either—and he could have, easily. But the conversation was starting to take on all the fascination of a train wreck.

"So . . ." Bad Luck said again, struggling to find the right word, as if she really, really wanted him to know how her mother had felt, but was being extra careful not to hurt his feelings.

How sweet, he thought. *How utterly absurd.*

How utterly pressed against him she was, like a hot lamination.

"So—"

He took a breath, and wished *he* had a margarita, because he couldn't take much more of this. She was crying seriously now, hiccupping between words, the tears spilling onto her cheeks, smudging her mascara and giving her a slightly bruised and helpless, damsel-in-distress look that he seemed particularly susceptible to, the way other men were susceptible to the plague, or dengue fever.

"So . . . so . . ." Her brow furrowed, her straight little eyebrows bunching toward each other.

Okay, great. She'd lost her train of thought and was now stuck like a broken record. A nicer man would have helped her out.

Hawkins was not a nice man. He helped himself.

Bringing his hands up to her face, he smoothed his thumbs across her cheeks and wiped away her tears, and the next time she said "So . . . so . . ." in her softly confused voice, her gaze imploring him to understand, he leaned down and kissed her, opened his mouth over hers and took the zero-to-sixty-in-0.5-seconds-flat trip down memory lane.

It was a helluva ride. Her breasts cushioned against his chest, her soft skin beneath his fingers, her mouth opening for him, letting him inside—and the sound of instantaneous surrender she made in the back of her throat that went through him with all the galvanizing force of a Top Fuel dragster on ninety-percent nitro. He felt the heat of her mouth all the way down to his groin, turning him on, stirring him up, when he had no business getting stirred by her at all.

But, God, she was sweet, the taste of her damnably erotic, a little *mezcal*, a little salt from her tears, and all Bad Luck.

He opened his mouth wider and shifted angles, so he could have more of her—more access, more of her tongue in his mouth, because it drove him crazy in the most exquisite way. She melted against him, opening herself even more to the kiss. It was such a tease of what he really wanted: more *her*.

And what a damn god-awful thing it was to find that out. He'd wondered what it would be like to kiss her again. He'd been wondering ever since he'd first set eyes on her at the Botanic Gardens, and now he knew—incredible, everything he remembered and then some, the giving way of her body, the way she rose to his touch, the unconscious roll of her hips into his.

Geezus. He was in so much trouble, and for a second, he thought about pulling away—and then he thought to hell with it.

Oh, yeah. His first year in stir, he would have given everything he had, including the 350 Chevy Malibu waiting for him on the outside, for her to come and kiss him like this, and it would have been worth it. There'd been nights when he'd skated so close to the edge of the abyss, it had only been Dylan's promises that had held him back and kept him alive—dark, fierce promises that had somehow kept him sane.

All because of her. So was he crazy, or what?

Probably, he admitted, because he wanted to kiss her anyway, despite the past and the havoc she'd wreaked on his life—all because he'd fallen in love with a crumpled-up little Tinkerbell who kissed like an angel. It was something he'd never quite understood. The last place he'd ever expected to end up in his whole life was in bed with a prom queen.

It was exactly where he wanted to end up tonight, though, and what was wrong with that? He didn't have to fall hopelessly, crazily in love with her. Hell, he wasn't a teenager anymore. He'd made love with lots of women without falling in love. Okay, maybe "lots" was stretching things a bit. He tended to be very particular about his lovers. He liked women, loved them at their best and was fascinated by them at their worst, but he didn't need to sleep with every one he met.

He just needed to sleep with this one, Katya Dekker. He needed to sleep with her tonight.

Closure, he told himself. That's what he was looking for, and maybe some absolution. She could have saved him once, saved him in a thousand different ways, and she'd abandoned him instead, left him to suffer alone and commit his sins of survival.

And he still wanted her, after all he'd been through.

So, great. He'd take her to the gallery, let her grab a

few things, talk to Alex Zheng—and then he'd take her home, home to his place, Steele Street. She needed to talk? Fine, he'd let her talk right up until he got her into bed, because that's what he needed. Sex. With her.

Hell, she'd practically fallen into his arms, so why not? It was the perfect plan. Straightforward, simple, with no complicated, extraneous objectives in mind, nothing to get all screwed up—especially his head. He wasn't going to let his head get into this at all. It was going to be sex, pure and simple.

CHAPTER

8

SIMPLE. RIGHT.

Hawkins turned Roxanne onto Seventeenth Street and slowly motored up the block.

Yeah. He'd had it all worked out in the bar at Mama Guadalupe's, but in his plan, she hadn't passed out cold, all slumped down in her seat, her mouth a little open, her hair a tangled mess going every which way, the hem of her dress almost up around her waist, which he was trying very hard not to notice.

One margarita. It almost didn't seem possible for someone to pass out on one margarita, even one of Rick's margaritas. She wasn't very big, but it was still hard to believe that she was down for the count—and that he was hell and gone out of luck.

Of course he was. What had he expected, really expected? She *was* Bad Luck, the stone-cold definition.

In truth, it was all for the best, and he knew it. He

couldn't have had sex with her and walked away. He was stuck with her, he reminded himself. Through the weekend at least. And he couldn't have had sex with her without his head getting involved, because there was a whole section of his brain with her name engraved on it.

He pulled to a stop in front of the gallery and shut Roxanne down. The night was quiet, with just a few people cruising in and out of the Oxford Hotel, and a few more heading down to the bars on Wynkoop. The gallery was dark, and she sure didn't have any keys on her. Hell, she barely had on her dress. So it was time for a little breaking and entering.

She stirred beside him, rolling to her side as if she were snuggling in for the night, and he knew it would be easier just to call it quits and take her to Steele Street. He could bring her home in the morning. But he really did need to talk to Dylan, and even Alex Zheng. He'd know who in town she'd kept in touch with all these years. Ted Garraty had been at the garden party. Who else had been there? he wondered. Who else from the Prom King Murder was still in Denver?

He used to keep track of the boys who'd been in the alley that night, but once he and Dylan had gotten involved in creating SDF, he'd become more focused on the future than his past, and gradually, he'd let them go. He'd have to get Skeeter working on tracking them all down again.

"I don't like you." Her voice came across the quiet interior of the car, dead serious, even if her words were a little soft around the edges.

He rolled his gaze in her direction. She was a

heartbreaker, all right, but right now she looked like hell, sleepily drunk, with mascara tracks running down her cheeks and her lipstick smeared—what was left of it, anyway.

"You're not very nice, and I'm—I'm angry with you," she continued.

Yeah. Furious. He could tell by the way she'd had her tongue halfway down his throat.

"I think you're real nice," he said, and he did. Nice to kiss. Nice to get naked with—not that he was getting anywhere with that, which was fine, all for the best.

"No, you don't. You th-ink I'm bad luck," she said around a yawn.

"Yeah, well, that, too." He knew better than to argue with a drunk.

Her sleepy gaze locked onto his, still so very, very serious, and he felt all his old discomfort come back.

"You th-ink I didn't really love you."

Okay. Time to bail out on this particular conversation. He opened the door and got out of the car.

Swinging around to the passenger side, he reached for the door handle, then stopped. He couldn't leave her in the car. He knew that. But he needed a moment to remind himself—again—that she was just a job.

Of course, he couldn't remember the last time he'd ever kissed anybody on the job.

On the other hand, just because it had happened once, didn't mean it had to happen twice.

Famous last words, he thought, when he opened the door and saw her doing God knew what in the seat. Stretching, yeah, that's what it was called when a woman in a too-short dress arched her back and lifted her hands over her head, yawned, and pressed one of her four-inch heels into the floorboards.

He called it stunning. Damn near paralyzing. She was nothing but silken, golden tan all the way up to her thong.

Dammit. He'd been wrong. He couldn't handle her underwear, not while it was still on her body, and he didn't even want to think about it coming off. He didn't dare.

Steeling himself, he leaned down to retrieve a set of lock picks out of Roxanne's glove box and unbuckle the seat belt, knowing he had to work fast or risk getting arrested—on both counts. It seemed damn near impossible, but he wore a forty-two-long suit jacket, and somehow there wasn't enough of it to cover her up. She should have been swaddled in the damn thing, damn near swallowed up by the material. Instead, the only part of her he couldn't see was her arms.

He slipped the set of picks into his pants pocket and reached for her.

"Come on, sweetheart. Let's go," he said, but actually getting her out of the car proved to be another of the night's long list of challenges. The *mezcal* had turned her body into a wet noodle, and the harder he tried to hold on to her, the slipperier she got.

"Hell," he muttered, finally just bending his knees and lifting her over his shoulder. He clamped his arm across her thighs, locked Roxanne, and headed for the gallery door—just in time to see a squad car turn the corner at Wynkoop and slow down as it headed for the curb in front of Toussi's.

It was uncanny, really, how badly the night was going

down. He didn't blame the cops. If he'd been a cop and seen a man hauling a woman around over his shoulder on a Friday night in LoDo, he'd have pulled over, too.

No, he blamed his ancient Chinese curse, Drunken Bad Luck—all five feet, two inches of it.

The cops stopped, and he waited while one of the officers hauled himself out of the squad car. He'd hoped it would be someone he knew—but no, of course it wasn't.

"Good evening," the cop said, approaching with the calm, measured tread of a seasoned veteran.

"Good evening, Officer." It didn't hurt to be polite to a man with a gun and the law on his side. Hawkins had both those things, too, but a concealed weapons permit and his Department of Defense ID weren't going to explain his current situation.

"Is there a problem?" the cop asked.

"No, sir. My date had a little too much to drink, but—"

"We didn't have a *date*," a muffled voice came from behind his back. He'd planted his hand firmly on her butt, holding the tail end of his jacket in place, protecting her modesty as best he could, but the policeman was still getting an eyeful of her legs. He couldn't tell if that was working for him or against him.

He smiled at the cop. "But I'm the—"

"And I only had *one* drink," the voice came again, sounding a little petulant, but not at all distressed, which was perfect. He could almost see the cop relaxing. "I'm the designated driver," Hawkins finished, "and I'm fine."

"Are *not*," she mumbled.

He ignored her.

The cop tilted his head a little to one side. "Are you okay, ma'am?"

Hawkins waited for her to say something, and waited, and waited. But, of course, given a chance to redeem him, she'd decided to button up tighter than a clam. Some things never changed. Then it came, a sniffle, then another, and a hiccup.

He wanted to groan.

"Can I see your identification?" the cop asked.

Hawkins went for his wallet, even though the guy's gaze had been drawn back to her thighs. He understood. They were irresistible, but for the most part, even a set of world-class legs like Katya's would not have their own ID.

One-handed, he flipped his wallet open, showing his Colorado driver's license and his DOD ID. Two months ago, he'd been on special assignment to the FBI and carrying Bureau identification, which would have been perfect for this situation.

"You live up on Steele Street, huh?" the cop said, taking the wallet and shining a small flashlight on his driver's license.

"Yes, sir." She was crying all over him in back, softly sobbing her heart out, getting his shirt all wet, which was a perfect match for the wet patch she'd left on the front from her previous bout of drunken remorse. Hell.

"Used to be a rough part of town up there and down here," the cop said.

"Yes, sir." He knew what the guy was doing—checking him out, getting a bead on him. There wasn't a law against carrying a crying woman around on your shoulder. It was just an odd enough situation to deserve a closer look—and the longer the cop looked, the more he wished he were out of the country.

"You sh-shouldn't k-kiss me," she mumbled, then hic-cupped. "Please, *oh, pul-lease*, don't kiss me again . . . you just don't *know*."

What in the hell, he wondered, was she talking about now?

The cop's eyebrows had risen half an inch, and he was eyeballing her like he wished he knew, too.

"I can't bear it. I *sw-swear* I can't. Not when you kiss me like that. No one else has ever, ever, ever—not the way you . . . and I can't . . . I just can't. Oh, *Christian*."

Geezus. Hawkins didn't embarrass easily, but she was coming damn close to doing it.

"Christian . . . uh . . . Hawkins? Right?" the cop fought a grin as he turned the wallet sideways to read the DOD identification.

"Yes." Now he really wished he were out of the country.

"Well, thank you, Mr. Hawkins," the cop said a moment later, handing back his wallet and not even attempting to hide the big grin spread all over his face. "You have a good night, now."

"You, too, Officer." He gave a short wave as the man walked away, then swore under his breath and walked the last few steps to Toussi's. The gallery's front door was big and old, and he figured it would take him about ten seconds to jimmy the lock.

"Bad . . . so bad . . . bad, bad, bad," she said, going back into broken-record mode.

He felt a tug on his shirt, felt the tail sliding up out of his pants as he tested the knob.

"Bad, bad, bad, bad—"

He gave her a little jiggle to get her back on track, then pulled out his first lock pick.

"Bad l-luck," she moaned on a hiccup, pulling the last of the shirttail up and out of his pants.

The material instantly went tight across the buttons. He could feel her wadding it up in her hands, feel her head turning from side to side as she dabbed away at her eyes and cheeks and, from all the sniffling, her nose.

He'd had worse on him, a lot worse, but *geez*, couldn't a guy get a break here tonight?

"Is that really . . . *really*, really what you've been calling me all these years?" she asked. "B-Bad Luck?"

"Sometimes," he admitted, sliding a second pick in on top of the first. The lock gave, and he twisted the knob open.

No lights were on inside the gallery, and Hawkins wasn't inclined to turn any on. Enough light shone through the windows from the street to keep him from running into anything. He closed and locked the door behind them and waited for his eyes to adjust. The gallery was packed with paintings and sculpture. The room was open to the second floor, with a balcony circling the room and a catwalk crossing it. A series of particularly large paintings hung from the ceiling, some of them swathed in sheeting. Others of a similar size—paintings of men, he thought, or maybe angels—were hung on the walls. There were a lot of them, powerful paintings, full of movement, dynamic even in the low light and obviously all done by the same artist—most of them seeming to be of the same man. He was guessing Nikki McKinney and Travis the Wonder Stud, as Kid had called the guy.

Kid had fallen for the girl, fallen hard. Hawkins remembered her from years ago, when she must have been about six years old and all the wild boys from Steele

Street had gotten busted into her grandfather's job-training program digging dinosaur bones. According to Kid, she'd turned into an amazing woman. From the look of her paintings, Hawkins had to agree.

Behind him, Kat let out a big sigh.

"Th-thank you," she said, her voice carefully solemn. "Thank you for bringing me home . . . thank you . . . thank. I thank-think I can take it from here."

"Think again, babe," he said, looking for the elevator or the stairs up to her apartment. *Hers and Alex Zheng's*, he corrected himself, though he hadn't changed his mind about the secretary not being her boyfriend, not after the way she'd kissed him—desperately, as if she hadn't been kissed in a long, long time, which was just another one of those things he didn't want to think about too much.

He finally spotted the stairs and the elevator toward the back of the gallery, and headed in that direction.

"What floor is your apartment on?"

"Five. Yes, definitelently-lentil-ly five."

Elevator, he thought, then felt her tugging at the T-shirt he was wearing under his dress shirt.

"Hmmm," she murmured quizzically, as if she'd just discovered something.

Hmmm, hell.

"Katya," he warned, reaching around with his free hand and gently extricating her fingers from the cloth.

"Do you know what this is called?" she asked, obliging him by letting go of the T-shirt and smoothing her hand over the muscle curving over his hip and down to his groin.

"Off limits," he replied with a grimace, catching her hand before she could go too far.

"I lived in Paris."

"So you said." He let go of her and quickly shoved the tail end of his T-shirt back in his pants, only to have her pull it back out.

"And I lived in New York."

"Come on. Stop it, honey." He tried to capture her hands again, but this time failed. His T-shirt came free again, and he swore under his breath.

"And I lived in Los Angeles, but I never saw anything like this." She smoothed her palm across the small of his back, across his tattoo, and all he could think was, if she stuck her hand down his pants, he was not going to be held responsible for the consequences.

"That's because I didn't get it in Paris, New York, or Los Angeles." They reached the elevator, and he hit the call button.

"You didn't tell me where you done it, or it done... had it done."

"No." He hadn't. It had been a hot, lazy summer in New Mexico. The woman he'd gone down there with had been ten years older than he was, an artist, and he'd been her favorite canvas during their whole brief and intensely educational affair.

The old cage elevator finally groaned its way down to a stop. Hawkins reached for the handle to slide open the door, and that's when she did it, slipped her hand into his pants, beneath his underwear, and down over his hip.

Son of a bitch. He knew what she was doing, tracing the lines of his tattoo, but that was only going to take her someplace she really shouldn't go, and get both of them in a whole lot of trouble.

"Kat, come on now." He grabbed for her hand, and she

giggled, which was better than her crying. "Okay, babe. Party's over. Come on." And when, he wondered, was the last time he'd tried to get a woman's hand *out* of his pants? Maybe never.

Juggling her and the elevator door, and praying she wouldn't start crying again, Hawkins managed to ease her down off his shoulder, before she either did him any damage or got him so turned on he wouldn't care if making love with her was the smart move or not.

The thought no sooner formed in his mind than he froze. Since when had he gone from having sex with her to making love?

Geezus. He couldn't be that stupid.

"Don't kiss me, Christian," she pleaded, falling against him again and executing a full-frontal, full-court, fulsomely arousing press up the length of his body, the whole thing, from stem to stern.

Against his will and every ounce of his common sense, he looked down at her mouth.

And took a breath.

No, he wasn't going to kiss her. What he was going to do was get her up to her apartment. Now. With that goal in mind, he hustled her the rest of the way into the elevator and hit the button for the fifth floor.

The elevator started up with a groan and a shimmy. It was a small elevator, unbelievably small, but he did his best to keep to his side and hold her on the other with his palm pressed firmly against her torso in that no-man's-land between her abdomen and her breasts.

Distance is what he needed, and a little cooling off time. A man had been murdered tonight, and he needed to clear his head and start figuring out why.

The elevator hit a rough spot, and before it shook itself free, she ended up back in his arms.

He didn't know how. He'd literally been holding her at arm's length.

"*Please* don't kiss me," she whispered, her voice kind of raw and throaty, as if they'd already been kissing the stuffing out of each other for the last couple of hours or so.

Without makeup, her face had lost some of its dramatic contrast, but none of its beauty. Her lashes weren't so dark. Her lips were a softer shade of pink. He could see a light dusting of freckles across her nose, which made her look younger—a lot younger, closer to eighteen than she had a right to look. Her hair was wild, absolutely wild, as if she'd been dragged across the pillows and rolled over on a mattress, the way a guy might, if he was . . . crazy, or lucky, or simply out of his ever-loving mind.

"*Christian.*" She breathed his name, her hands going to the buttons on his shirt and starting to undo them one by one.

He didn't stop her. He was too busy thinking, remembering, and wondering if she might have learned some voodoo hoodoo over the years, maybe in Paris or something, because he was not his normal, clear-thinking self. He felt a little bewitched, as if he were under some kind of spell. She'd had a margarita, but all he'd had was a beer—and a taste of her mouth, and her in his arms, and yeah, that was probably enough to fuck him up.

All because a long time ago she had stripped him bare, cut him to the quick, and left him. Not one word had she spoken to him after his arrest. Not one.

He'd sat there in court and listened to her testimony, watched her be so careful, watched her watching him, and he'd felt like he was seeing the whole thing from under a hundred feet of water, with no air and no light. The weight of what had been happening to him had been crushing.

And her mother. He'd felt the heat of that woman's hatred searing the skin off his bones and then charring what was left. Her fury had been a palpable presence in the courtroom, another entity he'd had to fight against to try and stay alive—and then he'd died anyway. That first night in Canon City, when the doors on his cell clanged shut and the catcalls started, he knew he'd gone straight to hell.

All because he'd made love to the prom queen.

She was pulling the rest of his T-shirt out of his pants and unbuttoning his cuffs, pushing his dress shirt off his shoulders. She was gone, over the edge, and a part of him wanted to just go over the edge with her. If he hadn't gotten busted, maybe they'd still be together. Maybe she would have still been his, and it wouldn't have mattered if she was drunk. He could have made love to her just because she was sweet and hungry and needed him.

Needed him inside her.

Needed him to anchor her world.

She still looked like the Katya he'd known. She still smelled like her, and felt like her, and tasted like her, and God knew she still had the same mind-blowing effect on him.

But she wasn't the same, and neither was he, and he'd

learned his lesson the hard way, the hardest way, and he knew better than to kiss her.

He moved his hand up to cup her cheek and smooth his fingers over her skin.

Hell, they wouldn't have still been together. They wouldn't have survived her mother, not this long. They probably wouldn't have lasted until Labor Day.

Yeah, he knew better than to kiss her, but he did it anyway—just let go of every freaking thing he'd believed in for thirteen years, tilted her face toward his, and brought his mouth down to hers.

Heat, as pure and simple as anything he'd planned, washed through him. He groaned with the pleasure of it, gave himself over to it. Her skin was damp, and he was breaking out in a sweat, and he suddenly knew it didn't matter that she was drunk and he was crazy. *In vino veritas*—in wine is truth. She wanted him, and deep, deep down inside, in a dark place where he'd locked, bolted, and chained the door and thrown away the key, he'd never stopped wanting her.

One of her hands slid through his hair, across the nape of his neck and up toward the top of his skull, holding him for her kiss. His brain was fogging. Her mouth was wet. He reached for her leg and drew it up around his waist, pushing up her dress, getting her closer, reveling in the silken softness of her thigh beneath his fingers. Her other hand was sliding under his waistband, heading south, driving him wild, and he knew—he knew she was going to take him in her hand, stroke him, get him even harder than he already was, and he was going to let her. Oh, man, was he going to let her.

At least that was his plan, until the elevator rattled to a bone-jarring halt and light flooded into the cage.

He froze, the hair on the back of his neck rising. There hadn't been any lights on anywhere in the building when they'd entered.

Well, he *did* have a gun in his pocket—along with everything else. The trick would be using it, if he needed it, because Katya hadn't noticed that their situation had changed.

"*Christian*," she moaned, her hand sliding the last few inches home.

He grabbed for her—too late. *Geezus*. Her palm was so soft, her fingers so delicate, her leg wrapping around his waist, her hand doing the same to his cock—and he was dying...*dying*...but he still slid the hand that wasn't holding her into his pocket for the Glock 9mm.

"If you like," a man drawled, "I can just shoot you now and put you out of your misery." The voice was unmistakable: Dylan.

Hell, he wanted to thrust into her hand so badly he couldn't breathe, but he'd be damned if he would do it in front of an audience.

"K-Katya?" Another man's voice entered the fray, sounding breathlessly shocked—and that would be Alex Zheng, the secretary. He didn't even have to turn around and look.

"Kat," he whispered against her lips, trying not to move too much for fear of what he might do, trying to extricate himself from her sweet grip, trying to find his brains, which he'd probably left in Roxanne, or maybe back at the Botanic Gardens. "Katya, honey. We have to stop."

Hell, they should never have started. Not this, with the two of them backed up against the elevator wall, with her clothes going up and his coming off. It was crazy. His shirt was only half on, his pants unzipped, and he didn't have a clue how she'd worked so fast.

"No," she moaned. "It's been so long, and no one has ever . . ." Her mouth slid over his, her tongue getting him wet, her teeth taking a gentle nip. "No one like you."

He didn't need to know that—honestly.

"You look like hell, and I've got a plane to catch. The— uh—elevator looks a little full. We'll take the stairs and meet you on the fifth floor," Dylan spoke up again.

Hawkins leaned on the fifth-floor button and felt the old elevator restart its ascent. When it had changed direction and gone back down to the gallery, he didn't have a clue. Probably somewhere between when she'd unbuttoned his last button and he'd completely lost his mind.

CHAPTER

9

THINGS COULD HAVE been worse. Hawkins knew it. He just didn't feel it. No, he felt like things were as bad as they could get. Not only had he completely lost his mind, there had been witnesses.

Fuck. He'd given up disintegrating in public after his first three months in prison, and if he sometimes had a hard night to get through, he got through it alone and in private.

Then along comes Katya Dekker, and inside of two hours, he's practically banging her in an elevator in front of her roommate—and Dylan, who had warned him.

He never ignored Dylan's warnings. Never. They'd saved his life too many times, but he'd thought he'd had this situation covered. At the gardens, he would have bet Roxanne's pink slip against him getting within twenty feet of Bad Luck, let alone getting between her legs.

He straightened her dress one more time, trying to

cover her up. It was hopeless. The damn thing was hanging by a thread, and two safety pins were not enough to remedy the problem. He'd taken his damp, wadded-up shirt completely off as the elevator had slowly ground its way up to the fifth floor; out of necessity, he'd let her keep his coat, which left him in a T-shirt and left her way too busy running her fingers up and down his arms.

"The first boy I ever made love with was arrested," she said, her index finger following a path of ink from just below his wrist to his elbow.

"Yeah, I heard." He finished buckling his belt. Damn, she really had moved fast.

"He looked a lot like you."

No kidding, he thought.

He dragged his hands back through his hair, trying to smooth it all into place. The way she'd been working him over, he probably looked like he was the one who'd been rolled across a mattress.

He looked at the top of the elevator door. The thing was slower than molasses in winter. The number three had been lit up forever, making him wonder if the damn thing even went to the fifth floor, or if it just spent a few minutes shaking and shimmying at three before dropping back down.

Finally the four lit up, then the five, and her apartment started coming into view, starting as a band of light at the top of the cage that slowly got broader and broader.

Color was his first impression. Neither she nor Alex Zheng was afraid of color, and possibly, in this instance, a little fear might not have been a bad thing.

The first wall he saw was brick, painted yellow with red and orange flames tinged with white, blue, and green roiling across it. The back wall was graffiti heaven, its big, fat, blue letters proclaiming JULIO RULES against a purple background. KING JULIO was written in huge white letters rimmed in gold across the loft's twelve-foot-high ceiling, the letters looking like clouds in a pale blue sky.

"Who's Julio?" he asked.

She fell against him, her mouth curving into a grin. "Suzi Toussi's latest boyfriend. He's very-very-very, but not so cute as you." He was glad to hear Julio was Suzi's idea of a good time and not Bad Luck's.

He held on to Kat, keeping her from sliding down his body, the direction she seemed inclined to want to go. He didn't know what to make of her comment. "Cute" was not a word people used to describe him.

"Son of a bitch," now, he heard that pretty often. "Mean motherfucker" tended to come to people's minds in certain parts of town and in certain parts of the world, especially if the people concerned happened to be on his shit list. It was usually a pretty long list, full of bad guys the Department of Defense wanted taken down.

Taking down bad guys, that's what he did. He did not get taken down himself—at least not until about three minutes ago. If it hadn't been for Dylan and Alex Zheng showing up . . .

God, if she were drunk, he might have actually started pouring his heart out to her, and wouldn't that have been awful?

French-girl voodoo, that had to be it.

Now all he needed was the antidote.

The elevator lurched to a stop, and when he glanced through the cage, he got exactly what he needed: the look on Dylan's face.

His boss was holding a manila envelope in one hand and a tiara in a plastic bag in the other, looking at a photograph he'd obviously pulled out of the envelope. The expression on his face was one of pure, cold fury.

Standing next to Dylan, also looking at the photo, Alex Zheng had gone white, no mean feat for a half-Asian guy. His hand was up near his throat in a purely feminine gesture of distress—which pretty much clinched Hawkins's gay theory for him.

Both men looked up as he slid open the elevator door. Alex Zheng's gaze went quickly over him and Katya, then came back to the tattoos on his arms. If possible, he turned even paler.

"Alex. Oh, Alex," Katya crooned, holding on to Hawkins as she stumbled off the elevator and into the apartment. "Did you see the fireworks? Are you okay? I've been so . . . so *worried* about you."

She reached for him, and he stepped forward to take her hand, which made a very cozy threesome, because she didn't let go of Hawkins.

"I'm fine, luv. I—"

"You won't *believe* who I ran into," she said, cutting him off with a breathless exclamation.

"Christian Hawkins," he said. His voice sounded a little strangled, as if he'd said "an ax murderer from Hoboken."

"Christian Hawkins! Can you believe it?"

Alex Zheng looked like he believed it all too well, as if it were his worst nightmare coming to life.

Hawkins knew exactly how he felt.

"What's going on?" he asked.

"More bad news," Dylan said grimly, walking toward the elevator and extending both the photograph and the envelope. "This and the tiara were waiting for us when we opened the apartment door. There's a piece of material in the bottom of the envelope. It looks like another part of her prom dress."

Hawkins took the photograph and the envelope, while still holding Kat up—or holding her at bay. It was hard to tell the difference. She was plastered against him, her hand running over the small of his back and occasionally dipping toward his waistband—which he kept putting a halt to as best he could—and she was still talking to Alex Zheng and holding on to his hand, and Hawkins wished they could all just spread out a little, let everybody get a little air.

"My *tiara?*" Kat gasped, letting go of Alex's hand to reach for the bag Dylan was holding. "Ohmygosh."

Dylan carefully held it out of the way, not letting her touch it. "I'm sorry, Ms. Dekker, but this is official evidence right now. I'm sure it will be returned to you later."

"Official evidence for—for what?" she asked.

"For Ted Garraty's m—" Alex started, then saw the look Hawkins was giving him and shut up.

At least the guy had *some* brains. Katya did not need to know Garraty had been murdered—not while she was too drunk to handle the information.

And she shouldn't have been in the same building with that damn tiara, let alone the same room. According to the testimony given at Hawkins's trial, it had gotten lost in the alley when the boys were chasing her, and it hadn't been seen since. He knew for a fact that she hadn't been wearing it when she'd gotten into his car.

He'd known they'd all been lying, the bastards, and as

far as he was concerned, the tiara narrowed down his list of suspects pretty damn succinctly.

Hawkins glanced down at the picture, an eight-by-ten full-color glossy—and turned to stone.

"Where did this come from?"

"It was inside the apartment door when we came in," Dylan said. "And to answer your next question, I have no idea when it was delivered, except sometime after four o'clock, when Ms. Dekker and Mr. Zheng left the apartment to go to the Botanic Gardens."

Hawkins stared down at the photograph, not believing what he was seeing, even though it was right there in his hand. The photo was thirteen years old, yet the rage he felt looking at it was as immediate as if the violation had occurred only moments ago.

He looked at the tiara in Dylan's hand. "Are you sure that's hers?" His throat was so fucking tight, he could hardly breathe, hardly speak.

"Y-yes," Alex answered, a blush creeping into his cheeks. "Triple fleur-de-lis with pink rhinestones, except for the one clear stone on the middle fleur-de-lis, which is obviously a mistake." At Hawkins's questioning look, he added, "I've been over the facts of the Traynor case many times."

Obviously, though how anyone besides an eighteen-year-old prom queen and her mother could see the one clear stone among all the pink sparkle and shine was beyond Hawkins.

"Can I see?" Katya asked, clinging to him with one arm while raising herself on tiptoe to look at the photograph.

"No," he said, holding the picture out of the way. She

didn't need to know about this, either, not while she was drunk.

"I'd say we've narrowed down our list of suspects for tonight's party at the Gardens," Dylan said with typical understatement.

One of the Prom King Murder boys, Hawkins silently agreed. *One of those lying bastards.* The pieces of her dress and the tiara all pointed that way. He forced his gaze back to the photograph and knew why Alex Zheng was blushing. If he hadn't been so furious, he might have blushed, too.

Geezus. There it all was in full color, him under her dress, a cotton summer thing with little straps, little buttons, little flowers, and a few rows of dainty white lace. He was doing God knew exactly what under that dress, and if there was any doubt, all a person had to do was look at her face.

She was in rapture, her mouth open, her neck arched, her fists clenched into the rows of lace—with her legs over his shoulders. Eighteen years old and getting ready to give it all up for him. He remembered. He remembered everything.

As for him, well, you couldn't see that much of him, except for his bare ass, one of his arms, and his back, and that's about all it took to make a positive identification. No wonder Alex had known who he was the instant he'd stepped off the elevator. Without his dress shirt covering his tattoos, there was no mistaking him.

Hawkins opened the envelope up wider. "You look in here?" he asked Dylan. Katya was chattering away to her secretary again.

"No. I pretty much got the general idea from just the one photo. Figured you could take it from there."

Dylan was nothing if not discreet, which had saved both their lives more times than Hawkins could count. He pulled the stack of pictures partway out of the envelope and quickly went through them.

It only got worse. One of those friggin' prom boys had been pretty busy with a camera. All he had to do was find out which one and do what he did best—take the son of a bitch down.

"What's wrong with her?" Alex interjected during a lull in Katya's breathless monologue about the tiara and the fireworks, and the fireworks and the tiara.

"She had one too many margaritas." Hawkins shoved all the photographs back into the envelope, not bothering to elaborate that just one margarita had been too much.

"No, I've—I've seen her drunk," the secretary begged to differ, "I've just never seen her like . . . like this." He made a small, helpless gesture.

"Why don't you take her into her bedroom," Hawkins suggested, peeling her off his body and handing her over to Alex. "Get her something to wear."

He wasn't going to leave her in the apartment, especially now, with some wacko breaking in and leaving his sordid calling card, but he could use a breather, a chance to clear the air and get his head screwed back on straight.

His coat fell open during the transfer, and there she was for all the world to see, practically half naked with her clothes falling off.

Alex quickly wrapped his arm around her waist, holding

her up. "What happened to her dress?" he asked, a definite edge coming into his voice.

"It tore, Alex, the new one I bought in L.A., but I was able to pin it together," Katya answered, twisting to one side. "See? Two pins."

"It tore during the explosion at the Gardens, when she fell," Hawkins added some explanation. "All I've been trying to do is keep her in one piece. It's all I'm going to do."

From the look Alex gave him, his line was obviously a little hard to swallow after the way she'd been all over him, and honestly, he'd be the first to admit that if she came on to him sober the way she was coming on to him drunk, he was going to take her up on her offer. He was no saint, and kissing her had done nothing but whet his appetite for more. As a matter of fact, kissing her had put a real edge on his appetite. They were both adults now. He could handle it, handle her—and she could handle him any way she wanted.

But Alex Zheng didn't need to know any more than what he'd already seen in the elevator.

As for himself, he'd seen plenty, too. Enough to change his plans for the night.

"I think we can all agree that it isn't safe for Ms. Dekker to stay here. If you could put a few things together for her, I'm sure she would appreciate it," Hawkins said, keeping his voice cool, calm, and professional.

"This isn't a matter for the Department of Defense," Alex said, agreeing to nothing.

Hawkins looked to Dylan.

"He wanted confirmation of who we were with,"

Dylan said, "and I gave it to him. His plan is to call in the police."

"Let me get her settled," Alex said, before Hawkins could tell him where he could put his plan. "Then I'll be back." Holding her close to his side, he headed for a door on the other side of the living room.

Hawkins cocked an eyebrow at Dylan, who shrugged.

"He's having a hard time accepting that he's not the one in charge of this deal."

Hawkins didn't give a damn. "Well, he better get used to it. I'm taking her back to Steele Street tonight, especially after this." He lifted the envelope. "Tomorrow I'll run down all the Prom King boys. What?" he asked, seeing Dylan's expression turn grim.

"Skeeter got a call from Miguel. The NRF dumped J.T. off the back end of a truck in a box and a body bag just after sunset. Miguel said Kid didn't sound too good, but he won't be able to get into Rosalia to get him out until tomorrow morning."

Something hard twisted in Hawkins's chest. Somehow, even with what they'd been told, a part of him had held on to the possibility that J.T. was still alive.

"Miguel also said the Marines were pulled out of Rosalia late this morning," Dylan continued. "Back to Panama."

So Kid had been left on his own—all day, and he'd be on his own all night tonight. Hawkins wanted to swear in frustration. If Kid had seen the body bag, he'd obviously opened the box. Hawkins hoped like hell that he hadn't opened the bag—but he knew Kid had. Hawkins would have opened it. So would every one of the guys who worked for SDF.

"What about Stavros?" This was going to be hard on old man Chronopolous. J.T. had been giving his father heart attacks since he was fourteen years old and running wild in the streets of Denver. Stavros's love had been there for his son, but not the ability to control him, not after Kid and J.T.'s mother had left for the bright lights of Los Angeles and a career as a wannabe actress in Hollywood.

"Skeeter's headed over there now and will stay with him for a while," Dylan said.

"I'll have to go back to Colombia. Finish the job." Revenge was a hard word, but the men of SDF were hard men; one of them didn't get killed without all of them having to be dealt with.

"We'll all go back," Dylan said. "Let's get this Prom King mess off our backs first, take care of old business, before we finish up the new." Dylan tied off the bag with the tiara inside and tossed it to him.

Hawkins caught the sparkling crown with one hand.

"How much trouble are we going to be in with Lieutenant Loretta if I have Skeeter dust the prints off this before we turn it over?" he asked.

"No more than we can handle," Dylan assured him. "General Grant put us here, so he can damn well back us up if we end up stepping on a few toes."

That was fine by Hawkins. Loretta might not like it, but he figured she wouldn't hold it against him—not for too long, anyway.

"I'm not one to give advice," Dylan continued.

Like hell he wasn't, Hawkins thought. He'd been giving them all advice since he'd first roped them all together into a gang of thieves.

"So don't."

"She's trouble, Cristo. Nothing but trouble, and her mother is meaner than a junkyard dog. Tonight looks like a setup to me, and you're the one getting set up. Not many people have the kind of power to pull this off. Could be that Senator Dekker didn't like the idea of you still being in Denver with her daughter moving back home."

"And she had Ted Garraty murdered to frame me?" he asked incredulously, then shook his head. "Hell, no, my luck isn't running that good." There were few things he would like more than to go *mano a mano* with Linebacker Dekker at her junkyard-dog worst, but she hadn't planted naked pictures of her daughter in the apartment, and she hadn't bought a hit on Garraty.

Dylan shrugged. He never put anything past a person with a motive. Never. Despite the choirboy face and impeccable manners, Dylan Hart was a cynic to the core. It was what made him tick, what had kept him alive.

"Well, will you do me a favor and at least *try* not to sleep with her?" His boss gave him a look that said he was only thinking about what was good for him—and Hawkins knew it. He knew getting involved with Bad Luck would only bring him more bad luck. It didn't take a rocket scientist to figure that out. Dylan was only giving him the advice of a friend, a good friend, the very best.

"Sure," he said, and had to wonder if he was lying through his teeth.

"Try?" Another voice intruded.

Both Hawkins and Dylan turned to look at Alex Zheng.

"There won't be any *try* to it," the secretary continued,

his voice shaking, his face livid. "She's crying in there, and as of right now, Ms. Dekker is *strictly* off limits to you both. I know all about you, Mr. Hawkins. Straight from the 'junkyard dog' herself, and she'll have you *keelhauled* if you set so much as another finger on her daughter."

"So you know the senator?" Hawkins asked. Cool. Calm. Professional.

"We're like this," the secretary said, holding up two entwined fingers as he came to a stop in front of the two men, his small frame trembling with anger. "My job is to keep Katya safe at *all* costs, and that *stunt* you pulled at the Botanic Gardens and the shape you've brought her back in is enough for me to get assault charges drawn up."

It was a ridiculous threat, but it still rankled the hell out of him.

"So who do you take your orders from?" Cool. Calm. Nonconfrontational. That was him—until he decided he needed to kick Alex Zheng's ass.

The secretary drew himself up to his full five feet, six inches in height. "My authority comes *directly* from Senator Dekker herself, and your associate is absolutely correct. She is not to be messed with—by anyone. So I suggest you leave the premises, before I call her and she has you arrested."

"Been there, done that, Alex."

"And I'm sure, from what I've been told, that it was an experience you would prefer not to repeat."

To hell with being cool, calm, and professional. He was going to kick Alex Zheng's ass right here, right now.

"Actually," Dylan interrupted, before he could deck the sucker, "I think Mr. Zheng might have a point."

Now what in the hell did that mean? he wondered,

glaring at Dylan. Then he saw her, his attention caught by movement in her bedroom doorway.

Alex was giving Dylan a rather smug look, while Katya was looking at her secretary from across the apartment, her expression one of utter betrayal, and yes, he knew the feeling well enough to recognize it in someone else, even at a distance. She'd just lost her best friend—to her mother.

"I have more than a point, Mr. Hart," Alex said. "I have a senator on my side, a senator who will be in Denver tomorrow morning to kick off her new campaign."

It was the last straw for Tinkerbell. Bringing her hand to her mouth, she turned and disappeared into the bedroom. A few seconds later, he heard it: the sound of someone stepping onto a fire escape.

Holy shit.

"Okay. You win this one, Mr. Zheng," he said. "But don't think that I won't be back."

Alex's surprised expression at winning so easily quickly turned to satisfaction. The guy was obviously too full of himself to notice the sound of Katya's escape.

Hawkins turned and headed for the door. By the time her secretary noticed she was missing, he'd have her long gone.

"So how long have you worked for Marilyn Dekker?" he heard Dylan ask Alex behind his back, running interference.

As soon as he cleared the door, Hawkins broke into a run. He slid down the stairs, vaulting the rail at every turn, doing the five floors in one tenth of the time it had taken on the elevator. He saw a back door next to where the stairs ended, and he was through it in record time—in plenty of time to watch her make her painstaking way down the fire escape.

The alley was poorly lit and quiet enough for him to hear her swearing and crying the whole way down. She'd taken off her four-inch heels, thank God, and had them in her hand, but it still seemed like an eternity before she finally got to the bottom.

The fire escape didn't reach all the way to the ground, and as she shimmied herself over the final platform—truly a sight to behold—he moved into place.

She slid into his arms, still cussing and crying and starting to hiccup again, and without setting her down, he hefted her back over his shoulder and started walking down the alley.

Roxanne was just around the corner, parked in front of the gallery, and Steele Street was just a few blocks north, and the whole night was stretching out in front of him with nothing but trouble in sight.

As soon as he closed the door behind Dylan Hart, Alex headed for Kat's bedroom, checking his Colt .45 semiautomatic pistol. He had to get her out of the apartment and someplace safe.

It was going to take him years to forgive himself for losing her at the Botanic Gardens—if he ever forgave himself. He'd gone soft, gotten too used to never having to protect her from anything more than a bad-news rock-and-roll boyfriend or the other shoppers at a Neiman-Marcus shoe sale.

But tonight. *Christ*. Tonight had been insane. Ted

Garraty murdered. Christian Hawkins, so help him God, whisking her away. Bits of her prom dress flying around like so much confetti. The damn tiara.

And the photographs.

Somebody was going to pay for the photographs. If Christian Hawkins didn't get to him first, Alex was going to take the bastard apart.

It was nothing short of a miracle that Hawkins and Hart had given her up and left. Invoking the senator's name was something Alex usually avoided at all costs, having spent most of the last five years with Katya trying to distance himself from the woman who had actually hired him, but it had been effective.

At least that's what he thought until he entered her bedroom, saw the open window, and instantly knew he was screwed. A soft curse left his mouth as he raced for the window. One look down into the alley proved he was too late.

Damn, oh, damn. He didn't waste a second dwelling on the awfulness of her disappearing again, but turned and ran for the door. When he reached the street, all he could do was stand there and swear. The chop-shop boys had aced him again. Dylan Hart, Hawkins, Katya—all of them were gone.

Muttering every curse word he knew under his breath, he reached for his cell phone. How a couple of ex-car thieves had turned into the kind of men with the security clearances Dylan Hart had flashed at the Botanic Gardens was beyond him. He only hoped they'd moved fast enough to catch her. The last thing he wanted was Katya on her own tonight. Just the thought was enough to make his blood run cold.

Hart had given him a business card before he'd left, and he punched the top number into his phone.

The call was picked up on the first ring.

"Hart."

"Zheng," Alex shot back, irritated as hell. "Where's Katya?"

"Under the protection of the Department of Defense."

"So you've got her?"

"Not me. Hawkins."

Alex bit back another curse, told himself to stay calm, and tried to take a nice, deep breath. This was his fault, he knew it, but he couldn't help but think that Senator Dekker and her staff had dropped the ball on these boys. He'd been briefed ad nauseam on the Jonathan Traynor III murder when he'd been hired, been given a folder on Christian Hawkins that was four inches thick, which had included profiles on all the boys who'd gotten busted with him out of the chop shop on Steele Street when they'd been teenagers.

A few of them had joined the military, a couple had gone to college, and two of them had been written off as basically harmless car salesmen—Dylan Hart and Christian Hawkins.

Jesus. Had anybody taken a look at these two guys anytime in the last five years?

They weren't car salesmen—and deep breathing wasn't working.

Marilyn Dekker was connected all over the Department of Defense. Someone on her staff should have been paying better attention. *He* should have been paying better attention.

"I want her back." And he wanted the tiara and the

photographs back. Letting Hawkins get away with them was just one more big mistake on his part. At the time, all he'd been thinking was how glad he was Hawkins was leaving.

"She's with the guy who headed up the Personal Security Detail for the Secretary of State when he did his tour of the Middle East last year," Hart said, his voice coming over the phone in clipped tones. "If you want to worry about something, worry about who shot Ted Garraty."

The click in his ear told Alex the conversation was over.

Fine, he thought, snapping his phone shut and shoving it in his pocket. He took a deep breath, then another, watching the traffic go by and trying not to panic—but he could tell it was going to be a losing battle.

TROUBLE. God, he was in trouble here.

Stretched out in one of the chairs in front of his fire-place, Hawkins had a straight line of sight to his bed, where he'd put her. There were no walls in his Steele Street loft, just three thousand square feet of wood floors and a hundred feet of fifteen-foot-tall windows looking out over the city. He'd left her dress on, but it wasn't covering a whole hell of a lot, and she kept kicking the sheets off the rest of her.

She was tossing and turning—and talking in her sleep, and man, oh, man, was she pissed off at her mother. But that was Linebacker's problem. His problem was the whole crazy night and how easily he'd lost control of himself.

He wouldn't last long anywhere under those circum-stances. Self-control was supposed to be his middle name. But damn, she'd pulled a number on him. No more, though. Not tonight.

Pushing himself out of the chair, he headed across the living area to the kitchen to start a pot of coffee. He had a long few hours ahead of him before dawn, and brooding about her wasn't getting him where he needed to go. He'd called in Johnny Ramos, a kid who worked in Steele Street's Commerce City garage, to watch over her for the rest of the night. Ted Garraty's murder would be all over the papers in the morning, but he and Mickey were going to get it out on the street tonight, see if the news rattled anybody, see if anybody remembered the Traynor case, and see if they could find Ray Carper. Mickey hadn't heard that Carper was dead, so chances were that the old guy was still hanging around somewhere. Hawkins also needed to go back to the Botanic Gardens. Poke around a little bit. See what he could find.

Fifteen minutes later, he poured himself a big paper cup full of strong, black coffee and snapped a plastic lid on top. He'd changed into a skintight muscle shirt, gray with the Chinese characters for "Fuck you" silk-screened on the front, a pair of jeans so baggy they barely clung to his hips, and his favorite pair of two-hundred-and-fifty-dollar stolen Nikes. He hadn't stolen them, but he'd bought them off the guy who had, a real deal at fifty bucks a pop.

She groaned, and he went over to check on her. He took a sip of coffee, then knelt down next to the bed and rested his palm on her forehead. The coffee was hot, damn hot, and so was she, but not fever hot. He looked down the length of her body. A damp sheen of sweat covered her skin, from the backs of her calves, in the tender hollows behind her knees, up her thighs, and over the incredible curves of her ass.

He wanted to eat her, to start at her pink-polished toes with his mouth and just not stop. Instead, he set his coffee aside, stood up, and shrugged into his shoulder holster. A well-worn black leather vest went over the top.

He checked his watch, waiting for Johnny, then let his gaze wander the rest of the way up her body and her torn and bedraggled dress. He could have put her in one of his T-shirts, but he honest to God hadn't trusted himself, and that was a hell of a thing, maybe the worst realization yet tonight. He wouldn't take advantage of her, but he was on a damn thin line as to whether or not he would try to seduce her.

Come on, Johnny, he thought, checking his watch again.

He turned his attention back to Katya and noticed her shooting-star tattoo was gone.

Perfect, he thought. It hadn't been a real tattoo, just one of those painted-on ones, and now it was probably smeared inside the sleeve of his favorite two-thousand-dollar suit. Whoever had named her Bad Luck had hit the nail on the head.

Oh, right, that had been him.

Hearing the elevator stop, he snapped the sheet up over her again.

"Hey, Superman," Johnny said, coming through the door. "*¿Qué pasa?*"

Johnny was a Hispanic kid whose older brother had died in a gang killing. He'd been in plenty of trouble in his seventeen years, and like Skeeter, he'd been on the street when Hawkins had found him.

"Hey, Johnny. Thanks for coming up. This is Katya

Dekker." He gestured at the lovely lump in the bed. "I don't want her leaving the loft. I don't care if you have to tie her up. She stays here."

Johnny eyed the nearly comatose woman, then gave Hawkins a big grin. "Sure, Cristo. You can count on me, man. I can keep her here. As a matter of fact"—he leaned in for a closer look—"I think she's out cold, *hombre*."

"She had a margarita at Mama Guadalupe's."

"Just one?"

"One."

"Oh, man." Johnny rocked back on his heels. "*Mezcal*. Sure, man. I can keep her here. You don't think she's gonna be sick?"

"Anything can happen," Hawkins warned him. "The least of which is her throwing up. So you be ready. Look, she's still here when I get back, and you're still with her, you can have Roxanne next Friday night."

Johnny brightened. "Sure, man. I can handle her."

He didn't want her "handled" at all and was just about to tell Johnny as much, when she let out a soft moan and rolled over, losing the sheet in the process.

"*Ay, caramba,*" the boy whispered, his eyes glued to the naked curve of her hip.

Hawkins quickly got the sheet back over her. "Remember your honor," he said, tucking the sheet in between the mattresses. "And hers. *No toques.*" Don't touch. *Don't even breathe on her, baby-boy, or the* mierda *is going to hit the fan.*

Satisfied that he'd done all he could, and that things would only get worse if he stayed, and that he'd only get more screwed up, he straightened from the side of the bed. Checking to make sure he'd remembered to load his gun, he headed for the door.

ONE *more endless night*, Nikki McKinney thought, glancing at the clock in her studio. Midnight had long since come and gone. Nothing unusual there. She always worked best at night. Returning her attention to her painting, she took a step back. The piece of canvas was large, eight by six feet.

She let her eyes wander over the image she'd created, breathing softly, letting her mind slide into the emotions it evoked, drifting from one wash of color to the next, from curves of paint to the more startling photographic image beneath.

Eventually, as always, she knew what to do next. Taking a piece of cardboard, she dipped the end of it in a tray of indigo blue paint, then lifted it to the canvas and scraped it in broad, dripping strokes down one side of a tortured angel.

He was bound and gagged, and in agony, and he was beautiful, probably the most beautiful man she'd ever seen. He was also sound asleep over in the corner on her studio floor, stretched out in a pair of cutoff jeans and a T-shirt on a pile of blankets.

The walls in her studio were covered in photographs and paintings of him, mostly as an angel, but sometimes as a demon, and sometimes just as a man. But she loved him best as an angel. She loved all her models best as angels. Travis James was her favorite, though, and had been for the last five years, ever since she was sixteen and he was eighteen and she'd first started painting him naked.

He was exquisite, with his shoulder-length blond hair and lean, muscular, rock-climber's body, the epitome of youth, man as God had envisioned him—both sexual and innocent, with a face designed for seduction and a smile that made the fall worthwhile.

He wasn't smiling in this painting, though. She'd put him through hell for this piece.

Finished with the blue, she dropped the cardboard in the trash with a dozen others. They were only good for one run through the paint. She picked up another and dipped it in a tray of white and made one long, diagonal curve across the canvas, coming from the top of one battered wing, through the angel's right shoulder and down across the front of his body into the abyss rising up at his feet—and suddenly, the painting was complete.

No fanfare sounded. It was simply done, just like that. Between one breath and another, two months' worth of work finally reached its end—thankfully, in time for her opening at Toussi Gallery tomorrow night, in less than twenty-four hours.

She should have been done with it weeks ago. She'd always planned it as the centerpiece of her whole show, the painting that would catch the critics' eye and hopefully vault her to fame and glory, or at least into a showing in Los Angeles or maybe even New York.

But life, and love, and heartache had intervened one hot, unexpected summer night in June, and she'd had a helluva time getting back on her feet, artistically speaking. Emotionally, she was still a mess.

Chaos, that's what had happened to her that night, Kid

Chaos, and she'd barely begun to sort through the wreckage he'd left in his wake, which was utterly ridiculous. He'd walked into her life a total stranger, and eight hours later, he'd walked back out a lover. That alone should have been enough to fuel some serious soul-searching, but the rest of it was even worse. She hadn't just fallen in bed with the man, she'd fallen in love.

And he'd left her. Just like that. Without so much as a by-your-leave. Her—the invincible Nikki McKinney, the oldest living virgin in Boulder, Colorado, until Peter "Kid Chaos" Chronopolous had nearly gotten her killed and then turned around and stolen her heart.

"Damn," she muttered under her breath. Here she was, thinking about him again, a bad habit she'd had absolutely no luck breaking. Every thought she had turned to him, and she didn't have a clue as to where he was, or what he was doing, or what had happened to make him leave her. Her only connection to him was through her new brother-in-law, Quinn Younger, who was sworn to some damn secrecy pact at the place they both worked. Even her sister, Regan, hadn't been much help, telling her only that SDF was part of some government operation and highly classified. All Quinn had promised was to tell her if something happened to him, and Nikki could think of few things that sounded more ominous. The last thing she wanted to hear was that Kid had been hurt . . . or killed.

It was crazy. She was crazy. Suzi Toussi had offered her the biggest opportunity of her life, and when Suzi had sold the gallery to Katya Dekker, that opportunity had hit the stratosphere, and she'd still almost blown it.

Katya Dekker. Struggling artists whispered her name

as a talisman. She was brilliant, becoming very high profile on the California art scene over the last couple of
years, and in her career, she had taken a dozen no-name
Los Angeles painters and turned them into stars.

Nikki wanted to be her first Colorado success. She
wanted everyone to see her work, to experience it. To
her, an unseen painting was only half complete, sterile. It
needed the emotional response of the viewer in order to
bear fruit—and that was the point of it all, the whole
point, to make the connection, not just with the work,
but with other people through the work.

She especially wanted to make the connection through
this piece, *Pathos VII*, and she'd almost let the opportunity slip away by wallowing in heartbreak and shame.
Twenty-one years of virginity, and she'd thrown it all
away on a one-night stand. What did that say about her
judgment?

Nothing good, she knew that much, but that wasn't
the worst. The worst was the pining. She longed for Kid,
for his touch, for the sound of his voice, in a way she
wouldn't have thought possible. It was unbearably needy
of her to want a practical stranger so much, all the time.
She wanted to kiss him, breathe him in, be with him, and
in her own twisted way, she'd managed it as best she
could—and almost blown her show in the process.

Reluctantly but inevitably, she shifted her gaze to the
far wall of her studio, her wall of Chaos, Kid Chaos. She'd
photographed him that night, during the shoot with
Travis for *Pathos VII*. He hadn't known what she'd been
doing, so all the shots were candid. He'd been taking in
the whole process of her work, the lights going, the mu-
sic blaring, her bank of cameras whirring and clicking,

Travis succumbing to the abyss she'd created—and she'd caught him once staring straight at her through the lens of her Nikon.

The shot was stunning—especially blown up to four by six feet and enhanced with all the skill she had at her very talented fingertips. She had a dozen of the painted photographs hanging on the wall and stacked around her studio, along with enlargements of all the other shots she'd gotten of him. They were all showpieces, but she wasn't putting any of them in her show. Not yet. He was still hers, even if only on canvas and paper.

She walked over to the wall and grazed her fingers across his face, across hawklike eyebrows, the smooth lines of cheekbones above the faint beard stubble along his jaw, across the curve of his lips. His gaze was narrow, fierce, piercing in its intensity, his alertness honed to a razor's edge. Every fiber of his being was ready.

Ready for what? she'd wondered at the time. An hour later, racing down a mountain canyon in a hail of bullets, she'd known only all too well. He'd been ready for anything, absolutely anything, if that's what it took to save her life.

He was a warrior who'd dragged his bag of lethal heavy metal up on the Hill in Boulder and changed her forever, and for a very short time, she'd thought he'd been hers. Waking up alone had cured her of that illusion. Not hearing a word from him since, in seven long weeks, had pretty much cemented her deduction: She truly had been a one-night stand.

How could she have been so wrong about what she thought had been between them?

The sudden ringing of the phone made her heart lurch

to a stop. Her gaze instantly went to the clock: a few minutes past four A.M.

In two steps, she had the phone in her hand.

"Hello?" she said breathlessly, her heart pounding. On the other side of the room, Travis stirred and pushed himself up to a sitting position. Their gazes met, and Nikki held up her hand. She didn't know who it was yet.

"Nikki? Nikki, it's Regan. Sorry we've been late getting home, honey, but we finally got the parts we needed for the plane in Hawaii." Her sister's voice was scratchy, as if she'd been crying, which didn't make sense. She and Quinn were on their honeymoon. "We made it to L.A. about an hour ago and should be home early this afternoon."

"What's happened?" Something was wrong. Nikki could feel it. Travis rose to his feet and started across the room.

There was a pause on the other end of the phone, then an indrawn breath. "Kid's brother has been killed. He's bringing the body back to Denver."

The shock of the statement left her momentarily stunned. Travis put his hand on her shoulder, letting her know he was there.

Kid's brother. J.T. Kid had told her he was working in South America, that they all did a lot of work in South America. So that's where he'd gone, to be with his brother—and his brother had been killed.

"Kid?" She reached for Travis, gripping his arm, barely able to get the name out.

"He wasn't hurt, Nikki. He should be home sometime today, maybe tonight...but I don't...I don't know what's going to happen, honey. I'll call you as soon as we get to Denver. Are you and Wilson okay?"

"Fine," she said, still stunned. "We're doing fine."

"Okay, baby. I'll see you this afternoon, then. I was so worried we might miss your show, because of the plane. But I'll be there, Nikki. I promise. Good-bye. I love you."

"I love you, too, Regan. Bye," she said, then heard the click of the line disconnecting.

She carefully hung up the phone, her emotions racing.

J.T. had been killed. Poor Kid. Oh, poor, poor Kid. Her hand came up to cover her mouth.

"What's wrong, Nikki?" Travis's voice was softened by sleep, but his hold on her was steady, reassuring.

She lifted her gaze to his. "Kid's brother has been killed. They were in South America. He's bringing the body home today."

"Ah, Nikki," he said, turning her into the warm circle of his arms, holding her close.

She lowered her face into her hands. Her heart was breaking, breaking in a thousand jagged pieces, she hurt so badly for him, but she couldn't deny that deep inside her blood was rushing faster and a small spark of hope had flamed to life, because Kid Chaos was finally coming home.

CHAPTER

WHEREVER SHE WAS, it was perfect, Katya thought. The bed was perfect. The sheets were perfect. The pillow over her head was perfect, and as long as absolutely nothing moved, she'd be perfect, too. The problem was, she was breathing. It was inescapable, and every breath brought a tiny bit of movement, and every tiny bit of movement brought a huge, wracking, throbbing, aching pain to her head.

She carefully opened one eye a bare fraction of a slit. There was enough space between the pillow and the bed for her to see all the way across a rather expansive room to a large bank of windows on the other side. The ceilings had to be at least fifteen feet high. The windows were framed in iron with a very industrial look, quite a contrast to the soft gray furniture grouped around an Oriental rug in front of a black marble fireplace. There was a fire going. She could feel the warmth of it floating across the room and taking the chill out of the air, and there was a chill in the air. From the angle of the sunlight streaming in through the windows, she figured it was about mid-morning—and she'd woken up in a strange bed.

That was a first.

A very disconcerting first.

Then she remembered something—an explosion, and a car named Roxanne, and a man... and a killer margarita.

Oh, brother. How could she have forgotten for even a second? Christian Hawkins, and this was undoubtedly his bed.

She turned her nose deeper into the sheets. *Oh, yeah, this is his bed*—soft, warm blankets, Egyptian cotton sheets, down pillows, and the smell of him wrapping around her senses. Heaven.

"Katya?"

The voice came from somewhere on her right. She recognized it instantly—and it was definitely Hawkins. She quickly calculated the odds of her spontaneously disappearing without a trace, and figured they were pretty slim.

Too bad.

"Are you okay under there?"

"Yes," she whispered into the sheets, then confessed, "No." She didn't have the strength to maintain a lie. She was completely wiped out, more tired now than she could have possibly been when she'd fallen asleep—or perhaps "passed out" was the more accurate description—and her head was breaking. It was what had woken her up, and what was going to make getting back to sleep impossible: the Headache from Hell.

"Do you want some tea?"

Tea?

"Chamomile. It'll help. Then we'll get a couple glasses of water in you. If you can eat some toast, I'll give you some aspirin."

A man with a plan that sounded like it could save her, which was his specialty, if she remembered correctly, and she was pretty darn sure she did. The night was quickly coming back to her in bits and pieces, like a jumbled-up puzzle. She let them all fall through her mind and fall into place, painting a rather tumultuous picture of the previous night, until one of those little memories leaped out and froze her solid where she lay under all those soft, warm blankets.

She'd stuck her hand down his pants.

Ohmigod. The heat of a sudden, fierce blush flashed across her cheeks.

She heard him walk away, heard the sound of him working in the kitchen and, far too quickly, heard him return.

"Kat?"

"Hmmm?" she answered softly, politely. The small sound echoed under the pillow like she'd yelled down the Grand Canyon, and she winced, which just about blew her head off.

"Come on, Kat. Let's get a little something in you." He'd moved closer. She could tell by the sound of his voice. Then she smelled the tea and toast, and miracle of miracles, it smelled good, like it actually could save her.

He was right, of course, she needed some sustenance, but that didn't make her unbelievably mortifying situation any better. She hadn't just stuck her hand down his pants. She'd . . . she'd . . . oh, God. She squeezed her eyes shut and prayed someone would tell her it just wasn't so, that she hadn't actually grabbed on to him and . . . and felt him up—which was as close to the truth as she dared to get. Oh, geez, what in the world had she been thinking?

She'd meant it as a rhetorical question, but her suddenly functioning memory banks were all too ready to supply an answer. She'd been thinking how warm his skin was, and how much she was fascinated by his tattoo, the clean, broad strokes of stylized feathers, the tips curling onto the backs of his hands, the wings themselves flowing down his back to the base of his spine, where they split and curved low around his hips, ending above his groin. She'd been thinking about all the times she'd traced those lines with her fingertips . . . and her tongue, and then suddenly they'd been kissing, his mouth so hot on hers, and her hand had gone way beyond the out-of-bounds territory.

Her blush deepened, as did her distress. It had been a lot like making love, being that intimate with him, and the last thing she wanted to face was even the remote possibility of still being attracted to him. It had been thirteen years, and she'd never heard so much as one word from him in all that time. What had happened had been too awful, and she'd assumed that like her, he would only want to forget.

Except that was a lie. She hadn't wanted to forget anything about him. Being wrenched away from him, losing him, had been as painful as facing Jonathan's death. Hawkins was who she'd needed to share her grief with, to find solace with—and he'd been taken away. He'd been the man she loved, even if he'd only been a boy.

"Katya?" His voice came again, a little more insistent.

Well, he wasn't a boy any longer, and God, yes, what she needed to do was pull herself together and get out of his exquisitely decorated downtown loft, before he had her arrested for sexual harassment, but she simply could not face him.

"Could you go away...please?" she mumbled under the pillow. Like to Siberia for a few days, so she could slink away like the coward she was and hopefully never, ever have to face him again.

After a long silence, in which she began to wonder if he actually had gone away, he spoke.

"No, I can't go away." He didn't sound any happier than her about it, which made her feel even more mortified. "We've got a lot of work to do today, and I need your help. If we can get a little food and water in you, you'll feel better. The toast is whole wheat."

Oh, God. He'd remembered her favorite toast. He was a saint, and she was a pervert, but she didn't have to be an idiot pervert.

Slowly, she slid her hand out to the side of the bed. "Toast," she mumbled.

"Tea first."

Fine. He wasn't going to be nice and do things her way, but she'd get through this. She always got through horrendously mortifying situations. But she honestly didn't think she could apologize for sticking her hand down his pants. She didn't have the courage to even mention it, let alone discuss it. All she could do was hope he hadn't noticed.

Yeah, right.

How could she have done such a stupid, crude thing? Just how desperate was she, really?

Once again, her brain was only too happy to supply the answer, and the truth was, it had been a long time since she'd met a man she wanted, and what she'd done hadn't seemed at all stupid or crude at the time. It had been lovely. Touching him had made her feel warm all over and hot inside, and so very alive—which just made it that much harder to face him.

God help her. She had to get out of his loft, the sooner the better.

Moving carefully, she slowly levered herself up on one elbow, letting the pillow slide off her head onto the bed. Her hair was half down over her face, which she considered a real plus, and she barely opened her eyes, the better to keep her head from blowing off.

"Tea," she agreed, putting her hand out.

She did not look at his face. The last thing she wanted was to make eye contact. Most of what she saw was the front of his shirt, and what she saw sparked her curiosity in spite of her hangover.

She leaned her head sideways a little to see past his vest.

" 'Fuck you' ?" she said, reading the Chinese characters on his shirt.

"Sure," he said, "but why don't you drink your tea first?"

It took a second or two for that to sink in, and when it did, her half-closed gaze inadvertently shifted to his, and another blush, even deeper than before, flashed across her face.

"I was just . . . just—" Not thinking. At all, she admitted to herself.

"Reading Chinese," he said, helping her out. "That's interesting."

"It's Alex, my secretary. He knows Chinese, and he . . . uh . . ." *Betrayed me*, she remembered. Sold her down the river to her mother. Oh, yes, it was all coming back now, but as awful as Alex's betrayal was, it was nothing compared to the trouble she was in, sitting in Christian Hawkins's bed.

One look at him, and a hundred other memories came flooding back. He'd kissed her. That's how everything had started. He'd kissed her in the bar at Mama Guadalupe's, and she'd melted with pleasure and need. Absolutely melted.

Her gaze dropped to his mouth, and her blush grew even hotter. No one kissed like Christian Hawkins—long, and slow, and wet, and deep, like his next breath depended on her kiss, his mouth molding to hers like they were made for each other, his body so strong and hard up against her, moving against her. She could have kissed him forever.

"Don't worry about Alex," he told her. "He's out of the picture, if you want him to be. Not even your mother can change that."

His words startled her out of her reverie, and with effort, she forced herself to meet his eyes again. He looked about twenty-two this morning, with his tough-guy clothes, tousled hair, and beard-shadowed jaw, and he obviously needed a reality check on one of the less pleasant facts of life, one she would have thought he'd known.

"My mother can change anything she wants," she told

him, because it was the truth. International oil crises, diplomatic relations with Third World countries, political agendas and media priorities, friendships, loyalties, her daughter's love life—Marilyn Dekker had messed with them all, repeatedly and freely over the years, with abandon and damn little conscience.

"Not this time," he told her with enough self-assurance in his voice to make her wonder if it could possibly be true. Could he possibly have some source of power great enough to subdue the Dragon?

She looked around his loft. He lived well, very well. She knew expensive furniture and a designer kitchen when she saw them, and he had both, but Katya didn't doubt for a minute that Dragon Dekker could ruin him all over again—if she found out what had happened. And with Alex on her payroll, she was probably already airborne and headed to Denver.

The thought was enough to clear her head in one startling blast of realization, and make her stomach churn with the next. Oh, God, she had to get out of there, away from him, immediately. She couldn't bear for him to be hurt again because of her.

She wasn't too thrilled about what her mother might try to do to her, either.

Damn Alex all to hell.

"I'm—uh—sorry, but I won't be able to help you with any work or anything for—um, who did you say you were with? The Department of Defense?" What in the world he thought she could do for the Defense Department was a mystery. *Not much*, was what she figured. Moving with glacial slowness, she started easing herself

off the bed. "Thanks for—uh—everything, though."
Whatever everything might be. She really wasn't sure,
but a nice thank-you always eased a parting—or an escape. "If you'll just call me a cab, I'll let you get on with
your day." *And I'll go find a hole to crawl in somewhere*,
probably at a hotel, since Toussi's was the first place her
mother would go.

Oh, no—She brought her hand up to her head. *Toussi's*.
She had a showing tonight. Nikki McKinney's.

She squeezed her eyes shut, dreading the rest of the
day and the thousand things she needed to do. How had
one margarita done so damn much damage? And how
was she going to elude her mother, fire Alex, finish getting ready for the show, and survive when her head was
cracking apart eight ways from Sunday?

"It's not going to work, Kat," her most immediate
problem said calmly. "You and me, we're a team from
here on out. You don't leave my side. I don't leave yours.
Not until we find out who was behind the mess at the
Gardens last night."

From another man, such concern would have been
sweet. From Hawkins it was downright daunting. She
didn't want to be a team with him. She didn't have the
strength for it. Not today.

"Thanks, but it's—uh—no big deal. Honestly." She
finally got both feet on the floor, which really wasn't an
improvement. "I'll call my insurance company, my
lawyer, and the Botanic Gardens, for goodness sakes. Find
out what in the world they were thinking with those fireworks. They've probably already called Oleg, the artist
whose painting I had donated. We'll get it all worked
out."

"I'm afraid it's a little more complicated than that."

"Complicated?" She peeked through her fingers, and inadvertently, her gaze drifted over his face, over the fall of his silky dark hair, the hard angle of his jaw, before finally coming back to his eyes, so intensely dark, so intensely focused on her. She'd fallen in love once with those eyes, with the way he'd looked at her, and with an awful, sudden certainty she knew it wasn't impossible for it to happen all over again.

Please, no. Falling in love with him again was simply not an option. It was too crazy. It didn't make any sense. She'd gotten over him. She'd made a life for herself.

"Here, have a drink," he reminded her, lifting the cup to her mouth.

She took a sip, and it was warm, and soothing, and wonderful—but it wasn't enough to keep the tears from filling her eyes and spilling onto her cheeks. She didn't have time for this. Honest to God, she didn't.

She watched him track the first wet streak down her cheek, saw the utter resignation of defeat come over his face. He swore under his breath as he looked away.

"You can't do this to me, Kat. Please."

It was a plea, nothing less, and hearing it from him only made her feel worse. He'd been right. She was bad luck for him. Bad luck to the core.

CHAPTER 12

DAMMIT, Hawkins thought. He was trying to be professionally disengaged here, but she was undermining him at every turn. Crying already, and he hadn't even gotten to the tough part.

He wiped his hand across his mouth and looked back up at her. Yeah. The tough part. He was going to have to get to that pretty quick, but not yet, and he couldn't just sit here on his heels and watch her cry.

Rising to his feet, he leaned down and scooped her up in his arms, making sure to snag a blanket as he did.

"I'm going to set you up over here by the fire, while I take a shower, and I want you to promise to drink your tea and eat the toast. I'll leave the aspirin for you. Do yourself a favor and take three. Okay?"

"Okay," she whispered, which was good enough for him. It had to be.

They needed to move quickly. Linebacker Dekker was

probably halfway to Denver by now, and the last thing he needed was a senator on his ass while he tried to figure out what the hell was going on. Skeeter had spent half the night getting him an updated list of the Prom King Murder boys, and all but two of them still lived in Colorado, most of them either in or near Denver, which made them all look as guilty as hell in his book.

Eight boys in the alley that night. Two of them dead. That left six to shake down—more than a day's work after a night spent cruising the streets, hitting the Gardens and coming up empty, and three hours spent stretched out on his couch, trying to sleep instead of think about the woman in his bed.

He'd spent time with J.T.'s dad this morning as well, and hell, compared to what had happened in Colombia and what Kid was going through down there, he was working a cakewalk. A shower could only help put it all into perspective.

KATYA watched him leave the room from over the top of her mug of tea. He was beautiful, yes, in that rough-edged way he'd always had, but he looked almost as bad as she felt, like he hadn't gotten any more sleep than she had gotten.

Bad luck—that's exactly what she'd been to him, and once, a long time ago, he'd been everything she'd ever wanted.

Another tear rolled down her cheek, and she silently swore at herself. She'd turned into such a baby, which wasn't like her at all.

But the man undid her. He simply undid her, and she

needed to figure out why. It couldn't be love. That was too absurd.

She took another drink of tea and forced herself to take a bite of toast. She needed to get herself together and get the hell out of his loft while the getting was good.

She shook four aspirin out of the bottle he'd left, then tossed them back with another swallow of tea. If her luck held, four aspirin on an empty stomach would outright kill her, which would solve a whole lot of her problems.

Wrapping the blanket toga style over one shoulder and under one arm, she forced herself to her feet, then almost fell back into the chair. After a second, she found her sea legs, so to speak, only to look down and realize she wasn't exactly dressed in her dress. Her four-hundred-dollar designer knockoff was little more than a rag held together by two shoulder straps and a matched pair of safety pins.

Well, hell. She couldn't catch a cab half naked or wrapped in a blanket. As a matter of fact, she probably couldn't catch a cab at all.

She had no purse, no credit card, no money, no identification—no dress—and no shoes. No keys to her gallery. No cell phone. No brains to have gotten herself into such a fix, and no clue as to what to do next.

Hawkins, on the other hand, had all those things, including brains and clues. All she had to do was find what she needed and borrow it all for a bit.

Great. Borrowing brains. She'd hit a new all-time low, and given the sheer awfulness of her months in Paris, when she'd hit rock bottom and then some, that was saying a lot.

Okay, she was exaggerating. As bad as this was, Paris had been worse, much worse. She might have lost a few brain cells last night, but she hadn't lost her mind, and she'd come damn close in Paris, all thanks to her mother. How one woman could do so much damage in the name of love was beyond her.

Just the thought of her mother was enough to spur her into action. Dipping her toast in her tea, and eating as she went, she shuffled—carefully—across the loft, dragging her blanket along with her and trying to jar herself as little as possible.

God, she was pitiful.

And he was amazing. Looking around, one thing was becoming glaringly apparent: He had incredible taste. The color scheme in the loft was muted, but not without its high points, and the art was stunning. She knew art. She'd found her salvation in it at the Louvre and the Sorbonne, and she was in the home of a serious collector—with money.

Two huge, abstract Caldwells flanked the sides of his carved oak entryway door. The door itself she recognized as the work of a local artisan, Tomás Alejandro, a guy whose studio was just a couple of blocks from Toussi's. Hawkins had a matched set of John Frank sculptures in front of the windows, and two huge panels of stained glass taking the morning light and painting the room in shades of yellow, blue, and green on one side, and red, rose, and orange on the other, with nothing but the sky and the Denver skyline in the middle. He did have an iron balcony running along the outside of his loft, and it was jam-packed with plants, potted trees, and cascades of geraniums and petunias, ferns, paintbrush, ivy, and violets.

She could live here, she thought, happily, comfortably.

His home was richly complex, but with ideas rather than stuff. There was a simplicity in its relative emptiness, all the open space, with his bed off to one side and the open galley of his kitchen off to the other, the clean wood floors, the great expanse of windows. Of course, this was from a woman who lived, literally, under the aegis of "King Julio" in gilt-edged clouds of garish color. Anything looked good compared to Suzi Toussi's apartment.

She heard a shower start up, the sound coming from behind the kitchen. So the bathroom was back there, and maybe his closet, because she didn't see any clothes anyplace else, and a man's closet was probably where he kept stuff like a very expensive black suit jacket with over five hundred dollars in one of the pockets.

She wasn't going to feel guilty about the money. She was simply borrowing it, not stealing. The same way she was hoping to borrow a shirt and maybe a pair of pants she could roll up.

Shuffling along, soaking her toast in her tea, and knowing she looked like something even an alley cat would hesitate to drag home, she headed for the door past the kitchen, the one that didn't sound like there was a naked man taking a shower behind it. Along the way, she set her teacup on the kitchen counter. Then she spied her black high heels, and as awful as the thought of putting them on was, she felt a little relief. At least she wouldn't leave barefoot.

When she finally got to the door and opened it, she realized she'd found his spare bedroom, not his closet. She flipped on the light. Whoa. He had a freaking arsenal filling up one wall. It was enough to make her feel a little dizzy.

He had more guns than a midtown SWAT team, big guns, little guns, handguns, rifles, automatic weapons.

All the more reason to get the hell out of here, girl, she told herself. Even after a whole night spent in his company, she didn't know a damn thing about his life, or who he had become, or what he actually did for the Department of Defense—though the huge rack of guns was giving her a lot of ideas, all of them very bad news.

Her hangover be damned, she strode over to a door inside his home arsenal and found what she'd been looking for: a walk-in closet. The black suit jacket was easy to find, and the five hundred dollars was still in the pocket. She borrowed two hundred and told herself not to forget to write him a note and leave it on his desk.

She quickly riffled through his clothes, through silk shirts and hockey jerseys, elegant suits and suede pants that had to fit him like a second skin—which gave her a moment's pause—before she found a beautifully tailored Italian dress shirt, hanging between an iridescent blue snakeskin jacket of indeterminate fashion nationality that had definitely seen better days and a denim jacket with the sleeves ripped out that looked even worse and had MARAUDERS embroidered across the back.

Well, that was just great. She'd spent the night in the bed of a member of the Marauders, Denver's most notorious motorcycle gang. No one but a member would dare to wear their colors, not and expect to live through the weekend, which gave his arsenal a whole new meaning.

She definitely needed to confirm his employment with the Defense Department—and if she couldn't, she was definitely in more trouble than she'd thought.

Taking off her dress first she slipped on the Italian shirt and folded the sleeves back, then secured the French cuffs with a pair of onyx cuff links she found on his dresser. A pair of button-fly jeans went on next, the bottoms triple rolled.

Shoving the last bite of toast in her mouth, she ran her fingers through his belts and found one with a big silver buckle to cinch around her waist. A sudden, searing pain somewhere deep behind her eyes brought her to a screeching halt. One hand went over her face, the other clutched the edge of his dresser.

Good God, whatever Rick put in his margaritas, it was lethal. Slowly, carefully, she breathed her way through the agony, until she could get on with the job.

She should have felt like a thief, pawing through his things and taking what she needed, but she didn't. She'd get it all back to him. She should have felt a lot more uncomfortable invading his inner sanctum, but she didn't. Mostly what she felt was curious, powerfully curious, and a little unnerved. He seemed to have a split personality, part biker-boy, part designer babe, part arms dealer.

On second thought, she grabbed another hundred dollars out of his suit jacket. Good hotels didn't come cheap. They really didn't, and she couldn't bear anything less than a four-star hotel, not today. She was going to need extensive room service—a massage, a jetted tub, perfect food and even better coffee, and she was going to need it fast. She and Alex and Suzi Toussi, not to mention Nikki McKinney and her model, Travis James, had been working on Nikki's show all week, but there were always a thousand last-minute details. Nikki had promised to have

Pathos VII finished for tonight, and it was going to have to be hung.

And now there would be her mother to deal with—which she could hardly bear. And Alex to fire—which was even worse.

On third thought, she stuffed another hundred dollars in her pocket for good measure. Then she shifted her gaze out the closet door and back to the racks of guns hanging on the far wall of his spare room. What, she wondered, did he do with all those guns? And after wearing a very expensive suit last night, what had he been doing wearing Chinese "Fuck you" this morning?

Was he really a Marauder? And lived like this? she wondered.

Bodyguard was still a better answer, a bodyguard for the DOD, which meant high-security work for heads of state and ambassadors. But DOD work wouldn't have paid for Tomás Alejandro doors and John Frank sculpture, let alone the Caldwells—unless he worked for some obscure section of the Defense Department she'd never heard about, the kind nobody ever heard about, the kind that operated without Congress's approval and were bankrolled with slush funds . . . like, maybe, one buried in Denver, Colorado.

Nah, she decided. Him working for a secret government agency was a little too far-fetched, even for someone who knew the government had layers that weren't exactly what they seemed.

So what had happened to him after his pardon? He'd been a car thief when she'd met him. A continued life of crime wasn't completely out of the question, not with a room full of guns.

She looked back at the top of his dresser. He'd emptied

a lot of pockets onto it. There was stuff everywhere: tickets, bank cards, access cards, a movie store card, what appeared to be a few other types of ID, receipts, pieces of paper, a couple of envelopes—keys.

No way, she told herself. Borrowing his keys was out of the question. She wasn't getting anywhere near Roxanne's ignition, but that still left plenty to explore.

Curiosity overcoming common sense, she opened the closest envelope and peeked inside—two tickets for the opera next Friday night, *Madama Butterfly*, Puccini, her favorite, which surprised her and didn't do a thing to improve her mood or her headache.

It had to be a date. With a woman. She turned the top ticket to one side—a woman he liked enough to spend a hundred dollars a pop for dress circle seats. Attached to the tickets was a message slip written to Superman from Skeeter in a bold script confirming a dinner reservation for two at Club Dove—on the same night.

Definitely a date.

He was seeing someone.

Someone he liked.

Someone he probably didn't call Bad Luck, and she'd bet the last hundred bucks she'd taken that he wouldn't be wearing his Marauder jacket or his Chinese muscle shirt when he took this woman to Club Dove.

Dammit. She didn't even want to think about how that made her feel. Of course he'd gone on and made a life for himself, and of course that life would include women, and all that kissing last night had just been . . . incredible. Dammit.

Dropping the opera tickets back on his dresser, she looked over some of the IDs. Slowly, her brow started to furrow. He had a library card, two platinum credit cards, and a card from the FBI that said he was Special Agent Christian Hawkins, complete with a photograph.

Now why would he tell her he worked for the DOD, if he worked for the FBI? Of course, the next ID she picked up said he worked for the State Department—in Saudi Arabia. There were two more credit cards issued from banks in France and Germany. The next few cards were bundled together with a rubber band, each of them confirming Christian Hawkins as a member of the U.S. armed forces—every branch. U.S. Army, U.S. Navy, U.S. Air Force, U.S. Marine Corps. It was enough to raise her eyebrows all the way up to her hairline.

Criminy. He even had one saying he worked for the National Security Agency. They all had his photograph on them, they were all current, and they all looked absolutely valid.

Yessiree, it was definitely time to get the hell out of Dodge. Whatever he was into, and at this point she was guessing major felonies and quite possibly gunrunning for somebody, maybe even the DOD, she didn't want any part of it.

She dropped the cards back on the dresser and turned to leave, when something pink and sparkly on a worktable in the other room caught her eye. Her heart came to a sudden stop, and her hand came up to her mouth.

Oh . . . my . . . God.

Her tiara. She'd forgotten about it.

Slowly, she walked out of the closet and over to the table. There had been a man with Alex last night, waiting in her apartment, and he'd given the tiara to Hawkins.

How in the world, she wondered, had her tiara ended up in her and Alex's apartment? And where had it been all these years?

None of the Prom King boys had ever confessed to having it. So why was it here? Now?

Fighting an awful premonition of disaster, she reached over the row of pistols laid out on the table and picked up the tiara. It was tagged and bagged like a piece of evidence and as she picked it up, the tag caught on a manila envelope underneath it. The envelope was from last night, too, she remembered. She tucked it under her arm as she looked over the tiara. When she turned over the tag, there was a note written in the same bold handwriting that had been on his dinner reservation: *Superman, It's clean as a whistle, no fingerprints. Skeeter.*

She looked across the hall to the bathroom door on the other side. Complicated, he'd said, and she was beginning to see exactly what he meant.

Glancing down at the tiara, she swore under her breath. None of this was good. It was all bad, the whole damn thing, starting with last night and continuing on until now.

She took the manila envelope out from under her arm and snapped it open. Whatever was in it, if it had something to do with her and the mess she was in, she'd prefer to know it now rather than later.

At least that's what she thought until she looked inside.

HAWKINS found her exactly where he'd left her, except she'd put on one of his shirts and a pair of his jeans. She'd been in his spare room and in his closet. He'd known immediately when he'd gone in to get a change of clothes. The scent of her perfume had lingered in the air, the way it no doubt lingered in his bed.

She didn't look happy, and considering what she was holding in her hand, he wasn't surprised.

Well, nothing about this was easy, least of all what he'd put off long enough. She had to be told about Ted Garraty.

"More tea?" he asked, bringing the iron pot and her cup with him from the kitchen.

She nodded.

He refilled her cup and poured one for himself, before setting the pot on the slate table in front of the fireplace and settling into a chair.

"You've seen these?" she asked, taking the opening gambit and lifting the manila envelope, her voice tight.

Oh, yeah, he'd seen them, spent quite a bit of time last night looking them over as a matter of fact, which hadn't done a damn thing to improve his chances of getting any sleep.

"Yes," he said, keeping his face expressionless, his tone of voice flat and professional.

"How long have you had them?" From the ice in her voice, he was guessing she thought he'd had them about, oh, thirteen years or so. That pissed him off a bit, but he kept his cool.

"Your secretary and my partner found them when they entered your apartment last night. They were inside the front door, along with your tiara."

"Alex saw these?" she gasped, her voice little more than a strained whisper.

Reaching over, he took the envelope from her and belled it open. A quick look inside netted him a score, and he pulled out the top photo.

"Just this one," he said, handing the photograph and the envelope back to her. Talk about ice. He was so cool, he was damn near glacial.

She looked down, and all the color she'd lost came flooding back into her cheeks. He understood. The look on her face in the eight-by-ten glossy made it the hottest picture in the group. There was less of her body exposed than in the other shots, but her expression was one of pure, raw pleasure, and he'd been the one giving it to her.

He wondered if now would be a good time to tell her about Ted, while she was already halfway into a state of shock.

"Who . . . wh-who," she started, stammering again, and he decided to wait a minute longer, let her catch up with the facts a little.

"Were any of the Prom King boys shutterbugs? Any of them into photography?" It was a question he'd wanted to ask her since he'd hauled her out of the alley behind Toussi's. There'd been a lot of buzz on the street last night. A lot of the people he and Mickey had talked to about Ted Garraty had made the connection to the Traynor case. A few of the old-timers had even brought up Lost Harold and the Jane Doe floater, remembering the whole crazy summer that year. No one had seen Ray Carper in the last couple of days, but they'd assured Mickey the guy was still around and that they'd get the word out: Superman was looking for him.

"No, not that I . . . you think one of them . . ." She lifted her gaze, her voice trailing off.

"Yes, I do," he said clearly. "I think one of the boys snagged your crown out of the alley, and later somehow got himself into a position to take these photographs. I have no idea why, or what he's done with them all these years, or why he suddenly decided to give them and the crown and a piece of your prom dress— Did you see the piece of material in the bottom of the envelope?"

"Yes."

"Well, I don't know why whoever it is decided to de-liver everything to your apartment last night. What about you? Do you have any idea why someone would do this?" He kept the part about him maybe getting framed for Ted Garraty's murder to himself for the moment.

"No," she said, her attention straying back to the pho-tograph. "No, I don't . . . except maybe blackmail."

His gaze accidentally strayed back to the photo, too, and he let out a short breath. *Geezus.* Just looking at it was enough to remind him of how she'd tasted. It's what he'd struggled with in the night, the memory of her and how he'd felt every time he'd been with her—like he'd slipped into a fantasy dream, her skin so pale, her curves so delicate against his much larger, darker frame. Every time they'd made love he'd felt washed through with sat-isfaction, and infused with magic. That she would give so much to him. At nineteen, he'd given her everything— and now, to top off an already shaky start to the day, he was a little more than halfway primed for more of the same.

Perfect.

Getting a hard-on was so professional.

"Has anyone contacted you, wanting money?" he asked calmly.

"No."

Of course not, he thought, shifting slightly in his chair. Extortion would have been too easy, and it wouldn't have addressed the problem of Ted Garraty getting double-tapped between the eyes.

"Have you kept in touch with anyone from that time in your life?"

"N-no . . . I haven't seen any of them in years."

Well, things were moving right along, he thought. They weren't getting anywhere, but overall, the interview was going pretty well. She hadn't cracked, and he hadn't caved in, leaped over the table, and ravished her.

God, he really did need his head examined.

"Any of your girlfriends?"

"No, not really. I tried at first, but it was difficult, and I, well, it was difficult." She passed her hand over her face, rubbing her brow. "Look, is this really necessary? My insurance company will investigate what happened, including the break-in at the gallery. I wouldn't want you to get in trouble for tampering with evidence, but really, shouldn't you have left all this at Toussi's and let the authorities handle it?"

Her faith in him was utterly demoralizing, just exactly what he needed to get his other problem under control.

"I'm going to send the tiara and the piece of dress over to Lieutenant Bradley at the Denver Police Department today," he told her. "Along with Skeeter's analysis. But I thought I'd keep the photos, just send a description." He'd be damned if he wanted half the cops in Denver ogling her, or a bunch of guys staring at his ass.

The photographs were grainy, but there was no doubt about who was in them. "Other than that, I am the authority on this case."

And he was. She could take it to the bank.

She let out a heavy sigh and looked up at him through her fingers. "Since when does the Department of Defense, or the FBI, or the U.S. Army, or the State Department, for crying out loud, get involved in charity art auctions?"

So she'd looked through his stuff. He wasn't surprised.

"Since I was called off a high-priority mission and assigned to be there. It took somebody with a lot of power in Washington, D.C., to pull that off."

"You mean my mother," she said wearily, then covered her face again. "You can't possibly work for all those government agencies you have identification for in your closet." She said it as a statement, but the question was clear.

"I've worked *with* all of them, and other than that, what I do is pretty much classified."

"How convenient," she said flatly, still hiding behind her hands.

Usually, he admitted to himself, but it wasn't proving very convenient this morning.

"Or criminal," she mumbled, apparently as an afterthought.

Well, he wasn't going there with her, not right now. There was only so much he could prove to her under their current circumstances. After that, she'd either come around to believing him, or she wouldn't.

"I'd like your cooperation on this, Katya. With your

help, I think we can clear this up in a couple of days." And be the hell done with it.

She slumped even further down in her chair, her fingers sliding up over her head, her eyes squeezed shut against the pain he knew she was feeling. She looked like a whipped puppy—with completely wild, long blond hair and slinky curves wrapped in a man's shirt and a pair of too-big jeans that still managed to look sexy as hell, which kind of ruined the whole puppy thing he'd had working.

"I can guarantee you my mother doesn't have anything to do with those photographs or the tiara, or that piece of dress material," she began slowly, "but it is entirely reasonable to assume she would hire bodyguards behind my back, sic them on me at her whim, and have me followed every freaking place I go." She stopped for a second and rubbed her fingers across her brow, and if he wasn't mistaken, swore under her breath before continuing. "Therefore, if you qualify as a government bodyguard, one whose assignments could be manipulated by a senator with deep ties to the military establishment, it's true my mother, much to her horror if she ever finds out the bodyguard was you, could have gotten you pulled off a high-priority mission and assigned to a security detail at my party."

Nicely said, but nothing he hadn't already known, except for the fact that her mother had her followed, consistently, relentlessly, despite her wishes. No wonder she'd been so adamant about not calling Linebacker last night—for all the good it had done her. With Alex Zheng on the senator's payroll, Hawkins figured Marilyn

Dekker had kept herself very well informed as to her daughter's comings and goings.

"It's not my usual line of work, but I've been a bodyguard for three U.S. ambassadors, the secretary of state, two envoys, and the occasional governor or congressman, and I can guarantee you are safer with me than you've ever been with Alex Zheng or with anyone else on this side of the Mississippi."

She looked up at that, her eyes peeking out from under her hands, blatantly curious. "Who's on the other side of the Mississippi?"

"The D-boys at Fort Bragg," he said with a grin. Even hungover, she was quick. "If one of them wants to take you out, we might have to run."

Miraculously, the faintest hint of a return smile curved the corner of her mouth as her gaze slid away. "I don't think I've got any Delta operators mad at me. They love my mother. She fights for them in Congress, and they know it."

Dragon Dekker, Hawkins knew Kat's mother was sometimes called, for her fire-breathing, saber-rattling support of the armed forces. She especially championed Special Forces, which benefited SDF, the irony of which had never been lost on him.

"Katya . . . I need your help to get to the bottom of this. I need to call up your old friends, set up a few meetings for today and tomorrow, just casual, social stuff," he said, outlining his basic plan, well aware that he still needed to work in the part about Ted being dead. "Ask each one to meet you for coffee, or a drink. Then when the time comes, I'll go alone and make your excuses, tell them I'm your secretary and hit them up for a charity donation or something. I want to keep it low-key, just check them out, see what they're up to." At least that's what he was telling her. "I'm sure the police will be contacting them, but with your help, I can get to them first." And Lieutenant Bradley could have whatever was left when he got finished with them.

She let out a heavy sigh and buried her face back in her hands—and just sat there, for a long time, without saying a word.

"I'm having a hard time connecting the dots," she finally said, looking up. "Fireworks, maybe some ruined paintings, my tiara, those pictures, a piece of my dress . . . you. What's the point of all of it?"

"I'm not sure yet."

"But you think we've got a perverted pyromaniac photographer on the loose, and you've already narrowed the suspects down to the seven Prom King guys?" She dragged one of her hands back through her hair. She only got partway before her fingers got caught in the tangles. Working her fingers free, she gave up on her hair and continued. "Most of whom I don't ever want to see again. So your answer is no. I won't be calling a bunch of guys who I thought were my friends, but who turned out to be terrible jerks, and asking them out for double cappuccinos. I don't care how drunk they were. I don't care that charges were never filed against them. Also, with you in control here and the police on the case, and Alex waiting for me at home, I don't see much need for a bodyguard, either, thank you very much. So if we can just call this quits, and call me a cab, and get me back to Toussi's before my mother gets there, or to a hotel, if she's already in residence, that would be great. I've got a lot of work to do today."

"Six," he said, figuring it was now or never.

"Six what?" she asked after a short pause, her gaze narrowing the slightest bit.

"There are only six suspects, six Prom King boys left. Ted Garraty was killed last night at the Botanic Gardens. Murdered."

The dumbfounded shock on her face made him feel like the world's biggest jerk. She'd had to be told, and he'd put it off long enough, but there had probably been a better way. He just didn't know what it could have been.

"Ted was—was murdered?" she finally choked out.

"A clean hit."

She stared at him for the longest moment, a dozen emotions crossing her face, each of them fleeting, each of them bounded by confusion and disbelief.

"I think," she finally said, "I think I'm going to be sick."

CHAPTER 13

WELL, THAT HADN'T gone too badly, he thought. Now she knew the worst of it, knew she was in serious trouble, knew she couldn't just walk away, knew she was stuck with him—and it had made her lose her toast, and her tea, and everything else she'd had in her stomach.

She'd kicked him out of the bathroom—he checked his watch—approximately one hour and ten minutes ago, which he would have found nearly unbelievable, except he knew all about her and bathrooms. They were her favorite place. They'd practically lived in the bathroom at the Brown Palace. It was where they'd showered, and made love, and where he'd watched her dry her hair, and lotion her legs, and pretty much all-around drive him crazy.

About ten minutes after she'd thrown him out, he shoved a suitcase full of her things and her purse in for her. She assumed her secretary had sent them over, and he hadn't had the heart to tell her Alex didn't have a clue where she was, and that he'd simply gone back to Toussi's last night and gotten all the stuff himself, without her secretary/bodyguard noticing he'd broken in and was basically robbing the place—one more reason he'd be damned if he left her with only Alex Zheng between her and whoever was behind this mess.

It wasn't that her secretary was completely incompetent. Hawkins had broken into far more secure places than a fifth-floor apartment in a run-down building. Between the two of them, he and Dylan had "tested the security" at two nuclear power stations and half a dozen high-risk overseas U.S. Air Force, Army, and naval bases for the home team. When it came to bad guys, they'd pillaged and looted their way through corporate offices, foreign embassies, private compounds, and public estates without ever leaving a trace.

The sound of a door opening at the far end of the loft brought his head up. She was coming out of the bathroom. Or so he thought. Nothing else happened for the next few seconds, except he slowly rose to his feet from where he'd been sitting in a chair by the fire.

He wasn't sure what he expected, but when she finally walked through the door, he knew he'd just been outclassed, outgunned, and kicked back down to the minors. All he could do was stand there and remember to keep his jaw off the floor.

This was it. This is what she'd done to him thirty days in a row, every single day without fail, all those years ago. She would go into the bathroom looking mussed, and tumbled, and warm from bed, looking imminently edible and like she was his—and she'd come out an hour later dressed to kill, like he couldn't have her on his best day, even if he won the lottery, saved the world, and was proclaimed King.

It had intimidated the hell out of him at nineteen. At thirty-three, he liked it. He liked it a lot. He liked the challenge of it: all that perfectly blown-dry, silky, "don't touch me" hair, the mouth he knew she'd spent five minutes putting lipstick on, the soft skin a guy was supposed to touch, but not too much.

And the dress. So help him God, he'd thought it was a shirt when he grabbed it out of her closet and threw it in the suitcase, a very red shirt. He'd even packed a pair of white pants to go with it.

But she wasn't wearing pants, white or otherwise, just the shirt, pulled down to the point where it passed the border into "dress" territory—so help him God.

She was The Slayer in a pair of black cat's-eyes sunglasses, Katya "The Slayer" Dekker. She didn't look like Bad Luck. She looked like sex and Red Hots, like double-dipped chocolate cherries and cool whipped cream—like she wouldn't melt on a hot day, but like she might, if you were lucky . . . if you did it right, like she might melt in your mouth.

She'd melt for him. He knew it down to his bones. She'd damn near done it last night.

But he wasn't going to touch her—not when he had her right where he needed her. Cooperating, he hoped.

All he had to do was keep from getting slain himself.

Right. That's all he had to do.

He did not have to let his gaze slip and slide around her curves like a set of slicks in the rain. He didn't have to stand there sending up silent prayers of gratitude to the gods of Lycra, or wondering what had happened to the laws of genetics. It was Saturday morning, coffee time, time to rock and roll.

"If you can book a couple of these guys in before lunch, that would be great," he said, holding up the print-out Skeeter had made for him with the current phone numbers and addresses for the Prom King boys. Four lived in Denver or close by, one was in Maryland, and one was missing, no current address available.

Without a word, she held out her hand, and he obeyed like a hound dog coming to heel, crossing the room on her command.

"There's been a change of plan," she said when he handed over the paper.

"No, there hasn't," he said, immediately wary.

"I'm going with you."

"No," he said more firmly. "You're not. You're staying here."

He couldn't actually see her eyes behind the dark glasses, but he felt the look she was giving him—and it was pure "don't mess with me" attitude. She hadn't had that look at eighteen, and though he admired it, he couldn't say he liked it, especially when it was directed at him. He needed to be in charge here.

"You'll get twice as much information twice as fast with me as you will without me," she said.

Possibly, but it wasn't a chance he was willing to take. "I don't want you anywhere near these guys."

"I did some thinking in the bathroom."

Dangerous territory, he thought, though he didn't say a word.

"And you've got two choices," she continued. "Take me

with you and get what you want; or go alone and find out your cover has been blown. I can make sure these guys don't talk to you, and I will."

Son of a bitch. She was serious.

"Don't work against me, Kat." It was as much a warning as a plea. He didn't want her hurt, and that meant he had to catch the bad guys as quickly as possible, before they could get to her. His gut was telling him it was him they wanted, nailed to a cross, just like last time—but that didn't mean she was safe.

KATYA watched the subtle play of emotions on his face, mostly anger and a whole lot of worry, which was fine. He needed to be worried. She *had* done some thinking in the bathroom, serious thinking, putting aside her horror at Ted's death, and Alex's betrayal, and the simple disaster of the auction going up in balls of flames—and what she'd realized was that he was in at least as much danger as she was, maybe more.

By his own admission, he didn't know who had gotten him assigned to the Botanic Gardens, and neither of them knew who had planted the tiara and the awful photographs in her apartment, but it would be ridiculous to assume the two events weren't somehow tied together—and that meant trouble, big trouble, for him.

She couldn't sit idly by, letting him handle everything, and just hope for the best. She couldn't . . . and still live with herself. She had to step in and do what she'd tried and failed to do during his murder trial. She had to try to protect him.

"I either go with you, or I go on my own. Your choice."

She wasn't budging on this, for her sake as well as his—but it wasn't easy holding her ground.

His gaze had narrowed to a dangerous degree. His jaw looked tight enough to snap.

"Fine," he said, not sounding any too happy about it. "My choice, my rules, which means I give the orders. *All* the orders."

She agreed with a short nod. He could give all the orders he wanted—that didn't mean she'd follow them.

Tim McGowan needed a haircut, and a shave, and a shower, and a clean shirt after the baby had spit up on him. Hawkins also figured he needed about two fewer kids than the five he had, or a wife whose high-powered job didn't send her to Europe or one of the coasts two weeks out of every four.

Tim had not been able to meet them for coffee. They'd had to go to his big house in one of Denver's more exclusive suburbs, and after about two minutes at his kitchen table, Hawkins had felt like he needed a shower, too. There'd been milk and cereal everywhere, kids everywhere, cartoons blaring, two dogs trying to eat as much of the cereal as they could wolf down before they got caught, and just an overall general stickiness to the whole situation.

Kat still looked good, though. She didn't have a Fruitio or a Crunch Flake on her anywhere, and he'd just peeled another one off his jeans and tossed it out Roxanne's window.

He downshifted for the red light and glanced in her direction.

"I don't think Tim is our man," he said.

"No kidding," she said, tilting her head and looking at him over the top of her sunglasses.

"You didn't think so, either. That's why you started with him, isn't it?"

"Tim was always a decent guy. He actually came to Paris to see me at the—uh—place where I was staying, to apologize, to make sure I was okay. The only reason he ran into that alley was to try and make the other boys back off."

"I don't remember seeing anyone trying to rescue you."

"Tim had asthma as a kid. Always carrying his inhaler around. He was probably the only one there that night that I could have outrun. When you pulled up, he was still at the other end of the alley."

Hawkins thought that over for a minute. It was possible, he decided. It had all happened so fast. One of the boys could have been coming into the alley instead of going out.

"He didn't seem too upset about Ted."

"He wasn't really part of that crowd of boys," she said, lifting her hair up to catch the breeze coming through the window. The day was definitely heating up. "We all just kind of ended up together prom night. I think he thought the other boys were all too spoiled, and too fast, and headed for too much trouble. What happened to Jonathan only proved him right. He's too nice to say it, but he probably feels the same way about Ted, bad apples coming to no good end and all that." She lifted her other wrist up and checked her watch. "I really do need to at least stop by the gallery. This is Nikki McKinney's first major show, and I'd like everything to go well for her."

"So Ted was a bad apple?" he said, ignoring her request. "You're killing me here."

A fleeting grin curved his lips. She was nothing if not persistent, but it was a no-go. They'd been over this at the loft, about a hundred times. She'd called Suzi Toussi in to help Alex Zheng get the show together, and that was as much involvement as he was willing to allow. Whoever had murdered Ted was still out there, and all the clues pointed to its being someone she knew, and worse yet, someone who knew her. She wasn't leaving his sight, and he didn't have time for an art show.

"He was a jerk," she said with a sigh, letting her hair fall back down over the front of her shoulder. "A terrible, disgusting jerk, and out of all of them, I guess he's the one I'd put my money on for taking those pictures, but he's dead."

"That doesn't mean he didn't take the pictures." The light changed, and he slid Roxanne up into first.

"No," she admitted, automatically bracing herself, her hand sliding onto the armrest on the door. "I guess not, but he sure as shoot wasn't the one who put them in my apartment."

"Why not?" He shifted up into second and then cast a quick glance in her direction. It was stupid, he knew, but he couldn't help himself. He'd noticed she always crossed her legs for second gear—and sure enough, she did it again. He didn't know what it meant, but he found it fascinating. Or maybe it was just the way she crossed her legs he found fascinating.

"Because the only thing Ted Garraty has been breaking into with any regularity is doughnut boxes. He must have gained about fifty pounds over the last thirteen years, and he wasn't just heavy. He was out of shape, dissipated. No way could he have climbed five flights of stairs, and he wouldn't have fit in Toussi's elevator."

She had a point. The elevator was small, damn small, wonderfully small.

He cleared his throat, shifted into third, kept his gaze straight ahead, and asked a question he already knew the answer to. "So who's next? Robert Hughes?"

"Bobba-Ramma Hughes," she corrected him.

"Bobba-Ramma?" He shot her a skeptical glance.

Her cell phone rang inside her purse, muted, insistent, maybe getting a little desperate, but like the last five times it had rung, she ignored it. They both knew who it was. Alex. He'd been calling every two minutes since she'd turned the phone on ten minutes ago. Suzi must have arrived with her assistants by now and informed him his boss was not coming in or coming home today.

"That's what he told me when I called," she said. "He's not plain old Bobby anymore. He's Bobba-Ramma, the Prince of East Colfax Avenue. Apparently, he decided against going into his daddy's stock-brokerage business and bought himself a high-end strip club, which sounds like an oxymoron if I ever heard one."

Skeeter had notated the club on the hot sheet, The Painted Pony, but nothing had been said about "Bobba-Ramma."

"You think he's our guy?"

"He certainly qualifies as a pervert," she said without hesitation. "He always has. He was suspended twice our senior year for exposing himself in the boys' bathroom, and once for exposing himself in the girls' bathroom."

Well, that was a new and unpleasant twist.

"What about the pyro part?"

"Yeah," she said after a moment. "I can see him liking the drama of starting fires, big fires, especially with explosions, but he's no murderer, not by a long shot. He's too self-absorbed. I can't imagine him being interested enough in anyone else to go to the bother of killing them. You know he's doing me a big favor seeing me this morning. God knows what he's going to think when I drag you in with me."

"He told you he was doing you a favor?" She'd done a good job on the phone this morning, played it perfectly, despite the fact that she'd been holding her head with one hand and the telephone receiver away from her ear with the other. She hadn't said much when it was all over, just handed him back the sheet with times, addresses, and meeting places written in the margins by the prom boys' names.

He'd been impressed.

"Sure did. He's just so, *so* busy, but it was just so *sweet* of me to call, and we were *such* old friends, so he was just going to *push* his schedule and make room for little old me, because it was just so *awful* about Ted."

The news had broken all over the morning papers. There had even been pictures of the fireworks exploding over the Botanic Gardens. Nothing had been mentioned about the quality of the kill shots: perfect, two hits, dead center between the eyes. To his relief, Katya's name hadn't been mentioned, either, but he'd still called Lieutenant Bradley and gotten a couple of undercover cops to be at the show, to keep their eyes open and make sure nothing bad happened.

"As far as I know, he's the only one with a motive for wanting to hurt me," she continued, "or ruin me, if that's what this is all about."

He quirked a brow in her direction. "What motive?"

"He wanted to be prom queen that year. It just ate at him all night long when I won."

"You're kidding, right?"

"Nope." She leaned forward to pop open Roxanne's glove box.

Hell. Hawkins felt like he was sliding toward the bottom of the social misfit barrel, a place he'd had more than enough of in prison, but he couldn't fault his guide. She was nailing these guys for him, giving him information it would take Lieutenant Bradley weeks to uncover.

She started rustling through the stash of pharmaceuticals she'd put in the glove compartment. She had all the legal painkillers out of his bathroom, and all the antacids, the combination painkiller/antacids, three herbal supplements guaranteed to cure what ailed her, and a bottle of B vitamins she was sure would set her right—if she could just get enough of all of it down, and keep it down. She'd also brought a box of crackers she'd set on the dash, an orange she was sure would rehydrate her as well as give her immune system a much-needed boost, and two bottles of mineral water she'd found in his refrigerator.

It had been like watching a general prepare for war this morning. She'd commandeered his loft, his phone, and every ounce of his attention. It was hard to keep his eyes off her. Hell. It was impossible. He'd had about twelve hours to get used to the idea of having her around, and he was starting to like it way too much, starting to forget that she was at the top of his "Ten Most Wanted" list for having fucked up his life.

So he just had to be careful, he told himself, just a little more careful.

FIRST Tim McGowan and now Bobby Hughes, Katya thought, rummaging through a few things she'd stashed in Roxanne's glove compartment. From Dudley Do-right to Psycho-boy.

"So do you think Bobby Hughes wanted the prom queen thing badly enough to nurse a grudge for all this time?" Hawkins asked from the driver's side of the car.

"Absolutely," she said without hesitation. She found the orange among all the stuff she'd brought with her from Hawkins's kitchen and his medicine cabinet in hopes something would help ease her amazing hangover. It had been a solid seven on the Richter scale when they'd left Steele Street, but Tim's beautiful, wildly rambunctious, and unbelievably loud kids had pushed it toward a ten. "Nursing grudges is what Bobby always did. He made sure he was the strangest ranger at Wellon Academy, then spent all his time complaining that people treated him like he was strange. There was no winning with Bobby. Never was. He hated his mother for being a flamboyant alcoholic and his dad for being a straitlaced stockbroker. Even though a lot of us Wellon kids lived around the Denver Country Club, we avoided going to the Hughes's, at least us girls did. The guys went there to get drunk. There was always plenty of booze, and

Bobby's mom didn't like to drink alone. Rumor had it that some of the Wellon boys even slept with her."

"Ted Garraty, maybe? Or Jonathan Traynor?" he asked after a short pause.

She looked up from her orange, startled.

"I guess . . . I guess that might be a motive for murder, but it was just a rumor, one of those kids' things that go around a school. I can guarantee you Jonathan never slept with her. As far as Ted, his name was never mentioned, that I remember."

"What about the other boys from prom night?"

She hated to think about it, let alone admit it, but a couple of those boys' names had been linked to Theresa Hughes.

"Stuart Davis practically lived at the Hughes house that summer. His mother taught at Wellon, so he was at the academy on a community scholarship."

"He's the ex-Ranger we don't have a current address for, right?"

"Right," she said, peeling the orange. "All you've got listed on the printout is the date of his discharge a few months ago."

"Any of the others?"

There were only three left, and one of them she was absolutely sure had not been involved with Bobby's mother.

"Greg Ashe did not hang out at Bobby's house, ever. He was homophobic, probably still is." She looked around for a place to put her orange peels and decided on the shifter console. There was a small, scooped-out part, and if she was careful, she could just fit the peels into it. His car was very clean on the inside, and the last thing she wanted to do was make a mess. "Albert Thorpe might have spent some time there. He liked to party, and Bobby's was a party house. Philip Cunningham, definitely. He was probably the only one at Wellon who actually liked Bobby, who thought he was funny instead of just weird."

"Don't we have an appointment with Cunningham after Hughes?" he asked.

"Cunningham and Ashe together," she confirmed. "They're partners in a construction company, and we see Albert tomorrow."

"So who do you think stole your tiara?"

He was in investigator mode. She could tell by the tone of his voice—flat and cool, with just a slight edge.

"I don't know. Anybody could have picked it up. I remember it falling off in the parking lot, before I ran into the alley."

"What about the piece of your dress? Who all was in on that?"

Her glance strayed to the orange in her hand. She was trying, really she was. It wasn't easy dealing with everything that had happened last night at the Gardens and having to relive everything that had happened that summer. The dress had been so beautiful, so perfect, and by the end of prom night it had been ruined, parts of it cut off, parts of it stained with her blood. What had started as a not very funny joke had so quickly gotten out of hand.

Souvenirs from the prom queen, they'd been shouting. Then Jonathan had pulled out a pocketknife and everything had gone wrong.

She'd been angry and telling all of them to leave her alone, but they'd all kept pulling and tugging at her, trying to cut off a piece of tulle—everyone except Tim. He'd pushed his way to the front and tried to shove people away, and then all hell had broken loose. Everyone had suddenly been fighting and she'd gotten cut, badly.

"They were all in on it," she said. "Except Tim McGowan, but I don't know how many of them actually got a piece of the dress. It was a little crazy."

After Jonathan's murder, the police had impounded the dress, and it had come out at Hawkins's trial how cut up it had been. She didn't remember the knife moving that fast, especially not after it had sliced into her arm, just above her elbow.

Like the tiara, none of the boys had admitted to having a piece of her dress. But neither had they admitted to assaulting her. Just a little fun getting out of hand, they'd all said. And chasing her into the alley? Well, they'd known they couldn't let her run around lower downtown alone at night. It wasn't safe, and hadn't they all been proved right? Some low-life guy in a fast car had literally roared up and snatched her away, practically kidnapped her.

They'd been worried sick about her, especially Jonathan, they'd said—and Jonathan had ended up dead, killed by the same greasy street boy who had stolen his girl.

A very impolite word crossed her mind at the memory. What a bunch of liars. She knew what she'd felt. She'd known she was in danger, real danger, and if it hadn't been for Hawkins saving her . . .

She looked at the partially peeled orange in her hand, then blew out a short breath and tossed it back into the open glove compartment.

"You're on the wrong track here." She'd thought it

over, had been thinking it over since they'd headed out to Tim's place. "This doesn't have a damn thing to do with my dress, or my tiara, or those photographs, or with Bobby Hughes wanting to be prom queen."

She looked over and caught his gaze for a second.

"How so?" He downshifted for another red light and brought the car to a stop.

"I'm an easy target," she began. "If someone wanted to blackmail me, they could have done it a long time ago, and if someone wanted to scare me, they wouldn't need to kill anybody to do it, but . . ."

"But?" he prompted when she paused.

She shrugged and glanced up. "But you're not an easy target. Anyone who wants to come after you is going to have to work real hard, and if they want to scare you, it's probably going to take more than killing Ted Garraty. So maybe we need to be watching your back instead of worrying about my old prom dress."

He didn't answer at first, just held her gaze for a long moment, then looked away.

"Even if you're right, we need to talk to these guys."

She was right, and he knew it, whether he wanted to admit it or not.

"I suppose," she agreed reluctantly. She didn't want to talk to the rest of the Prom King boys. Tim was a friend. They'd kept in touch—not regularly, but every now and then. It had been easy to talk to him, and nice to finally meet the group of wild Indians he called his children. Jonathan had been a friend, too: dear, sweet, overwhelmed, and underloved Jonathan. He'd never meant to hurt her that night. But the rest of the boys—there had been some real malice in the incident. It had all happened so fast, though, she'd never been able to pinpoint exactly where it had come from.

Just thinking about it was enough to make her headache worse. She reached for the box of crackers she'd put on the dash. Maybe eating a little something would make her feel better.

The light changed, and he shifted the car back into gear.

"You loved that dress," he said after a couple of minutes of silence.

Yes, she silently agreed. She really had loved that dress.

BY THE TIME they got to The Painted Pony, she was covered in cracker crumbs, and Hawkins's plan to be more careful was starting to include things like "carefully brushing her off," and "carefully taking her home," where he could "carefully kiss her mouth" and "carefully take her clothes off."

He was insane, and it was ridiculous, and it wasn't doing a damn thing to improve his mood, which had been a little tense from the get-go this morning.

He pulled to a stop in front of the Pony and looked at her. She'd still been a little green around the gills at Tim McGowan's, but the ride back into the city, the crackers, the vitamins she'd taken, the half bottle of mineral water, and the orange she'd finally gotten down were starting to work. Though she was far from perky, she was edging toward normal.

"This place is disgusting," she said, looking out the window at the strip club and taking a bite out of another cracker. Like all the other clubs along Colfax Avenue, the Pony looked a lot worse for wear in broad daylight. At night, its flaws would be camouflaged with flashing lights—kind of like the strippers themselves.

She took another bite, turning in her seat, and he watched a small avalanche of crumbs tumble off her dress onto the seat and the floor. Roxanne was as dusted in crumbs as she was, and he was trying not to let it get under his skin. Unlike Kid, who used his cars as combination garbage trucks and auxiliary refrigerators, he kept Roxanne clean, very clean, paying Skeeter a hundred bucks a month to detail the Challenger.

By the time he was finished hauling Bad Luck "The Slayer" around, it was going to cost him at least two hundred. There were orange peels stuck in the console, and one of the bags of herbal supplement—last year's Christmas present from Skeeter, along with the chamomile tea he'd tried to get down Katya this morning—was scattering itself all over the place.

One look at the leaves, twigs, and seeds inside had only reconfirmed his decision not to use it. Not Bad Luck, though. She'd taken one look at the bag, read the ingredients, and shaken half of it into her bottle of mineral water. The other half was now pretty well distributed over the dash, and every time he made a turn, a bit more of it sifted down to the floorboards.

She was an amazing slob, but he'd known that from their time together in the Brown Palace. Any hope that she might have outgrown her less-than-tidy ways had been shot to hell when he'd gone into the bathroom while she was making her phone calls.

Armageddon. Ragnarok. Doomsday. His bathroom had rivaled all of them. Oddly enough, he didn't mind it in the bathroom. Those memories were too sweet.

But his car was different. He liked his cars clean, all of his cars, but especially Roxanne. She was classic muscle, customized, one of a kind after all the work he and Skeeter had put into her—and Bad Luck was turning her into a Dumpster.

A small price to pay for her cooperation, he told himself, but it still grated across his nerves when she popped the last of the cracker in her mouth and proceeded to brush herself off in the car . . . *in the car!*

It was all he could do not to grab her hands and say, "Come on outside, baby, and let's brush you off in the parking lot."

But he knew if he touched her, the last thing he was going to care about was cracker crumbs.

"Okay," she said, still brush, brush, brushing. "If we've got to do this, let's get it over with."

Great idea, he thought, but he still didn't move. All he could do was sit there in stunned amazement and watch the crumbs fly around inside the car and settle on his shirt, on his jeans, and in his lap—and she didn't have a clue. There she was on her side, grooming herself for her next big entrance and destroying him in the process. A couple more minutes and he'd be completely *en croûte*.

When she finally finished and reached for her door handle, he got out of the car and brushed himself off . . . *in the parking lot.* Cripes, what was so hard about that?

Predictably, when he rounded Roxanne, the first thing he noticed was that Kat had crumbs on her butt. In his own defense, he told himself it wasn't just because the first thing he did was look at her ass. He'd noticed the crumbs because they really stood out on a red dress.

"You have crumbs on your butt," he said.

She immediately stopped and did that twisty-turn, hip-shot stance thing she'd done in Doc Blake's last night, trying to see her behind while she brushed it off. She did a pretty good job, too, only missing a few.

Rather than make a big deal out of it, he stepped forward, all chivalry and good intentions to finish up for her. But while he was brushing off her butt, she reached up and slid her hand through his hair, and suddenly there they were, with him standing too close and her half turned toward him.

"You've—uh—got some crumbs. . . ."

In his hair, right. He should have known, but in a real testament to his powers of prescience, he didn't give a damn about the crumbs anymore. They could have been standing in a hundred-pound sack of them, and he wouldn't have cared, because he could smell her lipstick: bubblegum.

Yeah, he was that close, with his hand on her butt and her hand in his hair, and everything else in the world begging the question: "How much would it cost him to kiss her?"

Five percent of his self-respect?

Ten percent of his eternal soul?

And did he really care?

Bubblegum lipstick—soft, pink, sweet, and on those lips. Just how much of a test was this supposed to be? he wondered.

He felt her breath on his mouth and started bending his head toward her.

"You . . . uh, we can't," she said, her voice as soft as her lips looked and without an ounce of conviction in it.

No, of course he couldn't, he thought, stopping his descent, but keeping his hand on her ass, because it just felt too incredibly good to give up. Kissing her wasn't in his plan. It didn't make sense. It was the first step on the road to perdition.

Or maybe the second, because the hand-on-the-ass thing sure felt like it could take him straight to hell.

"We're—uh—in a parking lot." Her voice slipped down to a whisper.

Actually, if that was the problem, there was no problem, because he could kiss her in a parking lot. He could kiss her anywhere, in a box or on a fox, in the rain, on a train. He could kiss her anywhere she and Dr. Seuss could dream up.

He thought kissing was great fun. He thought this lovely limbo he and Kat were in, half wrapped around each other but barely touching, was great fun, too, but he wanted to jack it up a bit, take it to the next level, and the next level after that, and the one after that.

She was right. Maybe he couldn't kiss her in a parking lot. Maybe he couldn't just kiss her.

So he backed off, carefully lifted his hand off her butt—no wandering—and stepped away.

He should have thanked her for saving his life.

"Close call" was the best he could come up with.

"Damn close," she agreed, completely avoiding his gaze, her attention all on straightening her dress.

Twenty-four hours ago, he would have bet a million dollars that he would not have reacted to her, but here he was, reacting all over the place to every single breath she took.

Fucking unbelievable.

Once they got inside the club, he had to admit she'd been right. The Painted Pony was disgusting, worse than disgusting. It smelled of stale cigarettes, spilled booze, and a few other things Hawkins didn't want to think about too much. He'd been in a lot worse places, but he didn't think the American Princess had.

The lights were low inside, but they weren't low enough to hide Bobba-Ramma's inch-thick eyeliner and false eyelashes, his bad dermabrasion job and the shaking of his hands, or the tracks up his arms.

But Kat had been right about him, too. He was no murderer. Like Manny the Mooch, Bobba-Ramma didn't have enough brain cells left to plan a homicide, let alone double-tap a guy between the eyes. He'd been partying way too hard over the years, done way too many lines, and was an alcoholic to boot, if whiskey on the rocks for breakfast was any indication.

"Ohh, yes. Poor Teddy-bear," Bobba-Ramma tsk-tsked.

"Teddy-bear?" she asked, and Hawkins had to give her credit. She knew her job was to chat Bobby-boy up, while his job was to look like a mean son of a bitch.

From the nervous glances Bobba-Ramma kept casting in his direction, he was doing a damn good job of it.

"Teddy," Bobba-Ramma said. "Teddy-bear Garraty. That's what we *all* called him." His eyes darted to the stage, where a young man in a pink negligee and a pout was shrugging his shoulders.

An annoyed expression tightened the club owner's

face, and he waved the young man back with a couple of angry flaps of his hand.

"I guess I don't remember that," she said.

"Go, Luke, *go*. Find it," Bobba-Ramma snapped at the young man, then rolled his pale blue eyes back at her. "No, no. Not all of you, from back then. All of us here, at The Painted Pony. He was a true, *true* friend to all of us."

And there was a motive for blackmail, if Hawkins had ever heard one. Anyone on the Denver Social Register who was a true, *true* friend to the likes of Bobba-Ramma and his Pony boys and girls was a mark just looking to get taken for a load of cash—but not necessarily murdered.

"Oh," was all Katya said, having a little trouble running with that information.

"Can I trust you?" Bobba-Ramma asked, leaning closer over the table, apparently oblivious to the fact that for every centimeter he moved forward, Kat shied away two.

"Of course," she said, looking like she could fall over any second.

"We do special revues for special clients . . . very special clients." Bobba-Ramma leaned even closer, and Kat just had to endure. There was no place left for her to go without toppling over. "They're by invitation only, and we serve dinner and everything for five hundred dollars a plate. They're all the rage, really, and Teddy-bear was a founding member. He'd been to one in Chicago, and thought Denver should have its own special show. Other clubs are trying to steal the idea, but nobody has better boys and girls than the Pony." A claim that had the unfortunate effect of making him smile, or maybe grimace was a better word.

"I'm sure," she agreed weakly. Bobby-boy's teeth were

a definite shade of green, as if he had an algae problem, like maybe his tank needed cleaning—with a fire hose.

"I don't know *what* we'll do without him," the club owner said. "Teddy-bear was more than just a member, he was a sponsor, and a truly fine revue needs sponsors. They're *very* artistic. Oh!" He brought his hand up to his cheek. "*You're* into art, aren't you? A gallery or something?"

Subtlety was not Bobba-Ramma's strong point. Hawkins could see what was coming next, and he was duly amazed that a guy on estrogen had enough balls left to do it.

"With Teddy-bear gone, there *is* a spot open for the next revue." He tucked a strand of stringy blond hair behind his ear, looking coy. "I'd be happy to let you come on a trial basis the first time, see if you like it."

Well, that did it for Hawkins. The guy was totally insane. Women who looked like Katya Dekker did not ever, *ever*, show up at private "revues."

"I could even give you a discount," the club owner said, sweetening the pot. "Teddy-bear gave me a small deposit last night to secure his place, and I could put that money toward your account."

Bingo.

Hawkins leaned forward on the table. "Did Garraty talk to anyone else while he was here?"

"Well, he was in quite a rush, actually. We barely had time to chat ourselves. Then Stuart just *barged* in on our conversation. *No* tact whatsoever. You can take the boy out of the suburbs, but you *cannot* take the suburbs out of the boy." Bobba-Ramma had clearly been offended.

"Stuart?" Katya asked. "Do you mean Stuart Davis?"

"The bruiser himself."

"What did Stuart and Ted talk about?" Hawkins asked.

"I don't know, I was busy with—Oh, Luke," Bobba-Ramma crooned, distracted by the young man in the pink negligee sashaying victoriously across the room. "You found it."

Luke was carrying a tiara, and if a sallow-faced, washed-up scarecrow could glow, Bobba-Ramma was doing it.

"You remember, don't you, Katya?" he said, breathless, his gaze fixed on the younger man and the prize. "Prom night?"

Good God, the guy *was* totally insane, Hawkins thought. How could she forget her prom night?

"*I* had the votes, but they gave the crown to you? Remember?"

Insane and delusional.

"Yes," she said, surprising him.

The club owner's smile turned slyly winsome. "It was a travesty, but I survived. I could have been the first prom queen queen in the history of Wellon Academy, but they lacked the vision," he said, taking the tiara from Luke and fitting it to his greasy locks.

"Yes," she agreed again.

Something in her voice set off a warning bell, and when he glanced over at her, the warning bell turned into a siren.

She was on the verge of hyperventilating again, her breathing getting shallow, her gaze fixed on Bobba-Ramma and his tacky little tiara. The metal was bent in a couple of places, as if it had been thrown against a wall and stomped on by a big boot. The stones were plastic, and the sight of Bobby-boy in the crown was so pathetic as to be downright scary.

Okay, they were out of there.

"Thanks, Mr. Hughes," he said, shoving back from the table and rising to his feet. He ignored Luke's lazy once-over and took Katya by the arm. "We'll get back to you on the revue." When hell freezes over.

"You're—you're leaving?" There was no disguising the disappointment in Bobba-Ramma's voice. "But . . . but—"

Hawkins didn't wait to hear what the guy had to say. He grabbed Kat and walked out of the club without a backward glance. He kept his hand on her the whole way across the parking lot, until he had her safely back inside Roxanne.

BREATHE or faint, Katya told herself when he closed her door, knowing it had to be one or the other. She was trembling inside, which she hated, and she couldn't get her seat belt buckled, which flustered the hell out of her.

"We're not very far from my place. Let me take you back," he said, when he got inside the car.

"No." She was going to see this through, no matter how awful it got, but she wasn't going to ride around in Roxanne without a seat belt. How *did* this thing work? There were too many straps, some for pulling down over your shoulders, some for wrapping around your waist. There was even one for pulling up between your legs. The only one she wanted was the waist one, the one she'd been wearing before, but all the others were ganging up on her with all their clips and buckles and whatnot.

"Do you want some help?"

"No." It couldn't be that complicated. It was just a seat belt.

"Bobby didn't seem too broken up about Ted," he said.

That was the understatement of the century.

"But I don't think he killed him, any more than I think Tim McGowan did."

She didn't, either. Where was that one clip? The one with the orange button that held the waist belt?

"Are you all right?"

"I'm fine . . . just fine."

When he didn't say anything else, she looked up. He knew she was lying.

She went back to struggling with the seat belt. "Okay. The tiara threw me a little." It was as much of an admission as she was going to make. "But now we know Stuart was in town last night. So maybe we've almost got this thing tied up."

"Not quite," Hawkins said dryly.

She stopped in mid-fumble, then after a second continued straightening out the clips and buckles, trying to find two that matched.

"Okay, maybe not tied up." Just because Stuart was an ex-Ranger who knew how to shoot a gun didn't mean he was a murderer. What she really hoped was that none of the Wellon boys had killed Ted. She'd rather it was just some random criminal who'd happened to shoot him.

But she didn't think that was the way things were going to lay out. And she didn't think she was ever going to get the dang-blasted seat belt figured out.

"Kat, you don't have to do this," he said, reaching over and patiently buckling her up.

"Yes. I do," she said, when he was finished and she'd let

out the breath she'd accidentally held. She wasn't going to walk away from this mess and leave him to handle it. She wasn't going to walk away from him, no matter how many perverts crawled out of the woodwork.

This time, she was seeing it through to the end. Maybe it was penance, or maybe it was just the right thing to do.

"Okay, then," he agreed, but she heard the reluctance in his voice. "Where do we go next?"

"Greg Ashe and Philip Cunningham." She didn't have to look at the list lying on the dash. "They're partners in a big development company down in Colorado Springs. Greg said they'd seen the news about Ted this morning in the paper, and they were both shocked. I got the feeling that hearing from me made him pretty nervous."

"Nervous works for me," he said, turning the key in Roxanne's ignition. The car did what it always did, came to life instantly with enough power and sound to qualify as a natural disaster or an act of God.

He gunned the motor, and she grabbed for the side of her seat and the console—as ready as she was going to get.

FROM across the street, Birdy took a long drag off his cigarette, then knocked the ash out the window of his low-slung Corvette. A tight smile curved his mouth.

He'd had no idea this was going to be so much fun, watching the two of them scramble around like squirrels looking for nuts.

Well, they'd found a nut all right. Bobby Hughes was so far over the edge, his last reality check had bounced. Still, he'd had enough brain cells left to call Stuart in a panic this morning to tell him Katya Dekker was coming to the Pony. Stuart had told Bobby to keep his mouth shut—but Birdy figured that thought hadn't stuck much beyond the phone call itself, if it had even stuck that long. Listening had never been one of Bobby's strong points. With Bobby, it was all about him, all the time.

But Bobby hadn't mentioned Christian Hawkins showing up. That part had surprised Birdy when the two of them had driven up about half an hour ago, and Birdy didn't like surprises that weren't of his own making. He'd made sure Hawkins would be at the Botanic Gardens last night, but he'd never dreamed he and Katya would hook up again.

What was she thinking? Didn't she realize Hawkins was probably the one who had murdered Ted Garraty last night? Everything had been set up to look that way, just like things had been set up thirteen years ago for it to look like Hawkins had murdered Jonathan.

The girl simply had no sense. She never had. It frustrated the hell out of Birdy. And what she'd been doing in those photographs—well, that just infuriated him. She'd made so many bad choices in her life, starting with choosing Jonathan over him, and then choosing Hawkins over Jonathan. Neither one of them had been good enough for her.

And now she was with Hawkins again—but not for long.

The last time he'd set Christian Hawkins up for a murder rap, it had been a real slapped-together job. Passions and adrenaline had been running high. People had been scared. There'd been blood everywhere, and he'd had to think fast on his feet. He'd been amazed when Hawkins was actually convicted, then irritated beyond measure two years later when it became apparent that he was going to be pardoned.

Talk about having to think fast on his feet. He'd had to scramble like hell to find that old deathbed skid-row bum, Manny the Mooch, and convince him to confess. It was amazing, really, how little money it took to buy a man's reputation and his life—not that Manny had ever had much of either.

This time, though, Birdy had been able to plan things out. There wouldn't be another pardon for Christian Hawkins. Hawkins's success with the Department of Defense just made it that much more satisfying, that much more of a challenge to bring him down.

The brute-powered muscle car Hawkins was driving pulled onto East Colfax, and Birdy went ahead and started the Corvette. He would have loved to follow them in their quest for justice, but he had a little blackmail to conduct, and his pigeon was due at the mansion in less than a half hour.

He doubted if there was another person on the face of the earth who'd managed to blackmail someone else for a murder he'd committed himself—let alone two—and he'd been doing it for thirteen years.

Sometimes he wondered why he worked so hard at his day job, when he'd shown a preternaturally young flair for serious extortion. More than a flair, actually. A true brilliance.

He did need Katya, though, for something. He wasn't quite sure what yet. Seeing her again had really driven the point home. He'd always planned on her being part of his little reunion party. He'd wanted to shake her up a bit. Now he was thinking he wanted to do more than shake her up.

He flicked his cigarette out onto the street and started putting the Corvette through its gears.

Choosing Christian Hawkins again might possibly be her last mistake.

CHAPTER

15

THE CORPORATE OFFICES of Cunningham Ashe Construction were nothing short of luxurious. According to Katya, old man Cunningham had built half of Denver before moving the company to Colorado Springs and joining forces with Greg Ashe's father. The trust funds ran rich and deep on both sides of the boardroom.

From where he sat in Greg Ashe's outer office, waiting for the man's secretary to track him down, Hawkins could feel every dollar of all that old money. The carpet was thick, the paneling cherry, and there were dozens of elaborately framed photographs on the walls. Like Tim McGowan, Greg Ashe had a passel of kids.

But it wasn't the photographs that were holding Hawkins's interest.

Kat was wandering around the office, all strappy red sandals and little red dress, and he was riveted to every step.

He'd borrowed J.T.'s car one night that summer, a GTO named Corinna, and taken Kat to the races. And what a helluva thing that was to be remembering. They'd made love in the backseat, hot, steam-up-the-windows love in the middle of the night on the drag strip at Bandimere Speedway. He'd clocked a quarter mile in six-teen seconds, and his prize had been undressing her in the backseat.

He'd taken his time.

Geezus.

She'd been so shy, and getting her out of her under-wear had taken some coaxing, but all he'd wanted to do was look at her for a long, long time—and have his pants unzipped while he did it.

"Here's one for marksmanship," she said, looking up at a framed certificate hanging on the wall. "That doesn't look so good, does it."

She was talking to herself as much as him, so he didn't feel overly pressured to reply, especially since he was kind of busy.

It had taken a while, but she'd finally relaxed and let him look, so pretty, and so woman to everything he'd wanted as a man. She'd let him touch her, tease her until he could hardly breathe, her own gaze heavy-lidded and half-glazed, watching him stroke himself—and just as he'd been ready to cover her, push up inside her, she'd surprised the hell out of him and gone down on him in Corinna's backseat, taken him in her soft, wet mouth and blown his ever-lovin' mind.

Her first time, and she'd gotten him so hot.

She moved along to the next framed piece. "And here's

another one, marksmanship again, that makes him the best in Colorado Springs for two years in a row."

He was so friggin' screwed.

With a monumental effort worthy of the Man of Steel, he shut down the old memory machine and tried to concentrate on what she was saying: marksmanship, champion, two years. Okay, he wasn't too worried. The shooter at the Gardens had been a professional, a guy who shot off hundreds of rounds of ammunition a day, every day—not a guy who won the annual skeet shoot at his country club once a year.

She stopped next to a small table and opened her purse, giving him a perfect profile view of pure, unadulterated heartbreak.

How could she not know he was thinking about sex? he wondered. It was all he'd been thinking about for the last eighteen hours, give or take a few minutes spent thinking about keeping them both alive. Oh, yeah, and twice he'd thought about food, once about her mother, and once he'd checked to make sure he had an extra mag for his Glock.

He was trying his damnedest not to think about Kid and J.T.

She stood there, going through her purse and talking about Ashe and Cunningham, filling him in while she searched for something, probably her bubblegum lipstick, and she was completely clueless that in his mind he already had her half undressed and was getting ready to go down for the count.

She turned and met his gaze, a fleeting smile on her face and sure enough, a shiny gold tube of lipstick in her hand. She was still talking about the guys they were going to meet, and he let her. Without moving a muscle from where he was sprawled in the chair, he let her ramble on.

He'd met women who knew the instant a guy's attention turned to sex. He'd met them and bedded them. Katya Dekker was not one of those women.

She finally ran out of conversation, and in the ensuing silence, the subtlest change came over her face.

Okay. That's all he'd wanted. He pushed himself out of the chair and headed for the door to go get some air. He'd just wanted her to know he was thinking about sex, about the two of them doing it, not all those times they'd done it before, but about doing it now, him asking, her giving, and the two of them getting hot and heavy up against the little wooden table she was standing next to at the side of the door. That's what he'd been thinking about—and now she was thinking about it, too.

AFTER way too many hours following the guy from one construction site to the next, Greg Ashe was off Hawkins's list of suspects, way off. He was a decent guy, a true-blue family man whose wife brought him his lunch. Hawkins knew a liar when he met one, and Greg Ashe was no liar.

The verdict was still out on Philip Cunningham. He'd skipped out on their meeting. Ashe made profuse apologies, but Hawkins could tell he was confused about his partner's unexplained absence. Cunningham had been told Katya was coming. Ashe said his partner had been looking forward to seeing her—which was probably as close to a lie as he'd gotten all day. But the guy was a no-show, and all Cunningham's secretary could tell them was that he'd received a phone call shortly before lunch and left.

Hawkins and Katya had tried his house, a mansion set in the foothills above Colorado Springs, but he wasn't there, either.

Night had fallen on their way back to Denver, and the lights of the city were stretched out across the plains all the way to the horizon. Skeeter had called a couple of hours back to tell him Dylan and Kid had made it home. Dylan was doing a quick turnaround to Washington, D.C., and Kid—hell—Kid was going over to his father's house.

God, what a night.

Angling for a break in the traffic, he slid Roxanne onto an exit ramp for downtown and started gunning down the motor. Kat had fallen asleep about halfway home. She was sitting turned in her seat, facing him, her face pale in the moonlight and the faint glow of the dash lights.

He'd promised her he would drive by Toussi's and give her a chance to see how the show was going—but only from within the safe confines of the Challenger. She'd talked to Suzi Toussi half a dozen times today, but Alex was still persona non grata, and despite his pleading, Katya had not spoken to him.

Three Prom King boys down, three to go—and so far Hawkins had struck out. Shortly after they'd left The Painted Pony, he'd put Skeeter on tracking Stuart Davis down. Cunningham was going to get a call first thing to-morrow, and by a stroke of luck, Albert Thorpe was flying in from Maryland in the morning and had said he'd be happy to meet with her.

They'd done all they could for the day, unless Skeeter found Stuart Davis. In that case, Hawkins would be making a midnight run on his own, after he got Katya safely ensconced at Steele Street. He figured with Stuart being one of the last people to see Ted, he didn't need an invitation to visit. Given the circumstances, he'd called Lieutenant Bradley right after he'd called Skeeter, and he knew she wouldn't hesitate to knock on Stuart's door in the middle of the night, either, if the police had found him.

A few minutes later, he pulled up across the street from Toussi's.

"Kat?" He reached over and gently cupped her cheek, his thumb smoothing across her skin. "Kat, we're here."

What he really wanted to do was one of those Snow White numbers and kiss her awake, but though she was the quintessential damsel in distress, he sure was no prince.

She stirred, and he removed his hand.

He watched her lashes slowly rise to reveal slumberous, sea green eyes—and he felt something, very near to where his heart might be, turn over.

"We're here, Kat. Toussi's." He gestured out the window. "Looks like it's going pretty good."

There were cars parked up and down the street, and what looked like dozens, if not a hundred people inside the gallery, everyone schmoozing. A low murmur of the noise inside the place drifted out onto the sidewalk, and other people were arriving even as they watched.

Yawning, she rolled to her other side in the seat to look out the passenger door window.

Kat Dekker. Hell. He'd spent the whole day with her, and he could still hardly believe it.

More curves than a cyclone—his gaze went over her, from where she had her feet tucked under her to the tip of her perky little nose—and yes, it was perky, damn perky, but she wasn't. Never had been, not even at eighteen.

For all the little-blond-bombshell packaging, she was and always had been sultry. He'd had pretty girls before her, the prettiest in west Denver, and he'd had some very elegant, sophisticated, and downright gorgeous women since. Somewhere in there, she should have been wiped off his memory banks.

But she hadn't been, not even close.

He let his gaze slide down her arm to a point just above her elbow, almost on the underside of her arm. If a person didn't know where to look, they would never notice the scar. It had faded with the years.

He had to keep himself from reaching over and touching it, from wrapping his hand around her arm.

"I should be in there," Kat said. "Nikki's an amazing talent, and there are certain people I want to make sure she meets."

"Suzi can handle it," he assured her. "She's a pro."

She went perfectly still on her side of the car. Then her head swiveled around, and she pinned him with her gaze.

"You know Suzi?"

Amazing. He knew that tone of voice, had heard it a few times from a few women, and all he could do was hold her gaze and fight a grin, and wonder if this just wasn't a hell of a thing.

"I've—uh—bought a few pieces from her over the years."

"You *dated* Suzi Toussi?"

Now, how the hell, he wondered, had she gotten that out of what he'd just said?

It was true, but how had she known?

"A few times," he admitted. What did he have to hide?

A question that Kat didn't seem to care about, because she was shutting down on him, big-time. First with the crossing of the legs, then the crossing of the arms, then her mouth settling into a hard, hard line, and then the fixing of her gaze out the windshield.

Absolutely amazing.

What could he say? That he never would have made love to another woman in his whole life if he could have had her?

Actually, he could have said that, because he was sure it was true. No one had ever felt like her. He would have been true to her.

But none of that seemed particularly relevant to their current situation. Christ, he'd gone to prison because of her, and the fact was when he'd gotten out he'd laid half the women in Denver before he'd kind of come to his senses and figured out that setting some sort of record wasn't going to change a thing.

"Is she the one you're taking to the opera?"

Unfuckingbelievable. He didn't know whether to laugh or get really pissed off.

"You told me last night she was in love with a guy named Julio."

The little shrug she gave him spoke volumes. "I think they broke up, and knowing Suzi, she's probably looking for a new boyfriend . . . or an old one."

And Katya thought that he might be interested?

"*Gee-zus*," he swore, sliding down in his seat. She'd always had the most amazing way of turning him inside out, and he'd be damned if she hadn't just done it again. She couldn't possibly be jealous—unless she remembered more of last night than she'd let on.

"I think we need a reality check here. How about we go get a cup of coffee or something? Maybe some dinner."

A major reality check. *Cripes.* And he was starving. He straightened back up in his seat and reached for the ignition. Jealous. That didn't make any sense at all, no matter that he'd been feeling the same way. He knew he was nuts when it came to her, a file folder with way too many unopened documents, but he'd thought she'd have more sense sober.

"How about Chinese food?" he asked. "And a cup of coffee?"

She didn't answer, so he decided for the both of them, and an hour later they pulled up in the alley called Steele Street with takeout from Chang's Imperial Palace and a couple of coffees from Jack's Joe—if what she'd ordered even qualified as coffee. He doubted it. A double-chocolate, single-shot grande latte with triple whipped cream sounded more like a warm milkshake than a caffeine punch.

But to each his own. He'd gotten a double-shot espresso, straight up, and basically wasted as much time as possible getting home. He didn't know what the two of them were going to do all night. He figured his best bet was calling Skeeter up to the loft and the three of them playing Parcheesi or something. He knew he didn't want to be alone with Katya. He didn't trust himself not to get in over his head. He'd thought he could count on her to shoot him down if he got too many ideas, but that had been before the Suzi Toussi conversation.

A freight elevator big enough to haul automobiles to the seventh-floor garage clung to the side of the reinforced brick building like an upended suspension bridge, with its exposed guide rails and open-cage construction. Hawkins keyed a combination into the control panel, and when the lift door opened, drove Roxanne up onto the platform. They'd installed a newer, fully enclosed automobile lift on the north side five years ago, but the only one who used it with any regularity was Dylan, whose need for speed usually superseded the aesthetic advantages of slowly crawling up the side of 738 Steele Street with a view of the city and the mountains opening up to the west.

As the elevator started its journey skyward, he punched a few keys on Roxanne's onboard computer, calling up Skeeter. This close to home, the damn thing ought to work. Kryptonite, Skeeter was always telling him. He was like kryptonite to the computer's motherboard. Everybody else at Steele Street had one of Kid's inventions installed in their cars, and they all worked. His was the only one that needed to be within ten feet of the main office to fire up.

Skeeter would have already tracked them onto the elevator and would know they were home.

"Skeeter—Kid and Dylan?" he typed in and got an automated reply. Hell, Skeeter wasn't going to save his ass tonight.

"*Shadow to DOD.*" The message flickered across the small screen embedded in the dash, the first part referring to Dylan. "*Superman to Colorado Springs. Kid Chaos to Stavros's. Captain America to Stavros's, then to Toussi Gallery for McKinney show. Skeeter to dinner. In case of emergency, dial 111–111–1111.*"

And Skeeter would come running, probably from the Cuban deli on the corner.

Hawkins had figured Kid would go to his dad's, and he knew why Dylan hadn't wasted any time heading to Washington, D.C. They were going back to Colombia, and Dylan would want the authorization to do what had to be done. Captain America was Quinn, heading over to his new sister-in-law's show after paying his respects at the Chronopolous home.

Maybe he'd have Kat try to call Cunningham again, try to set up a meeting for early morning. He wanted this thing narrowed down. One of the Prom King guys was dirty and all but aching to get caught. Why else leave all that crap at her apartment?

Well, he was happy to oblige, the sooner the better.

He glanced over at Kat, and his gaze narrowed.

She'd taken the lid off her coffee.

Why?

The lids were designed to keep the coffee in the cup. A person didn't need to take it off to drink.

Of course, if a person was more interested in spooning the whipped cream out with their stir stick than drinking the coffee, there might be a reason to take the lid off, but not in a car—not in Roxanne.

The old freight elevator hit a rough spot and shimmied for a few seconds until it screeched its way past the sticking point. He watched out of the corner of his eye while she licked cream off the stick and balanced the cup away from herself, making sure it didn't spill—and he was duly grateful when it didn't.

They went through the same sequence of events at every floor, successively negotiating every one, thank God.

When they stopped at the seventh floor, he swung out of Roxanne and went over to open the cage. The seventh was where Steele Street kept their main offices and a whole lot of the cars they all drove most of the time. The garages took up a number of the lower floors. The eighth floor was the armory. His apartment was on the eleventh.

It took less than a minute for him to walk over to the freight door, pull it open, and turn back toward Roxanne.

Geezus. He tilted his head to one side to better see into the interior of the car.

How in the hell...?

He took a step forward, and tilted his head to the other side, beginning—just beginning, mind you—to get some idea of just how much freaking whipped cream there was in a triple order.

Plenty. More than enough to slide a bit down the windshield and still have some left over to drip off the ceiling. Enough to land on the front of her dress and leave a bit on her nose. Enough to get in her hair, and way too much to clean up with the tiny little napkin she was wiping around all over the place, making it all just so much worse. There was enough to leave a dollop on the steering wheel, which she was dutifully scooping up with her finger and sucking off while she tried to dab a chocolatey-looking spill off the dash.

Wow. She was amazing. Like Godzilla in Tokyo. Total destruction.

He crossed the elevator and leaned down in the passenger side window, resting his arms on the door.

She swung her head around, looking guilty as hell, the empty cup in her lap, her eyes wide, her finger still in her mouth, eating the evidence. She had a whipped-cream mustache, and it was all too much, way too much for him to handle anymore. He gave up. He was done, with nothing left to fight with, absolutely nothing.

She started to speak, but it was way too late to talk.

"Hawkins, I'm so—"

"Shhh, Kat," he said softly, leaning farther in, his hand sliding around the back of her neck, his mouth coming down toward hers. He licked the whipped cream off her upper lip, then sucked the whipped cream off the tip of her nose and slid his tongue across her cheek.

"Christian . . . I—" Her breasts rose on a quickly indrawn breath.

He didn't stop. He laid a wet trail down the side of her neck to her cleavage.

Mocha. God, she had coffee and chocolate all over her—and whipped cream.

He raised his head and looked down past her lap. A smear of whipped cream was sliding off her thigh. He caught it with his hand and licked it off his fingers, and then he kissed her, with the sweet taste still in his mouth.

A soft sound came up from her throat, and he knew exactly what it was: surrender. Just as well. The war had been lost.

He pressed her back in the seat, his mouth more demanding. He'd wanted her for so long, all those agonizing nights in Canon City. He'd wanted the smell of her, and the taste of her. He'd wanted that sweet Kat softness, the softness of her mouth and skin, the softness of her touch, the tenderness of her kiss, the way her hands had moved over him, sometimes with gentle reverence, exploring, and sometimes with desperate need.

There was one thing he knew about their time together: She'd been as fascinated with him as he'd been with her, physically, emotionally, and she hadn't been afraid, which he'd found amazing.

She should have been afraid. He'd been nothing but trouble, and always on the lookout for more, too dumb to be afraid of anything. He and the rest of the Steele Street regulars could outrun the cops and outsmart the gangs, which had left downtown Denver an open field for the lot of them. They'd made a living; they'd made some enemies, and they'd drawn some lines none of them had ever crossed.

But he was the only one who had spent a month in the Brown Palace making love to an American princess—and he wanted to do it all over again. Thirty days and thirty nights of trying to get enough of her.

Reaching down inside Roxanne's door, he pulled a lever under the passenger seat. The seat went back, reclining all the way, and he climbed through the window after her, easing himself down on top of her, heading for the backseat.

Moving the empty cup off her lap, he slid his hand up under her dress. *Oh, yeah*, this was what he'd wanted.

"Haw-kins," she gasped, and he covered her mouth with his own, still so sweet.

Rolling onto his side in the passenger seat, he pulled her against him, his hand sliding over lace panties, under them.

"Hawk—"

He kissed her again, working a number on her lips, sucking her tongue inside his mouth, opening his wider over hers—taking her.

Pulling her thigh up over his, he reached down and pushed off one of her sandals, then ran his hand all the way down her foot, massaging her instep, her sole. She sighed in his mouth, the sound dragged up from deep inside, her leg sliding higher up his hip. Her hands were on his chest, either holding on to him or pushing him away. He couldn't really tell, not yet.

Maybe she didn't know yet, either, but her mouth was sweet under his, her tongue teasing him, turning him on like it was hardwired to his groin, getting him hot like her underwear got him hot.

Man, she'd had a big day, real tough, and his had been kind of a toss-up between sucking eggs and hitting the fan—and this was exactly what he needed, what he'd wanted to give her since she'd stuck her hand down his pants and pretty much sealed his fate. He was doomed. He wasn't going to work her out of his system, not anytime soon, probably not ever—and he wanted her. Every cell in his body was primed for making love to her, for drowning himself in her. He lifted his mouth from hers and kissed her bare shoulder, licked her skin.

"Hawkins, please..." she murmured, her breath warm against his ear.

Please what? he wondered, stopping. After a long few seconds of silence, he pressed another kiss to her shoulder and raised his head.

Some things a guy just had to know.

Meeting her gaze, he ran his hand back up the side of her dress, under her arm. "Please what, Kat?" He found the zipper tab and started pulling it down. "Please make love to me, Hawkins, because no one else ever, ever, ever..." He repeated her words, knowing exactly what she'd meant, because no one else had "ever, ever, ever" done it for him, either. He'd had great sex, yes, but nothing like the way she'd done him, from the inside out with so much love in his heart he'd thought he might die from it.

A guy only gave that away once, and he'd given it to her.

He slid his hand through the zipper opening, leaning his mouth down to her ear. "You know I'll do it for you, Kat," he whispered, giving her a kiss and sliding his nose across her skin. "I'll do it for you every time, if that's what you want." And he would, a hundred different ways and start all over again.

He grazed her jaw with his teeth, felt her tremble. A shuddering sigh left her, and he felt her hips rise toward him, the smallest movement, but he felt it.

"You—you don't even like me."

Well, that wasn't precisely true, and he was bound to like her even more once he got her naked, but *that* was not the right thing to say—even if it was true.

And it was. There was something very likable about a

naked woman in your arms who was melting all over you, ready to take you inside, especially if you thought she was the most beautiful woman you'd ever seen and her mouth was sweet, and her hands were on you, and you knew, deep in your heart, just how good it was going to be between the two of you.

What wasn't to like about that?

"No," he countered. "The problem here is that I like you too much." It was a flat-out admission and his cue to back off. Maybe take stock of the situation, reclaim a little pride, but he didn't take his hands off her. He didn't lean back and give her some room, and he didn't lift his head from the curve of her neck.

Quite the opposite—he opened his mouth on the soft, sweet skin beneath her ear again. He tasted her with his tongue. He slid one hand up her body and moved her hair back over her shoulder, letting the silky strands drift through his fingers.

It was just one big mistake after another: using his other hand to slide down over her bottom and press her into his hips, helping her with that decision, grazing her throat with his teeth, letting her scent seduce him.

Geezus, how he'd missed her, her tenderness, her willingness, the mind-blowing softness of her mouth, and beneath the ice, the heat. She'd been so young, so sweet, and the most amazing lover he'd ever had, including every one he'd had since—not the most skilled, but the most amazing. She'd spoken French to him, whispered in his ear, and damn near set him on fire. He'd loved it.

He'd loved her, like no one before or since.

He tightened his hold on her and slid his mouth over

the top of hers, claiming her. He wasn't going to let her go, not tonight.

K̲AT wanted to cry, and if she had been able to catch her breath for even a second, she might have—but she wasn't going to be able to catch her breath, not with Hawkins kissing her, touching her.

He had magic hands, utterly magical, and the taste of his mouth left her breathless. No man had ever tasted like Christian Hawkins: darkly delicious, primal male, answering a need in her she hadn't known she had until the first time he'd kissed her. She'd wanted him so badly all day, even more than she'd wanted him that first night so long ago, and she'd wanted him so badly that night, she'd all but thrown herself at him.

She'd been so frightened then, in pain where her arm had ached, distraught over what had happened to her and to her dress—and she'd been enthralled, absolutely mesmerized by the heart-stoppingly beautiful boy who had saved her. He was the most fascinating mix of street toughness and natural elegance she'd ever seen, six incredible feet of raw, lean power, silky dark hair, and cheekbones—tattooed, carrying a knife, rough talking, and yet so careful with her. He was so sure of everything, of facing those boys, of the wild car he drove, of what to do with her, sure of everything from the instant he walked into the alley until he walked her to her hotel room door. He hesitated there, and she'd been so afraid he would leave, she'd hardly been able to speak.

But she'd gotten the words out, and he agreed to stay a while, until she felt safer, felt better. Room service had saved her. She'd ordered three times: dinner, dessert, and champagne. He thought it was all pretty cool.

She thought he was cool. Self-assured enough to openly appreciate the hotel suite and the incredible food, and so gorgeous she hadn't been able to take her eyes off him—something he'd finally noticed.

"Do I have ice cream on my face?" he asked over cherries jubilee, leaning across the table with a curious grin.

She'd ordered the dessert just to have the waiter flame it up and hopefully impress him. She'd really wanted to impress him. He was everything she'd never had, everything she wanted to be—wild, free, not living by anybody's rules.

"No," she said, embarrassed to have been caught staring—again.

He laughed then, leaning back in his chair and running both of his hands back through his hair. Amazingly, for a guy who ran around on the streets of Denver and seemed to have more than a passing acquaintance with the alleys, he'd been wearing slacks, not jeans, and the oddest, silkiest palm-tree shirt that would have looked affected on any other boy. On him it had looked so laid-back cool.

"God, I'm going to be in so much trouble," he'd said to the ceiling, then let out another short laugh and brought his chair back down onto all four legs. "I had two more cars on my list to pick up tonight. Two cars Sparky isn't going to get, and that's going to get me on his list—which is not such a good place to be."

"I'm sorry." She hadn't known what else to say, even though it was a bald-faced lie. She wasn't sorry for anything that had brought him into that alley, into her life. It had only been a week later that she'd finally correlated "picking up cars" with "stealing cars." By then, she was too addicted to him to care.

"Creed and J.T. are going to wonder what happened to me," he'd said, leaning back over the table and idly picking up her hand.

There was nothing idle about her reaction. It was the first time he'd touched her since he'd grabbed her in the alley, and she was electrified by his touch.

"It's getting late." He started to rise to his feet, and panic set in. She couldn't let him go. She'd never see him again if she let him go.

She rose with him, her hand still in his.

"How about more champagne?" she'd asked, and immediately felt foolish. It was such an obvious ploy.

He'd grinned and dipped down to better see her face. Even though she wore heels, he towered over her.

"Are you trying to get me drunk?"

"No." She'd looked away, embarrassed. "I'm sorry. It's just . . . well—thank you, Christian. Thanks for taking me to the doctor, and for what you did. It was . . . very brave." And that sounded too stupid to bear.

Her blush deepened, and she swore at herself. *Very brave . . .* God, like he was a little kid or something.

He didn't say anything for a long time, and she just couldn't bring herself to look at him, not after saying something so dumb.

He still had ahold of her hand, though, and during the long silence, he slowly slid his thumb over the ridge of her knuckles—and her heart started to race.

"Only girls who kiss me call me Christian," he'd said, entwining his fingers with hers. "Everybody else calls me Hawkins. Just Hawkins."

It was all the encouragement she'd needed.

"And how many girls have you kissed, Christian?" she'd asked, daring to glance up at him.

"Just two." His grin had broadened. "Just *mi abuela*, my sweet little grandmother . . . and now you."

He'd bent his head down to hers and brought his other hand up to cup her face, and within half a minute of his mouth touching hers, she'd known he was such a liar.

Oh, God, he'd known how to kiss. He'd played with her mouth. He'd seduced her completely, without touching her anywhere else—and he'd forgotten nothing.

Nothing. No one kissed like Christian Hawkins. She opened her mouth on his and just breathed him in, tongues sliding, lips pressing. With everything about him so hard, the inside of his mouth was so very, very soft . . . wet. He tasted faintly of espresso, which was so very Hawkins, something rich, dark . . . sensually intense.

His hands were hot underneath her dress. Her underwear had disappeared. She was barefoot—and with just his kiss, he'd already taken her past "Oh, God, should I do this?" to "Please, God, don't ever let him stop."

She wanted him, desperately. She wanted what he offered, what he could give her, and she was willing to risk her heart to get it.

And that's exactly what she was risking. Nothing less. She knew him, knew herself with him. No half measures would do. She would end up giving him everything, and he would take it all and then some, and when he left, she'd be left with nothing.

But, God, it had been so long, so very long since a man's touch had made her melt from her core.

Between their bodies, she felt him unbuckling his belt,

and a whole new level of thrill went through her. Her options were dwindling fast. Not that he wasn't a gentleman. He was, and no one had more control of himself than Christian Hawkins—just the thought of all that control was enough to make her melt another degree. It had taken her years to take another lover. She hadn't done it until long after he'd been released from prison. God only knew what might have happened to her, if he'd never been released.

He'd spoiled her young, though. She'd thought all men knew not to give up on a woman. She'd thought all men loved making love, loved every touch, every kiss.

She'd been wrong.

But not about Hawkins, never about him, not from the first moment she'd seen him and ran straight into his arms, not about taking him into her bed—and hopefully not about taking him again in the front seat of a 1971 Dodge Challenger R/T named Roxanne, seven floors up in a garage freight elevator.

Was she insane?

Or just shamelessly desperate?

She felt him slide his zipper open, and she dragged her mouth from his. Their eyes met in the darkened interior, and she knew it didn't matter if she was wrong or not, or if they were jammed together in the front seat of his car, or spread out on her bed at home. His gaze was dark with need, his hand sliding up between her legs, and all she could do was watch his face—so beautiful, his hair silky long and damp on the edges, his eyes so deep set, so thickly lashed, so intensely focused on hers.

He touched her then, his fingers so sure, so unerring, and pure, sweet pleasure poured into her. With a soft gasp, she brought her mouth back down to his, moving against him, her hips pressing into his hand.

"*Christian . . .*" she sighed, loving what he was doing to her, loving being so close to him, half on top of him with no place else to go.

She tunneled her fingers up through his hair, holding him for her kiss, for a hundred kisses, and she began undoing the buttons on his shirt.

HE'D been friggin' nuts, Hawkins thought, to come through the window after her. Five more minutes and he could have had her in his bed, his king-size bed with pillows. Instead, they were going to end up doing a pretzel fuck in a bucket seat—because there was no other way this was going to end except with him inside her.

She fit in Roxanne, and she fit him like a glove, but he didn't fit. He had one foot jammed up against the windshield, his other leg half under her. Not that it mattered. Nothing was going to stop him now. She was hot, and wet, and all over him, and this was the way it had always been between them. Instantly incredible.

The faintest taste of bubblegum lingered on her lips, so sweet and lovely, but not the taste he needed, the taste he'd driven himself crazy thinking about all night long with that damned manila envelope and the pictures of the two of them in his hand—his right hand, and yeah, he'd been holding on to himself with his left, but he couldn't say he'd had all that much fun. With her lying in his bed, and not being able to touch her, the whole thing had been an exercise in futility. Not that he hadn't gotten off. He had, but it hadn't even begun to take the edge off his frustration.

He'd wanted her, and in addition to all that lust making him horny, it had demoralized the hell out of him. She'd lain there on his bed, nearly comatose, a little pile of drunken bad luck, and all he'd been able to do was watch her and ache.

Some things a guy liked to think he'd outgrown, and some things he had, but not her.

"Kat, help me," he said against her lips, his hands going to her hips and trying to lift her on top of him. He didn't mind if he ran into a few things getting organized, but he didn't want her to get knocked around. He just wanted her on top of him, especially since he'd gotten her out of her underwear in record time, but he was only able to manage getting her on top if he slid farther down in the seat and put one leg out the window and braced the other against the dash, making enough room for her to get her knees on either side of his face. Thank God she wasn't being shy about it, because the maneuver was already clocking in at a high ten for difficulty.

More sliding down and more pulling her up his body finally . . . finally got him what he wanted. He opened his mouth on her, found her sweet, hot center with his tongue, and proceeded to slowly drive them both out of their minds.

She gasped, almost a sob, and a huge wave of tension lifted away from him as he just gave himself up to the wonder that was her. *Sweet Jesus*, this is what he'd wanted, what he'd needed, the part of himself he'd held on to so desperately, the part of himself he'd shared with her—sex, pure and simple and the sweetest thing on earth, her giving it all up for him, her responses triggering his own, the two of them getting lost in each other.

Her hands were in his hair, his were on her hips, sliding over hot, satiny skin, until she came in a torrent of soft cries and trembling shudders—and it was better than he'd remembered, filling him with the deepest, bone-deep satisfaction. He kissed her again, and again, so softly, and she cried out each time, melting on top of him, until she slipped away down his body.

Cradling her against his chest, he smoothed her hair back off her face and kissed her cheek. "Backseat, sweetheart," he murmured in her ear, then lay back down and gave her a little boost so she could crawl over him—and, oh, yeah, that alone was worth the price of admission.

Maybe the whole car thing hadn't been such a bad idea after all, he thought, following her.

She slid down into the seat, and he slid in right after her, the condom package between his teeth and total victory in his mind. She was his. She'd always been his—and nothing happened in the next few minutes to shake his conviction. She had her hands all over him while he put the condom on, her voice whispering a whole litany of sweet nothings that seemed to mostly be made up of his name, which he loved more than she could possibly know.

Yeah, everything was going just fine, right up until he slipped her leg up around his waist, and started to push into her.

That's when his wires got crossed, when he blew a fuse and short-circuited every commonsense synapse he had in his whole friggin' brain. She was so hot, so slick; sliding into her, he felt like he was dying and on his way to heaven. There had to be a name for what happened to guys in this situation, maybe Electromagnetic Vaginal Impulse Syndrome, because when he thrust into her, his whole brain was instantly fried, as if he weren't connected to reality at all anymore.

He thrust again, and it just got better, and with the next thrust even better, like he was sliding into a hot, silky sea and knew he was going to drown and didn't give a damn. And then it suddenly all got so much worse.

"I love you, Kat." The words whispered from his lips without a single connection to conscious thought, sanity, or his will. They just came out . . . and kept coming. "God, I missed you . . . missed you so much."

Geezus, he was holding on to her so tight, his arm low around her hips, lifting her into him, his head buried in the curve of her neck, and he was pouring out his soul. Damn, damn, damn.

"*Kat . . .*" He ground himself against her with every deep thrust, wanting . . . wanting . . . getting so strung out, his mouth all over her—endless minute after endless minute, until she gave him everything he wanted, her body going stiff beneath his. Her head went back on a groan, and her back arched off the seat. God, he'd never seen anything more beautiful, never felt anything more exquisite than the cascade of her contractions tightening around him, and it undid him. He dropped his head between her breasts, his breath caught, his release so fierce and hot.

It was like being in never-never land, what she did to him, the place she took him, and it took a long, long time to come down. When he did, she'd long since stopped kissing him, stopped caressing him, and had curled up and fallen asleep.

Oh, God, Kat, he thought, carefully pulling her on top of him so she wouldn't get crushed. She settled in, and he got as comfortable as possible in a backseat that had to be pushing a hundred degrees. Steamy didn't begin to describe it. It had been jungle love. Tropical jungle. And he'd given himself over to it body and soul.

So what in the hell, he wondered, was he going to do now? Damn.

CHAPTER 16

INSIDE THE TOUSSI GALLERY, on the biggest night of her life, Nikki saw Kid Chaos walk through the front door, and her heart jerked to a sudden, painful halt. Oh, God. Her hands gripped the stair rail where she stood in a crowd of people above the main gallery floor, looking out over dozens of her paintings and over a hundred patrons and potential clients.

Kid... her heart started up again on an equally painful jolt. She could hardly breathe, her gaze running over him, hardly believing it was really him. He looked so different from when he'd left, older, and so very tired her heart broke even more. His hair was longer, still short and dark, but long enough to muss up, and it looked like he'd dragged his fingers through it a dozen times. He was dressed with a casual elegance she wouldn't have thought him capable of the night they'd met, when he'd been wearing camouflage pants and a colorfully clashing Hawaiian shirt. Tonight he had on a white suit jacket and a fine black mesh T-shirt, with jeans and cowboy boots, a style that passed for semiformal in Denver, but nothing seemed to quite fit him, and she realized he'd lost weight, a lot of weight—*oh, God*.

The rest of him was the same, though: the six feet of pure predator, the hawklike gaze and chiseled cheekbones, the lean angle of his jaw, and the nose that gave the clean lines of his face an unexpected boyish appeal. He'd been hurt, and her heart twisted at the sight. A small patch of hair above his right ear had been shaved off, and she could see a couple of stitches, which only reinforced the awful truth. He'd finally, really come home, but under the worst circumstances imaginable.

She started down the stairs, then stopped when a woman she didn't know approached him with a smile and a glass of champagne in hand. He took the drink and smiled back, and suddenly Nikki didn't have a clue what was going on, a clue what to do.

It would be so easy to run across the room and throw herself into his arms, but what if he wasn't here to see her, but because Quinn was here? Quinn and Regan had gotten home mid-afternoon. They'd seen Kid, spent the early evening with him at his dad's house—but Nikki hadn't expected him to show up here. She'd felt so left out, knowing he was in Denver and not having the right to go to him. He'd been gone for almost two months, and he hadn't called her once. Not while he'd been gone, and not today.

Not once.

A smart girl would think about that for a minute, no matter how heartbroken she was for him. The last thing he needed was some girl he'd slept with one night to throw herself at him, expecting something he wasn't willing to give, especially when he seemed to be charming the socks off the willowy brunette with the champagne.

The brunette leaned in close, said something in his ear, and he tilted his head toward her, another brief smile flashing across his face.

Nikki's grip tightened on the stair rail, her fingers turning to ice, everything inside her freezing into a cold hard lump of pain. It was too much. She hadn't smiled since he'd left her, and he was smiling with another woman? Had he brought the brunette to the show? Could he be that cruel?

Honestly, she didn't know him well enough to know the answer, and that hurt, that she'd given her heart to someone she didn't know. God help her, she'd never been jealous in her life, but she was jealous now, and it was an awful, awful feeling.

She wanted to run and hide, just disappear, but she couldn't do that and face herself in the morning. So she steeled herself instead and started down the stairs. There were other people she needed to meet here tonight. Unbelievably, and for reasons unknown to her, Katya Dekker had not shown up, and Nikki was trying not to overanalyze what that might mean to her career. Suzi Toussi and Alex Zheng had done their part in keeping her introduced to all the right dealers. Now she needed to hold up her end and charm them if possible, or at the very least make a little polite conversation. She did not need to fall apart over a man she barely knew.

She did need to make damn sure their paths didn't cross.

She couldn't bear that. Really, she couldn't, not while that woman was practically hanging on him and he didn't seem to mind.

KID couldn't breathe. The gallery was unbelievably crowded, and he didn't see Nikki anywhere. And then this woman—who was only trying to be nice, bringing him a drink and all—was confusing the hell out of him. He couldn't hear half of what she was saying with the band playing and all the noise in the room, and he didn't want to be rude, but he didn't have a damned thing to say to her. He didn't have anything to say to anybody, except Nikki. She was the reason he'd come. She was the one he needed—and he didn't see her anywhere.

He'd seen Quinn and Regan leaving by the back door as he'd been coming in the front, too late to get to them through the crowd. They were going back to his dad's. They'd said they wouldn't be gone long, but he hadn't been able to wait. He'd had to bail out. Skeeter had said Hawkins might come by the gallery, too, some kind of problem with a murder last night. Not the usual SDF op, but connected with the orders Hawkins had received to leave Colombia. Dylan had talked to him about it on the plane from Panama City, but he'd been so exhausted and hungover, he hadn't heard even a tenth of what Dylan had said—except the part about all of them returning to South America.

To finish the job.

The thought was enough to make his stomach churn.

He knew what it would be like when they went back to Colombia, knew what they would do, and he was afraid it wouldn't be enough—and that scared the hell out of him. Creed had said he and J.T. had been set up. Finding the people who had done it was going to be harder than finding the people who had tortured Creed to within an inch of his life, and killed J.T. Bringing them to justice might be even harder—but for the rebels who had killed J.T., justice would be swift and exacting.

A picture of his brother's body flashed across his brain, and he felt a sheen of sweat break out across his brow. Struggling for a breath, he looked down at his champagne glass, then shoved it into the chattering woman's hand and walked away.

He had to find Nikki.

He crossed the room twice, working his way through the crowd, searching faces, and was just about ready to give up and leave, before he stopped breathing altogether, when suddenly, there she was, in a group of people in front of a huge painting of Travis James, the wonder stud and her favorite model. He recognized the painting from the night they'd first met, but it was the sight of her that stopped him cold in his tracks.

God, she was so beautiful. Even trying hard to remember everything about her, he'd forgotten. Looking at her, it was hard to believe he'd touched her, kissed her, made love to her and had his body inside hers. He'd never met anyone who affected him the way she did. She wasn't very big, but she was powerful in a way he'd found strangely daunting and utterly fascinating. She exuded an energy that lit her from within. She was heat, and light,

and warmth, and more than he'd ever known of love before—and he hardly knew her at all.

He glanced around the gallery again. This was her night.
The place was full of her paintings, most of them of Travis,
who was a nice enough guy, but Kid would have liked him
better if he wasn't so naked everywhere, especially in
front of a girl he was sure he'd fallen in love with in less
time than it usually took him to ask someone for her
phone number.

She excused herself from the crowd and started making her way back across the gallery—alone—and he knew
he had to make his move or leave. There was no middle
ground.

He started forward, but had only gotten a few steps
toward her when he was waylaid one more time by the
woman with the champagne.

"Hi, again," the brunette said, all bright teeth and span-
gly beaded dress. "I didn't get your name. I'm Pamela."

She held out her hand, and Kid stared at it for a second
before habit kicked in and he took it with his own.

"Uh . . . I'm . . . uh"—out of the corner of his eye, he
saw Nikki approaching—"I'm Kid, well, Peter," his voice
trailed off.

He was staring at Nikki so hard, she had to feel it, had
to know he was there. Finally, she glanced in his direction, and the rest of the world fell away. Nothing else existed, just the two of them, him frozen to the spot, and
her . . . growing suddenly pale, and a spark of . . . anger? . . .
coming into her eyes.

This wasn't good. He hadn't planned for anger, which
had been damn dumb on his part. He could have kicked
himself. Of course she was angry. He'd up and left her,

and though he'd told her he was leaving and how much she meant to him, he never had been sure that she was exactly awake when he'd said all those things.

From the look on her face now, she hadn't been.

He started forward again, and realized the spangly-dress woman still had ahold of his hand.

Geez. "Uh—excuse me." He got his hand back and crossed over to where Nikki was still stopped in the middle of the room, only to find that he didn't have anything to say.

Well, that wasn't exactly true. He had a thousand things to say to her, a million thousand, just none of them were coming to mind.

"Hi" was the best he could come up with. When she didn't say anything right away, he tried a little harder. "I've been out of town for a while."

"I know," she said, her voice a little shaky, her gaze angled somewhere past his shoulder. "I'm . . . I'm very sorry about your brother."

He was going to have to ignore that. He couldn't talk about J.T. Not at all, not to anyone. He hadn't even been able to talk to Dylan about him.

"I was in—uh—South America." He should have called her, dammit. He could see what a big mistake that had been now, not calling her when he'd had the chance, the couple of times he'd been in Panama. It wasn't like he hadn't thought about calling her. It just hadn't seemed right to drag her into what had been going on. "The orders came down the night we—uh—were together, and I was hoping we could kind of pick up where we—uh—"

She glanced up at him, both of her eyebrows arched in

a look that was half confused, half a complete mystery, but didn't look good.

"...left off," he finished lamely. The expression on her face changed ever so slightly, but with the change he recognized it for exactly what it was: anger again. He started to feel the sand slipping out from under his feet, like a big old wave was sucking him back into a riptide.

"What I mean is—" God, he was stupid. He'd said it all wrong.

"I know what you mean," she said through her teeth. "I know exactly what you mean."

He caught her by the arm as she turned to leave. He couldn't let her go. Not yet. Not when just looking at her was enough to tear him up inside. Not when she was angry with him.

"Nikki," he said, his voice hoarse, his hand tightening on her arm.

Her skin was so soft.

"No, Kid." She glared at him, her cheeks flushed. "You can't just walk in here and expect—" She stopped suddenly, the color fading out of her face, a stricken look coming over her. "I'm sorry, so sorry, but I can't—"

"Nikki?" Another voice intruded, and Kid glanced up. His jaw immediately tightened.

Travis, the blond-haired, blue-eyed wonder stud, stopped next to her, close enough to slip his arm around her waist. Kid felt his already short leash get shorter.

"Kid." Travis greeted him with a nod of his head and an easy smile Kid didn't misinterpret for an instant, but he wasn't going to let the situation deteriorate into a dogfight, not if he could help it.

Of course, no one knew better than he did what a

goddamn big "if" that might be. He hadn't exactly been in charge of himself lately.

"Travis." He returned the other man's greeting and tried not to think about how many hours the model had spent naked in Nikki's studio. Tried not to think about Travis's hand on her waist or what might have happened between the two of them since he'd left.

He didn't want to hurt the guy. Really, he didn't. Nikki would hate him for sure if he busted up her angel—and despite the warning in Travis's gaze, Kid didn't have a doubt in the world about which one of them would get taken down. He could have come right out and told the guy, "Don't fuck with me tonight. You're too nice a guy to get in the middle of what I'm dishing out," but he didn't.

The important thing tonight was to win, and winning meant leaving with Nikki. To that end, he backed off, letting his hand slide down her arm, until he held her hand in his—a nominally less dominating hold, but still a connection. He wasn't going to let go of her, no way, not unless she absolutely shot him down.

"One dance," he said, turning his attention to her. "That's all I'm asking. Just one dance. It's my birthday." He had to work not to wince as those last words came out. It was true, but it was also about as lame a thing as he'd ever said.

Okay, it was worse than lame. It was pitiful, and if she turned him down after such a pitiful plea, it could only be because she was sleeping with Travis. He didn't have any facts to back up his conclusion, but his intuition was telling him it would be true—and then the night might get ugly. Whether Travis had only the purest of sexual motives and instincts or not, and according to Nikki he always did, Kid was probably going to deck the guy.

Her hesitation wasn't lost on him, or on Travis, who after a few more seconds of her silence, dropped his hand from her waist.

"Good to see you," he said with another nod, before turning back into the crowd.

Kid was so grateful the guy had left he couldn't move at first, only stand there holding on to her hand and wishing she would look at him.

She didn't.

But neither did she remove her hand from his.

Stalemate. He took a deep breath and led her toward the dance floor. She was wearing the most outrageous shoes, high-heeled platform boots with short cuffs around her ankles, purple patent leather with silver swirls.

And the dress.

The dress made him hot all over. Like the black skirt she'd been wearing the day he'd met her, the dress just barely covered her butt, and he meant just barely. It was sleeveless, backless, and almost sideless.

Squares of pink and purple satin, and silky string, that's all there was to the whole damn thing. He didn't have a doubt in the world that she'd made it herself; the squares of cloth were hand-painted. He just wished she'd made more of it—until he turned her into his arms and slid his hand across her bare back. Her skin was smooth, and soft, and warm, and touching her triggered a thousand sensory memories. The boots added inches to her height, making her head fit perfectly against his chest.

He pulled her close, felt her soften against him, felt her hand slide up to his shoulder, and for the first time in days, the knot of tension that had been holding his heart in a vise began to ease. It was dangerous, letting go of the tension, but for her he was willing to do it, on the chance he could draw some of her inside himself, some of her heat, some of the life pulsing through her.

Gathering her closer, he bent his head to hers and eased her backward in a slow dance of swaying hips and barely moving feet. She felt like heaven in his arms. If it had been up to him, he wouldn't have moved at all, just held her, just run his hands over her and buried his face into the curve of her neck, remembering.

But tonight was about winning, and he wanted to win more than just the memory of making love with her. He wanted to lose himself inside her. He wanted to forget who he was for a while, and she was the one, the only one, who could give him that kind of oblivion.

A brief smile curved a corner of his mouth. She smelled like Nikki, a little like paint, as if her dress might not have had time to completely dry. She also smelled warm and sweet and so very female. Her scent wrapped itself around him, seeped into his pores, filled him, and another layer of tension melted away.

This was going to work. Finally, he could see a path out of the abyss. Maybe everything was going to be okay.

A sigh left him, and he kissed the top of her head, then let his mouth slide lower—to her temple, her cheek, to the tender skin of her neck. God, it was heaven to hold her, to feel the softness of her skin with his lips, to take a taste and feel her tremble. He opened his mouth on her ear, let his breath warm her, let his teeth gently graze her lobe—let his body tell her how much he wanted her. How much he'd needed her.

Even in the tropical heat of the Colombian jungle, he'd been frozen inside. Those last few days after Hawkins left had been hell—pure hell, and then it had turned into a nightmare. The sight of J.T. inside the body bag was burned into his memory. It followed him into sleep. It was waiting for him when he woke up—but Nikki could save him. He had to believe it, had to believe in her. She was all he had left.

He slid his hand lower on her back, underneath her dress and down to the base of her spine, caressing silken skin, rediscovering silken curves. A tremor went through her, and even knowing he was out of line, he turned her away from the crowd and slowly brought his hand all the way back up, until his open palm rested on her rib cage and his thumb softly caressed the underside of her breast.

She went very still in his arms, her breath catching against his chest, and he gave up all pretense of dancing.

"I missed you." He felt safe telling her that much. "I missed you so much it hurt." What he didn't feel safe telling her was that he still hurt, everywhere, all at once, all the time, and if she couldn't save him, he was afraid he'd be lost forever.

Her hand tightened on his shoulder. "I missed you, too." Her voice was so soft that if he hadn't been holding her in his arms, he wouldn't have heard her.

But he did hear her, and it was all the reason he needed to give in to more of what he wanted.

"Is there someplace we can go?" He didn't want to sound desperate, but he was afraid he did.

"After the show?" she asked, looking up.

Taking a breath first, he plunged ahead. "No. Now. I—uh—really want to kiss you." That didn't sound so bad. Kissing wasn't so bad. "*Really* want to kiss you," he admitted, and tried a smile. He meant it to be reassuring, but from the look on her face, he might have just scared her off.

He didn't blame her. If she was smart, she would run as far away from him as she could get. He was a mess. He knew it, and he wasn't at all sure how much longer he could hide it—and the longer they stood there, the harder his heart started to pound. What if he'd blown it? Christ, he wasn't even sure he could get back to Steele Street on his own. He needed help. He needed something, and he'd wanted it to be her.

Fuck. He hadn't planned this out very well. His dad was so broken up, he hadn't been able to stay at the house, but he could have gone to Superman's. Dylan had left straightaway for Washington, D.C., and hell, Quinn had just gone back to the one place he couldn't handle tonight, but Hawkins was around—somewhere. Hell, even Skeeter wasn't bad in a pinch. A little nutsy, but dependable, and definitely one of the guys. Skeeter knew the score, better than he did sometimes.

But he'd wanted Nikki. God, how he wanted her.

She was looking him over pretty good, her gray-eyed gaze focused on his, taking his measure, which was damned demoralizing. No way did he look worth taking a chance on tonight.

"Come on," she said, surprising the hell out of him.

Taking his hand in hers, she led him across the gallery to a door in the back, and when they went through it, she turned around and locked it behind them.

"We should be safe in here for a couple of minutes," she said. He heard a switch get flipped, but nothing happened. "Oh, no lights, sorry. I think this is an office, or maybe a closet. It feels kind of small, doesn't it?" And she sounded kind of nervous.

A lot nervous.

His night vision was excellent, and with the help of a window that looked out on the alley, there was enough ambient light from the city that he could see just fine.

A small office, maybe, he silently agreed, or a storeroom. There was a lot of art piled against the one wall, an office chair shoved into the corner, a closet rod full of clothes next to the door, with a desk underneath the clothes.

She hadn't let go of his hand, and when she turned back around, she was practically in his arms—and looking very unsure about being there.

"Kid, I—"

He lifted his hand to her face, touched his fingers to her lips. He didn't want talk, not about anything. Talking wasn't going to get him anywhere. What he needed was her mouth, her body. What he needed was her all over him, until he couldn't think.

That's what he wanted—not to think. He smoothed his thumb across the top of her cheek, then ran his finger down the length of her nose. Another grin lifted the corner of his mouth.

He'd "painted" her that night, with an empty brush,

smoothed the soft, superfine bristles across her skin and marveled at his self-control—which he had damn little of tonight.

But she knew what he wanted. He'd been mostly honest.

He rubbed his thumb across her mouth again and felt his breath tighten in his chest. He'd told her he wanted a kiss. She knew.

He lowered his mouth to hers, telling himself to take it easy, not to push too hard, too fast, not to devour her. He was twice her size, and he wanted to make love to her, not hurt her.

Her tongue slid across his, the first intimate touch, and he brought his other hand up to cup her face, knowing he'd never been so miserable and so happy at the same time in his entire life. It tore him up, but he knew this was what he'd wanted, what he'd longed for, to have her mouth be so hot and sweet under his.

He opened his mouth wider, asking for more, and she gave it to him, moving deeper into his arms. A welcome surge of pleasure washed through him, the cleanest thing he'd felt in days, and he let himself fall, just fall off the edge of the earth. Her tongue was delicate and soft, and having it in his mouth again felt like a miracle.

God, she felt so good. He pressed himself against her, rubbed against her.

"Nikki," he murmured, kissing her lips, her cheeks, her eyelids. Everything about her was so soft and smelled so good. She was everything he'd needed, her hands sliding up over his shirt, her breath so gentle on his skin.

Go slow, he told himself, even as he slid her dress up

over her hips, a very short trip, especially when she stopped him with her hand on his.

Fine. He'd just wanted to touch her. He'd just wanted to breathe without it hurting in his chest, but kissing her was working. He let another barrier fall away, opened himself up a little more, just to take her in, just to get closer to her heat.

Wrapping his hands around her waist, he lifted her onto the desk and moved between her legs, getting there, closer to where he needed to be. Everything about her turned him on, which was such a relief. He hadn't been sure he would still function. Everything had gotten so screwed up.

Everything.

So goddamn screwed up.

He pulled her against him, fighting off a little surge of panic.

She was warm and giving, and that's what he needed to think about. Nikki. Not J.T.

Another surge of panic sizzled into his veins, and he held her tighter, kissed her harder—too hard. He could tell by the little sound of distress she made deep in her throat, where he was trying way too hard to put his tongue. She pushed against him, and for a second, just a second, he wondered if he was going to let her go. He was locked onto her like a heat-seeking missile, and so help him God, all he wanted was more. He did not want to back off, and it crossed his mind that if he just kept at it, just kept pushing, she would loosen up, just give in and let him do what he needed to do.

Oh, shit. He broke off the kiss and froze where he stood, pretty much horrified by his last train of thought.

His head was resting against hers, his heart pounding. *Shit*. He was holding her way too tightly, and he immediately loosened his hold—but he couldn't let her go. He couldn't. *Geezus*, he was so freaking whacked. He had a pocket full of condoms, a hard-on, and a full-blown panic attack jacking his heart rate up into the danger zone. He was sliding off the deep end into nowhere, and if he let go of her, something terrible was going to happen. He didn't know what. He just knew it would be terrible—which was so fucking irrational, he was afraid it was already too late for him.

Nikki could feel his heart pounding, hear him hyperventilating, and it scared the hell out of her. Something was wrong with him. His face had been flushed in the gallery, and his smile had been weak, barely a curve—but God, he was so beautiful, and his mouth, his mouth had been everything she'd missed, everything she'd wanted since he'd been gone, up until his kiss had gotten so fierce.

He was like tempered steel beneath her hands, his whole body rock hard. There was no softness left in him, no protective layer. He'd been honed down to sinew and bone, and all of it was frighteningly focused on her.

"Kid?" She whispered his name, so scared he was going to break right there in her hands. He'd gone so rigid.

He'd been trying to take her clothes off, hardly five minutes after showing back up after walking out of her life, and she didn't know what in the world to think about that. She wanted to kiss him. She felt like she wanted to kiss him forever, but she didn't know what she wanted after that—and she was sure she was supposed to have more pride than to let him strip her naked in a closet.

Or maybe not.

There was an edge to him, and she could imagine all the reasons why.

"Kid?" she whispered again. He'd gone so still, she couldn't stand it.

Turning her face, she kissed him again, a soft touch of her lips on his cheek. When he didn't respond, but just stood there, his head bowed, his eyes closed, a shiver of panic skittered across her brain, and suddenly, she knew she didn't dare lose him, not like this. She knew what she'd felt when he'd made love to her: cherished. He'd been so sweet, so careful.

That wasn't the way it was going to be tonight. She'd been a virgin the first time they'd made love, but she hadn't been naive. She'd unraveled too many men in her studio to be naive about them. He'd been taking her clothes off for a reason. The only mistake she'd made had been in underestimating just how serious he'd been about doing it.

Kissing him again, she pulled her dress up and pressed his hand to her breast, let him feel her heartbeat, which even though it was racing was a darn sight mellower than his. Then, without another thought, she pulled the dress completely off over her head and let it puddle into a silky pile next to her hip.

That got his attention. His hand closed on her, so gently, and his mouth slid down to kiss the curve of her ear. A tremor went through him.

"I won't hurt you, Nikki," he said, kissing her again. "I promise, I won't hurt you."

He wouldn't deliberately hurt her. She knew that, but neither did she delude herself into thinking he was going to be the tender lover she'd had before—before his brother had died doing God knew what in Colombia and Kid hadn't been able to save him.

"I won't hurt you, either," she whispered against his throat between kisses—and she meant it from the very bottom of her heart. She would hold him tonight, love him the best way she knew how, and hope she could save him from himself.

CHAPTER 17

TRAVIS'S GAZE went back to the closet door for about the hundredth time. He had a pretty good idea of what was going on in there. He'd seen the look on Kid's face and known exactly what he'd come for: his woman, any way he could get her, even if it was in a damn small, over-crowded storeroom-cum-closet, during the middle of the biggest night of said woman's life.

If it had been any other guy, he wouldn't have worried. Nikki was tough. She always held her own—but not with this guy. Kid Chaos had sliced and diced her heart. Travis had been hearing about it every day for the last two months. Nikki McKinney, the oldest living virgin in Boulder, Colorado, had finally given it up for a Marine sniper on a hot summer night in June, and the guy had walked out on her.

Travis couldn't have called that one. Hell, no.

Kid had broken her heart and confused the hell out of

her—even though he'd apparently left because of some mission he'd been on. Travis had dissected the whole encounter with her, from the first kiss to the postcoital drift into sleep, and he'd assured her nothing had been wrong—except for the guy leaving while she was asleep. He'd figured the sex had gone okay without her telling him everything. He knew Nikki better than anyone, well enough to know she was at heart a sensual creature, and he'd figured the guy couldn't have been a complete klutz. But she'd been glad to get the reassurance, and God knew she'd wanted to talk about it—over, and over, and over.

He was fine with that.

Kid had given her a great orgasm, and Travis had to admit he liked the guy for that. Her first time, and she'd come. That was great, a classy move. It wasn't always easy for a woman her first time—or even her hundred and first, if it came to that, unless a guy cared enough to figure it out and take his time. And it was never easy for a guy to take it slow his first time with a woman. The excitement level was usually over the top before he even got her clothes off.

Yeah, those first times tended to get wild real quick.

But this dragging her into the closet after two months without a word, because the guy was hurting over his brother dying, he didn't know about that. There'd been nothing but pain written on Kid's face tonight, but man, that was a lot of freight to drag into a closet with a condom—and Kid sure as hell had better have a condom.

Travis felt for the guy, really, but he loved Nikki. They were soul mates on the artistic plane. They'd taken each other places no one else would ever see, unless someone caught a glimpse of it in Nikki's paintings, and the look in Kid's eyes tonight had told Travis he was bordering on dangerous, that he was living up to his name—Chaos—in spades.

But hell, he still couldn't convince himself to go over and knock on the closet door.

He swore softly and forced himself to look somewhere else. It was a strange night all the way around. Alex Zheng, the gallery guy, was so wired that Travis was afraid he was going to explode, or disintegrate, or something. The guy was a nervous wreck, and Katya Dekker, the world-famous, highly influential, very-important-to-Nikki's-career Katya Dekker, had been a no-show. That had freaked Nikki a little.

Hell, it had freaked her a lot. But given the disaster at the Denver Botanic Gardens last night, no one was really surprised Katya hadn't made it. Some guy had been murdered during the art auction, and Katya had lost an Oleg Henri painting.

As for himself, he'd been hit on so many times tonight, he'd been ready to leave, until Kid had shown up. He couldn't leave now, but he sure wished a lot of these people would understand that just because there were about fifty life-size, nude paintings of him hanging off the walls and from the ceiling, he wasn't for sale.

What he and Nikki did—it didn't have anything to do with sex, except for pieces like *Narcissus by Night*. But even *Narcissus* was about private sex, internal sex, a sexual state of mind—not the deed.

So he was doing his best to look interested in paintings of himself, which was nothing short of weird, and trying not to make eye contact with anyone, which meant he'd been spending quite a bit of time looking at the walls and daydreaming about going climbing in the morning. He might just head up to the Flatirons tonight, camp at the base of some gnarly pitch, and be ready to go at first light.

Yeah, that sounded good.

He looked around the gallery again. There was an old elevator toward the back of the gallery, and a door leading to the alley next to it. Something about the door had been drawing his attention all night. Maybe it was the potential of it, the potential of escape.

He checked his watch. He'd give Kid and Nikki half an hour—okay, forty minutes—and then he was going to check on her. If she was fine, great. He'd go back to Boulder alone.

That settled, he found his gaze going back to the door yet again—but this time it opened.

The gallery was air-conditioned, and the air from the alley was still supercharged from the sweltering day. It flowed into the room like a river of heat, cutting through the chill, and winding its way across the gallery, riveting him to where he stood. It smelled like the city, all hot bricks and steam, and it had brought a messenger.

One hell of a messenger.

She stood in the doorway, backlit by a street lamp, the glint of metal following the curve of her hip.

Chain mail, he realized. She was wearing a chain mail miniskirt over a pair of black silk tights, with a metal knife sheath in place of a zipper. The tights were rolled up on the bottom, revealing four inches of bare leg above a pair of thick-soled, brown leather work boots. She had a black ball cap pulled low over her face, a pair of mirrored sunglasses, a Chinese tattoo on her upper right arm, and a silver ponytail that came out of the back of the cap and fell down the front of the skintight black muscle shirt molded to her curves. A pack of cigarettes stuck out of the hip pocket on her skirt, and she had one cigarette hanging from between her lips. As he watched, she struck a kitchen match off her chain mail and lit up. He could almost hear her inhale, and when she exhaled, she did it through her nose.

Man, she was all smoke and mirrors and *so* not his type, and he couldn't for the life of him figure out why his gut was clenching at the sight of her.

She looked around, cool like ice, checking out the whole gallery scene, before she made her move, and unbelievably, her move was to head straight for him.

He felt her gaze lock onto him from behind her mirrored shades, and he got an odd impression of handcuffs, for no reason he could logically explain, any more than he could explain the odd thrill heating his skin.

He was so fucked, Hawkins thought, reaching up into Roxanne's back window for the container of crab wontons. He had shrimp dumplings and noodles with sesame sauce balanced on the console, spring rolls in the front seat, which he could just reach, if he stretched his arm around by the driver's door, and a container of jumbo prawns on the floor along with cashew chicken and tofu with vegetables. He'd done quite a bit of damage to all of it, propped up in the backseat with a pair of chopsticks in his hand and Kat sleeping on his chest.

But he was still screwed.

I love you, Kat? Where had that come from? And why had he felt so freaking compelled to tell her?

It defied all logic.

She mumbled something unintelligible, turning her head the other way and readjusting herself on top of him, and he looked down at her, a sigh lodged in his chest. Wasn't it the guy who was supposed to fall asleep after sex, while the woman lay awake analyzing and worrying the whole thing to death?

Yes, it was. He knew it without a doubt. What he didn't know was why it never worked out that way between the two of them.

She was limp, draped over him like an exhausted kitten, her mouth partly open, her lipstick gone, her mascara smudged beneath her eyes—the whole of her so lovely it broke his heart. Five feet, two inches of golden curves and a tiny tan line across her ass.

Hell. He checked the wontons, counted only three, and put them back in the window. She probably loved crab wontons, and her stomach had been growling for the last fifteen minutes. He went instead for the shrimp dumplings, stretching the chopsticks over to the console and snagging the little wire handle on the container.

He'd just put one in his mouth when he felt her stir again, as if this time she might be waking up.

Chewing slowly, he watched and waited, practically holding his breath—just one more act of pure idiocy he was at a loss to explain. He always kept breathing, always, under the worst of conditions, under fire. He breathed.

But oh no, not with her. She was a threat of unknown capabilities, unknown force—and he'd told her he loved her.

Geezus. What if he really did? What then, Superman?

She yawned, her warm breath making a hot spot on his chest—and yeah, that's about all it took for him to start getting real interested in her waking up, and with both of them naked and her on top of him, there was no way to hide it.

Damn.

He was starting to feel uncomfortably vulnerable, something he would have thought it would have taken a guy pointing an AK-47 at him to accomplish—not one smallish woman whose only weapon was a one-way ticket to heaven.

Before she even opened her eyes, a slow smile curved her lips.

"Mmmmm. Food. Smells good."

"Open your mouth." God, how he loved those words.

She obeyed—which gave him a really nice feeling—and, using the chopsticks, he placed a dumpling on her tongue. She sighed in pleasure.

Oh, yeah. Open your mouth, Kat. Lick me. He sighed himself, but he didn't think he'd be getting any of that tonight. He wasn't going to ask, and he wasn't at all sure it would cross her mind.

He wished it would, though. He really did. Just the thought of having her mouth on him was enough to make his erection complete, and given her position, there was no way for her not to know it. Perfect. Again.

So, he wondered, what, if anything, was she thinking now?

He didn't have to wait long to find out.

"Do we still have some tea?" she asked, looking up at him from under a tangled fall of blond hair, her green eyes lazily slumberous.

Yes, as a matter of fact, they did. It had cooled down considerably, but there was still a Styrofoam cup full of the stuff in the bag on the floor.

He pulled it out, opened the lid, and handed it to her.

Rising slightly, she took a long swallow, then handed it back, and without so much as a subliminal suggestion on his part, she started sliding down his body, one of her hands going between his legs and the other sliding up his chest, under his arm, and over his biceps, where her fingers curled around him—as if she needed to hold him down to keep him from getting away.

Yeah. Right.

In fact, he had no intention of going anywhere. She'd pretty much frozen him in place with the possibilities of what she might have in mind.

She was cradled between his thighs, and he had a perfect view of anything she came up with. No, he wasn't going to move, not an inch—at least that's what he thought until she did exactly what he'd been dreaming about, starting with a kiss and then another, before her tongue came out and lit him on fire. *Geezus.* He braced one arm against the driver's seat and gripped the backseat with the other, dropping the damn tea, his hips rising off the seat on a surge of pleasure so intense, if he'd been standing it would have put him to his knees.

Oh, God, be careful what you wish for, he reminded himself, his gaze riveted to the utterly compelling sight of her going down on him—her hand encircling him, her mouth all tantalizing softness and flickering movement.

Her hair slid over his belly, the long blond strands catching on the dark hair arrowing down his lower abdomen, and as he watched, she ran her tongue up the length of him.

Good God. His hips rose again, and he gripped the seat harder. No wonder he'd fallen in love with her at nineteen. She was a witch, with a witchy, spellbinding mouth.

She was relentless in her tender onslaught, and he was very quickly floating somewhere near to where nirvana must be, his body suffused with pleasure, moving in rhythm with her, his thought processes on permanent vacation.

But there was a point where a guy had to interject a little reality check for a girl's sake, and he'd reached it.

"Kat," he said, his voice hoarse, his body strung tighter than a compound bow. "Kat . . ."

She had to know what was going to happen; try as he might, he'd hit an unmistakable rhythm—and it felt so incredibly good, so sweet and deep, his whole body alive like she'd plugged him in to a low-voltage electrical current.

"Kat . . ."

Her only answer was to slide her hand across his shoulder and up to his face. She gently traced his lips, silently telling him to *shhhh*, and he caught her fingers with his mouth.

It was irresistible. It was perfect, one of those physical fantasy moments where the brain and the body simply meshed. He sucked on her fingers, and she sucked on him, the current complete and completely sensual, the two of them so incredibly in tune, everything so sweet.

She had to love him. He felt loved—loved in every cell of his body.

Taking her hand in his, he slipped her fingers from his mouth and ran his tongue down the center of her palm. He sucked on the inside of her wrist, laved the tender skin of her forearm, and he kept pulling her up, until she had to release him and give him her mouth. He wanted her kiss like nothing else in the world. He wanted to be covered by her.

He slid further down in the seat, licking her lips, tasting himself on her, consumed by the pure eroticism of making love.

"Condom?" he whispered.

"No, not this time . . . please," she murmured, rubbing herself against him, running her fingers through his hair, breathing on him—absorbing him. "You're safe with me, Christian."

And she was safe with him, or he never would have let her take him in her mouth. As for the rest of it, he trusted her, more than trusted her. She was a part of him. They were both sheened with sweat, their bodies so hot, he felt like they were fusing, melting into each other, a sensation that only increased when she slid down on him, taking him inside.

God. Kat on top. He pulled her mouth down to his and just lost himself in kissing her, in thrusting into her, in letting her ride him.

When she tightened above him, her cry caught in her throat, he still didn't stop. He just kept going, pumping into her, holding her mouth to his for an endlessly deep kiss, until the wave of his release washed over him and dragged him completely under with her.

CHAPTER 18

ALEX ZHENG was beside himself, completely beside himself. He didn't know where Katya was, and she wouldn't answer her phone, and he seemed to have lost the artist—*the* artist, Nikki McKinney, the woman everyone had come to see, the new sensation all the dealers were here to meet, and then, just to make things worse, someone was smoking, *smoking*, in the gallery.

He couldn't see the culprit, but he could smell the smoke, and it simply wasn't allowed.

But that wasn't the worst of it. Not even close.

How had he let Katya get away from him last night? And with Christian Hawkins of all people. He was dead—which brought him around to "the worst."

He brought his hand to his chest and pressed on the sudden pain near his sternum. Heartburn or heart attack, it didn't matter. By the time Senator Dekker got done with him, there'd barely be enough left to bury.

And she was coming, *coming to Denver in the morning*. He and Katya hadn't planned on seeing Marilyn during her brief stop.

But Marilyn wanted to see him now . . . in chains.

Oh, God, the pain got worse, and he pressed harder. He wanted nothing more than to get on a plane to L.A. and go home to Max, beautiful Max, with his long dark hair, incredible mouth, and strong shoulders.

But not even Max could save him from Marilyn Dekker.

He'd called her; he'd had to, but that didn't make having to face her any easier. Even worse, unbelievably, the Dragon had gotten the same manila envelope full of pictures that had been waiting in the apartment for him and Katya last night.

He didn't want to think about it. Really, he didn't. He'd been shocked enough for both of them. Not about the sex. There'd been nothing at all unusual about what Christian Hawkins and Katya had been doing, and quite frankly, Mr. Hawkins had been one very beautiful boy thirteen years ago—very beautiful. God, the tattoo on his back and the way it curved around his hips had been nothing short of mainline erotic. No, Alex had been shocked that the pictures had ever been taken and were circulating now, especially after what had happened at the Denver Botanic Gardens.

Someone was out to either get Katya or ruin her—and he'd lost her.

Shit.

And then the whole thing with Dylan Hart, whose security clearances had not only impressed the hell out of him, but also scared the hell out of him. Mr. Hart had made connections on a cell phone Marilyn Dekker couldn't have made from a secure line in her office.

So who the hell was Dylan Hart? Or for that matter, Christian Hawkins? He knew what they'd been thirteen years ago, but as far as he could tell, the information that had been gathered on them since was worthless. The only chop-shop boy that anyone had kept current with was Quinn Younger. Of course, his face had been plastered all over every newsmagazine in the country when he'd been shot down in his F-16 over northern Iraq a few years back. With that kind of publicity, it hadn't exactly taken a rocket scientist to follow his career.

And he'd been here tonight, in the gallery. Apparently, he was married to Nikki McKinney's older sister.

Alex dropped his face into his hand and shook his head. Denver was *such* a small town. Practically inbred. He couldn't swing a dead cat without hitting one of these chop-shop boys, and he couldn't get a damn bit of information out of any of them. He *knew* Quinn Younger knew where Christian Hawkins was—but the man had been completely closemouthed, very grim for someone at a gallery opening, and his wife, Nikki McKinney's sister, hadn't been much better. She'd looked quite sad.

Something was going on. A lot of things were going on, and Alex was out of the loop. It was a very uncomfortable, and he feared dangerous, place for him to be. If Katya needed him, he wasn't going to be there for her— but at least she had her red Gucci dress with the matching sandals, and her Kate Spade bag with all her little accoutrements, and her shampoo, and everything else a girl would need for two or three days out of town—as if *that* was any sort of consolation for having lost her. Dammit.

Hawkins had returned to the apartment in the middle of the night and taken it upon himself to pack the overnight bag Alex had refused to put together. It hadn't taken any great Sherlock Holmes–type detective work to figure it all out, either, because the man had actually had the audacity to leave him a note.

Alex wasn't given to much self-doubt, but that had thrown him. Hell, he'd been right there in the apartment all night long, and he hadn't heard a thing.

So who were these guys?

And where was Katya?

He needed to warn her about her mother changing her plans and fitting a little mother/daughter visit in as a *top* priority. He needed to explain to her, explain a lot of things. He'd never betrayed her, not once in five years, and a fine line it had been, working for the Dragon and being a true friend to Katya. But he'd walked the line. He swore he had, and he wanted Katya to know.

And she had to be warned about her mother. He would never forgive himself if the Dragon snuck up on her. Katya didn't deal well with her mother under the best of circumstances. Under the worst of circumstances, it might be more than she could bear.

Jesus Christ, where was she?

He'd implored Suzi Toussi to contact her, but Katya wasn't taking anybody's calls.

He'd gone to the police, but some Nazi lieutenant named Loretta Bradley had very coolly shut him down, basically telling him Katya Dekker was in a secure situation and the investigation was out of his hands.

Like he didn't know that?

Well, he had until morning to get it back in his hands, or all hell was going to break loose—with him at the center of it.

Now where in the hell had Nikki McKinney gotten herself off to, and who in the hell was smoking in his gallery?

KID lifted his mouth from their kiss and looked down at Nikki, still not believing what she'd done. God, she'd taken her dress off, just pulled it off over her head and blown his mind, which was perfect. His mind needed blowing.

He put his hands on her, slid them up over her breasts, cupped her. *Geezus*, she was soft, probably the softest thing he'd ever touched in his whole life.

She stretched up and opened her mouth on his neck, laying a trail of kisses along his skin. He took a breath, hoping he could do this. He wanted so badly to make love with her, but, man, his head was in a bad place.

He squeezed his eyes shut, as if that would somehow block out the awful sense of panic buzzing at the back of his brain. It didn't.

Tough it out, he told himself—and really, what kind of a thing was that to have to be thinking when a guy had the hottest girl in the world in his arms, and she was practically naked?

His hands started trembling, and he didn't know what would be worse: to lift them off her body and not have her to hold on to, or to leave them on her and have her know he was shaking like a leaf.

She had to know it already, but all she did was slide her hands around to the front of his jeans and start unbuckling his belt—and that helped, that got his attention.

Honest to God, if anyone had asked, he would have said it was physically impossible to have an erection and a panic attack at the same time, not that he'd known what a panic attack was, except from talking a guy through one once during a combat mission. Now he knew, up close and personal, and it was awful; he'd known what one was ever since this evening, when he'd gone to his dad's.

He hadn't been able to take it, watching his old man break up.

But he could take this—having her take off his pants. *Oh, yeah*, he could take it just fine. She finished with his zipper and slid her hands around over his bare ass, pushing his jeans and briefs a little lower as she did.

Then she pushed them even lower, and they just kind of slid off him the rest of the way to pool around his boots. He'd lost a lot of weight in Colombia, gotten downright scrawny, but he hoped she wouldn't notice that.

He hoped she would notice that he was suddenly hard as a rock—and that was great, just great. So was having her hands all over him, sliding up under his T-shirt, rubbing his chest, kneading his shoulders, smoothing back down his torso and over his ass again, holding on to him like she meant it—yeah, that felt good.

Incredibly good.

He rocked against her, sliding up against all her soft, satiny skin, and miracle of miracles, he felt the panic ease. He'd needed her so badly.

She started to push his jacket off his shoulders, and before it got too far toward the floor, he reached in his pocket and pulled out a fistful of the condoms he'd made sure he had with him before he'd left Steele Street. As the jacket came the rest of the way off, and he was toeing out of his boots, she happened to notice what was in his hand.

He followed her gaze from his fist up to meet his own, and a sudden, unexpected blush coursed over his cheeks. A fistful of condoms either looked pretty stupid or pretty damn presumptuous.

"Um . . . how many of those things do you think you've got there, cowboy?" she asked, the tiniest grin playing about her lips, her eyebrows arched, her head cocked to one side.

Yeah, he was a cowboy all right, kind of a desperate, horny cowboy.

He looked down at his hand and surprisingly found himself fighting his own grin.

"Eight," he said, making a fair guess. Okay, that was stupid, but what was even stupider was that there were still more in his jacket pocket.

"Eight," she repeated, opening his fist and carefully taking the packets out of his hand. She made a little pile of them on her dress. "I don't think we'll need eight to start." The briefest smile curved her lips as she ran one delicate finger up the length of his cock.

It was hot in the closet, but it instantly got a whole lot hotter.

Probably wouldn't need eight to finish up with, either, he silently agreed with her, feeling so friggin' foolish and so freakin' turned on—and oh so much better. All she was wearing was a little pair of white lace underwear and her spike-heeled, silver-splashed, purple go-go boots—and somehow, that was all really working for him, even better than if she'd been completely naked, and he got the idea that she knew it, that she'd done it on purpose—which just made it work all that much more.

"You're the only man I've been with, Kid," she said, looking up at him again from under her lashes, her finger making another lazy trail back down him. *Geezus*. It wasn't a coy touch, or a coy glance, not at all, not from those hands, or from those eyes, so discerning, so unafraid, so beautifully gray. She simply knocked him flat out. She had from the first instant he'd ever seen her.

And she hadn't slept with Travis. The relief he felt was absolutely humbling—but that wasn't all she was telling him, and he knew it. She was being careful, and he liked that she was careful. He liked it a lot, mostly for her, but also for what he was beginning to think it might mean for him.

"My job," he started. "Well, in my job, they're always poking and prodding at us, checking us out, and—*Geezus*, Nikki."

She'd wrapped her hand around him, run her thumb over the top of him, and while he was still absorbing that eye-crossing pleasure, she ran her whole hand down the length of him—and back up.

God. He leaned down and kissed the top of her head, rubbed his lips over the silky, spiky mess that was her hair, and just soaked in the intense sweetness of having her stroke him. It was so perfect, exactly what he'd dreamed about all those endless nights in Colombia. He'd been so lonely for her. Hell, so lonely for anybody, but he'd wanted her, just like this, turning him on, sharing something that had more to do with life than all the death that had surrounded him.

And he'd ached for her, just ached to have her touch him like she was touching him now.

"I've got a clean bill of health, Nikki," he swore to her, and she looked up. "I hadn't been with anyone for a long time before you, and no one since." His voice was hoarse, and he felt like he was spilling his guts, confessing things that made him look a whole lot less than cool, but he also didn't think being sexually cool would have been a plus with Nikki. She certainly hadn't been sleeping around.

No, she'd saved herself for someone special. She'd saved herself for him, and from the look in her eyes, he'd just told her what she'd needed to hear, needed to know.

That sweet, lazy smile graced her lips again, and the next time she brought her hand up him, her mouth was there to take over the job—hot, silky, wet...mindbending.

He groaned, his head falling back, his hips thrusting forward as she plied her tongue in one of the most sensual explorations of his anatomy he had ever experienced. He'd watched her work. He knew she knew men in their most intimate details, and she brought all that knowledge to bear with infinite finesse, infinite tenderness, all but turning him inside out with pleasure—so sweet and keen. She left no part of him untouched, unloved by her lips, and her tongue, and her hand and fingers, exploring, applying pressure, rubbing him in exquisite, surprising moves he hadn't even known he would love.

When she finally lifted her head, he slid his mouth down over hers and proceeded to drown himself in the taste of her, sealing his lips over hers and drawing her tongue into his mouth—again, and again, and again, exerting just enough pressure to make having her as vital as his next breath.

He finished toeing out of his boots and kicking off his jeans. Then he broke the kiss and pulled his T-shirt up over the back of his head.

"Scoot back," he said, helping her move further onto the desk and following her up, filled with a sudden sense of urgency. They ended up in the hot, dark place underneath the clothes, naked and wrapped around each other, her underwear off, and his hand going between her legs to tease her, please her—and please himself, while they kissed and sighed and kissed some more.

All women were soft, but kissing her, touching her, was unlike anything he'd ever experienced, ever felt, and he knew it was because he was in love in a way he'd never before imagined. He hadn't known a girl would ever make him redefine himself. That a girl would push him beyond what he'd known, the way she did. She was a genius with a paintbrush and a camera, twenty-one years old with a gallery full of people at her feet—and she was making love to him in the closet.

He went as slowly as he could, which wasn't very damn slow, because he just wanted to be inside her, as deeply inside her as he could get, for as long as he could get it. God, she was sweet, and a little small—and yeah, he needed the "magnum"-sized condoms, but that only made it all that much more incredible.

"Are you okay?" he asked softly, trying to be careful, murmuring the words against her cheek as he kissed her.

"Mmmmm" was the only sound she made as she adjusted her hips under his. He could feel her little go-go boots resting on the backs of his thighs and sliding up toward his ass as she tightened herself around him, trying, like him, to get even closer.

And then she did get closer, moved an infinitesimal degree and nearly brought the house down.

"Oh, geez, Kid," she gasped. "Oh, God."

Geezus was right. A couple more moves like that and it was all going to be over—and he was ready, so primed for taking her to completion. He sealed his mouth back over hers, sucking on her tongue again and matching the rhythm of their bodies, letting himself sink into the act, letting himself be consumed by the heat and power surging through him, letting her love burn through him—until there was only her, coming with a soft cry, holding him, her body tightening beneath his and taking him with her.

The pleasure was intense, soul-shattering, almost more than he could bear. It stripped him down to his core, and in the aftermath, when it faded and left him naked and unprotected in her arms, something deep and terrible broke inside him. He felt it happen, like the San Andreas fault opening up in his chest, a giant, jagged cut straight down through the middle of him.

He sucked in a breath against her lips, tried to stop it—but it was too late . . . too late.

Nikki felt him suddenly go still in her arms, so still she

worried that she'd somehow hurt him. Then she tasted it, the warm, wet saltiness of his tears.

Oh, God. They were streaming down his face onto hers, running over her lips and breaking her heart. Not a move, not a sound escaped him.

Only the tears.

She held him, not moving herself, feeling some awful premonition in the rigidity of his body, as if he might crumble if she so much as dared to breathe.

She didn't know what to do for him, how to help him.

When he kissed her, lightly rubbing his lips over hers, she thought for a second she was wrong. That he was okay, just suddenly sad, but it would pass. She kissed him back, and he moved his mouth to her cheek, and in the split second before he spoke, she knew her hope had been misplaced.

"They cut him up . . . into pieces." His voice was so soft, so raspy, his arms holding her so tightly.

She knew who he meant, and the horror of what he was saying flooded through her, leaving her speechless.

"They dropped him off in a body bag, and the bag . . . it didn't look right. It looked too small to be J.T. So I thought—I thought there had been a mistake. But when I looked, it was him."

Oh, God. Oh, God. They'd cut his brother to pieces.

"I didn't tell Dylan . . . or Miguel—but I have to tell Superman. He needs to know what they did."

Superman, yes, whoever he was. They needed to tell Superman, someone who could help him. She tightened her arms around him, loving him and knowing it wasn't enough. Nothing could be enough.

He kissed her cheek again, just the softest brush of his lips over her skin.

"I'm sorry," he said roughly. "I'm so fucking sorry."

It wasn't her he was talking to, and Nikki knew it. She knew the words were for his brother.

"So sorry," he repeated, and then a racking shudder went through him, and another. A sob broke free from deep in his chest, an agonized sound Nikki felt all the way down in her gut—and all she could do was hold him.

CHAPTER 19

TRAVIS WAITED, breath held, as the girl crossed the gallery, heading straight for him. She wasn't as tall as she'd looked standing in the doorway, but she was still all legs, slim hips, and nothing short of amazing breasts. Even more fascinating was the way she moved, like a catwalk model, all languid grace and rolling hips—but with an unerring sense of purpose.

And the closer she got, the more he realized it was her purpose he found unnerving, much more so than her looks. She had a black leather purse bandoliered across her torso. It looked heavy, and if he wasn't mistaken, it clanked when she walked. What in the hell that meant was a mystery.

"Hey," she said, coming to a stop in front of him, her chain mail letting off a little susurrus of sound. "You must be Travis, Nikki McKinney's friend."

"Hi." He stuck out his hand, hoping she would take it.

Up close, she wasn't as old as she'd looked, either. Not even close, which was kind of a downer. She didn't look old enough for any of those fleeting ideas he'd had watching her cross the gallery. Sixteen at the most, seventeen and he'd eat his socks. She was a baby—one very tough-looking biker-babe baby.

"I'm Skeeter," she said, taking his hand. She had working hands, calloused, strong, her grip as firm and unflinching as any guy's. Her biceps flexed when she shook his hand. "Skeeter Bang. I'm looking for my friend, Kid Chaos. I tracked him here, found his car outside in the alley, but"—she gave a little shrug, looking around—"I don't see him, and I really need to find him."

A friend of Kid Chaos's, now why wasn't he surprised? Like Kid, Skeeter Bang—and that was a helluva name—looked like she could kick ass and take names while she was doing it, even though the longer he looked at her, the more he wondered if fifteen might be closer to the mark than sixteen. Either way, she was way out of his territory.

She'd tracked Kid here, Travis silently repeated, wondering what that was all about, and wondering how in the world to explain to a fifteen/sixteen-year-old that Kid was in the closet, probably getting laid.

"Well, he's here . . . with Nikki," he said, deciding to go for a condensed version of the facts. "They kind of hooked up."

"Okay." She nodded thoughtfully, then took a long drag off her cigarette and blew out the smoke. Travis had to work not to cough—or lecture. "That's good." She leaned over and knocked the ash off her cigarette into a discarded plate perched on a granite table. "So Nikki, she's a nice girl?"

The question was asked with a casual nonchalance, but it definitely had an underlying edge that said she expected a real answer and he'd be wise to give it—which frankly amazed him. He knew what he looked like, and women from eight to eighty usually cut him a lot of slack because of it. But not this girl. She wasn't handing out unearned props to anybody, and unlike everyone else in the gallery tonight, she could give a damn that he was the model in all the paintings.

God, what a challenge. A grin curved his mouth. Not a sexual challenge, he reminded himself, just a kick-in-the-pants challenge.

"Define nice."

"Sure," she said, without missing a beat, except to take another drag off her cigarette. "Nice girls don't run around on their guy."

Easy enough. "Kid's the only guy Nikki's ever had."

One eyebrow arched above the mirrored sunglasses. "She never had you?"

Lots of people thought that question, and every now and then, someone got up enough balls to ask—usually another of Nikki's models who was hoping to get lucky—but coming from a fifteen-year-old, Travis found it damned disconcerting.

"We're friends." Not lovers, he could have added, but he didn't.

He didn't know how, but even from behind her sunglasses, he could tell she was weighing his answer, checking him out, like it could possibly be any of her business.

"He was worried about that, while he was gone."

Well, that explained her interest, and Travis guessed he wasn't surprised.

"He never said it, actually," she continued, "but I could tell he was worried about you stealing his girl."

"So why didn't he call her?" That seemed a fair enough question. Certainly Nikki had asked him it a hundred times.

Skeeter Bang shrugged and sucked another hit off her cigarette. "He was in a bad place . . . very bad." Her voice broke a little in the cloud of smoke she exhaled, and she glanced away toward the floor. "Look, I'm just here to make sure he's okay."

"Sounds like you think he might not be."

She shrugged again. "I was with him earlier tonight, at his dad's, and I . . . I couldn't help him. I was hoping Nikki could. If you'll just tell me where he is." She glanced back up, and though all Travis could see was himself reflected in her glasses, he got the impression she was on the verge of tears, which, unlike some guys, didn't make him panic. It just made him feel badly for her.

"Well, he and Nikki kind of disappeared into that closet over there." He gestured toward the door on the west side of the gallery. "And though I'm just as concerned about Nikki as you are about Kid, I guess I figured the two of them would work things out without me interfering."

She followed his gesture. "Yeah," she said, stabbing the end of her cigarette into the plate. "I'm sure you're right." But she went ahead and started over to the door anyway, without giving him a backward glance.

Travis followed, not sure if he meant to stop her from going in, or if he just wanted to be there if she did. Either way it was a moot point. She didn't even touch the knob when she got there, just laid her ear up against the door and listened.

As an invasion of privacy, Travis figured there were worse, but he sure as hell wasn't going to put his ear to the door. At least that's what he thought, until she reached for him, her hand closing around his wrist in a gesture he didn't misinterpret for a second. Whatever she heard, it made her need somebody to hold on to; it made her feel the need for support.

Moving closer to her, he, too, put his ear to the door, and it didn't take more than a couple of seconds to understand her distress.

Ah, Christ. The guy was crying, breaking up.

He stepped back, looked down at her, and swore again. She was crying now, too. Big tears running down her soft little cheeks, and suddenly he was in the middle of Kid's brother dying, too. In it up to his neck.

"Nikki is the best thing for him right now," he said, hoping to reassure her. "She knows all about guys crying." Right, he thought dryly. Nikki knew how to take a perfectly normal guy and deconstruct him, until he was in tears. She'd done it more than once. Never to him, though. For all he gave her, he knew better than to let her have everything her way.

"Will she take care of him tonight?" Skeeter Bang asked, and on that point, Travis could be one hundred percent positive.

"She's crazy in love with him. If it was up to Nikki, she'd never let him out of her sight again. Come on, let's get you something to drink." Turning his hand around in hers, he led her away from the door. Neither Nikki nor Kid needed them hanging around.

"I don't drink," she said, following him nonetheless.

She shouldn't smoke, either, but that hadn't stopped her.

"I was thinking orange juice."

"Oh, that would be nice."

Yes, nice and healthy, a shot of antioxidant to counteract that damned cigarette.

"So you know about Kid's brother?" she asked.

Travis nodded. "I know he was killed, somewhere in South America."

"Yeah. I didn't really know J.T. that well." She wiped at her cheek with her free hand. "He only came home a couple of times in the last couple of years, since I've been at Steele Street. The rest of the time he was in Colombia or Panama. But he was cool. Cool to me. He invited me down to Panama, said to have Kid bring me down with a couple of friends, and we could use his house, even if he wasn't there."

Travis knew J.T. was Kid's brother, and Steele Street was where they worked. Quinn Younger, Nikki's new brother-in-law, the man who had stolen the fantasy love of his life, the eminently brilliant and luscious Regan McKinney—now Regan Younger—worked for Steele Street, too. Now what work they all did was apparently some big secret, but it had gotten J.T. killed, and he'd seen where Kid had been injured—a couple of stitches to his head. The guy had lost a lot of weight, too, which made Travis wonder just how much jungle-running he'd been doing in the last seven to eight weeks, before disaster had struck.

"Johnny and Gabby and I were going to take him up on it, but I guess we won't be going now. Not that it's important. It's just, I guess I wish I could have known him better. Kid is such a mess over this."

At the bar, he got her an orange juice on ice and sat her down in a quiet corner, where he could keep an eye on the closet door. He had no idea what in the hell might happen next, but the night had definitely taken a turn— for better or worse, he didn't have a clue.

The party was starting to break up, though, people leaving in pairs and small groups, most of them heading out to one or another of LoDo's rightly famous clubs or bars.

"So what happened to Kid's brother?" he asked. Nikki hadn't known, only that he'd been killed.

"I don't know exactly. I haven't gotten a clear picture of it yet—maybe I won't, but I've been getting the feeling it was awful. I've been getting that feeling for a couple of days now . . . and all Kid brought home was a bag of bones."

The last bit of information shocked him, as did her delivery. If he wasn't mistaken, there was a hint of vengeance in that tightly controlled tone of voice. "And he hasn't said what happened?"

She shook her head. "Only that there was a fire. He's been pretty messed up since he got off the plane this afternoon. He hasn't talked to anybody, not even his dad. I was hoping he would talk to Nikki."

"He will." Everybody talked to Nikki, sometimes as a form of self-defense, if nothing else. He'd seen her go into a chatterbox mode under stress that almost defied the laws of nature.

"Hey," she said suddenly, swiveling around in her chair, her gaze going to the alley door as if she'd heard something. "Just a sec."

She got up to leave, and he was right behind her, not about to "just a sec" while she walked out the back door.

There were a dozen cars parked in the alley, but she went straight to an older-style Porsche painted an odd, flat black.

"Hey, Nadine," she said, and he could only assume she was talking to the car, because there was no one else in the alley with them. She was digging in her purse, and after a minute, her hand emerged with a small electronic device that easily fit in the palm of her hand. She licked the bottom of it, rubbed it on her shirt, then grabbed on to the Porsche's door handle and swung herself a little ways under the car. When she came back up, her hand was empty.

Next, she pulled what looked like a PDA out of her purse and coded in a series of numbers and letters. A small flash of red light burst from underneath the car, just one flash, and she put the handheld computer back in her purse.

"Did you just put a tracking device on that car?"

"Yeah. I don't want to lose him, and if he needs help, I want to be able to find him."

So the car was Kid's.

"I thought you already tracked him here."

"Sure," she said, pulling another cigarette and a match out of her skirt pocket. "But that was . . . well, that was just following my nose. If he leaves downtown, I want to have a better lock on him."

She struck the match, lit the cigarette, then stuck out her hand. "Thanks a lot."

And what? She was leaving? Just like that? He didn't think so.

"I'll walk you to your car."

"I don't have a car, not tonight anyway. I'm walking. It's just a few blocks."

Walking? Alone? On a Saturday night at eleven o'clock through the alleys of lower downtown? He wanted to ask her if she was nuts, or if she really wasn't old enough to drive.

On the other hand, a walk sounded good. He'd been cooped up in the gallery for over four hours, and he'd be damned if he'd let a little kid wander around out here alone.

And she was a little kid, despite the cigarettes and the French exhales, despite the chain mail and her way too savvy comprehension of what was going down with Kid Chaos.

"I'll go with you."

"You don't have to, really. I'll be fine," she protested.

"Probably," he said, though he didn't believe it for a minute. "But I wouldn't be. Come on."

TAKING a drag off her cigarette, Skeeter gave him a quick once-over. She knew she was safe on the streets, but she wasn't so sure about him, and if he walked her home, she'd probably have to trail him back to the gallery or give him a ride to make sure he was okay.

Stifling a sigh, she flicked her cigarette into the alley and squished it with her boot.

"Okay. Sure," she said. "It's not far."

She hadn't had any trouble picking Travis James out of

the crowd. Besides the dozens of paintings of him hanging all over the gallery, he practically glowed—just like Kid had said. He was all golden skin and golden hair and Caribbean blue eyes, and way too pretty for anybody's good, even in a starkly black suit and a blue silk shirt, which was all beside the point.

In the low light of the gallery and the alley, he looked like Creed—a lot. She was surprised Kid hadn't mentioned it, but maybe a guy might not notice. Creed was taller, his hair the same length, to his shoulders, but not so blond, his eyes a stone-cold serious gray, and Creed looked as bad as he was, too tough to fuck with, but the resemblance was there. Skeeter bet there wasn't a woman in the gallery who hadn't been thinking about fucking this guy—and probably half the men had been thinking the same thing. He was that beautiful.

Which was still beside the point.

She'd found Kid. That had been the point. She'd tagged Nadine. That had been the point. And she'd reassured herself that Kid was with someone who cared enough to take care of him.

That had been the point.

Quinn and Regan had gone back to Stavros's, but like Kid, Skeeter couldn't take any more of the older man's pain, not tonight. She'd spent most of the day with him, and yesterday she'd been down in Colorado Springs at the hospital with Creed, holding his hand, praying for him to wake up. They had him so drugged.

She'd driven Betty, a 1967 Dodge Coronet with a 327 under the hood, which was always a risk. The cops tended to notice bright red cars, and she'd lost her license a couple of weeks ago for street racing at the Midnight Doubles. She'd won, but geez, without her license, driving around just got a bit too damn risky.

She was more than licensed to walk herself home, but she couldn't say the company was bad. Travis seemed like a nice guy, and like Nikki McKinney, Skeeter could really appreciate the sheer artistry of his face and body.

She'd like to draw him, though she could guarantee he wouldn't come out looking like one of Nikki McKinney's high-art angels in her hands. She'd pump him up a little, get him a little more stark, put him in tights and Lycra and call him . . . hmmmm. What would she call him?

The Avenger, yeah, that's what he'd be, maybe the Scarlet Avenger, except he'd look better in blue. Maybe she could call him Kenshi the Avenger, give him his own *Star Drifter* story line.

"So how far are we going? Where do you live?" he asked.

"At Steele Street with the guys."

"Not with your folks?"

It was an unexpected question. She wasn't sure why he would think she lived with her parents, but she went ahead and answered it. "I have parents, yeah, but they've got . . . problems."

"What kind of problems?"

She didn't have to tell him any more. She knew that, but there *was* something really nice about him, something warm, like when he'd held her hand, something she trusted, which was weird. She didn't trust too many people outside of the Steele Street regulars.

"Drugs, mostly, and alcohol, and poverty, and my dad had real issues with anger management, so I kind of moved out one day a few years ago, and a while later, I kind of moved in to Steele Street. I don't hold anything against my mom so much. I was kind of a weird kid, like a changeling or something, and Steele Street is a whole lot better place for me to live."

"A changeling?"

"I'm smart," she told him with a short laugh. "Really smart. *Weirdly* smart."

He stopped, and pulled her to a stop beside him. The look he was giving her was very thoughtful, and very curious. "How weird?"

"Well," she started, taking a moment to consider just how much to tell him. Surprisingly, she decided to tell him more than most. "To begin with, in about thirty seconds, Kid and Nikki are going to leave the gallery."

They'd crossed the street, but were still in line with the alley, and he turned to look back.

It took more than thirty seconds, more like a minute, but there was no denying when Nadine roared to life and eased out of the alley heading up Wazee.

He turned back to her, his gaze still so very thoughtful. "You do that often?"

"Often enough to freak some people out."

"Like your parents."

"Like my parents," she agreed.

"But not the guys at Steele Street."

"Hell, no." She laughed aloud. "It takes more than a slightly clairvoyant teenage girl to rattle the guys' cage."

Looking down at her, Travis wished he could say the

same, but he felt like his cage was getting rattled but good, and it didn't have a damn thing to do with her clairvoyance.

It had everything to do with what she was making him feel, and how god-awful young he was afraid she might be.

CHAPTER

20

ALEX HAD FOUND the cigarette. After everyone had gone, and there'd been nothing left but him and the party trash, he'd found it in a plate on the Lewis table—a cigarette butt.

He drained his glass of champagne and poured another. The culprit would ever remain a mystery, though he'd seen a rather punk-looking rocker chick in the gallery toward the end of the show.

Kids. Hell.

He slumped further down in his chair and passed his hand over his face.

The night had actually been a roaring success. They'd sold over half the paintings and booked two more showings for Nikki McKinney, who had finally shown back up, right at the very end—shown up just long enough to whisk one very gorgeous and very distraught young man out the back door.

The night had just been seething with angst, no small measure of it his own. *Damn it*. Marilyn Dekker. He didn't have the strength for it. Really, he didn't.

Facing the Dragon required balls of steel, and his balls felt like raisins—old raisins.

How in the hell was he going to tell the senator that he didn't have any idea where her daughter was, except possibly she was with the man who'd gone to prison for killing Jonathan Traynor III, was beyond his ability to imagine. It was just too awful.

He drained his glass again and was reaching for the champagne bottle for a refill, when the small snick of a door closing upstairs froze him solid in his chair.

Oh, fuck.

It wasn't a good sound, like maybe one of the gallery guests who was just getting around to leaving. Oh, no. It was a sly sound, a dangerous sound, faintly murderous from where he sat like a sitting duck on the main floor.

Well, hell. That's why he carried a gun.

Swinging out of the chair, he pulled out his Colt and headed for the back wall, his gaze strafing the upstairs balcony.

No one was in sight, but the balcony was dark, low lit, with plenty of shadows for hiding.

If he'd had a choice, he would have called for backup. As it was, he was just grateful that wherever Katya was, it wasn't with him.

Moving as stealthily as possible for someone who had to have been sighted, he slid up the inside rail of the stairway. He saw nothing, heard nothing, which made him think whoever it was had been going into his and Katya's apartment, not coming out.

At the door, he listened carefully, then moved in, his gun at the ready. The lights were all on, which he'd done deliberately at the beginning of the evening. A small package tied with a pink bow was waiting just inside.

Shit.

Somebody had been there and made another delivery. Ignoring the package, he cleared the rest of the apartment and found Katya's window open, but no perpetrator.

Hell. He was really starting to hate that window.

Sheathing his pistol, he went back to the package. He might have called Lieutenant Bradley, but she hadn't exactly been all that helpful to him. So, being very careful to check for wires, he slowly opened the box.

What was inside made his heart sink way down deep into his stomach, where the whole mess of his insides churned in a nauseating knot.

It was another part of the dress, *the* dress, and it was covered in blood—rusty, dried-out, thirteen-year-old blood.

Shit.

Sitting down on the floor, he dropped his head back to rest on the door and pulled his cell phone out of his front pants pocket. There was only one number to call, the number on Dylan Hart's business card. He'd tried it earlier and gotten an answering machine, but at least it picked up and he could leave a message—which was more than Katya was letting him do. It was time for somebody to let him into the game.

TRAVIS stood on the street with Skeeter Bang, outside an old brick building that looked like it might once have been a garage. There were big bay doors, three of them, running down the west side of the building, a couple of big WEATHERPROOF signs stuck in the windows, some Dumpsters parked against the wall, and one very nice, rather artistic iron door opening out onto the street. There was also a big freight elevator clinging to the side of the building like a geometrically constructed spider web, and they were waiting for it to descend.

Given the amazing cars Quinn drove, and the kind of money he seemed to have, Travis had expected the place to be a little more upscale.

"Sorry," she said. "There's a faster elevator on the other side, but this one gives such a great view of the city." She gave a little shrug. "It's going to take a few more minutes, but really, you don't have to wait."

"Actually," he said, glancing down toward the end of the block, his attention drawn by the sound of voices. "I think I do."

A group of guys had crossed the street, talking loud, taking up a lot of room, and walking like they owned the squalid stretch of turf that was just a few blocks too far north to qualify as a cool part of LoDo.

Hell. With luck the elevator would get there before the gang-bang posse, but listening to the damn thing screech and rumble didn't give him much hope.

"Hey, hey, Skeeter Bang-bang!" one of the guys yelled out, and Travis's "not much hope" got downgraded to "no hope."

He felt her stiffen beside him, her gaze going to the end of the block. She swore under her breath, which didn't do a damn thing for his confidence.

He wasn't going to mention it, but really, if she was going to have a bit of the sight, wouldn't this have been a better thing to have gotten a heads-up on than Nikki and Kid's escape?

Like a swarm of wasps, the gang zoomed in on them, surrounded them, a few outriders floating on the edge, the king wasp front and center, demanding all the attention. He wasn't the biggest, just the toughest looking, with his homeboy pants sliding off his hips, his shaved head, and enough tattoos on his arms to qualify him as a piece of art. There must have been about a dozen guys altogether. Too many to fight, too many to outrun from a dead standstill. Travis didn't exactly see his life flash before his eyes, but his adrenaline was definitely pumping.

"What's shakin', baby Bang?" the leader asked.

In the two seconds before Skeeter answered, she did something amazing, something Travis wouldn't have thought any fifteen-year-old could have done. It was all so subtle that if he hadn't been fixated on her, trying to get a clue as to how freaked he should be, he would have missed the actual transformation. As it was, he saw the whole thing take place in the space of a single breath.

Turning to face the gang leader, she straightened her spine and broadened her stance, actually putting one of her legs in front of him in a damned proprietary move that told him to stand still and shut up, she was in charge—so subtle, so smooth, so damned unexpected.

"Hey, Gino, I heard you bet against me the other night," she said, the accusation turning the tables on the punk, the edge in her voice downright cutting.

Attack certainly wouldn't have been his first choice of moves—Christ, he'd practically minored in Conflict Resolution—but she hadn't hesitated. He noticed something poking out of one guy's jacket pocket, and he started to wish he had a gun, not that he could actually imagine himself using it, actually blowing a hole in one of these guys.

Kid had a gun, and Travis knew for a fact that he had blown holes in people with cold, deliberate precision. The guy was a sniper, ex-Marine. Kid had lots of guns, but he was safe with Nikki, probably heading to Boulder, which Travis wished to hell he were doing—with Skeeter Bang at his side—instead of standing in front of a dilapidated old building on a deserted street, getting ready to get the crap beat out of him—and that was probably the best-case scenario.

These guys had guns. He could practically smell them, and there was that suspicious bulge in that one guy's pocket.

"You cost me, Skeeter baby. You cost me big." The guy postured in front of her, his body language one hundred percent street cool. He had it working with the hand jive and the body dips, but there was real aggression behind all of it.

"Get a clue, Gino, I was driving Quinn's COPO Camaro," Skeeter shot back. "What did you think was going to happen? That I'd let Billy Thompson take me in the quarter mile with that piece of crap Honda he's been screwing around with for a year?"

Hell, no. Travis didn't even know what she was talking about, and he would have bet on her.

"You should've been watching the sheets, babe. You could've held back. Could've saved yourself a whole lot of trouble," the gang leader said, his words an undeniable threat.

Travis watched the brim of her ball cap tilt, as if she were giving Gino a careful looking-over. When the brim leveled off again, a small "fuck you" smile curved her lips.

"The day I throw a race is the day it's got something a helluva lot more important than your money riding on it."

She was giving him a heart attack. Right here. Right now.

Gino made a move toward her, and in the next instant, she'd pulled a switchblade out of the sheath on her skirt. The edge glinted in the light from the street lamp, looking razor sharp.

"Don't tempt me, Gino. You know how this all works. You fuck with me, Superman fucks with you, and you'll never get it up again."

Oh, shit. Not with the knife, honey. This was a bad dream, a nightmare, and he was stuck in it with a girl.

The standoff lasted a small eternity, with neither side showing any sign of backing off. He would have backed off. Hell, if it hadn't been for needing to take her with him, he would have backed off like a track star. He had enough adrenaline surging through him to outdistance these guys right off the blocks.

Just when he thought the tension was going to snap like a slap shot and all hell was going to break loose, somebody said something in the back.

"The fuck you say," another guy responded, his gaze going straight to Travis, which Travis didn't find at all encouraging. Then the second guy leaned forward and said something to the kid in front of him, who also moved his attention from Skeeter to him.

Something was happening. Travis watched the ripple

of information work its way through the gang and up to Gino, with everyone seeming to back off a little, just sort of melt back toward the street.

When Gino got the word, the change was startling. The aggression went out of him like air out of a balloon, all the body tension, all at once, leaving him loose. Loose enough to slide back a step or two without it looking like a retreat.

"Hey, Creed," he said, flashing a mouthful of friendly white teeth, finally deigning to acknowledge his existence. "Didn't recognize you, man. Been a few years, hasn't it, bro?"

"*Creed Rivera*," Travis heard someone say in the back. The kid who got the news kind of ducked, shooting Travis a quick glance, as if he expected a blow. Another guy leaned in, said something in his ear, and the two of them peeled off from the crowd and took off down the street, not getting far before they broke into a run.

"Yeah, a while," Travis said, wondering who Creed Rivera was and how long these guys were going to believe he was him.

Long enough, it seemed. Gino took another step back, giving Skeeter some cryptic hand sign and a big grin.

"Next time, baby Bang, my money's on you."

"Hey, that's great, Gino," she replied, giving him what looked to be a genuine smile. "Really great. We'll kick some ass, okay?"

"Yeah, babe."

In seconds, the whole gang was back down the street.

"So what was that all about?" he asked, flummoxed by the whole event.

"Gino lost a grand at the Midnight Doubles a couple of

weeks ago—and apparently, it wasn't his grand to lose, so he's strong-arming everyone on the north side, trying to save his ass."

"You race cars?"

"Only illegally, so don't be shouting it out anywhere. Okay?"

"Sure." God save him. She'd pulled a knife, and he, for one, didn't have a doubt in the world that she would have used it. He couldn't imagine that things would have gotten better after that—quite the contrary. A shudder went through him, which made him feel foolish. She wasn't shaking, not anywhere. She was watching Gino and his boys.

The gang of punks disappeared around the next corner, and she turned to him then, still smiling, and put her hand on his face. She tilted her head, and her smile broadened.

"I knew you looked like Creed. Kid didn't mention anything, but I saw it."

"And who's Creed?" He liked having her hand on him, but he hardly had time to enjoy the feeling before she removed it.

"Creed Rivera was running these streets back when Gino boy still lived with his mother."

An explanation that only confused him. "I'm just guessing here, but Gino looked older than me."

That got him a laugh.

"I know," she said, still grinning. "Aren't people funny? He's looking right at you and backing off, because his brain is telling him you're Creed, and the whole time his eyes are telling him no way can you be Creed. You're younger than he is. Fascinating."

Fascinating—almost as fascinating as her smile. She had a beautiful smile; her lips weren't full, just very soft looking, and she had pretty teeth, the kind a guy wanted to run his tongue over. He wished she would take off her sunglasses and her ball cap. All he could really see of her were her cheeks, and her mouth, and her nose, which was a very delicate, very cute nose, indeed. But it wasn't enough. He wanted to see her eyes.

"How old are you?" he asked, surprising himself with the bluntness of the question. He'd wanted to know, but he hadn't meant to ask.

"Probably older than you think," she said, turning around and opening the cage door on the freight elevator.

He hadn't even noticed when it had arrived, which frankly amazed him, because it was loaded with one of the hottest cars he'd ever seen, a lime green Dodge Challenger with a big black racing stripe running up over the hood.

"Which means you're not fifteen?" he said.

She laughed again, disbelievingly. "You thought I was fifteen?" She stepped into the elevator and gestured for him to follow.

"Yeah." He nodded, getting in behind her.

"Well, you're off by about five years. I'll be twenty next week."

Thank you, God—he sent up a silent prayer of thanks, shot through with relief. She was still young by his standards—he usually went for older women, even a lot older women—but there was definitely something about her that was flipping his switches.

She pressed a large button on the cage wall, and with a rattle and a screech, the elevator began to rise.

She came back around the car, trailing one hand along the hood, when something caught her eye.

"Man, oh, man, Superman," she said, bending at the waist to peer in the driver-side window. "What kind of trouble did you drag home tonight? Cripes, will you look at this?"

She reached in and pulled out a dress, a little red dress with the zipper undone, the whole dress, without a woman in it—which simply lit up his imagination.

She held it up to herself, which fired up a couple more of his fantasy files.

"So what do you think?" she asked, angling her gaze up the side of the building. "You think we've got a naked woman running around up there?"

Yes. That's exactly what he thought.

She let out a short laugh and looked back inside the car.

"Oh, this is going to cost him big-time. Will you look at this mess?"

Obligingly, he bent down and looked through the open passenger-side window—and immediately got a whole lot clearer picture of what had happened with the red dress.

Sex.

He could smell it. Sex and chocolate, and Chinese food.

Wow. There was a pair of red satin underpants not two feet from him, hanging off the gearshift. The matching bra was draped around the inside door handle. He saw one red high-heeled sandal and a guy's shoe. A pair of boxer shorts had been eighty-sixed into the driver's seat, and the back window sported a couple of cartons of Chinese food. A few more cartons had spilled, one in the backseat, and two on the floor.

And the sex. Had he mentioned that? The car was still hot with it, really hot with it. Steamy.

Steamy enough to turn him on. He couldn't help it. He was afraid if he closed his eyes and breathed too deeply, he'd have an instant hard-on.

"So what do you think?" she asked, but he didn't think she really wanted to know. "I usually charge him a hundred bucks to detail Roxanne here, but this"—she made a short sweeping gesture—"this has got to cost more like two, two-fifty. What do you think?"

"Two hundred and fifty dollars to clean a car?"

"Yeah, that's what I thought, too," she said, as if he'd just agreed with her. "Two hundred and fifty. You hungry?" She reached in and grabbed one of the unspilled cartons and broke open the fresh pair of chopsticks lying on the dash.

Wielding the chopsticks like an expert, she offered him a piece of food across the interior of the car. He couldn't resist. He'd take anything she wanted to give him, but he did have to lean way in to get the food. So there he was, right in the middle of the aftermath of Superman's lovemaking with the woman in the red dress, with the punk-rocker chick feeding him steamed dumplings. The whole thing was enough to make his head spin a little.

She fed herself a dumpling and pulled out of the driver-side window to walk around the back of the car.

He followed her lead, and the two of them leaned back on the trunk to finish off the food, while the old elevator groaned its way skyward.

She was right about the view. It was spectacular, the lights of Denver spreading up into the foothills.

"Do you want to see what's in those cartons in the back window?"

"Sure," he said, though he really didn't think it was a good idea for him to get in the car.

Crab wontons and spring rolls—two of his favorites, well worth the effort of getting them, but it still felt slightly illicit to be eating this guy Superman's dinner. When the elevator finally docked on the seventh floor, his whole idea about Steele Street was transformed.

There were cars, unbelievable cars, rows of them, a million dollars' worth of truly exquisite cars: muscle cars, sports cars, Jaguars, Porsches, hot red cars, two gull-winged cars he didn't even know what to call. And the bank of offices built along the north wall looked expensive and modern. He could see tons of electronic equipment and elegant furnishings through the windows looking out onto the garage floor. The place was a high-tech dream.

He had a car, a Jeep. It started when he turned the key, and it stopped when he stepped on the brake. It usually, but not always, got him where he wanted to go without too much trouble, and that was about it.

"Hop in, and I'll give you a ride," she said, opening the driver-side door on the Challenger, after opening the freight cage door.

"No, thanks. I'll just walk." He wasn't getting inside that car with her. No way. Not that he thought he was in any danger of getting lucky. It was the weirdest thing, but he was getting absolutely no vibe of sexual awareness off her at all. None. *Nada*. And it was driving him a little crazy. Hell, he'd had gay chicks hit on him just for the cheap thrill of it—but he was getting nothing off Skeeter Bang.

She started the Challenger, and a big grin instantly split his face. God, what a cool car. It roared and rumbled, and made the elevator shake. He could feel the power of the engine all the way from the bottoms of his feet to the top of his head. It made him wonder if maybe he just had never really given cars a chance. To have one like Roxanne would just be too cool.

Roxanne. Nadine. He wondered if every car at Steele Street had a name. Somehow, he figured they did.

She parked the car in a washing bay and walked over to meet him, where he was standing next to a navy blue GTO.

"Corinna," she said, running her hand over the roof of the car. "A 1967 with a Ram Air 400 and a four-speed. J.T. won her back from Hawkins a couple of years ago, but I guess . . . well, Kid will have her now." Her voice broke a little, and when she got to the front of the car, to the grille, she lifted her hand off the sleek blue finish and offered it to him. "Thanks. It was real sweet of you to walk me home. If you want, I can give you a lift back to the gallery."

Sweet? And she was kicking him out?

He took her hand, but he didn't take the hint. "You live here?" He looked around the garage.

"Up on the eleventh floor, across from Superman."

Without being all that subtle about it, she retrieved her hand.

"Shouldn't I, like, see you to your door or something? This is an awfully big place."

"Actually, my friend Johnny is going to be here in about a half an hour, and we're going to give Corinna a tune-up, rotate her tires, maybe blow her out on a run to Colorado Springs, check up on a friend down there."

Definite brush-off, but at least the Johnny thing didn't sound like a date. Rotating tires?

"So your schedule is pretty packed through the middle of the night, up until dawn?"

She at least smiled at that. "Yeah, pretty packed."

Well, he obviously had nothing left to lose.

"I'd like to see you again."

She didn't say anything for so long, he started to wonder if he'd accidentally spoken in a foreign language or something.

"No," she finally said. "I don't think that's a good idea. I don't think I want to do the Beauty and the Beast thing with you."

He'd been dumped by girls before, a number of times, but he'd never not even gotten out of the starting gate with one, and she thought he was a beast?

Somewhere in her cold, cold heart, she must have taken a little pity on him, because when he just stood there, struggling with her flat-out rejection, she spoke up again.

"Look, you don't even know me, okay?"

Finally, something he could latch on to.

"That's the whole idea behind seeing each other again," he said, though he thought that idea was pretty self-evident. "To get to know each other. It doesn't have to be a date or anything. It can just be coffee."

"Okay," she said, way too quickly. "I'll give you a call sometime."

Liar. She was lying through her teeth, and for the life of him, he couldn't figure out why that hurt. Something must have shown on his face, because she let out a big, heavy sigh and reached up and took her glasses off. Her head was tilted down, and he still couldn't see her face because of her hat. But then she reached back up and pulled it off her head, careful to pull her ponytail through the back, and then she stood there, looking him straight in the face.

She had blue eyes, real pretty blue eyes, kind of a silvery blue, instead of a deep, dark blue. And she had a scar that ran diagonally across her forehead, cut through her right eyebrow, and ended at her temple just an inch or less from the corner of her eye. It wasn't pretty. It hadn't faded with time, and being an EMT who spent many of his weekend nights scraping car accident victims off the highways and putting them into ambulances, he could just imagine how much blood she'd lost when it had happened. She must have been blinded by the blood. It had to have run into her mouth and down her chest, and the whole thing must have hurt so badly, she must have thought she was going to die. She must have been terrified by seeing so much of her own blood soaking her clothes.

"Guys like you—" she started.

"Guys like me?" Now he was mad.

"Guys like you," she continued patiently, "have lots of choices. You know that's true." She smiled at him, as if he were going to buy that when she was shutting him down. "And though I admit that I can be a bit of a novelty for—"

"Novelty?" Now he was really pissed off. Novelty? What kind of a jerk did she think he was?

Oh, right. He didn't need to wonder. She was telling him straight-out what kind of a jerk she thought he was.

"The truth is," she continued, still so damned patient, which just pissed him off that much more, "there's no reason for us to get to know each other."

"I'd like to kiss you." That was a reason, but where it had come from, he didn't have a clue. It was true, but he sure hadn't meant to tell her.

What annoyed him even more was that she took his pitiful confession in stride.

"Gino wants to kiss me, and you don't see me inviting him to come up here and hang around all night, either."

What was this? "Guys like him" now included slimy psychopaths like Gino? He was more than shot down. She'd ground him into dust.

And he still wanted to kiss her.

Shit. There was nothing to do but walk away—which he did, just turned on his heel and headed for the elevator.

She didn't stop him, either.

By the time he got to the street, he'd decided to just chalk up the whole strange night to the bizarro zone. Skeeter Bang. What kind of name was that?

And how had she gotten hurt so badly?

And why did he want to kiss somebody who thought he was such a jerk?

She was right. He had lots of choices. There had been

at least two women who had wanted to take him home from the gallery. Two who'd made it pretty damn clear, which always left him cold. He knew he was slow to hook up with a new person, but he liked to set his own pace. He didn't have sex with strangers, never had, didn't imagine that he ever would. It always took a few dates before he felt comfortable approaching a girl that way—which surprised a few of them, because he had this small home business on the side, Boulder Sexual Imprinting, Inc., a business based on his master's thesis on human female sexuality, but it was business, not personal. It was work, and he was very careful to stay within certain boundaries when he was with a client. The process was sensual, without a doubt, and wouldn't have been very effective if it wasn't, but when he was working with a woman on her sexual imprint, he was very careful to keep his responses out of the process. Extremely careful. Sure, he had women who were addicted to the process, but as far as he knew—and he was very intuitive about such things—none of them were addicted to him, or fixated on him, which was a sign of good clinical therapy.

It was the process they loved, the process that healed. He just happened to be particularly adept at facilitating that process. He knew how to touch them, how to soothe them, but he did have to wonder sometimes if his client base was getting a little inbred.

Either way, the business was doing fine, and his social life sucked. He hadn't been with a woman of his own for a long time—and tonight wasn't going to be any different. It was just going to be him and his much-loved, maybe overly loved, poster of Regan McKinney in her lavender underwear—a photo he'd all but begged Nikki to blow up and give him.

Actually, he had begged, and had never regretted a minute of his groveling.

Regan was married now. He probably should give the poster up, but he just wasn't ready to part with it. She was a goddess, all lush curves and pale blond hair, who had never had a tan or lifted a weight in her life, and she'd been his fantasy ever since the day she'd walked in on him naked in Nikki's studio, when he'd been eighteen. He hadn't even had the brains to cover himself up. All he'd been able to do was stare at her, and all she'd been able to do was stare back, and he would have sworn something had passed between them. He'd been swearing it for five years, but he'd never once gotten her to admit to anything, or gotten her around to his way of thinking. Too young, she'd kept telling him, but a few times, definitely a few times, she'd come close to giving in. One night in particular, last Christmas, he'd been saying good-bye to her and Nikki at the door, when their granddad, Wilson, had hollered for Nikki. With the two of them standing there, with just the Christmas tree lights on and a couple of candles, he'd taken her hand and asked her why there wasn't any mistletoe. She'd smiled, started to say something polite, and he'd kissed her, just bent his head down and kissed her.

Her mouth had opened for him. He remembered that in every detail, the way he remembered the feel of her breasts against his chest, and the way she'd smelled. He had never wanted to let her go, but the sound of Nikki returning had made Regan pull away. For himself, he had trusted Nikki to catch what was going on and get lost, but older sisters weren't like that, he guessed.

Nonetheless, he'd leaned forward again, still holding her hand, and whispered in her ear, "Come home with me, Regan, please. We'll have such a good time. I promise."

The memory brought a fleeting smile to his lips. As he recalled, he'd promised her a few more things, too, like a fireplace, a sheepskin rug, and a vibrator, and his most sincere declaration that she would love all of it, especially him, and the vibrator, together, in any combination she might want to try.

She'd melted against him with a little groan he still heard in his dreams, the closest she'd ever gotten to surrender—but in the end, she'd turned him down again.

And now she was married.

He stopped walking and turned around to look back at Steele Street. Well, he'd kind of walked and worried his anger away, and maybe Skeeter Bang had been right. Maybe he didn't have any business kissing her—or anybody, for that matter.

Maybe Regan was what had gone wrong with Tracy, who'd dumped him in June, because, she said, he was too disengaged in their relationship. He knew for a fact that Christmas night with Regan was what had gone wrong with Lisa. He'd woken up about a week after that night, looked at his girlfriend, and just gotten an awful empty feeling, like there just wasn't anything left between them, no reason to keep on seeing her or sleeping with her.

So here it was the end of August, and he was horny and alone, and had just gotten his ego crushed by a biker chick in work boots. There was probably some justice in there somewhere, but he'd be damned if he could see it.

"*Pssst*, Creed." A voice came out of the alley to his right.

Pssst? Hell. He turned to look, and at first couldn't see anything. Then a shadow disengaged itself from the wall, a very rumpled, bedraggled shadow that smelled like grain alcohol and hot summer garbage.

"Yeah, Creed. It's been a while," a raspy voice intoned. It·was a guy, an old guy, very dirty and very drunk. "Just heard you were back. You remember me, don'tcha? Ray, Ray Carper."

"Sure, Ray, yeah. How's it going?" This did not seem the time or the place to tell anyone he wasn't Creed Rivera.

"Not so good. I think I'm dying." The old guy laughed, and coughed, and hacked, and then hacked some more. "Friggin' doctors. They don't know crap. I told them what was wrong with me. I got elbow cancer, but they won't do a friggin' thing about it."

"Elbow cancer, man, that's rough." The stench was damn near overwhelming, but Travis didn't move away or blow the guy off and leave. He did check the street both ways to make sure he wasn't being set up for a mugging, but he also got the feeling Creed Rivera was the last person anybody on this side of town would try to mug.

"Yeah, I can hardly move my fucking arm."

"Here." He pulled a twenty out of his pocket and gave it to the old man. "Give them this and tell them to treat you better."

Ray pocketed the twenty and laughed again, which started another hacking fit. When he got it under control, he let out a small chuckle. "Yeah, I'll tell 'em, Creed. Tell 'em you're gonna kick their ass, if they don't fix my elbow."

"You do that, Ray." He turned to leave, but the old guy stopped him with a hand on his arm.

"Wait a minute, I got something for you, something important." He started digging through his jacket pockets. "I heard Superman was looking for me, and I still got the goods."

Superman again, Travis thought. This Superman guy led a pretty complex life.

"You're lucky you caught me, though. I been thinking about going south, maybe to Florida." Ray kept searching his pockets, until he pulled out a fat, dirty envelope. "Yeah. Here it is. I kept it all these years, all of it. You look it over, you and Superman, see if I wasn't right." He pressed the envelope into Travis's hands. "The damn cops are worse than the damn doctors. You know I tried to tell them, tried to tell them everything, but they didn't listen to old Ray."

"Thanks, Ray," Travis said, taking the envelope. He didn't have a clue what the old guy was talking about.

"That poor little whore shouldn't a died like she did. Those boys were just too rough with her. I saw it that night, saw the whole goddamn thing, but nobody wanted to listen to old Ray."

Travis froze where he stood, his blood instantly running cold. *Oh, shit.*

"Who, Ray?"

"Jane. They called her Jane Doe, but her name was Debbie Gold. Least that's what she called herself. She thought it would make her money turning tricks, if she had a name like Gold, but all it did was get her killed."

"Do you know where she is now?" Good God.

"Six feet under, boy. She's been six feet under for thirteen years, her and that Traynor boy, and old Lost Harold. The same damn wild ones did them in, except maybe for old Lost Harold. I never knew for sure about him, but it looks like one of 'em got their own back last night at the Gardens. You look that over and see if I'm not right, that's all," Ray mumbled, wandering back into the alley. "You just look it over."

Travis tightened his hand around the envelope and watched the old man disappear. When Ray was gone, he took off for his car at a slow jog, then he picked up the pace, wishing Creed Rivera had been here to get his own damn envelope.

In a couple of minutes, he was back at the gallery, where he'd parked his Jeep. He slid into the driver's seat and hit the glove box to get the flashlight out from inside. His overhead light didn't work. Hell, half the stuff on his Jeep didn't work.

He tore open the envelope, careful not to rip anything inside. It was all newspaper clippings. One new one from this morning's paper talking about the murder and the fireworks at the Denver Botanic Gardens, and a bunch of old clippings dated thirteen years back, all from the same summer: some wino kicking the bucket down by Union Station, the death of a Jane Doe they'd dragged out of the river in June, and the arrest of Christian Hawkins for the death of Jonathan Traynor III in July. The name that caught his eye, though, was the only one he knew: Katya

Dekker. It was all over the clippings, half the time in the headlines.

She'd been at the Botanic Gardens last night, too, with a painting from Toussi's. He didn't know who in the hell Superman was, but he obviously had some connection with Katya Dekker—and from the looks of things, the connection was murder.

He didn't know what to make of Ray Carper's envelope, but someone who knew Katya Dekker a whole lot better than he did might. He looked toward the gallery and caught sight of a light still on.

Alex Zheng, he decided. That's who needed the envelope.

CHAPTER
21

KATYA'S RISE UP from the soft drift of sleep was a languid affair, a lazy meandering of her mind from one pleasant thought to another, the limp relaxation of her body, the comforting sensation of overall well-being. It had been a long, long time since she'd awakened with a sense of such rightness with the world.

Maybe she needed to drink double-chocolate mocha lattes more often before going to bed. She'd always been afraid that the caffeine would keep her awake that late at night, but maybe the triple whipped cream—

Her eyes popped open on a flash of sudden and total awareness, her every cell coming fully awake, the full extent of her current situation hitting her all at once, with startling clarity. It wasn't the whipped cream in the latte that had wrung her out until she was limp and then hung her out to dry. It was Hawkins. Christian Hawkins.

Oh, my God, what had she done?

Or rather, what hadn't she done?

Very carefully, holding her breath, she slanted her gaze to the right.

What had she done or not done, indeed?

As a question, it was beyond stupid. What she'd done was as obvious as the six feet of purely nude, purely male, tattooed elegance lying next to her, as obvious as the heat coming off him and keeping her warm on what was a very gray and rainy morning.

She remembered that about him. How he'd always run hot. Even that long-ago summer, she'd loved lying close to him, feeling his warmth and the power that so naturally emanated from his body, feeling the latent energy in the muscles of his arms as he'd held her. He'd been the most beautiful boy she'd ever seen.

Now he was the most beautiful man. Not even Nikki McKinney could improve upon his perfection. The harsh angles of his face were softened by sleep and the morning's pale light. His hair was thick and silky, and the color of midnight spread across his pillow. Beard stubble darkened his jaw.

The sheet was pooled low around his hips, revealing most of his tattoo, and she was—she glanced down at herself—she was perfectly naked.

A blush coursed down her body. She felt it start in her cheeks and flow past her knees to her toes. She'd lost her clothes in his car, long before they'd made it to his bed. As she recalled, she'd worn his shirt to get up to his loft— and maybe it had all been inevitable.

There was a reason they'd been so inseparable all those years ago. It was more than the sex, though this slow death by never-ending orgasm thing they had going was a powerful motivation for not leaving—ever. But even before the sex, she'd fallen in love at first sight. She'd been running so fast from Jonathan and the other boys, running her heart out, scared to death. She hadn't heard anything—her heart had been pounding too hard—but she'd seen the car come from out of nowhere, and the huge cloud of white smoke filling the alley. Then she saw him, walking out of the cloud, like an angel, a dark angel, and she knew that whatever was going to happen next, it wasn't going to be the atrocity she feared. She knew he wasn't going to let the other boys hurt her.

He'd caught her in his arms, and in that split second when he looked down at her and she saw his face, she'd fallen in love.

She let her gaze drift over him again, wondering what in the world she was supposed to do now. Running was what she usually did, what she'd been doing for thirteen years, and it still seemed like the only logical answer, but somehow, she didn't have the heart for running anymore. All her years of it had only brought her right back where she'd started—so maybe this time she should tough it out.

She took a steadying breath. Okay, she could buy that, but she didn't have to tough it out naked. Talk, that's what they needed to do. Not what they'd been doing— *oh, God.*

On his side of the bed, Hawkins lay perfectly still, perfectly content—except for the tidal wave of tension rolling off the other side of the bed.

She was thinking way too hard over there.

Now was not the time to be thinking, not of anything. He really needed to take the high ground here and save her from herself. He needed to be selfless.

He needed her under him again.

Oh, yeah. One more time for old times' sake, that was the strategy move on a lazy Sunday morning with the rain beating down on the windows. With the sky all gray and the world all quiet, making love was the only thing that made sense.

Without giving it another thought, he rolled onto his side and snaked his arm around her waist, dragging her across the mattress and under him in one easy move. She started to say something, but he stole the words with his mouth. It took all of five seconds for her to buy into his plan, five seconds of soft kisses on her lips and his hand sliding up to palm her breast.

His body was crazy for hers. All she had to do was breathe to turn him on. How could he have forgotten how easy it was to be with her, to be inside her? There wasn't any tension when they were making love. It was all languid sensation, a melting into her he'd never experienced with anyone else. Years ago, he'd thought that meant true love. He wasn't sure what it meant anymore. He only knew he wanted it, craved it like air.

Easing her leg up around his waist, he fitted himself to her, tested her, then slipped inside all the way, just to feel her surrounding the whole length of him. There was nothing like it, not on this earth. The slick, heated warmth of her seeped into him, starting at his cock and radiating out to the very nether regions of his brain. God, she made it hard to think.

He opened his mouth wider over hers, pulled her

tighter, felt her softness consume him, and he kissed her—long, and wet, and deep, over and over, making love to her mouth, to her tongue, and her lips, and her teeth. He just wanted her, wanted all her wet softness, all her sighs of surrender. He wanted the smell and the taste of her, the feel of her against him, and it was all more than was good for him. He knew it, and he still indulged, pulling out and thrusting into her as slowly as he could possibly manage, just to feel the magic of her body wash over him—again, and again, and again.

A guy could die doing this, and not give a damn. It felt so good.

"Mmm, Kat," he groaned, dragging his mouth down to her jaw, grazing her with his teeth.

Her hands were all over him, sliding up under his arms and then back down over his torso, caressing his skin in rhythm with his thrusts, her fingers moving down between his thighs.

He opened his legs wider and whispered in her ear, then felt her hand slide back around and come up from underneath, cupping his balls, gently kneading him, tugging on him —so lightly, her fingers so delicate.

He bit her neck, sucked on her. *Oh, yeah, this is it.* Perfection—and they'd slipped back into it effortlessly.

He didn't even want to come. He wanted this to last forever, for them to stay in this hazy, erotic limbo, where his mind was fogged with the heat of her body, with the pleasure rolling through him, with her soft bites to his shoulder, the glide of her tongue over his skin and the rhythm of her hips moving to meet his.

No, he didn't want to come. He wanted to fuck, like this, for as long as they could make it last—utter, mindless sensation. It was so sweet, and hot, and healing, a place out of time. He licked the inside of her mouth and softly bit her lips, then sealed his mouth over hers again, sealing them together with the same breath.

Katya felt like she'd fallen into a fever-dream. Her world had gotten so small as to have almost disappeared. There was only him, the weight of him holding her down, his thrusts making him a part of her, fueling needs that had been denied since the last time she had been like this, naked in his arms, being consumed. He filled her, not just with his body, but with his pleasure and the sheer power of his desire. His hands were on her, gliding over her skin, holding her, strong and sure, leaving no part of her untouched. He'd known exactly where he wanted to go, and he had taken her there with him.

It was all so achingly lovely, to just feel him inside her, on her, all over her. She slid one hand down his chest, her fingers tunneling through the soft, dark hair that covered him to his groin. She loved the way he felt, all hard, lean muscle moving on top of her, each flex and thrust of his hips pushing him deep inside her.

She knew him, knew this could go on endlessly, until they transcended conscious thought, until they reduced themselves completely to taste and touch, sight and sound and scent. It was eroticism poured into her skin. It was stamina and otherwordly delights. It was strength and the willingness to surrender. It was amazing. It was the reason she had called him Superman.

Long minutes flowed into each other, sliding across the day, until she no longer existed outside of him. His heat was hers, infusing every pore. The taste of him was the taste of her. She moved, and he moved with her, as one, until he tightened his arm low around her hips and pulled her up against him. All movement stopped then, except for the slow slide of his other hand up the middle of her torso and between her breasts, until his hand came to a stop at the base of her throat. His palm was so hot, pressing her back into the bed. It was a brand; it was bondage. It was dominance of the most primal kind imaginable, and it demanded submission. His gaze held hers, dark and glittering, his hair falling down on either side of his face as he pulled her even tighter against him.

Oh, God—oh, God—oh, God. He pressed down from inside her, and heat flashed across her body. Sweat broke out on her upper lip and brow. Oh, God. He pressed again, and a tremor started deep, deep inside her. He felt it, she could tell by the darkening of his gaze. A feral smile curved his lips, then his eyes drifted closed and his head went back. He moved her against him, pumped into her, his teeth bared, a low growl coming from deep within his chest, getting her hotter, making her wilder. She wanted him. She wanted this, all of it, desperately. Her legs tightened around him, and with his groan echoing in her ears, she felt the first pulsing jerk of his release, his cock so hot and hard inside her. Molten heat pooled in her groin, and when he thrust into her again, she was with him, drowning in ecstasy, suffused with pleasure so deep, she felt it in her bones, down to her soul, so full of him, he was a part of her.

An hour later, she roused from sleep again, this time fully and completely cognizant of her situation. She was in love. In love with the same man she'd always been in love with—God save her.

He'd fallen back into a sound sleep beside her, and she didn't want to wake him, so she didn't touch him—but she looked.

Looked her fill, he was so beautiful. The rain had stopped, and the sun was shining in the huge windows, heating up the loft. He'd kicked all the sheets off his body, leaving himself open to her gaze.

She remembered the first time she'd ever undressed him. Her hands had been shaking. They'd been kissing on the couch in the suite at the Brown Palace, something they'd ended up doing almost every night since the night he first saved her. He'd even made her laugh a few times, and twice he damn near stopped her heart—once when he slipped the strap of one of her summer dresses off her shoulder and put his mouth up near the top of her breast, and once when he slipped his hand up under her dress and came close to doing what he'd done last night—but not close enough.

He'd been very gentle, very leisurely about everything, and when he'd stopped kissing her, stopped touching her, and just held her, she'd been filled with a sense of loss. It hadn't been enough, not of him.

She'd run her hand over his arm, tracing the dark lines of ink that ran along his skin, trying to figure out how to tell him she wanted more.

"Where did you get this?" she'd asked instead, following the curve of one line with her fingertip.

"A place to the south of here," he'd answered with only the slightest hesitation. Then he added, "Would you like to see the rest of it?"

The question had been simple enough, but somehow, she'd known that seeing his tattoo was going to be one of the great adventures of her life.

She hadn't been too far off the mark. By the time she'd helped him get his shirt off, she was definitely in uncharted territory. She'd known he was in very good shape, but she hadn't realized he was totally ripped, until she saw him without his clothes.

"They're ... wings," she'd said, surprised by the realization. The dark lines snaking and curling up his forearms had not fully told the picture. From the back, with his arms outspread, she could see that the lines made feathers, not all of them perfect. Some were curled on the ends, or lifted with an arch, as if a wind was blowing across him, literally ruffling his feathers.

She was headed to California in the fall as a fine arts major, and she knew art, body or otherwise, and his tattoo was exquisitely done. The black, open line work was very graphic, rather than realistic, but the design was definitely a pair of wings. She could actually tell which way the wind was blowing across his body: from left to right.

"This is amazing," she'd said, sliding up behind him on the couch and taking hold of his hand. She'd lifted his arm again, stretching it out, suddenly oblivious to the fact that he was half nude. All she could see was that he was beautiful, his body a work of art layered under a work of art, the wings enhancing the sculpture of the muscles beneath his skin. And he was muscular, lean and highly defined.

She'd moved her hand over him, along his arm and up over his shoulder, then down the smooth, hard muscles

322 ◆ TARA JANZEN

of his back—until she came to the rather abrupt barrier of his pants.

"Oh," she'd said, and nearly pulled his pants out a bit to see down inside. "There's more." Curiously, he didn't seem to be wearing any underwear. She didn't know what to think about that.

"Some," he'd agreed, turning back around.

Her reverie had instantly ended. He wasn't a piece of sculpture, he was a man, or nearly so, and she'd been rather forward sliding her hands all over him, even if it had been in the name of art.

"But . . ." He'd shrugged, and she'd known exactly what he'd meant. She probably shouldn't go looking down his pants, not anytime soon, for if the back of him had elicited a purely art appreciation response, the front of him made her think purely and solely of sex again.

He was gorgeous, not just his face with his rather elegant nose and chiseled cheekbones, and that mouth, which she so wanted to kiss again and again, but his whole body, his chest covered in fine dark hair, his abs the proverbial six-pack. Just looking at him was enough to make her mouth go dry.

She wanted to touch him, nuzzle his neck, lick his skin—get into him, get onto him—and she was at a loss in knowing how to make that happen, or in judging how dangerous giving in to those desires might be.

He took her hand in his again, his so large and dark compared to hers, the veins prominent across the back and easily traceable up the whole inside of his arm.

Oh, how she wanted to kiss him—everywhere.

"This isn't about sex," he'd said, startling her with his frankness. "This thing with you and me."

"It isn't?" She didn't know whether to be disappointed or not.

"No." He'd shaken his head, then glanced up at her from under the swath of silky dark hair falling over his eyes. "This is about trust."

"Trust," she'd repeated, not quite understanding.

"I can get sex anywhere—"

Yes. She nodded her head. She believed that. He probably had girls and women lined up outside his bedroom door, taking numbers—oh, damn.

"But I'd like something different with you."

Uh-oh. This had all the signs of being the "Gee, I like you as a friend" speech.

He glanced away, and she could've sworn a soft flush of color had washed over his cheeks.

"I don't have any problem with taking my pants off for you." He'd looked back up, capturing her gaze with his own, and she'd been riveted to her spot on the couch. Stripping was definitely *not* part of the let's-be-friends speech. "But I don't want you getting in over your head."

Too late. She'd just lost her breath. He was going to take off his pants, and just the thought was enough to get her wet. She could feel it, and the sensation damn near paralyzed her. It had never happened to her before, not like this. Oh, he was way too late. She was in way, way over her head.

His smile had returned then, a flashing curve of white teeth and wry self-awareness.

"I'm already drowning over here," he'd confessed, his smile broadening, and she'd wondered if she was ever going to get another breath. "All I have to do is look at you, and I'm slain, princess, but I can handle it. *Nothing* is going to happen here that you don't want, and I don't mean maybe want. I mean nothing's going to happen tonight that you don't really, really want."

He had a good point, but she didn't think there was any "maybe" about what he made her want, and nothing could have surprised her more. She'd never considered herself particularly sensual or sexual, but she could smell him, almost taste him, even from a distance, all warm and male, and it was doing crazy, crazy things to her imagination, like an aphrodisiac-laced pheromone. She was half on fire and half on slow simmer, and if he didn't kiss her soon, she might just die from wanting it so badly.

"I don't know what's going to happen here, and neither do you—"

No. She shook her head. No, she didn't. He was absolutely right about that.

"—but even if . . . even if I was inside you"—and here the blush of color had come back into his cheeks—"and you said no more, go away, it would be over. Right then. I can promise you that."

Inside her? A soft, deep flash of heat exploded under her skin and washed through her entire body. Had he really said that?

Boys didn't say things like that. They just groped, and pawed, and complained when they didn't get what they wanted, or they looked hurt, which was even worse.

"I'm a virgin," she'd all but blurted out for reasons she could no sooner explain than she could explain the theory of cold fusion—which she couldn't, not at all.

"I feel like one," he'd confessed, a slow grin curving his mouth. Then he leaned down and kissed her again. "I won't hurt you. I know how to be careful."

And he had known. By the time he'd carried her to the bed, she'd been so ready for him, needing the taste of him in her mouth, the heat of him inside her.

She still needed him. The reasons hadn't changed. He was Hawkins, and she'd needed him from the first moment she'd ever laid eyes on him.

And now she'd gone and done it, really done it. Whatever bond had been broken thirteen years ago had now been reforged, even stronger for knowing what the loss of it had cost her.

So if love was supposed to be the answer to all life's problems, why did she feel so doomed?

"You're thinking too hard again," he mumbled into his pillow, not bothering to open his eyes. "I can hear the gears churning in your brain."

"Can not," she countered.

"Can, too. It's what woke me up." He rolled over onto his back and stretched.

She swallowed softly. God, he was beautiful.

"I think we need to talk."

"You want to do it in the shower?" he asked around a yawn.

"No. No, I—well, I think we should get dressed."

"No," he said, adamant, opening his eyes and pinning her with his gaze. "We're not getting dressed and having a talk. If you want to talk, we're either doing it in the shower, naked, or doing it right here, naked."

"You can't set rules like that for a talk," she said, exasperated. She did not want to talk naked. She was already too vulnerable, and he was . . . nothing but trouble when he was naked.

"Rule one—we do it naked. Rule two—nobody leaves the bed, until we're done talking."

"Oh, for pete's sake. I'm trying to be serious here." She shot him an irritated glance, but then wasn't quite able to pull her gaze away.

He was watching her, watching her like a hawk.

"I am never more serious than when I'm naked, babe."

She knew that. He'd proved it to her again and again, all night long, and then again an hour ago.

"I didn't mean we needed to talk about . . . sex." He was impossible.

"And I think that's the perfect place to start." He rolled to his side and propped his head up on his hand. "Sex. With you. I like it, a lot."

With effort, she stifled the huge sigh welling up in her throat. He was *completely* impossible. She was struggling with all sorts of feelings and the whole mess of falling in love with him again, if she even dared to call it that, and she couldn't just be a one-man band and sort through all of it without him.

"There's got to be more than sex," she said, feeling like she'd already lost control of the conversation and not knowing where to go from here.

"And I think you're underestimating what happens between us when we make love. It's not a simple thing, Kat." He was damned serious. She could tell by the tone of his voice and the unflinching steadiness of his gaze.

"No, it's not simple. It's—are you sure we have to do this naked?"

"Being naked is the compromise, Kat. You want to talk? Fine, we'll talk. If it's up to me, we get up, get dressed, preferably after a long, hot shower we take together, and then we spend the day moving all your stuff in with me, and from there, we just go on living our lives, except we live them together, instead of apart."

"Just like that?" She couldn't help but sound skeptical.

"Just like that."

"And how long does that last?"

He took his time in answering, took a deep breath before he did answer, but his gaze didn't waver from hers, not once. "It lasted thirteen years without us even seeing each other. Being two reasonably intelligent adults, I think we should be able to do better than that with a little effort."

More than thirteen years? His plan sounded more like a marriage proposal than an offer to shack up, and she truly didn't know what to make of it.

"Maybe we should go back to talking about sex."

"No." He shook his head. "We've moved on."

This was her cue to run. She could feel it, feel the need twitching in the muscles of her legs. She needed to get out of that bed and run like hell, or she truly, truly was doomed.

But she owed him the truth.

"I can't breathe." That was the truth. She was starting to hyperventilate.

"Ah, hell, Kat. Sit up," he said, sitting up himself and giving her a hand. "You know, you're not much help here."

She knew. He couldn't pick a worse person to live with. Given a choice, four days out of seven, she wouldn't live with herself, which was actually an improvement. There had been years when seven days out of seven she hadn't wanted to live with herself. She just hadn't been able to get away.

"I'm a mess," she told him—more of the unvarnished truth.

"I know, honey. Here, try this—lift your chest, don't collapse your lungs." He demonstrated, then moved his hand to her sternum and gently pushed upward. "Yoga could help, or medication. Have you tried medication?"

"I've got a record."

That got his attention.

"A criminal record?" His brows furrowed.

"In France." She nodded, her breaths still coming short and shallow. Next, she was going to cry, which really sucked, but there wasn't a whole lot she could do about it. It was an old, familiar cycle: stop breathing, start crying, get all fucked up.

"For what?" To his credit, he had the decency to sound absolutely incredulous.

"Escapee."

The change that came over him was very sudden, very frightening. "What did she fucking do to you, Kat?" His voice was harder than granite. "Where did she send you in Paris?"

"The Bettencourt School for Girls. Actually, it was more like a prison, a very exclusive, very expensive prison for *les incorrigibles*. Well, no, I guess, actually, it was more like an asylum. They locked us in our rooms at night and gave us lots of medications, and I—" She stopped for a second, tried to think of the right words, but there was no coming up with the right words for what she was trying to say. "I didn't do so well on the drugs, but she thought, she actually thought I was *insane* for loving you—and now . . . now here I am, loving you all over again, and I—and I can't breathe."

HAWKINS felt like his skin was on fire, like his hair was in flames. Her mother had committed her to an insane asylum? It was amazing, for someone who was on fire, how coolly he could weigh the costs and benefits of assassinating a United States senator. He could take Marilyn Dekker out. He wasn't the shot Kid was, but he could take her out.

But where would that leave Kat? he wondered, still so coolly assessing, still with his head, and his skin, and his heart in flames.

Probably worse off, he decided. An assassinated mother, even a monster of a mother, would be too heavy a burden to bear.

"Okay," he said, his voice amazingly calm. "So here's what we do. We chuck all this and move into a little thatched hut in Bora-Bora. We live on fish, and fruit, and canned ham—they love canned ham in the islands—and we spend our days swimming and rubbing coconut oil on each other, and that's all we do, forever, for the rest of our lives."

She just looked at him, no doubt struck dumb by his brilliance, or something, because she wasn't saying a word, until she suddenly burst into tears and threw herself into his arms, knocking him backward into the bed.

He caught her, and he held her, and he let her cry, and cry, and cry, and he let her use his sheets to wipe her eyes, and her nose, and God knows what, because he had plenty of clean sheets, and he only had one Kat.

CHAPTER 22

THE WORLD SMELLED faintly of paint . . . and jasmine. Kid stirred and immediately knew he was lying in silk sheets. They slid across his skin, nearly as soft and fine as the woman wrapped in his arms.

He bent his neck, kissed the top of her head, rubbed his lips through the softness of her hair. Precious, precious woman. She'd saved him in the night. He still felt awful, but he didn't feel like he was dying, and because of her, he no longer felt like he wanted to die.

They'd come to her studio last night and made a bed on the floor, but not until she'd fed him. He'd kind of forgotten about food for a couple of days, and eating had been enough to restore him a little. Sharing the food with her, having her straddle his lap and kiss him while they ate, had been the real ticket, though.

Being with Nikki made him feel like he was part of something bigger than himself, and that had been healing.

He'd had girls before, but with Nikki he wasn't alone, and he didn't know what else to call that except love. He loved her, every square inch of her, inside and out and all the way down to the bottom of her soul.

She snuggled against him, still so very asleep. A soft rain pattered on the windows, with only a gray morning light slanting in low to the floor.

Dylan wouldn't be wasting any time in Washington. The one thing Kid remembered him saying was that he'd be back in less than twenty-four hours. Other than that, he hadn't made any guarantees.

That was fine.

Kid didn't need anybody's guarantees or the U.S. government's approval. With food and the first decent sleep he'd had in weeks, he felt like his head was finally getting back on straight. He knew what he had to do in order to be able to live with himself. General Grant and the Defense Department were just going to have to back off and let him do it.

Skeeter had told him yesterday that Creed was out of the picture. It could be weeks, even months, before he was cleared for deployment—which meant more than ever that he needed to talk to Superman. That's what he needed to do—but not this morning.

This morning he needed Nikki.

Needed her like his next breath.

Pulling the sheets up over them, he settled deeper into his pillow, buried his nose in her hair, and just breathed her in, filled himself with her, with the softness of her skin and the sweet, sleek strength of her body lying so close to his.

Nikki woke to the feel of his hand sliding down the middle of her back. She woke to the heated strength of his body and the knowledge that she might never get enough of him.

He'd talked to her in the night, whispered to her of love, of need, and of his brother. He'd told her about J.T., how he'd lived, how wild he'd been, about the chop shop on Steele Street, about how he'd grown up to be a Force Recon Marine, before he'd hooked back up with Dylan and Hawkins, with Quinn and Creed, and once— just once—he'd spoken of vengeance, of going back to Colombia and finishing the job that had gotten his brother killed.

It had scared the hell out of her. It still did. She'd been a total fool to get involved with him, to give him her heart, because he was going to break it into a thousand separate pieces, and she wasn't sure if she had the strength to survive that. Her parents had died in South America eighteen years ago, and she was still dealing with that mess.

She painted, she created. Her whole life was about exploring acts of creation—and she'd fallen in love with a man who was capable of defining the force of de-struction, a man who intended to become a force of destruction.

How had that happened?

And how was she ever going to let him go, knowing what he'd be going into?

His stomach growled, and in spite of her fears, she grinned against his chest.

"Are you hungry?"

"Starving," he admitted.

"Come on, then, before we get distracted." She gave him a quick kiss and pushed herself up off the bed, reaching for his hand. He'd lost so much weight, she wanted to feed him even more than she wanted to make love to him.

At least that's what she thought until he stood up and stretched, his arms over his head, his feet apart in the pile of midnight blue silk sheets.

Oh, wow.

"Don't... move," she said, backing toward her camera shelf. Grabbing a 35mm, she quickly checked it for film, then grabbed a digital as well and slipped the strap over her head.

"Ah, Nikki, come on," he said, half a grin curving his mouth. "You can't... oh, come on." He blushed and turned his back to her as she started firing away. "Nik, really. I'm naked."

"Precisely, beautifully." She worked her way around him, her camera eating up film.

He kept turning, until he just gave up and faced her, planting his hands on his hips and all but daring her to take his picture.

She loved it.

After a second of holding his ground, he got all embarrassed again and put one hand over his face—classic. Then he dragged his hand up through his hair—even better than classic. Then he came after her.

"Kid," she squealed, laughing as she nimbly dashed

around the small table she had set up in the kitchen corner of the studio. It wasn't much of a contest, though. With a couple of moves, he trapped her between the refrigerator and the sink, and food suddenly plummeted to the bottom of his priority list, at least for a moment.

He picked her up, and she wrapped her legs around his waist, while looking down and kissing his face. In between kisses, she took her cameras off and set them on the counter.

He was so sweet, his mouth so sweet. She kissed his lips, his cheeks, the side of his nose, ran her lips over his eyebrows, those wild eyebrows that gave his face such a hawklike countenance.

Stepping backward, he sat down on the kitchen chair with her straddling his lap again.

"Food, wench," he growled against her skin, biting her neck.

She giggled and leaned over to open the fridge. "We've got pudding cups and—uh—pudding cups. I'll call for a pizza."

"At nine o'clock in the morning?" He looked up.

"Pizza Courier delivers twenty-four/seven," she said, reaching a little farther for the phone.

A speed-dial connected her, and a couple of minutes later, an extra-large pepperoni, sausage, and Canadian bacon Chicago-style pizza was scheduled for a nine-thirty A.M. delivery.

"You know the drill," she said into the receiver, opening the fridge back up and grabbing the carton of pudding cups. "Put it on my tab, give yourself a five-dollar tip, knock once, and go away."

"You've got rules for pizza delivery?" Kid asked.

"Sure do, cowboy." She hung up the phone and ripped the covering off one of the cups, then ran her tongue over the inside of the foil. "When I'm working, I don't like to break the mojo, don't want to chitchat with the pizza boys, just want my food, so I set up an account, and they bill me once a month."

"Sweet," he said.

"Mmmm," she agreed, dipping a spoon in the pudding and holding it to his mouth.

He took the first bite, and the next, and the next, until she ripped the lid off the third cup. Then she took about every fourth bite, while they worked their way through another two cups. By the time they'd finished all the pudding and she got half a pizza down him, he'd made love to her again and fallen back asleep on the pile of silk sheets.

Then she got out her cameras and got serious.

THE house was in an uproar, maids opening up long-closed rooms and whole wings of rooms, phones ringing with last-minute organizing, caterers scurrying, staffers everywhere. Big Jon and Lily Beth Traynor were back in Denver, and their first political event of the season—a campaign kickoff for Marilyn Dekker—was due to begin in just a few short hours, a fact which did not in any way interfere with Big Jon's regular morning ritual.

Albert watched as the older man poured himself a tumbler of whiskey and set about inebriating himself for the day. The bedroom suite was on the west side of the house, overlooking the south gardens and the glassed-in pool house where Albert had often swum as a teenager with the other Wellon Academy kids.

"You see the paper yet this morning?" Big Jon asked, then in typical style didn't wait for an answer. "Damn shame about Ted Garraty."

"Yes, sir. A damn shame."

Big Jon's hair had long since turned white, but he was still broad through the shoulders and handsome in a beefy, big-man way. Jonathan had been far more delicately built, almost slight, and at eighteen had still been inches shorter than his six-foot-two-inch father. He'd also been far less driven, possibly his biggest fault in Big Jon's eyes—but then there'd been so many faults, all of them announced in Big Jon's booming voice, repeatedly, year after year, until Jonathan had finally found a little surcease from all his failures in drugs.

Albert had seen it coming for years. Dear, sweet Jonathan had simply been no match for his father's ambitions. The senator had needed a different kind of son, one whose mind did not balk at the harsher necessities of life.

Albert never balked.

"You know I never held it against Marilyn," Big Jon said, returning to the inevitable subject of his son's death while topping off the tumbler. Coming home to Denver always brought Jonathan's murder front and center— which is why Albert did his best to keep Big Jon in Washington. "She's a trouper, and we've accomplished a lot for this great nation of ours over the years."

Accomplished a lot for yourself, Albert silently corrected. Big Jon had been forced to give up his presidential aspirations after the scandal, and so had left politics only to find he had much more maneuvering room in the private sector. He'd made a fortune lobbying Congress on behalf of the American military-industrial complex. He'd also built a fine web of corporations and partnerships that effectively hid the sizable number of weapons manufacturing companies he either personally owned or oversaw through their boards. He had connections from the State Department to the Department of Defense and personally knew half of the current administration's cabinet members.

He'd done very well for himself, especially the last few years, and Albert took great pride in being a big part of that success. As Big Jon's right-hand man, he had steered the big guy through a lot of rough shoals. He'd been the son Big Jon deserved—bright, ruthless, motivated.

"But that daughter of hers is a tragedy in the making, if you know what I mean," Big Jon finished up and took a good long swallow of whiskey.

Albert knew exactly what he meant. He'd heard it all a thousand times.

"She used my boy," Big Jon said, and Albert worried for a second that they were going to head straight into petulance and skip anger altogether.

Big Jon was prone to petulance and brooding in Denver, but today it simply wouldn't do. When Big Jon got all petulant and regretful, he got sloppily, idiotically drunk and stopped functioning altogether. Albert didn't have the patience for idiocy today.

"She used him and threw him away. He went bad because of her, and got in over his head. That's what killed him, not the bullet he took."

"Christian Hawkins killed him, Jon," Albert said,

knowing that's what the big guy wanted to hear. It's what he always wanted to hear.

Big Jon took another drink of whiskey, then wiped his mouth off with the sleeve of his robe. "The courts said he didn't, Albert, but I think you've got the right of it. The bastard killed my son, and Katya Dekker all but put the gun in his hand and helped hold it to Jonathan's head."

"You say the girl might be here today with her mother?"

"Possibly. I didn't want to offend the guest of honor by telling her who she could and could not bring," Albert said. In fact, he'd practically guaranteed Katya's presence at her mother's side, sending the senator a gentle reminder of all the sacrifices the Traynor family had made on her behalf. Big Jon had lost his son and his chance at the presidency, the least he deserved was a long overdue, personal apology from the girl who had been the cause of the whole tragedy. If Katya Dekker wanted to be back in Denver, she first needed to do penance at Big Jon's feet.

"As long as Marilyn had her locked up over in Paris, I didn't worry about her too much," Big Jon grumbled, "and I figured living in California wasn't too much different from being in the loony bin, but the girl's a menace, and I'm not going to have her flaunting herself around my stomping grounds. She can get out of Denver, or be ruined. I'm not settling for anything less. It's past time for somebody to bring her to heel."

Albert's thoughts exactly.

"Damn shame about Ted Garraty," Big Jon went on, repeating himself. He topped off his tumbler again before walking over to his desk. "You were all a damn fine bunch of boys. Damn fine...except for Robert Hughes. His screws were always a little loose."

"Damn fine," Albert agreed.

"Garraty was going to donate to Marilyn's campaign, so make a note for me to send my condolences to his family."

"Yes, sir."

"Where the hell is Herman?" the big man grumbled, looking around for his valet.

"I think Lily Beth is using him in the drawing room."

Big Jon harrumphed and pointed toward the closet. "Well, I want to wear the gray suit today, Albert. You know the one I mean."

"Yes, sir." He knew exactly which suit Big Jon meant.

"Could you get on the laundry again about the starch in my shirts? Herman tells them, but they're still not getting it right. They'll listen to you."

"Yes, sir." Albert headed for Big Jon's closet.

"And I'm going to need a reservation for next week in D.C. for a private dining room. You pick the restaurant. I've got some Saudis coming in, and you know how nervous the Saudis get in Washington."

Albert knew exactly which restaurant to call: the one currently giving him a ten-percent commission off the top of the tab. There wasn't a maître d' in Washington, D.C., who didn't know the score and how he allocated Big Jon's business. He wasn't above using Big Jon's name to throw his weight around.

Inside the closet, he went straight for the rack of gray suits.

"My brown shoes need some buffing. You know the

ones. Can you remind Herman he was supposed to take care of that yesterday?"

Yes, he could, and yes, he knew the exact pair Big Jon was talking about. When you were riding a man's coat-tails to the top, it paid to know the state of his shoes.

SKEETER woke on a start, her eyes wide open, her heart pounding.

Oh, hell. Oh, hell. Oh, damn. She swung out of bed, her feet hitting the floor at a dead run. Steele Street was under attack. An overwhelming wave of danger had crashed into her dreams and set off every alarm signal she had in her brain. And when she raced to the window, the swarm of police cars on the street down below bumped the alarm up to red alert.

She grabbed her hat, her customized PDA, and her cell phone on her way to the door, and punched a series of numbers into the phone at the same time as she lit up every number in her Class A phone book. Racing out the door, she hit "Send All" and dashed down the hall to Superman's. She heard his cell alarm go off even as she started pounding on the door.

"Hawkins!" she yelled. "Superman!"

Inside Hawkins's loft, Katya watched in amazement as Christian burst from pure somnolence to action figure in the space of seconds. He literally hit the floor running.

"Get your clothes on," he shouted back at her from the door.

At first all she could think was that the world was coming to an end, and she didn't have any clothes. She'd left her dress in the car. By the time she remembered her suitcase was in the bathroom, and figured out it wasn't Armageddon, just one person pounding, he'd swung open the door and dragged a girl inside, a girl wearing a ball cap pulled low on her face, a pair of black leggings, and a white sport bra.

He was still buck naked, but the girl didn't even bat an eyelash.

"Who else is here?" he snapped, sliding a big bolt home on the door.

The girl was frantically entering code on what looked like a PDA keyboard, and every couple of seconds, a different-colored light flashed. "Johnny left for Commerce City about five o'clock this morning. Quinn spent the night in Evergreen. Kid is still in Boulder. That means it's just us." The girl looked up from the tiny screen, her gaze landing on the bed, where Kat was still stuck in non-motion mode. "Just the three of us. Hi."

"Hi," Kat managed, trying hard to even think as fast as these two, let alone move as fast. But Hawkins was right. Whatever was happening, she wanted to face it dressed.

She slipped off the bed, wrapped in one of his sheets, and padded her way down the hall. Partway to the bathroom, she heard a truly crude curse escape him, and she stopped long enough to turn around and see what was going on. He'd grabbed his pants from last night and was shucking into them next to the windows.

"*Kee-rist*, there must be ten cop cars out there."

"Double Christ," the girl breathed. "*Marines*. Where in the hell did they get Marines?"

"Buckley Air Force Base would be my best guess. Well, hell . . . a fucking stretch limo just pulled up."

"Shit," they both swore at once.

Even before everything they'd just said could fully sink in, an unmistakable sound rattled through the building. The old freight elevator was going down.

The man and the girl both looked at each other.

"Nobody has that kind of authorization," Hawkins growled between his teeth. "Raise Dylan. Tell him we need General Grant on board *now*."

He raced back toward his spare room, passing Kat by, but the girl took a moment to stop and notice her.

"Superman, we've got a bunny in the headlights here."

He came back out, took three long strides to her, kissed her hot and solid, and then pushed her toward the bathroom. "Get your clothes on, Kat. I've got a real bad feeling that your mother is coming to call, and I'd sure hate for her to find you naked when she gets here."

That was enough to galvanize her, enough to almost make her sick. Alex had called her mother—how could he have done this to her? He knew. He knew everything.

As she slipped by the girl into the bathroom, Hawkins handed out a gun. The girl took it and slipped the holster over her shoulder, while punching numbers into her cell phone.

"Geezus, Hawkins. Don't tell me we're going to shoot it out with the cops?"

"Hell, no," he said from inside the spare room where he was picking up a pistol and some ammunition.

"Double geezus, not the Marines?"

He gave her a look that said *Are you nuts?*

"Then we're firing on the limo?" An idea that, judging by her voice, didn't make any sense at all.

"Damn straight."

Kat shut the door and dove for her suitcase, her blood

racing. She not only didn't want to be naked, if her mother showed up, she did *not* want to look like she'd been rolled over and tumbled in his bed all night. That was none of her mother's business. Absolutely *none* of her business.

HAWKINS came out of the closet with his Glock loaded and headed straight for Katya's purse. "Skeet...I just want you to look all twitchy and unreliable and armed." He turned Kat's phone on and hit the redial. The number for Toussi Gallery came up.

Skeeter shot a glance toward the door. "I *am* twitchy and unreliable."

"Yeah, right." He put the phone to his ear and heard it ring. "Just play it up. Buy us some time, if we need it. Make them nervous."

"I'm not drawing on a Marine." She was adamant.

"You won't be drawing on anybody. You don't have any ammo."

Skeeter started to sputter, but he cut her off with a raised hand. "Get Dylan. Get General Grant. Get us somebody. Okay?"

A guy on the other end of Kat's cell phone picked up, and he took a good guess. "Zheng?"

"Yes!"

"Hawkins."

"Yes! Thank God! Why didn't you guys pick up the phone yesterday! She's on her way. *On her way.* Do you copy? You have to get Katya out of there!"

"Too late for that, and I'm guessing you mean the senator? Your boss?"

"Boss, my ass. Yes, Marilyn Dekker hired me to watch out for her daughter, but hell, you know Kat. How long do you think I held out before I was her man? Figuratively speaking . . . of course."

"Of course. So you didn't rat her out to the senator two nights ago?"

"Hell, no. If I had, she would have been here this time yesterday. You've got to know that."

Yeah. Hawkins guessed he did.

"So what happened? Or was it just the newspaper coverage that brought her to Denver?"

"I wish." Alex let out a big sigh. "Senator Dekker had a campaign stop already planned for Denver this morning, but . . . Look, where are you? I've got some stuff you really need to see. A lot of stuff."

"You know the alley called Steele Street? Four blocks north of the gallery?"

"You're right here? In the neighborhood? All this time? Hell." He sounded so dejected.

"Halfway up the alley is a door. Key in nine-three-seven-one-eight, and I'll have Skeeter override the biometric reader. We're on the eleventh floor. Watch out, we're covered on the street side with cops and Marines." Hawkins hung up and looked to Skeeter. "Well?"

She shook her head, and punched in another set of numbers. After about five seconds, a big smile split her face. She tossed the phone to him.

"Dylan, it's Christian," he said. "All hell is breaking loose here. I think somebody wants my ass pretty bad. Did General Grant ever come up with a name on our last assignment?"

"He got as far as a company called Western Armament

Corporation, before he got stonewalled. What do you mean all hell? Senator Dekker?"

"And a platoon of Marines I'm guessing she pulled out of Buckley for a morning drill around Steele Street."

"She brought the Marines?" Dylan didn't sound like he believed it. Hell, Hawkins didn't believe it, and he was looking right down at them on the street below.

"And ten police cruisers."

"Shit. I'll call Lieutenant Bradley first. At least you won't end up in jail—for very long."

"I don't want to end up in the friggin' brig for very long, either."

"General Grant can get them pulled off. That just leaves you with the senator."

"The hell it will."

"Christ, Hawkins. It'll take me half a day to get a senator off your ass."

"Then get on it, please."

"Just stay put. They can't get into Steele Street."

"Dylan. They are *in* Steele Street. They commandeered the old freight elevator. Any minute now, we are going to hear the Corps storming up the stairs singing 'From the halls of Montezuma,' and unless I figure out a way to chain myself to the plumbing, I don't think *staying put* is going to be an option. The few, the proud, and the brave are here to haul my ass away, and judging by the size of the detachment, that's exactly what's going to happen."

Silence, then, "Where's Skeeter?" Dylan was definitely concerned now, and frankly, Hawkins was glad to hear it. Steele Street was supposed to be friggin' impregnable— and it was, unless somebody had the codes and was able to bypass or compromise the scanners. It was an inside job. The only question was—inside what? And the answer to that had to be the Department of Defense. No one at Steele Street would compromise their security. No one.

"She's with me."

"Do you still have Ms. Dekker?"

Have her, had her, going to have her again—at least he'd planned on it until the troops had arrived.

"Yes."

"Kid and Quinn?"

"I'll get to Kid, but let's keep Quinn on the outside. He'll be more help there."

"Okay. I'll do what I can on this end. Either way, I'll be back tonight." Dylan hung up, and a few minutes later, Hawkins saw about half the cops get back in their cars and leave.

He punched in another number. Yes, it was eleven o'clock on a Sunday morning, but he wanted his lawyer.

"Francesca?" he asked when she answered.

"This had better be good, Christian. It's Sunday."

"I need a house call. Immediately."

It took her all of two seconds to decide. "Sure. I could use a couple of grand. I'm starting my clock."

A couple of grand. Hell. But yes, he could easily see that racking up today.

There was some good news. Skeeter had managed to access the freight elevator through the computer connection to the main office on the seventh floor, and it was now stuck between floors, but given its age and condition, she wasn't sure how long her freeze would hold.

In one of the spookier moves of the morning, Alex Zheng showed up about three minutes after Hawkins had called him, making both him and Skeeter wonder if Alex should be called The Flash.

So approximately fifteen minutes into their whole ordeal, they'd cut the enemy in half, gotten an ally on board, had two reinforcements heading into the city, and were just getting down to the stuff Alex had brought, when the bathroom door opened.

Geezus, Hawkins thought, picking his jaw up off the floor. How did she do that?

She was all sleek and lovely, and hot, and perfect again. All "don't touch my mouth" and "don't touch my hair," when he knew he'd done nothing but touch her all night long. She was dressed in black slacks and a sleeveless black top, her black spike-heeled sandals, and big silver hoop earrings.

He hadn't packed any silver hoop earrings. Where did she come up with this stuff?

She looked cool and creamy, like that double-dark-chocolate, triple-whipped-cream mocha latte she'd spilled all over Roxanne, and it was all he could do not to tell her to lock herself back in the bathroom and not come out until the whole thing was over.

He didn't want her mother anywhere near her, and he'd bet his first million that her mother felt the same way about him.

CHAPTER 23

THE FIRST THING to give way was the old freight elevator. They actually heard it break free and drop half a floor, before the cables caught and saved all within from certain death—which wasn't really a bad thing. It was just damned inconvenient.

Alex—who had not been kidding when he'd said, "I've got some stuff you really need to see. A lot of stuff."—had already shown him and Kat and Skeeter the bloody piece of prom dress, which had made Kat almost faint, and quite honestly, had almost done the same thing to him. It had a lot more blood on it than the first piece. He'd forgotten, over the years, just how badly she'd been hurt.

"You were a prom queen?" was all Skeeter had said, but she'd said it half a dozen times, at least. "An actual prom queen? So that crown last night was yours?" A question that, for some reason, had prompted her to hit him on the shoulder, and Skeeter never pulled her punches, figuratively or otherwise. "You should have told me, Superman. A friggin' prom queen."

"Friggin' prom queen" sounded more like an expletive than a compliment, or like what Bobba-Ramma would have been, but Katya seemed to know the girl was impressed.

Hell, who wouldn't be. Ten minutes in a bathroom to go from emotionally exhausted, wild-woman lover to cool downtown chic chick? That had to be some kind of a record.

"Now here's the strange stuff," Alex said, emptying an envelope out on the kitchen table. "A man named Ray Carper gave these newspaper clippings to Travis James last night on the street. Travis brought them straight to me."

"Who's Travis James?" Hawkins asked.

"Nikki McKinney's model," Skeeter said, surprising him. "He walked me home from the gallery last night. Ray must have heard we were looking for him and come up to Travis on his way back to Toussi's, thinking he was Creed."

"Why would Ray think this guy was Creed?" Hawkins asked at the same time as Katya said, "Creed Rivera? I remember him being a lot . . . well, tougher looking than Travis. Bigger."

"Yeah," Skeeter said to Katya. "He is." Then she turned to Hawkins. "He's a dead ringer, though, Superman."

"Creed's blond now?" Katya asked.

"No," both Hawkins and Skeeter said.

"For God's sake . . . It *doesn't* matter," Alex finally interrupted. "That is not the point here, people. The point is *what* the old man gave Travis. Look."

He spread the articles out on a table.

"Now, I'd guess you all know the case as well as I do, maybe even better, though it's about all I've been working on for two days—besides the McKinney show," he quickly amended. "Which went beautifully, by the way."

He hadn't won Katya back over yet, but she at least gave him a nod.

"Anyway, there are some interesting connections here, if everything else the old man said is true."

"What else did he say?" Hawkins asked, skimming the articles. He remembered most of the ones about the Traynor murder, but there were also some about the Jane Doe that summer, and then yesterday's headlines about Ted Garraty. There was even a clipping about Lost Harold.

Alex pulled a sheet of paper out of his pocket, snapped it open. "This is what Ray Carper told Travis. We went over it and over it, and I think he did a pretty good job of remembering." He looked at the paper, starting at the top. " 'That whore shouldn't a died like she did. The boys were just damn rough with her. I saw it, saw the whole thing, but nobody wanted to listen to old Ray. They called her Jane Doe, but her name was Debbie Gold. She's been six feet under for thirteen years, her and that Traynor boy, and old Lost Harold. The same damn wild ones did them all in, but it looks like one of 'em got their own back last night at the Gardens.' "

Alex looked up from the paper. "I was able to get a copy of the coroner's report on the Jane Doe they pulled out of the river on July first that summer. Don't ask," he said, before Hawkins could even get the question out. "It states that the body had been decomposing between three or four weeks, the best estimate he could come up with, given the corpse's waterlogged condition. So sometime between June third and June ninth, approximately, a group of guys who'd been hanging around LoDo, these 'wild ones' Ray was talking about, roughed up a whore who was turning tricks for them. She died, and they threw her in the South Platte. And if Ray is right, one of those guys was Ted Garraty, good friend of Jonathan Traynor the third."

"Jonathan would *never* have killed anyone," Katya said, coming to her friend's defense. "And he would *never* have had sex with a prostitute . . . or . . . or any girl."

Well, that was a new twist she hadn't shared before, Hawkins thought.

Alex's eyebrows had risen. "The senator's son was gay?"

Katya nodded.

"And he never came out?"

She shook her head.

"Prom night was June fifth that year," Hawkins said. "Well within the time frame for the night of the whore's murder."

"You think the same guys who were after Katya in the parking lot did the whore instead?" Skeeter asked.

It's what Hawkins was beginning to think, but all he said was "We need to find Ray Carper." All those years ago, when he'd talked to Ray, Hawkins had thought he was talking about Katya and her struggle in the parking lot—a girl getting worked over by a group of boys, the one who died, he'd said—but Katya hadn't died. Ray hadn't shown him any newspaper clippings back then.

He'd never mentioned Debbie Gold or Jane Doe, just a girl in a pretty dress.

"If he was between Toussi's and Steele Street last night, he's probably still in the neighborhood," Skeeter said. "He doesn't get too far from Coors Field."

"We need to bring him in—except right now, we can't get out."

"Quinn knows him. Let's have him pick up the old guy and take him over to the Oxford Hotel."

"Make it so, Skeeter."

The girl started punching more numbers into her phone.

"There's more," Alex said. "Jonathan Traynor was murdered just four days after the dead prostitute floated to the surface of the river—something that could spook any boy into a bad case of the guilts, if he was guilty of murdering her, or knew the people who had murdered her, like maybe a group of boys whose first attempt at a gang bang didn't go so well on prom night."

"Quinn—" Skeeter started to say, when they heard it: the Marines, marching up the stairwell.

Hawkins turned to Katya. He very much wanted to tell her how much he loathed her mother, for everything she'd done, for everything she was doing, but he didn't.

He looked back to Alex. "Do we let them in? Or make them go through my Tomás Alejandro doors?"

"They get in either way, and if we let them in, we can save the doors."

He was right, but Hawkins didn't have to like it. "Skeeter, finish up with Quinn. I want you in the back, up against a wall; pull up a chair, stay out of trouble. Kat—"

God, Kat. Your mother is coming in here like the Four Horsemen of the Apocalypse, and I want you anyplace else but here.

"Kat, why don't you take a bar stool behind the kitchen counter. Alex, you and I are the forward guards."

He walked over to the doors and threw open the bolt. Hell.

Then everything went suddenly quiet. It didn't last long, but when the marching started up again, the Marines were heading back *down* the stairwell.

Thank you, Dylan . . . and thank you, General Grant.

Yet Hawkins knew they'd only dodged the bullet. There was every possibility the Marines would be back . . . just as soon as Kat's mother figured out how to circumvent Grant's hastily concocted—and timely— orders. And if not the Marines, Marilyn Dekker would find another band of merry men to get the job done. The woman was relentless—possibly insane. The Marines, for crying out loud.

"How many people does the senator have with her right now?"

"Five—her secretary and four sycophants," Alex said.

That made him laugh.

"Any of them armed?"

"Two."

"Well, suddenly, we have an even playing field."

Alex just looked at him as if he were delusional. "You never have an even playing field with a senator. Never."

"She can't be feeling too confident." Hawkins checked his watch. "Twenty-five minutes ago, she had an army, and now she's down to the honor guard."

"Tell yourself what you want, she already fired my ass

and is considering charges, and she actually likes me. You, on the other hand, are the bane of her existence."

"She told you that?"

Alex lowered his gaze for a second, before bringing it back up and casting a guilty glance in Katya's direction. "I was fully briefed on all aspects of Katya's life, including what the senator thought was your current situation. She never lost sight of you, although her information about you being a car salesman is obviously no more than a very good cover for whatever the hell it is you actually do."

"So you don't think she's the one who got me assigned as Kat's bodyguard at the Botanic Gardens two nights ago?"

"I don't know. If she did, she didn't tell me, which wouldn't make sense, because she was very concerned about Katya returning to Denver. Your name came up in any number of conversations we had, and I was told to guard against any contact being made, doing whatever it took."

"Like maybe setting up a murder that would inevitably include my name, or possibly frame me and get me tossed back into the state pen?"

"No."

Alex didn't elaborate any more beyond his one-word answer, which made Hawkins fairly inclined to believe him.

"Are you a shooter, Alex?"

"No," the man said, paling slightly. "An ex-cop, yes, but not a shooter, not the way you mean."

"Well, I am," Hawkins told him, his meaning clear.

"And if they take me out of here, I'm holding you personally responsible for Kat's well-being."

Alex paled even more. "I can't imagine that Senator Dekker has gone to all this trouble without at least getting an arrest warrant and possibly the keys to Leavenworth."

Despite the situation, he had to grin. "I can't, either." And that was the bitch of it, but he was starting to like Alex. Efficiency, intelligence, and that nifty speed-of-sound move he'd made this morning were easy to like, not to mention his blunt honesty.

When the knock sounded on the door, he checked his watch, then glanced at Skeeter. "Where's Kid?"

She looked at the GPS on her PDA. "I-25 and I-70, the Mousetrap," she said, referring to the elaborate intersection of the two main freeways running through Denver. It was a toss-up whether or not Kid would get to Steele Street before Hawkins got hauled downtown.

No one bothered to answer the door. Hell, Dekker's entourage had already broken into the building. It was pretty obvious they were coming in whether they got an invitation or not.

Sure enough, there wasn't a second knock before the cops and politicos breached the door.

Hawkins immediately realized that he had not sufficiently prepared himself for the sight of Marilyn Dekker up close and personal. He spent enough time keeping up with current affairs and going in and out of Washington, D.C., to know what she looked like, so it wasn't the way she looked per se that twisted his gut. It was that she was on his turf with her pageboy helmet of brown hair, her squared-off shoulders, those damn skinny legs, and her sensible shoes. He hated her beige three-button suit, her nude hose, her pearl earrings. He was sure she smelled like mothballs but was damned if he was going to get close enough to confirm his suspicion. He hated the tight, pinched line of her mouth and her squinty pea green eyes. He hated the sanctimonious tilt of her chin and her righteous confidence.

He watched her march into his loft, and he tried, so help him God, he tried to find one single aspect of her outfit, or her face, or her personality, or spirit, or even her aural sheath that he didn't loathe—because she was going to be the grandmother of his children.

It was enough to make a guy lose his lunch.

Lieutenant Loretta Bradley was keeping step with her, and when Marilyn stopped and took an imposing stance in the middle of his living room area, the lieutenant proceeded forward alone. She was a large woman, not overweight, just tall and big-boned, with a nice solid face, her nose a little too big, but with eyes to match of a beautiful, almost golden brown. She kept her hair short and colored anything in the red range. Over the years he'd seen it go from chestnut to carrot, to almost pink once.

No one had laughed.

"Cristo," she said calmly.

"Loretta," he acknowledged her greeting.

"I've got a warrant for your arrest, and your fingerprints all over a Remington .308 we found at the Botanic Gardens the other night."

Well, that sucked.

"Read him his rights, Carl."

While Carl read him his rights, Hawkins took a min-

ute to breathe and think through this latest unfuckingbelievable turn of events.

"The only Remington .308 I ever shot was at Quantico, three months ago."

Loretta met his eyes without flinching. "That's what
Dylan thought."

Dylan. So the wheels were turning and the lieutenant,
evidently, was open to slowing things down and letting
Dylan catch up to the situation.

"So," she continued. "Dylan called a friend of yours.
Gunny Howzer? And this Gunny told him that the gun
had been stolen shortly after your visit."

"So why are you here?" Hawkins looked directly at
Marilyn Dekker, before meeting Loretta's eyes—and seeing true regret.

"You know the drill. We're still gonna do the dance. So
do you want the drama of the handcuffs, or would you
like to come quietly?"

He wanted to scream something truly obscene, put his
fist through the wall, and then grab Marilyn Dekker by
the throat and shake her until she turned blue.

"No drama."

"May I have your weapon, please?" she asked.

He gave her the Glock.

"Have you called Francesca?"

"She's on her way here."

"Well, you can call her again from the station. I'm sure
she won't mind the extra traveling time. What's she
billing now? By the millisecond?" the lieutenant said
deadpan.

"That's hilarious, Loretta."

He looked down, and a corner of her mouth was

twitching, which just torqued him. This wasn't funny. It was god-awful.

"Okay, then, let's go."

He turned, met Katya's eyes for a second, before turning a very meaningful gaze on Alex. His message, he hoped, was clear, and by the slightly wild-eyed look he got in response, he felt sure the message had been received: Anything happens to her, something *definitely* happens to you.

THERE was something bracing about being in Marilyn's presence, Katya thought. For one, she never hyperventilated in her mother's presence. Never. She didn't dare. Falling apart emotionally was something far better indulged in with friends and lovers, people who cared more about you than themselves—which left her mother out of the loop. Another nice thing about being in Marilyn's presence was the playing rules. They were never ambiguous, and they were always adhered to by all parties. Politeness was a virtue above truth. Decorum the order of the day.

Kat was so glad she'd dressed in black.

"Katya, really, you're far too old for this sort of goings-on." After a moment of gloating while Hawkins had been marched out the door, Marilyn had turned her attention back to her daughter. "The man is a criminal at best, and a murderer at worst. I don't care what they said at the pardon. I would have thought you would have learned your lesson last time. Why you *insist* on slumming with him every time you get within a hundred miles of our home state—the state, mind you, that has given us the privilege of serving it in our nation's capital—is, well, it's disgusting, is what it is."

My God, her mother truly was amazing. She'd called out the Marines to give her a dressing-down.

"I actually thought you were in danger. The man is not what he seems."

"He isn't?" Kat played dumb. Marilyn expected so little of her, and she'd found over the years that it was best to meet those expectations. The huge success she'd had with her galleries had never really registered on her mother's radar. It was a refined, sophisticated, cultured career that fit in well with Marilyn's own image as a refined, sophisticated, cultured politician—and that was all that was required of it. Success would have almost been crass in Marilyn's eyes, so Katya kept her success to herself.

Truly, her mother wasn't interested.

"No, my darling. He isn't. Oh, I've missed you." Marilyn started across the loft, her arms outspread, and Kat actually did brace herself for the perfunctory embrace, the air kisses, one hovering above either cheek, that ensured no one lost any lipstick and no one gained any on their face. It was a set piece between them, known in Katya's book as "The Greeting," and it always followed, never preceded, "The Edifying Lecture."

Marilyn always opened with a lecture. Lecturing created a comfort zone for her. She liked telling people what to do, and she was always right—in which she took boundless comfort.

Of course, she made everyone else feel like hell, but

Marilyn didn't put a lot of stock in other people's feelings, especially when her own were so much more interesting.

Katya endured the near brush of lips to her cheeks. She endured the tight little squeeze her mother gave her arms, and then it was over and Marilyn was moving back around to the front of the counter.

"Don't worry, dear. Obviously, the man holds some sort of fascination for you, but that can be taken care of," her mother continued, and for a second, Katya thought she might hyperventilate no matter how well she'd braced herself. Her mother's idea of having something "taken care of" was her worst nightmare.

Or rather it used to be her worst nightmare. Watching Hawkins being hauled off by the police was her actual worst nightmare as of about three minutes ago, and she was *not* going to sit idly by while he went to jail. The best thing she could do for him was to keep her mother occupied and away from him, let her feel like she had everything under control. Contrarily enough, that's when Marilyn was the most manageable and the least dangerous.

And Kat needed to make a phone call—just one.

She had reached for her phone, when she noticed her mother getting agitated. A little warning skittered up her spine, and when she glanced over at her mother's entourage, she noticed all of them, four men and one woman, watching her mother's every move, as if they were anticipating disaster. Kat recognized two of the men as aides; the woman, Linda Goodrich, was her mother's personal aide. The other two men looked like hired muscle, except of course they wouldn't be for hire. They'd be government guys.

"You should know some evidence has come to light," Marilyn said, pacing a small area in the middle of the loft, her voice very tight, very controlled.

The comment was obviously directed at Kat, and out of a keen sense of self-preservation, she responded.

"Evidence?"

"Yes." The word was very short, very curt. "It's what made all this so necessary this morning, so very, *very* necessary."

As Kat recalled, her mother had used those same words recently on the news to condone a U.S. military invasion of a small Third World country in Central America: *very* necessary.

"I want you to know that I will *not* let these acts go unavenged." Her mother's voice actually trembled, and Kat began to understand why her aides were looking so uncomfortably nervous. Trembling senators were dangerous senators, and the word "unavenged" was nothing short of alarming. "You should have told me, Katya. You should have told me. I could have had him taken care of in prison."

Oh, God. Her alarm spiked. There it was again, something her mother could have "taken care of," and it apparently had something to do with Hawkins. Her nervous skitter of warning rose to a high crest and began taking the shape of a tidal wave.

"The same way he had that man taken care of in prison down in Canon City." Her mother turned on a dime and marched to the other end of the coffee table. "Not the one he killed outright, but the other one."

"Wh-what in the world are you talking about?" She barely got the words out, she was suddenly so breathless.

"Katya." Alex started forward, a look of deep concern on his face, but her mother called him off.

"Stay out of this, Zheng. You have been dismissed, and it's time she knew. I've protected her from the truth long enough."

And if that wasn't enough to make Kat's blood run cold, she didn't know what was. Marilyn's idea of protection inevitably came down to some sort of emotional blackmail/mental torture/freaking manipulation scheme that involved anything but the truth. It was as if her mother had been born with a genetic predisposition to spin-doctoring. Everything she said had a spin to it. She actually considered it one of her greatest natural assets— this ability to skirt the truth in any situation.

"I know he got off for killing Jonathan." Her mother was actually picking up her pace now. "And if there were any way possible, I would get the case reopened to see that justice was done. Big Jon has suffered the pangs of hell knowing his son's murderer got off scot-free. The pangs of hell, I tell you. It's why he left public life, and as he has agreed to become my new campaign manager, which includes him making a rather large donation, I feel I owe him justice."

Oh, yes, Marilyn could be bought, and it truly didn't take that much money to do it.

"And this thing with Ted Garraty," her mother continued. "Well, I'm sure Christian Hawkins did that, too, and I hate to say it, but he probably did the world a favor. Now, Kat." She held up her hand. "I know that sounds harsh, but the world is a harsh place, though God knows I've tried to protect you from those realities."

Kat bit her tongue.

"Ted Garraty was a deviant," Marilyn said. "A pervert, and the world is a better place without him."

A deviant?

"Uh, how do you know about Ted?" she asked. She couldn't imagine that her mother had been to The Painted Pony.

"Why, I've kept track of all the boys, Kat. Watched them over the years, waiting for them to step out of line in any way that could be prosecuted. Despite . . ." Her mother hesitated for a moment, an unusual enough occurrence to rivet Katya's attention. "Well . . . despite the way things were handled at the time, the whole lot of them should have been thrown in prison for what they did to you, and honestly, only a couple of them have proven to be of any worth to society whatsoever."

Katya didn't know what to say. Her mother had just admitted to a mistake—a mistake that had weighed on Katya since Jonathan's death. Her feelings had been so summarily dismissed at the time. Sleeping with Christian Hawkins had completely destroyed her credibility, as her mother had pointed out at the top of her lungs over and over during those awful days. No one had listened to her. No one had wanted to hear how unhappy Jonathan had been. No one had wanted to believe Christian had been a hero on prom night, not a criminal, not a seducer

All they'd wanted was quick justice and for everybody and everything about the case to simply disappear, whether it was to Canon City or the Bettencourt School for Girls—and her mother had just admitted that things had been mishandled. Katya couldn't help but feel some long-awaited relief.

"And as far as deviants are concerned," her mother continued, "there were worse in the lot than Ted Garraty."

And that had to be Bobby "Bobba-Ramma" Hughes she was talking about, Kat thought. She wondered which two of the prom boys her mother thought had turned out useful, but didn't ask. She wanted to know about "unavenged acts" and who her mother thought Hawkins had killed in prison.

"What man in Canon City are you talking about, Mother?" She never called her mother "mom." It just wasn't done.

Her mother gave her a pained look, as if she would have done anything to have protected her from this, but alas.

"Linda," she said, "give her the photos."

Linda Goodrich, a medium-sized brunette with a law degree from Harvard whom her mother was grooming for great things ahead—unlike herself—stepped forward without hesitation and handed Kat a file folder across the kitchen counter.

Kat noticed Skeeter rise out of her chair and start forward, a very grim expression on her face.

She turned back to the folder and flipped the top open—and blanched. There were photographs of dead men stapled to both sides inside. Her heart stopped for one shuddering second as she looked from one eight-by-ten photograph to another. One man appeared to have been beaten to death; the other's cause of death was unclear. But he was dead, his mouth gaping in a rictus of pain, his legs drawn up, his head thrown back.

"Christian Hawkins freely admitted to the beating that killed Clive Lennox. Unfortunately, the death was ruled self-defense, and there were witnesses who attested to the fact. Of course, they were all convicts, so who's to say what really happened?" Marilyn asked, her voice full of doubt.

A hand reached across the counter and snapped the folder shut. When Katya looked up, it was into Alex's eyes.

"He was nineteen years old and in prison, Kat," he said, his voice low and furious. "You know what the guy looks like. Don't be naive. It doesn't suit you, babe."

"This is none of your concern, Mr. Zheng," her mother said from across the room, her tone one that would brook no argument.

Another hand slipped into view and picked up the folder. Katya let it go and looked up to see Skeeter, who walked the folder back around the counter and handed it to Marilyn.

"I think your daughter's seen enough, Senator."

"And you are?" Marilyn looked down her nose at the polite but horribly underdressed girl.

"Skeeter Bang, Senator Dekker." Skeeter held out her hand. "I voted for you in the last election."

"Oh." Marilyn couldn't help herself. She smiled and took the girl's hand. "I think it's so important to appeal to the younger voters in my district."

"Yes, ma'am." Skeeter pumped her hand up and down, and Marilyn handed the folder back to Linda.

"How did the other man die?" Katya whispered to Alex. The photos had been gruesome, utterly awful, and she hated to think Hawkins could have had anything to do with them—but Alex was right. She couldn't afford to be naive, and she hadn't been naive, not even at eighteen.

She'd known what would probably happen to him, and it had almost destroyed her.

"It was a hit," Alex said after a long moment. "Contracted for on the outside, probably by Dylan Hart, I think now; he's got more connections than your mother. The dead man, Wes Lake, had it in for Hawkins in a real bad way. One of them was bound to end up dead."

"Well, it's just so lovely to meet you, Ms. Bang, but my daughter and I have an appointment." Marilyn's voice rose enough to interrupt her and Alex's conversation.

"Appointment?" Alex asked, turning to face her mother, his voice suddenly unsure.

"Yes," Marilyn said succinctly. "The weekend's events have only brought Big Jon Traynor's losses more sharply into focus. My campaign kickoff is today, and now we can add a little pleasure to our business. He has often expressed a desire to see you again, Katya. You were Jonathan's dearest friend, and I think he deeply misses those days when you and Jonathan were always around the house. We're not getting any younger, Kat, and sometimes it does seem to have all gone by so quickly."

Well, that cinched it. Kat was entering the twilight zone, full speed ahead, no brakes.

CHAPTER
24

DAMAGE CONTROL, that was the issue here, not giving in to her heart's desire and asking her mother if she was completely nuts.

A nice little visit to the new campaign manager would have been pushing her boundaries to begin with. That the campaign manager was Big Jon Traynor was awful. She did not want to go, but she was going—quietly and without a fight—for Christian's sake. Far safer for him to have her mother ensconced in the Traynor mansion, absorbed by her upcoming campaign, than to have her thinking too much about Hawkins. Marilyn had done quite enough damage there for one day.

Damage Kat was determined to mitigate. She couldn't bear to think of him in jail. Again. For something he hadn't done. Again.

So she called her lawyer, discreetly, during the hubbub of leaving the loft, with Alex flashing the bloody piece of dress and all but demanding that he be allowed to go with her, and Marilyn demanding that he simply disappear, because there was worse than what she'd already revealed—which Kat didn't even want to think about—and that it was all his fault it had come down to this to begin with.

"George?" she said when the phone was answered.

"Yes?"

"It's Katya. My fiancé has been arrested and taken downtown in Denver. His name is Christian Hawkins. The arresting officer is Lieutenant Loretta Bradley, and I want him out of there yesterday. Whatever it takes."

"Consider it done. Anything else?"

"No, and thanks, George."

"You can thank me when you see the bill."

Kat flipped her phone shut just as the shouting match was winding down. Her mother had won, naturally.

But Kat had just won as well. She defied anyone, even her mother, to go up against her Denver lawyer and come out in one piece. George Dale was ruthless, and he was connected all the way to the White House. He'd be down at that precinct before she and her mother got to the Traynor mansion.

With Alex completely freaked out, and Skeeter looking none too happy, Kat left with her mother. Like a lamb to slaughter, because it suited her purposes. And like a lamb, regardless that she was seething inside and worried sick over what her mother might try to do to Christian, she bore it in silence.

She expected the ride to the Traynors' to be a strain, and her mother didn't disappoint.

"Some very disturbing...information...has come to light," Marilyn began once they were in the back of the limo. "Very disturbing. It could disrupt the whole campaign. Linda?" She held her hand out, and her aide pulled a manila envelope out of her briefcase.

Thousands of different types of things came in manila envelopes. Millions, actually, but Katya had this niggling little suspicion of what might be in this particular manila envelope. She couldn't believe it, of course. It was too awful to even bear contemplating, let alone to actually have to endure. No, the reality of her mother having received copies of the same photographs of her and Christian that had been in her apartment was simply unacceptable.

With trembling hands, Marilyn opened the envelope, and Katya thought, *Oh, please, Mother, really. Do we have to actually look at them, with Linda and your four goons sitting here with us?*

The answer became all too obviously clear, when Marilyn pulled the photos out of the envelope and dropped them in Katya's lap.

"Do...do you know what this could do to my reelection if these got out? We barely survived the last scandal you created, and now you're embroiling us in a whole new, sordid mess. Really, Katya."

Katya flipped through the photos, slowly, one by one. She was beyond being shocked by them at this point. They actually looked pretty tame compared to last night. Quite tame, really.

"No, Mother. I don't know what this could do to your campaign. This is obviously not you in these photos. What do you think, Linda?" She started to hand a couple over to the aide, who tried to look shocked rather than smug, but hell, there wasn't a person in the car who hadn't seen these pictures and probably made copies, and Kat knew it.

Marilyn was too quick for her, though, snatching them back before Linda got ahold of them.

"Don't be smart, Katya. It doesn't suit you."

God, did her mother even listen to herself?

"Ruin me is what they can do, and then where will all of our hard work have gone? Hmmm? Did you think of that?"

No, she most certainly had not been thinking of her mother's hard work while those photos were being taken.

"What did you think you were doing? What, Kat?" Marilyn's voice was rising.

Kat wanted to say "Fucking my brains out," but she showed a little discretion instead and simply put both of her hands over her face and slowly slumped down in the seat.

Her mother was insane.

"I've spoken with a private detective, one in Washington, D.C., and he has assured me the photos can be doctored so it looks like rape. With a rape charge on top of a murder charge, not to mention the old murder charges, and maybe I can get the prison to reopen the Lennox and Lake cases, I think we can put him away for life this time."

Completely and totally insane. Someone should tell CNN.

Peeking out from under her hand, she checked her watch. Almost noon. At one o'clock, she'd call George back and see where they were with Hawkins. The instant he was out of jail, she was dumping her mother. She didn't have a choice, really. It had become a matter of survival—Christian's survival—and that's all that mattered.

It wasn't until they turned on to Speer Boulevard that Katya felt her first spark of hope about going to Big Jon Traynor's.

The sound roaring up behind them was unmistakable: horsepower, lots of it, with headers. A quick glance out the window showed the limo being flanked by a flat-black Porsche on one side and a big, green, mean machine with a black racing stripe running over the hood on the other.

Roxanne was on the loose, with Skeeter behind the wheel and Alex holding on for dear life, his eyes as round as demitasse cups. She didn't know who the guy driving the Porsche was, but neither did she doubt that he was on her side.

LAWYERS in love were fascinating, Hawkins thought. It was like watching vultures fight over carrion, with him being the carrion, and the two vultures being Francesca, his lovely, plump, middle-aged, really-ought-to-know-better, very expensive lawyer, and George Dale being the reserves sent in by his most lovely Kat. While they argued brilliantly, set bail, and made veiled remarks, they were also falling in love at first sight. He'd never seen Francesca so lit up, and he couldn't imagine that a balding, middle-aged senior partner from Dale, Preston, and Doyle normally conducted his business with a ridiculous grin plastered on his face.

The two of them were simply having too much fun—and it was three fucking o'clock.

"Can we leave yet?" he asked, his patience running so damn thin, he could see through it. He was amazed they couldn't.

"No," they both chimed in unison, then thought that was somehow significant. Their smiles broadened.

Oh, brother. And he was paying three hundred and fifty dollars an hour for this?

"How about if *I* leave?"

Francesca looked over at him, as if she'd just noticed. "Sure, Cristo. You're clear."

He could have left, and she hadn't told him? He was docking her for that, just for the principle of the thing. "Can I take your car? Maybe Mr. Dale here can give you a ride home."

And he was charging her for the setup. He could tell she was thrilled.

"Of course," George said, brightening.

"Keys, Francesca?" He held out his hand.

Five minutes later, he'd made a call to Skeeter and was heading to Big Jon Traynor's house.

NAUSEATING was the best word Katya could come up with for the luncheon Big Jon and his wife, Lily Beth, served Marilyn's campaign finance committee. It wasn't the food. It was the company. Besides the Traynors and Marilyn and her staffers, there were at least a hundred other people at the tables, people who'd made big donations and wanted a piece of the campaign action, shakers and movers. One of them was Philip Cunningham. Sharp-faced, with a blade of a nose and a thin mouth, and still red-haired and freckled, he was easily recognizable as the gawky kid they'd all called "Stork." He'd arrived late and had sat at another table, but the way he was watching her out of the corner of his eye was enough to churn her stomach into knots—and still it was nothing compared to the way Big Jon was watching her.

She hadn't realized the man hated her. The last time she'd seen him had been at the trial, and she'd probably just been too shell-shocked to notice. But he hated her; she could feel it every time their eyes met. He was standing at the head of the main table, introducing her mother in glowing terms to the people who would be doing her money-grubbing for her over the next eighteen months, and every now and then his gaze fell on her and chilled her to the bone.

As far as she was concerned, either Philip or Big Jon could have planted the pictures and the dress pieces or done any number of things to frighten or destroy her— but she couldn't imagine either of them killing Ted Garraty just to give her a scare. There had to be a motive, and the only one she could come up with was the old "Dead men tell no tales" one.

Maybe Ted had been trying to blackmail Philip for the death of Debbie Gold. Of course, that left a big hole where Big Jon was concerned, as she doubted if the then-senator had been running around on the streets of LoDo with his son's friends, picking up prostitutes and throwing them in the South Platte River.

No, that was never going to wash, even though Katya knew very well that senators weren't saints.

So that brought her back to Philip, who kept nervously glancing her way and dabbing at the sweat breaking out on his brow with his napkin. He looked like a heart attack waiting to happen. If seeing her made him that much of a wreck, no wonder he'd bailed out on their meeting yesterday.

Of course, the question was why seeing her upset him so much.

"Ms. Dekker, you have a phone call." One of the serving maids leaned down quietly to deliver the message.

Katya was only too relieved to have a reason to escape. She scooted away from the table with a whispered apology and followed the young woman out of the Traynors' ballroom.

"I'm sorry, miss, but the call came in on the billiards room line, and it's a ways into the south wing."

Katya remembered the billiards room and the south wing. The pool room was there as well, and for teenagers, it had been a natural gathering place.

"Normally, we'd be able to route the call to a more convenient place, but with all the people here today, I guess all the lines are busy."

That was fine with Katya; the farther away from the campaign finance committee she could get, the better. The only people who knew where she was were Skeeter and Alex, which made her doubly anxious to take the call. She figured they must have news about Christian, and taking the call also gave her an opportunity to call her lawyer again.

When she'd checked in earlier, George was already down at the station extricating Hawkins from the mess of lies her mother was trying to drown him in. He'd told her everything was going well. There wouldn't be any problems, which had relieved her immensely, but it was going to take a little more time, which had made her nervous. She wanted him out of there, and she wanted the hell out of Big Jon Traynor's.

She didn't know where Alex and Skeeter and the man driving the Porsche had gone. They'd all roared by when her mother's limo had turned into the Traynors' driveway, and though she hadn't seen them since, an earlier call to Alex the last time she'd checked in with George had confirmed they were all out there, somewhere—and if she walked out the front door, someone would be there to pick her up.

It was the one solid, comforting thought she'd held on to every time Philip or Big Jon had leveled a glare in her direction.

She was going to have to disown her mother, if it worked like that, completely disavow any connection whatsoever. A name change would help, and in her heart of hearts, she had to secretly admit she was hoping for Katya Hawkins.

The Traynor mansion had over forty rooms spread across more than twenty thousand square feet. It was more of a small castle than a home. The house was old, so the rooms weren't large, but they did make a bit of a maze. After the maid pointed her in the right direction to the south wing, Katya went in search of the billiards room, certain she'd be able to find it. The house had been added on to over the years, with rooms stuck on rather at random. Though the stone front of the house had retained its architectural integrity, the back of the house was a labyrinth.

When she heard the sound of breaking balls, she followed it, thinking possibly one of the Traynors' other children might be home. Jonathan had been the oldest by far, but there had been six more after him.

She rounded the corner into the billiards room and stopped, surprised. The guy playing pool by himself couldn't possibly be a Traynor. He was too old for one thing, and he was an Army Ranger for another, if she believed the tattoo on his arm. No son of Big Jon Traynor would ever have joined the Army.

Then something about him struck her as familiar.

"Stuart?" she said, wondering what in the world Stuart Davis was doing in the Traynors' billiards room.

He jerked his head up, obviously startled, then a big grin spread across his face. "Katya."

Stuart had never been the brightest bulb in the basket, and it took him a couple of seconds to remember that the last time they'd actually been together was the night he'd torn off half her dress trying to run her down in the alley.

She hadn't forgotten, though, and it must have shown on her face, because after the initial smile of recognition, his face sobered.

"What are you doing here?"

"I was—uh—having lunch with the Traynors. Big Jon is my mother's new campaign manager."

"You're probably not supposed to be down here." He looked enormous in his fatigues, his biceps bulging out from under his olive green T-shirt, his chest huge, the whole way he held himself telling her he was nothing but solid muscle from his skull on down—which she was sure didn't bode all that well for her.

Suddenly, Philip didn't look nearly as suspicious as

she'd thought. Stuart, on the other hand, looked like he could kill people with his bare hands.

"Yes," she managed over the growing lump in her throat. "I'm...ah...sure you're right." She turned to leave and was thanking her lucky stars up until she got halfway back down the hall.

Another man stepped out of a side room, blocking the end of the hall and holding a cell phone up to his ear. "Yes, sir," the man said into the phone. "I've got her."

"Albert?" That made the afternoon complete—a complete and total unnerving disaster. She didn't know why Stuart Davis and Albert Thorpe were lurking around Big Jon's billiards room, or why she'd been sent down here, but she doubted if she had a phone call waiting, and she was smart enough to figure out none of this could mean her any good.

SKEETER didn't like the setup. Alex knew, because she told him as much about every five minutes, and they'd been staking out Big Jon Traynor's place for over two hours.

Kid Chaos didn't like the setup. Alex knew, because he told Skeeter as much through the earpiece of her radio about every fifteen minutes from where he was doing recon in back of the Traynor place.

"Kid doesn't like what he's seeing," she'd say.

"What's he seeing?"

"Not much. A couple of silhouettes moving inside."

Well, hell. He didn't like what he was seeing, either, which was *nada*. Katya was in the house and he was not, and it was damn hard to see inside a mausoleum like the

Traynor mansion when you were parked discreetly down the block, even if you were using the single-lens scope Skeeter was so generously sharing with him, but not generously enough.

Kid Chaos, Skeeter Bang, and Alex Zheng. Chaos, Bang, Zheng—hell, they sounded like a comic-strip fistfight, and in the case of Skeeter, she looked like a comic-strip hero, with her long platinum ponytail, her mirrored sunglasses, and her ball cap pulled low. Her muscles actually rippled under her skin. She wasn't overbuilt. She was just sleek, and then there were her breasts. Alex was not a breast man. He was gay. But she had beautiful breasts, and he'd noticed. He'd also noticed how much she smoked.

"That's about your hundredth cigarette," he said, eyeing the flimsy-looking thing she was sucking on. "Or have you switched to something else?"

"It's a cigarette," she assured him. "Mexican. I found them on Roxanne's dash, a pack of Faros."

"Roxanne?"

Skeeter patted the hood of the car they were sitting on.

Of course, Alex thought. Roxanne. He gave the car a once-over and couldn't fault the name. She did look like a Roxanne.

"How long until Hawkins gets here?"

Skeeter checked her watch, looked toward the end of the street, and said, "Five seconds."

Before he could voice a doubtful response, she was proven correct. A car turned onto the block and pulled to a stop behind them in about five seconds.

It was a helluva thing.

Hawkins got out of Francesca's car and walked around

to the front of Roxanne. He shook hands with Alex and gave Skeeter a quick one-armed hug.

"Fill me in."

"There's over a hundred people in the house," Skeeter said. "And they've been having lunch since about twelve-thirty. It's kind of hard to follow the action through all those little mullioned windows with the gauzy curtains, but Kid is doing a little better in the back, where the additions onto the house have bigger windows—and we've been warned off by the maid twice and the cops once."

"Anybody we know?"

"Yeah, Officer Sean Evans, so there hasn't been a problem since. I had him call Lieutenant Bradley."

Hawkins looked down the street, letting his gaze go over the windows of the Traynor mansion, methodically, one by one.

"Lunch, right?" he said to Skeeter.

"Right. With her mother and the campaign finance committee for the reelection of a United States senator in one of the cushiest neighborhoods this town has to offer. Very classy. Very upscale. Very privileged."

"So why does it feel so bad?" It wasn't a rhetorical question, and Skeeter knew it. She knew a lot of things. They never used her in ops, except as a communications coordinator or for stakeouts, but she'd started taking over the office very shortly after Hawkins had brought her in off the street a couple of years ago. He'd just wanted to give a spooky little wallbanger, a graffiti artist, a chance to regroup, a chance to take charge of her life. Instead, she'd started taking charge of theirs.

"Well, after you left, the old bat dragged out some photos of Clive Lennox and Wes Lake, the body shots. Used them for shock value. From the look on Katya's face when she saw them, I'd guess the senator only got about half of what she wanted."

"Meaning?" He barely got the word out around the sudden lump of fury lodged in his throat.

"Well, dead bodies are always shocking, and it can't be easy knowing somebody you love had a hand in it, because I can tell you, that picture of Clive has *not* improved with age."

"Don't fuck with me, Skeeter." Shit, pictures of Lennox and Lake. Fuck. And it wasn't the pictures he hated, it was the friggin' stories behind the pictures.

Shit.

"But Alex came to your defense rather succinctly, kind of gave her the facts-of-life speech, and she didn't dwell on it after I took the pictures away."

Hawkins took a long, deep breath, making a conscious effort to keep his hands relaxed at his sides. "I hate that woman."

"So even if absolutely nothing criminal is going on in there, I'm still seeing red flags everywhere. The very fact that, against all her wishes to the contrary, Katya Dekker has ended up back in her mother's sphere of influence means she is getting the life sucked out of her. Been there, done that, Hawkins. It's a weird cycle to break."

Okay. He'd asked; she'd delivered.

"What does Kid think?"

"Kid?" she said into her lip mike. She listened for a moment, then grinned. "Kid doesn't know what the fuck we're talking about. He just wants to know if we're gonna go in there and kick some ass today or not."

Hawkins let that scenario play out in his mind: he and

Kid doing a takedown in the Denver Country Club neighborhood, rescuing a bona fide debutante from the evil clutches of a senatorial campaign finance committee. Somehow the scene was lacking something—like any semblance of reality.

"Alex?"

"We are *not* going to launch an invasion and do some sort of takedown on the Traynor mansion. Nor are we going to kick anybody's ass," the Asian guy said, clearly appalled by the idea. "So just get those thoughts out of your head."

Hawkins slanted a look over at Alex. Hell, was he reading minds like Skeeter now?

"That said, I agree with Skeeter. Kat needs to be rescued. I can't believe she went with her mother to begin with, unless she was thinking that by cooperating, she could keep the heat off you. But Marilyn isn't the only one in there I don't trust."

"Who?"

"I think Philip Cunningham arrived with the last group. I couldn't get ahold of the scope at the time"—Alex shot an accusing look at Skeeter—"so it was hard to get a positive ID, but if it *was* him, I don't like it."

"Cunningham," Hawkins said, a cold thread of doom winding through his gut. "You would recognize him?"

Alex nodded. "Unlike all you street hoodlums, the Prom King boys have been easy to keep track of. Marilyn sends me an update about every six months or so, including recent photographs."

Hell, Hawkins thought. He should have spent a lot more time talking to Alex Zheng, instead of letting his proprietary instincts get the best of him.

"Do you know where Stuart Davis is?"

"Not since he left the Army. After his discharge, he sort of fell off the map."

"What about Albert Thorpe? We had an address for him in Maryland, but he said he was flying into Denver this morning and we'd arranged a meeting—which we obviously missed."

"Albert 'Birdy' Thorpe works for Jon Traynor, seldom leaves his side, so if Traynor is in there"—Alex pointed toward the mansion—"so is Albert."

"Skeeter?" Hawkins asked.

"I followed his paper trail to Maryland and a company named Western Armament Corporation," the girl said.

It took a second for the name to register in Hawkins's mind, but when it did, sheer, absolute dread washed through him. Western Armament Corporation was the name General Grant had given Dylan this morning. Someone who worked there had been responsible for getting him and Dylan pulled out of South America and assigned to Katya's garden party—and that someone was probably inside the Traynor mansion right now, with Katya.

"Traynor has the controlling interest in Western Armament, and a house in Maryland—big, like this one," Alex explained, solidifying all of Hawkins's worst fears. "It could be he writes off the house and the staff on Western's books."

Shit. The situation had all the earmarks of a total freaking disaster—with Katya in the middle of it.

"No takedown?" Hawkins asked, still preferring an out-and-out assault.

"No." Alex was adamant. "Discretion is the way to go on this one."

"So it's a one-man job," Hawkins said.

"One man," Alex concurred.

"One man." Skeeter nodded in agreement. "Superman."

CHAPTER
25

"ALBERT," KATYA SAID, swallowing back her fear. "How great to see you. I'm sorry we missed our appointment earlier this morning. My mother showed up in town, and I just didn't have time to call and cancel. I hope it didn't create too much inconvenience for you." Politeness, politeness, politeness—it was her only hope.

Out of all the boys she'd seen so far, Albert Thorpe had changed the least. He was still tall, dark, and blandly handsome, with blue eyes, an athlete's build, and a vacuous smile meant to charm.

Other than Bobby Hughes, though, Stuart Davis had changed the most, and Kat couldn't help but keep glancing over at him, just to keep him in her sights, in case, God forbid, he made a move for her. He was built like a lowland gorilla, and all she could think was *Steroids, Stuart?*

"It wasn't a problem," Albert assured her. "I was going

to change our meeting place to Big Jon's anyway. He wanted to see you again, and he can be very persuasive."

"Well, yes." She let out a breathless laugh. "I know my mother is hoping he'll persuade a few million dollars out of people in the coming months, quite a few million."

"Let's go back into the billiards room," Albert suggested. "I know Big Jon would like you to see his new Charles M. Russell paintings." He gestured for her to precede him, and Stuart led the way, the two of them effectively herding her back the way she'd come.

Inside the billiards room, Albert motioned toward the paintings.

"Big Jon loves all this Old West stuff." He gave an indulgent laugh. "I went to your gallery in L.A. once. You weren't there, but your collection was great. Truly superb. Not a Russell or a Remington in sight."

"Thank you," she said as politely as she could, considering that her heart was going about a million miles an hour. "So you work for Jon Traynor?"

Albert nodded. "I work for a military research service that's part of a multinational conglomerate in which Big Jon holds one helluva lot of stock. I do things for him on the side. He does things for me on the side. Together we're a good team, and we've both been waiting for justice for a long time."

"Justice?" That didn't sound good.

"We aren't going to hurt you, Katya," Albert said, dismissing her question, his smile doing anything but charm her. She wondered what her chances were for getting into the solarium without one of them getting her, or God forbid, Stuart tackling her. "But we needed to talk with you, needed to set a few things straight. And frankly, after Bobby called yesterday—"

"Bobby Hughes?" she interrupted. "Bobba-Ramma?"

"Yes," Albert confirmed. "After he called and said you were dragging a man around with you to all these little get-togethers you seemed so intent on organizing, we did some checking—and once again, prom queen, you have chosen the wrong side. What is it with you and the bad guys? The street scum murders Ted Garraty and you run off with him into the night? What kind of judgment is that? I know you struggled with math, Katya, but I always figured you had some natural intelligence somewhere inside your pretty little head. At least I did, until you shacked up with Christian Hawkins in the Brown Palace that summer, and now this?"

"This what?" she asked, buying time, she hoped.

"This running around with him all weekend," Albert said, clearly disgusted. "It just looks bad. Christian Hawkins murdered two of our friends, and he is going down. Now, if you're smart, you'll let him go down alone."

So Hawkins had been right: This whole thing was about framing him.

"And if I'm not smart?" Quite possibly, her mother had been right about being smart not suiting her. In this instance, it didn't suit her at all.

"You've seen the photographs Ted took. Hell, Kat, just how many millions of other people do you want to see those photographs?"

He was going to blackmail her with nude photos? Not bloody likely. Those eight-by-ten glossies might scare her mother, but they didn't scare her. They made her angry, had shocked and dismayed her, but they didn't scare her. She was an art dealer, for heaven's sake. If Albert released them to the media, she'd do one better and put them up for sale in her galleries as erotica. Maybe she'd even have Nikki McKinney do some of her gorgeous enhancements.

Nonetheless, there was one aspect of what he said that made her skin crawl. "Ted took the pictures?" The very thought was so disgusting, she feared she might be sick. Maybe she'd release them to the media herself, just to spread them around, lessen the onus of some perverted little Ted, dangling out some high-rise window somewhere, snapping photographs of her and Christian.

The more she thought about it, the better she liked the idea. She'd much rather the photographs were in the public domain than some deviant's dirty little secret.

"Yes, and had prints made for all of us." Albert let out a short laugh.

"Is that why Ted was killed? Because of something to do with the pictures?" She backed toward the door into the solarium, holding Albert's gaze with her own.

"I don't think so." A new voice entered the conversation, and Katya jerked her gaze away from Albert to see who it was.

"Philip," she gasped as she saw the man standing in the doorway to the billiards room, but Philip's gaze remained fixed on Albert.

"It didn't have anything to do with the pictures, did it, Birdy?"

Philip still looked awful. His face was flushed, and beads of sweat were forming on his brow, as if his tie were too tight. She could see his Adam's apple working in his skinny neck.

"I'm tapped out, Birdy," Philip continued, his voice distressed. "I can't do this anymore. I guess when we started, I thought we'd get to an end somewhere. But there's never going to be an end, is there? You'll just keep at me, until there's nothing left, and it won't matter anymore that Christian Hawkins took the fall and Manny the Mooch died a liar. That'll all be a waste, all that work, because you'll never get enough. You'll just keep at me."

"I don't know what you're talking about, Philip," Albert said, his brow furrowing in concern and confusion. "Maybe you should go back upstairs where you belong."

But Philip wasn't going anywhere. Whatever he was talking about, he was truly distraught.

"Was Ted trying to blackmail you? Was that it?" Philip asked.

"Hell, no," Stuart said. "He was gonna squeal about the girl."

Both men turned and looked at the ex-Ranger, who was looking damned fed up with all their wrangling.

"You idiot," Albert snarled.

The look of disgust slowly faded off Stuart's face, but Kat had heard enough, and she kept slowly inching herself closer to the solarium door.

WHAT'S the situation?" Hawkins whispered, sidling up to Kid in the dense foliage along the back of the Traynor estate.

"Two men going in and out of the solarium," Kid said, watching the back of the house through the scope on his sniper's rifle. "One of them is big, cut like he's juiced on steroids or something, a huge guy, and he's wearing BDUs, with a big old U.S. Army Ranger tattoo on his bicep."

Shit. Hawkins reached in his pocket for the lip mike and earpiece Skeeter had given him and slipped them on.

"Tell Alex I just found Stuart Davis," he said to Skeeter over the radio.

"The other guy is slick," Kid said, "wearing a suit, spending a lot of time on the phone. I can't follow them when they go back inside the main house. It's too damn dark in there, like a cave, but for the last two hours, it's just been them, wandering in and out of the swimming pool area, like they're waiting for something."

"Or someone."

Kid nodded and handed him the rifle. "They're inside now."

Hawkins checked the back of the house through the scope. He had about half a dozen doors to choose from to get inside, and two of them were open, including the one on the solarium, which told him no one inside was expecting any trouble.

"It'd be real easy to draw them out," Kid said.

And kick their asses. Hawkins finished Kid's thought for him.

"No. For all we know, they're harmless," he said, handing back the rifle. "Just a couple of guys who were once involved in a bad murder case visiting an old friend and hanging around the pool."

Kid snorted in disbelief, shouldered the rifle, and took another look. "No, they're not harmless. The Ranger is as twitchy as Skeeter on race day," he said, then winced and pulled his earpiece out real quick. After a couple of seconds, he put it back in. "Sorry, Skeet, but you know how you get."

"And the other guy?" Hawkins asked.

"The Ranger is looking for trouble, and the other guy is making it. This whole situation feels bad."

"Yeah. That's what I'm thinking," Hawkins said, wondering if he'd have better luck going through the front door and getting her, or sneaking in the back. "Skeeter grabbed the radio bag, but no flex cuffs. What have you got?"

Kid dug in his pocket and came up with a handful of condoms and three flex cuffs.

"Cherry-flavored?" Hawkins grinned, eyeing the prophylactics.

"Yeah." Kid grinned back, looking over and meeting his gaze for the first time, and at once, he sobered.

Hawkins did, too, feeling the same thing he suddenly saw on Kid's face, the agony of losing J.T.

"Skeeter didn't have to call you in on this. I guess I should have gotten back to you and told you to stay put."

"No," Kid said. "Keeping moving is the best thing for me. I'm good to go, but we need to talk."

"Let's get through this, then," he said.

Kid nodded. They both knew what they had to do.

"I'm going in alone for a sneak and peek," Hawkins told him. "If I get into trouble, you're the one I expect to rescue my ass."

Kid nodded again, and Hawkins moved out.

So did you kill Ted, Stuart?" Katya asked. "You're an Army Ranger. You probably know your way around a gun, especially one stolen off the Marine base at Quantico."

"You're trying to dig your own grave here, Katya," Albert warned. "The fingerprints on that gun belong to your boyfriend, Christian Hawkins. You'll have to ask him why he decided to murder Ted. The way we figure, he's coming after all of us who were there in the alley on prom night, and I can guarantee you, we're not going to let him gun us down one by one in whatever vigilante fervor he's gotten himself worked into. He's in jail now, and he's going to stay there. Christian Hawkins is not getting off this time. There'll be no pardon, no getting out. Case closed."

Katya ignored him, concentrating instead on Stuart, the weakest link in the three-man chain, though Philip seemed to have already crumbled. "What about Debbie Gold, Stuart? Did you kill her, too?"

"I don't know any Debbie Gold," the ex-Ranger said confidently, as if that alone absolved him from the crime.

"How about the Jane Doe hooker that summer? The one they found floating in the South Platte River?"

"Oh, no," Stuart said, backing up a step. "You're not pinning that on me. Birdy,"—he turned toward Albert—"you're supposed to fix this. That's why I've been doing all this stuff for you all these years, so's you could fix this. She was still breathing when I got off her, and she was dead when I put her in the river, I swear, or I never would have done it. Isn't that the story, Birdy?"

"Will you *shut up*!" Albert snapped at Stuart, then turned on Kat, his face clouded with fury. "I was hoping not to have to kill you, Katya, but you're not leaving me much choice."

Well, she sure as hell hadn't meant to force him into killing her, and as a matter of fact, she was pretty sure she hadn't.

"No, Birdy," Philip said, coming farther into the room. "The killing has got to end. Murdering Ted, that was just too much."

"I *didn't* kill Ted," Albert said, his voice dangerously low. "*Stuart* killed Ted."

"Only because you told me to kill him. A clean shot, that's what you said, and that's what you got."

"A clean shot?" Philip repeated, his voice sounding weak. "I gave you a clean shot once."

"Shut *up*, Philip." Albert was almost screaming now.

"Don't make it any worse on yourself than it already is, Albert," she said with more confidence than she felt. "We have an eyewitness who is willing to testify about the Debbie Gold murder. He saw all of you, what you did, how you did it, and where you threw her into the river." And didn't she just sound oh-so-cool, like she wasn't terrified down to the tips of her toes.

The longer she talked, the closer she was working her way toward the solarium door. If she could just get through it, she could lock them in the house, while she made a run through the backyard.

The locks on the solarium door worked both ways for a reason: in case someone wanted to do a little skinny-dipping in the pool without being interrupted. Everyone knew Big Jon did his laps naked every morning, and it had been bandied about the neighborhood more than once over the years that Big Jon really wasn't all that big.

"And this guy has—what?" Albert asked, his charming smile turning into a sneer. "Just been hanging around for thirteen years, waiting for some big break in the case, before he spilled his guts?" He didn't look in the least convinced. "I don't think so, Katya. There's no eyewitness, though I have to give you a couple of points for trying."

"Ray Carper," she said, edging behind a wing chair. "He says you killed Jonathan, too."

Stuart was actively stalking her across the billiards room now, his predatory instincts having been ignited by her cautious retreat. When she decided to go for it, she really was going to have to make her move fast. If Stuart got one of his meaty paws on her, he was going to break her clean in half.

"Ray who?" Albert asked.

"Carper," she repeated. "Ray Carper. He's the eyewitness, and he's in a room at a downtown hotel right now. You've got the nude photos; I've got Ray Carper. I'd say you'd be better off dealing with me rather than killing me. Think about it, Albert. If I end up dead at a luncheon put on by Big Jon Traynor, how long do you think my mother is going to let you continue to exist? I can guarantee you, she will go down in a ball of flames to avenge my death, and she'll take Big Jon, his family, his business, and everybody who's ever said a kind word about him down. It will be scorched-earth policy all the way, and when Ray Carper spills his guts, you and Stuart and Philip, and whoever else was involved in Jonathan's and Debbie Gold's murders are going to be destroyed, no matter what it takes. She will not consider nuances of guilt. She will wipe you all off the face of the earth. She will have you excommunicated, deported, discharged, and disbarred, and *then* she'll start getting mean." Kat had stopped moving, but she couldn't stop talking, and the

more she talked, the more something awful and wonderful and disturbing started taking hold of her inside. "My
mother will gut you with her bare hands, Albert. She's
terrible that way. You know she is. She will not rest, not
for one second of any day, until you have been annihi-
lated."

And it was true, Kat realized, painfully, terribly true.
Her mother would do all of those things, if Albert and
Stuart killed her.

And Albert knew it. She could tell by the look in his
eyes, which were nearly as disconcerted as hers felt.

"You'll wish you were dead long before she ships you
to hell. It'll be your worst nightmare, Albert, worse than
your worst nightmare."

He was thinking about it. She could tell. He was
weighing the whole big mess and trying to think his way
clear of it, and keeping his eye on Philip, who had gone
strangely silent.

Well, there was no way clear of it.

"No. She won't go that far," he said, but didn't sound
too sure about it. "Not even close. She stuck you in the
Brown Palace for your last few months of high school,
because she couldn't be bothered to stay in town or
maintain a home for you, and she shipped you off to the
loony bin in Paris after the trial. Tim told us when he
came back. He told us all about the Bettencourt School
for Girls. That it was a nuthouse, a very expensive nuthouse. I actually felt bad for you, Katya."

Albert was wrong about her mother, and maybe, so
help her God, maybe she'd been wrong, too, because she
knew in her heart that her mother *would* do her worst to
anyone who hurt her daughter. Look what she'd done to

Christian. What she was still trying to do to Christian. Marilyn was hell-bent on destroying him, because her mother loved her. Loved her with a passion Kat had never truly understood, and Marilyn believed Christian had hurt her.

All those terrible, awful things her mother had done to her all her life had come from love. It was so weird, but it was true. Kat knew it now deep in her heart. All the harassment, the embarrassing intrusions, the damn bodyguards, Alex, even the horrendously horrifying Bettencourt School—all from love. Brilliant, ambitious, fiercely competitive Harvard Law School alumna Marilyn Dekker, who appreciated nothing more than the nice solid accounting of a person's checkbook and status, had somehow been saddled with a child whose head never came out of the clouds, someone who failed at things, someone who didn't take being on top, being the best, nearly seriously enough to get anywhere in the world. Even worse, Kat *had* gotten somewhere in the world, in her world, but her world was so far outside Marilyn's, her mother didn't even recognize her success.

It all suddenly struck Kat as so sad, she knew she was going to cry, right there in front of three guys who she most definitely was *not* going to let get away with murder, hers or anyone else's.

"This is bullshit, Albert," Stuart said, backing off. "You're getting everything all screwed up again, just like you did with Jonathan."

"Shut *up*," Albert ground out between his teeth.

"No, man, I'm not gonna shut up," Stuart barked back. "You said that Hawkins dude was going to take the fall for Jonathan, and two years later you get him out, man, with that dumb confession you bought off some LoDo wino named Manny the Mooch. *Jesus*, Albert, you're always telling everybody how smart you are, but that was the dumbest thing I ever saw."

"He was getting out anyway, you idiot. Somebody was tearing the case wide open. Manny was how I got the case closed again, and I did it to cover your ass, too, Stuart, and yours, Philip. If the two of you had half a brain between you, you would understand."

"I've got more than enough brains to know who's the real idiot here, Albert, and it isn't me. I didn't kill Jonathan, you did, and that was real dumb, 'cuz no matter how freaked out he was by the bitch floating up in the river, he never would have squealed."

"No." Philip finally spoke up again. "Birdy didn't kill Jonathan. That was me. I shot him."

Katya couldn't believe what she was hearing. It literally made her head reel.

"You didn't shoot anybody, Philip," Albert sneered. "You didn't have the balls. I had to actually put the gun in your hand and help you squeeze the trigger. If you hadn't been so drunk, you would have known he was already dead from the heroin I'd shot him up with."

"But . . . but—" Philip sputtered.

"But I've blackmailed you for over half a million dollars for a crime you didn't even commit? Is that what you're trying to get out, Philip, old boy? Well, don't bother." Albert said, drawing a gun out from under his suit jacket. "You've all just become horrible liabilities I can no longer afford."

A strangled sound drew every gaze in the room to the door leading from the hall.

Oh, my God, Katya thought.

"You killed my son?" It was Big Jon, standing in the doorway, his face ashen, his hand over his heart. He was leaning on the jamb. "Birdy?"

Albert didn't hesitate. He swung the gun until it pointed straight at Big Jon Traynor.

HAWKINS heard the shot, then another, and everything inside him froze solid for one thousandth of a second, before he took off down the hall, running, his gun drawn.

"Jesus Christ, Albert!" somebody roared from inside the last room. A commotion started on the floor above, a lot of running feet.

As he turned the corner, Hawkins saw two men slumped on the floor in the last doorway. One was a big guy with a full head of white hair. The man lying over him was much thinner and had red hair. Hawkins didn't stop for a second, just stepped over the two bodies and entered the room low, with every cell in his body focused on his first shot—but there was no one inside. Then he saw a high-and-tight buzz cut peaking up from behind a billiards table.

"You're fucking nuts, Albert!" Stuart Davis yelled again.

Hawkins could see where a round had cut across the felt on the table. Albert was a lousy shot, and unless he'd managed a two-for-one, probably only one of the men behind him was hurt.

He heard a groan coming from the doorway and started to turn, but then came the wail.

"Katya!" A woman cried out amidst all the running feet

pounding down the stairs and getting closer. "Where's Katya?"

God, it was Marilyn Dekker, and she'd just delivered some very bad news. Katya wasn't with the rest of the lunch crowd.

He went for the ex-Ranger.

"Freeze, fucker," he said, jamming the Glock up against the back of Stuart's neck, right on the old brain stem. "Where's Katya Dekker?"

Stuart was smart enough to know what the word "freeze" meant. He went total mannequin. Hardly a breath escaped him, until he said, "Albert took her through the solarium."

Hawkins gave fleeting consideration to flex-cuffing the guy, but his instincts were screaming at him to find Kat. So he ran through the door into the pool area, and had just caught sight of her being dragged out the door on the other end, into the backyard, when he got hit by a locomotive.

His head bounced off the pool deck, and he slid into the water with two hundred pounds of ex-Ranger rhino on his back and the world going black.

Kid breathed softly through the chaos of the shot and the confusion, people running around inside the house, their shadows dancing across the curtains, their shouts carrying into the yard. Out of the corner of his eye, he'd seen Hawkins get hit and go into the water—but that would have to wait. There was only one thing to do now.

Only . . . one . . . thing—and he was breathing his way

into it. Settling his cheek against the stock, quieting his muscles, quieting his heartbeat, and lining up his shot.

He was only going to get one, and like every shot he took, it had to be perfect, a cold zero. His target had a struggling woman in his arms and a gun to her head.

It was the only truth Kid knew. It was the only one that mattered, and 2.5 pounds of pressure on the trigger later, the man's life left him in a vapor trail of pink blood and disintegrated flesh. A millisecond later, the shot sounded in the air.

But the man was already gone, his body crumpling to the ground, a clean hole right between his eyes.

KAT stood frozen in shock, unsure of what had happened. Albert had been dragging her along, swearing a blue streak at her, and then he'd suddenly been silent. His arms had loosened from around her.

She looked to the ground, saw him, but wasn't sure what she was seeing. Blood was pouring out of the back of his head, but it took a moment to register.

Then it hit her. Albert had been shot. He was dead. He'd shot Big Jon or Philip, she wasn't sure which, then turned to shoot Stuart, and now he was dead.

She looked up and saw a man with a rifle coming out of the bushes and trees at the far back of the yard, and for a second she feared she was next to be killed. But he ran on by her, going all out, his legs pumping, his face stark with some emotion she couldn't name. He didn't even glance at Albert, and yet she knew he was the one who had killed her would-be kidnapper.

When the man dropped his rifle on the ground, tore through the solarium door, and dove into the water, she started moving again, and much to her surprise, she moved toward him, slowly breaking into a run herself, until a sense of panic overtook her and forced her legs to move faster.

Even when she finally reached the solarium and saw the fierce struggle going on in the water, the blood, the thrashing bodies, she still wasn't sure what had driven her so hard to be there, until she noticed another body drifting toward the bottom of the pool.

Oh, God. Her heart stopped beating, but she didn't hesitate. She dove in, stroking hard for the bottom. Someone grabbed her foot and jerked her around. She kicked, hard, and felt her heel connect with something solid. Then she was free, and within moments she had her arms under Christian and was dragging him toward the surface.

He started coughing up water as soon as they broke into the air, and with a superhuman effort, she got him to the shallow end of the pool.

The fight in the water came to a sudden stop, with someone out in the middle of the pool yowling in pain. She looked, and it was Stuart, floating oddly, doing half a sidestroke toward the edge of the pool.

The man with the rifle broke free of the water and swam after Stuart, catching him at the pool deck. With a mighty heave, he helped the ex-Ranger get out of the water, but it cost Stuart dearly. He landed on the arm that was sticking out at an odd angle, and with a guttural groan, he passed out cold.

The younger man strong-armed himself out and jogged to the shallow end to help her get Christian out of the water. Christian had coughed all his water up, and was taking in deep gulps of air, but he wasn't moving much. He had a bloody gash on his forehead.

The three of them sat there for a moment, Katya cradling Christian's head in her lap, all of them catching their breath. The sound of a lot of people running and talking and yelling kept getting closer.

"Is he alive?" she finally asked, tilting her head toward Stuart, who hadn't moved.

"Yeah," the younger man said. He had dark hair and dark eyes. His face looked drawn and tired, and she wondered if he was okay. "I had to break his arm to slow him down, but he'll live."

She didn't know how. Stuart looked twice his size. Stuart's arms *were* twice this guy's size.

"You killed Albert." It might have been a stupid thing to say, but it was all she could think.

"Yeah," he agreed, again without much emotion. "I killed him."

"Kat," came a tired voice from her lap. "Kat, are you okay? Did he hurt you?"

"No," she said, turning her attention to Christian, meeting his gaze, and for a moment, the rest of the world drifted away, and it was just her and Christian—then all chaos descended. Half a dozen people poured into the solarium—Marilyn Dekker and Lily Beth Traynor, Marilyn's security guys, a couple of other men who had their guns drawn. Outside, a massive exodus was taking place across the side yard leading to the driveway.

That was the sensible thing to do when a person heard shots, Katya thought—run away. But her mother had run to her.

"Katya!" Marilyn cried, then fell on her knees beside them and embraced them both.

CHAPTER
26

IT WASN'T ENOUGH, Nikki thought. It was never going to be enough. She'd taken twenty-eight rolls of film of Kid over the last ten days, and it wasn't going to be enough.

She stood next to him under the hot summer sun, watching his brother's coffin being lowered into the ground. His father, Stavros, a large man with craggy features, was on Kid's other side, his face a canvas of devastation. Kid's mother, Jennifer, a pretty blond woman, was between her ex-husband and Kid's oldest brother, Damian, sobbing, an endless stream of tears running down her face.

Quinn and Regan were there, along with her grandfather, Wilson, and a lot of other people Nikki didn't know. The whole Chronopolous family had come to the cemetery after the funeral service, and there were dozens of aunts, uncles, and cousins. Some of the other men at the graveside worked at Steele Street, Regan had told her. Others had come from Washington, D.C., from the State Department and the Department of Defense. A few people were there in uniform, with all branches of the military and the Denver Police Department represented. One man in particular was impossible to miss: Creed Rivera, the man who had been with Kid's brother in Colombia. He'd been injured—tortured, Regan had whispered to her—and was only standing with the help of a cane and a friend. The strain of staying on his feet showed in the fierce tightness of his jaw and the trembling of his arms, but he refused to sit—not while J.T. was being laid to rest.

In an odd, disturbing way, he looked like Travis, except bigger, and street tough, like Travis might look if he'd done the things Regan had told her Creed Rivera had done, if he'd survived what Creed had survived. It all gave Nikki chills, because she knew Kid had done the same things.

Nikki hadn't seen Creed speak to anyone since he'd been brought to the church, not even to the man helping to keep him on his feet. He was strikingly beautiful, though, beautiful enough to paint, despite his bandages and bruises, but definitely rough-edged, the prettiness of his features mitigated by the hard mask of his face. His eyes were a pale blue-gray and absolutely cold, like arctic ice. His hair was streaked by the sun and tied back at the base of his neck.

She did know the man holding on to Creed. Regan had told her his name was Christian Hawkins. Nikki couldn't remember how or where they'd met, other than he must have been one of the juvenile car thieves sent to work in her grandfather's dinosaur digs so many years ago with Quinn, but she knew him. She knew him in her bones. She knew his tattoo. It came out from under the white cuffs of his shirt, darkly inked curves snaking onto the backs of his hands, and every time she glimpsed it, a frisson of recognition went through her.

She'd have to ask him about it, but not today. Today it was all she could do to hold herself together.

Kid was leaving her.

She wiped her palms on her skirt for about the hundredth time and forced herself not to ball the material up in her hands. It had been like that for her all day—damp palms, tight nerves, moments when she couldn't catch her breath—and it had all started this morning, when she'd awakened to the sound of Kid cleaning his weapons.

Her studio kitchen table had been covered in guns, a rifle, assault weapons, two handguns, all of them broken down into pieces, and he'd been going over every piece with a soft cotton cloth. He'd been to Steele Street the night before, and the heavy duffel bag lying open at his feet had been full of ammunition of every size and grade.

He was a warrior, and he was going to war. The knowledge had hit her like a blow.

It wasn't personal revenge, he'd promised her. He had a job to do, a government mission to bring his brother's murderers to justice. He'd have a partner, Christian Hawkins, going with him, and everything was going to be fine. He'd be home in a few weeks, he promised.

But he'd lied. Every word had been a lie. She knew it, even if he didn't. She'd done nothing but watch him since he'd walked back into her life. She knew the driving force behind his long silences—and it wasn't justice. It was vengeance.

It invaded his dreams and spoke to her in his sleep—the crying out of J.T.'s name, a pained groan that curled him in upon himself and shut her out, the deep sadness that flooded his gaze every morning when he awoke.

She loved him. He was like breath and beauty and life—and every fiber of his being was intent on death.

His hand tightened around her shoulders as the first shovelful of dirt hit the coffin, and she wanted to sob with the heartbreaking sadness of it all, knowing all they'd had left to bury was J.T.'s charred bones—bones Kid had brought home.

As the grave was filled, people began wandering back to their cars, the crowd thinning, until only the men from Steele Street were left talking quietly in a group. Two of them, her brother-in-law, Quinn Younger, and Dylan Hart, broke away after a few minutes.

Christian Hawkins looked up and caught Kid's gaze, and in that instant Nikki knew it was over. He wasn't just leaving her. He was leaving her *now*.

"Kid" was all she got out, before her voice failed her. She wasn't ready for this, for being without him.

"It's all right, Nikki," he said, turning her into his arms, holding her, pressing a kiss to the top of her head. He lifted her face and kissed her mouth, once, twice, then whispered in her ear, his voice rough with emotion. "Being with you . . . it's not like anything I've ever known, Nikki. I love you. I know I've told you that about a thousand times. But it's true, and nothing's going to keep me from coming back."

She wanted to believe him, with all her heart she wanted to believe him, but as he walked away, she knew it would be a miracle if he survived in South America, and a miracle if she survived without him.

IT WAS ANOTHER perfect day in a South Pacific paradise. A blue green sea stretching to the horizon, the soft froth of breakers crashing into the island's surrounding reef, the silence broken only by the distant sound of birds.

Hawkins lay half asleep on the double chaise longue sitting on the end of a dock that stretched thirty yards out into the lagoon. A thatched tiki roof cast him and Mrs. Christian Hawkins in a pool of shade, a cool pool of gray amidst the blazing splendor of sea and sky.

Mrs. Christian Hawkins. He liked it. He liked it a lot.

There had been times these last two months when he'd wondered if he was going to make it to this point. Times when he and Kid had pushed too hard, taken too many chances. They'd gone back to Colombia within days of finishing up the Prom King murder mess. Albert was the only one who had died that day at the Traynor mansion. Stuart was in jail awaiting trial, and Philip was out on bail while the judicial system and his lawyers tried to figure out precisely which crimes he'd committed, and which ones had been committed against him. Big Jon Traynor had survived being shot but, according to Marilyn, was struggling with the truth of having employed Jonathan's murderer for thirteen years.

Those problems seemed miles away with the trade winds gently blowing through their bungalow.

Katya had hated for him to leave her for the job in Colombia. She'd cried salty sweet tears all over him for days, but in the end, she'd let him go with hardly a sniffle.

Not so Nikki McKinney. She'd been almost frantic by the time they'd left, which had only made it that much harder on Kid. Hawkins understood. Nikki was young, barely twenty-one, artistic by nature and spoiled by design, and she hadn't done well with the thought of Kid leaving again.

A lot of that had to do with Kid. Hawkins had been going to do a job, to honor his friend. Kid had been filled with far more powerful motivations, far more dangerous needs.

Hell, he was still filled with them. Hawkins didn't know when Kid would get enough and come home—which must have been Nikki's fear.

It had been hard, and fast, and dirty, what they'd done. He'd known what it was going to be like going in, and he'd had no regrets coming out. Sometimes the world was a hard place, and in those places, only hard men survived—and even they didn't always make it.

J.T. hadn't, and neither had the hard men who had tortured and killed him—all except for two.

Two of the bastards had gotten away.

Creed had recovered enough to replace him, and Creed and Kid were still after the last two rebels. Creed had needed to go and be part of it. Hawkins understood that. He understood it better than his own need, which had been to leave and get back to Katya. He'd always been the last man standing, the last one to leave a bad situation—but not now. She'd been a siren lure, and toward the end, getting back to her had become more important than getting the job done—which had been his wake-up call to get the hell out of Colombia, before he got himself or Kid killed.

Creed was fresh, though, fresh and running on the bloodlust of revenge. Hawkins didn't pity the poor bastard guerrillas when they caught them—and they would catch them. Neither Creed nor Kid knew the meaning of the word quit.

He'd been learning it, though, been thinking about it a lot—quitting. He had enough money for him and Kat to get by for a few years, or even longer, depending on how they decided to live. Katya still had the galleries, and he could see himself in the art world. He loved art, had a collector's appreciation that could be honed into something more.

And if he never slit another throat, he wouldn't miss it—which was not exactly what he wanted to be thinking about on such a totally excellent day.

"So, naturally, I agreed with the old guy," he said, picking up a conversation they'd sort of let drift off. It was one of the luxuries of being with her in this place, letting things drift off, picking them up later, with no one else getting in the way of their stream-of-consciousness honeymoon. "A man's got *no* use for a woman, I told him.

None." Belying his own words, he rolled onto his side and licked his way up her rib cage to under her arm, stopped to tickle her with his tongue, then continued on down to her elbow. She tasted like saltwater and coconut oil. She smelled good enough to eat.

She giggled when he tickled her. God, how he loved that sound.

"Did you tell him you practically had me tied naked to the chaise longue out here in this little thatched hut on the dock?"

"No." He nibbled his way down to her wrist. "There aren't that many women on the island. I think it's better if the old geezer figures he doesn't need one."

"That's the last time I let you go into town for a six-pack on your own. You just get up to mischief."

"Town?" He laughed. "Honey, it's a dive shack and a pop stand. Oh, God, will you look at the time? Three o'clock."

"Christian," she said with a laugh. "My temperature was *not* up this morning."

"Well, *mine* was. Now where's that sexual device?" He looked over the side of the chaise longue, hoping to hell it hadn't fallen in the water. That was the thing about living in a little thatched hut on a dock out in the middle of a lagoon. Everything ended up in the water.

"Sexual device?" she queried with a lift of her brow. "You mean the pillow?"

"Aha." He found it underneath her sarong. "Lift up."

She did, and he shoved it under her very pretty, bikini-clad bottom. Then he untied the two sides of her bikini. She was already topless.

"I don't have to elevate my pelvis until afterward."

"That's what you think." He grinned, already kissing his way down the smooth, satiny skin of her belly.

She was ripe for this, for making a baby. He knew, just like he knew so many things about her, and the more he knew, the more fascinated he became.

He took his time, teasing her, before he slid his tongue into those soft, sweet folds that simply drove him crazy every time he touched her. She instantly tightened beneath him, then melted back onto the pillow with a little moan of pleasure.

Damn, he was good at this, and that gave him absolute boatloads of pleasure. Pleasing her had become his favorite pastime.

"Christian?"

"Hmmm?"

"This isn't how you make a baby." Her voice was so soft and breathless, yet serious. Sweet thing, she was giving him advice.

He lifted his head. "Yes, it is, honey. This is how you make a boy baby," he said, then went back to doing what he did so very well, thank you, and she lifted her hips ever so slightly for him. He loved reading her: *to the left, Christian, please, up, down, oh, right there, Christian ... yes ... yes ... yes.* He loved following all her little hints and silent directions, listening to her body language and following the path she wove into her own pleasure. He loved being the instigator of it all, the catalyst.

"With your tongue?"

Of course with his tongue, he thought. Everything with his tongue. His tongue had been made for exploring her.

Then he remembered the subject under discussion,

and lifted his head again. Honestly, how they were going to get anywhere with all these interruptions was beyond him.

"It's in the book, Kat. Haven't you been reading the book?"

She giggled, which he took as a no.

"Step One," he said. "Bring the woman to orgasm, which will change the pH of all her most lovely secret places. That's where we're at right now, the middle of Step One."

She just grinned at him, obviously *not* taking all of this nearly seriously enough.

"Step Two, proceed to intercourse." He crawled up her body, balancing himself on the chaise. "Step Three, continue intercourse until ejaculation. That's my part." He leaned down and kissed her, long, slow, wet, and deep. Then he kissed her again, short and sweet. "Thanks to you, I think I'm getting pretty good at my part."

She laughed again, and he truly had to wonder when sex had gotten so damn funny—but he was grinning while he wondered.

"Step Four, don't let the woman move for at least half an hour. May elevate pelvis if so desired."

"Do you want a boy, Christian?" she asked, more serious now.

"Boy, girl, it doesn't matter to me." He leaned back down and kissed her nose, licked her lips, and whispered, "I just like making you come."

She looked up at him, her eyes all dreamy with love, and for a second he felt struck through the heart, the emotions he felt for her like a breath caught in his throat.

"Kat?"

"Hmmm?"

"I love you, Kat."

"You already said that today," she murmured. "This morning at breakfast, and again at lunch, and twice over pineapple snacks."

"Yeah, I know, but this time I mean it. I really mean it." And he did, with all his heart, and he needed her to know it, to believe it as strongly as he did.

"That's what you said yesterday."

"I know, but this time it's different, Kat. I swear. This time it's like sunlight on your skin." He reached over the side of the chaise and picked up the bottle of coconut oil. "This time it's like the ocean flowing through your veins."

He saw the dreaminess disappear from her eyes, saw her gaze narrow in concern. He didn't care. He was heedless. He was in love, and he went ahead and popped the top on the bottle.

He looked down the length of her body, all those curves just running into each other and taking off again. It was enough to drive any man crazy with love.

"Christian," she warned.

"This time it's like the tides, Kat. Inevitable." He slowly upended the bottle and squeezed a small stream of oil over her breasts, down her torso, onto her legs, back up between her legs.

"Christian . . . honey." She wrapped her hand around the arm of the chaise. "The last time you went crazy with the coconut oil, you slid off me into the water."

"I know, but this time it'll be different."

"You mean like the day before, when we both slid in like a couple of greased pigs and could hardly get back up on the dock?"

"Yeah." He grinned and squeezed on another layer, because he loved the way it smelled on her, loved the way it felt on her, loved the way it felt on him when he was inside her. "It's so sexy when you say greased pigs."

She fought a grin—and lost, fought a laugh, and lost that one, too. "You know you're going to hurt yourself, don't you? If you don't get this coconut oil thing under control?"

"Don't worry, babe," he assured her, a very confident smile on his face. "I can handle coconut oil. I'm Superman."

Oh, yeah, Kat thought, when he finally slipped inside her, filled her. He was Superman.

ABOUT THE AUTHOR

Of a mind that love *truly* is what makes the world go 'round, Tara Janzen can be contacted at www.tarajanzen.com.

Happy reading!

Don't miss
Quinn Younger's story in . . .

Crazy Hot

Now on sale

Read on for a preview

Coming soon . . .

Crazy Wild
Creed Rivera's story
on sale February 2006

Crazy Kisses
Kid Chronopolous's story
on sale March 2006

THE MISSION:

CRAZY HOT

TARA JANZEN

CRAZY HOT

Now on sale

NOTHING MOVED in the shimmering heat.

Good God, Regan McKinney thought, staring over the top of her steering wheel at the most desolate, dust-blown, fly-bit excuse for a town she'd ever seen. The place looked deserted. She hadn't seen another car since she'd left the interstate near the Utah/Colorado border, and that had been a long, hot hour ago.

CISCO, the sign at the side of the road said, confirming her worst fear: She'd found the place she'd been looking for, and there wasn't a damn thing in it. Unless a person was willing to count a broken-down gas station with ancient, dried-out pumps, five run-down shacks with their windows blown out, and one dilapidated barn as "something."

She wasn't sure if she should or not. Neither was she sure she wanted to meet anybody who might be living in such a place, but that was exactly what she'd come to do: to find a man named Quinn Younger and drag him back to Boulder, Colorado.

Quinn Younger was the only lead she had left in her grandfather's disappearance, and if he knew anything, she was going to make damn sure he told the Boulder Police. The police never had believed that Dr. Wilson McKinney had disappeared. Since his retirement from the University of Colorado in Boulder, he'd made a habit of spending his summers moseying around the badlands of the western United States, and according to the results of their investigation, this year was no different.

But it was different. This year Wilson hadn't checked in with her from Vernal or Grand Junction, the way he always did, and he hadn't arrived in Casper, Wyoming, on schedule. She'd checked. It was true he was a bit absentminded, but he'd never gone two weeks without calling home, and he would never, ever have missed his speaking engagement at the Tate Museum in Casper.

Never.

He loved nothing better than to rattle on about dinosaur fossil beds to a captive audience and get paid for doing it. At seventy-two, nothing could have kept Wilson from his moment of glory—nothing except some kind of trouble.

Quinn Younger, she mused, looking over the collection of broken-down buildings. Sheets of tar paper flapped on every outside wall, loosened by the wind. Half the shingles on the roofs had been blown off. The two vehicles parked in front of the gas station were ancient. Over fifty years old, she'd bet—a pickup truck with four flat tires, and some kind of rusted-out black sedan up on blocks.

If Quinn Younger did live in Cisco, he was stuck there, and nothing could have made less sense. He was a former Air Force pilot, for God's sake, a national hero. He'd been shot down over northern Iraq enforcing a no-fly zone and made the covers of *Time* magazine and *Newsweek,* and the front page of every major newspaper in America. His survival behind enemy lines and daring rescue by the Marines had become the stuff of contemporary legend. He was a one-man recruitment poster for the United States military.

Not a bad turnabout for someone who at sixteen had been on a fast track to juvenile hall and probably the state penitentiary, until a judge had put him in her grandfather's field crew for a summer of hard labor digging up dinosaur bones. Wilson had been damn proud of the young man, one of the first to be pulled off the streets and out of the courts of Denver and given a second chance with him. Outlaws all, Wilson had called that first crew of boys, but over that long, hot summer, he'd begun the process of turning outlaws into men—and at least in Quinn Younger's instance, he'd felt he'd succeeded.

Regan wasn't so sure. Not anymore. She'd met Quinn Younger once that summer, if one awkward encounter constituted a meeting, and despite his subsequent rise to fame and glory, the image of him as a shaggy-haired sixteen-year-old car thief with coolly assessing eyes and a slyly artful grin was the image lodged in her brain. Looking at Cisco did little to change the impression. Neither did the cryptic entry she'd found written on her grandfather's desk calendar, the entry with Quinn Younger's name in it that had brought her to this nowhere spot in the road in Utah.

With an exasperated sigh, she returned her attention to the buildings. The town was eerie, damned eerie, but she'd come a long way, and the least she had to do was check the place out. If Wilson or Quinn Younger was there, or had been there, she was going to know it before she left.

Ignoring her unease and a good portion of her common sense, she put the car in gear and pulled back onto the road, heading for the gas station.

SHE'S stopped in front of Burt's old place," Peter "Kid" Chronopolous said, looking through his scope.

Quinn glanced up from under the hood of the '69 Camaro parked in the barn and wiped the back of his hand across his mouth. "Stopped?"

All kinds of people drove by Cisco. Every now and then somebody pulled over to the side of the road and got out their map to figure out where in the hell they'd gone wrong. Damn few people pulled into town and stopped—with good reason. Out of the seven buildings still standing, not a one of them looked anything less than forbiddingly deserted. Other than the shop and living space the SDF team had built into the barn to use as a safe house, the buildings were deserted.

"Yep." Kid's gaze was still trained on the gas station through the scope. "And now she's getting out and going in." The younger man's voice stayed calm and steady, but Quinn sensed his heightened sense of readiness. Most lost tourists, especially lost *women* tourists, would not go wandering into Burt's place. Most, however, wasn't all, and Quinn wasn't inclined to jump to conclusions. Not one damn thing had happened in Cisco in the two weeks he and Kid had been stuck there. A woman in Burt's didn't mean their luck was changing or that the action was picking up, not by his standards.

"Take her picture and send it through the computer," he said, returning his attention to the Camaro's engine. The car was barely street legal as it was. Changing out the pulleys to work with the boost had pushed it right to the edge. Kid could have his fancy Porsche. Quinn was putting his quarter-mile money on the Chevy.

"I'm on it, but I think you better take a look," Kid warned.

Quinn lifted his head again, looking over the engine at the twenty-three-year-old ex-Marine. Kid—who for numerous reasons was also known as "Kid Chaos"—was the newest member of SDF and he was definitely jazzed. His eye was glued to the scope; his body was tense and alert. Of course, the boy had been roughing it with Quinn since the middle of June. Possibly it was merely the sight of a woman, any woman, that had gotten his juices going.

Or maybe Roper Jones, the man currently at the top of General Grant's Most Wanted list, had tracked them down.

Setting aside his wrench, Quinn straightened up from under the hood, testing his left leg before trusting it to completely hold his weight. He limped across the shop floor and turned on the laptop Kid had rigged up to half a dozen cameras around Cisco.

Despite a serious addiction to fast cars, extreme sports, and general mayhem, Kid was a certifiable electronics wizard—an electronics wizard with way too much time on his hands since they'd been holed up in the desert, waiting for the heat to die down in Denver. Kid had wired the ghost town to within an inch of its life for twenty-four/seven surveillance. Getting hurt in their line of work came with a few interesting consequences, the least of which was Kid watching over him like a mother hen, and if lately Quinn had been feeling like he'd washed up on the wrong side of thirty with not much to show for it but a friggin' barn to live in and a busted leg, well, he had no one but himself to blame. He'd made some bad choices—especially that last damn choice he'd made in the rail yards on the west side of Denver when he'd gone up against Roper and his goons.

Quinn typed in a couple of commands, activating the cameras in the buildings. When the camera in Burt's came on, the image of a woman filled the screen.

His brow furrowed. The only female assassin he'd ever seen had been sleekly fit and buffed on steroids. She'd also moved with the prowling gait of a hungry panther. Not this woman. She was randomly picking her way through the dust and the tumbleweeds inside the gas station, peering over countertops and around half-fallen beams. A broken chair caught her unawares in the shin, and she swore under her breath.

Colorful, Quinn thought, his lips twitching in a brief grin. *Definitely lost tourist material*.

No trained hunter would swear because of a measly shin hit. No truly trained hunter would have run into the chair in the first place. After rubbing her leg, she continued on, looking around with curiosity and caution, but not with deadly focus—and not with a weapon in her hand or visible anywhere on her body.

In short, she did not look like a killing machine. What she looked like was a schoolteacher—the luxury model. And oddly, to someone who didn't know many schoolteacher types, she looked faintly familiar.

Her honey blond hair was piled into a ponytail on the top of her head, but a lot of silky swaths had tumbled back down, giving her a mussed-up, just-out-of-bed look. She wore a soft-looking lavender shirt and a pair of jeans, both of which appeared to be standard mall issue, and both of which revealed a perfectly average, if decidedly nice, and very nicely endowed, female form.

Plenty there for Kid to get excited about, Quinn thought. Maybe even something there for he himself to get excited about, if he'd been in the market for that kind of excitement, which he wasn't. The only female in Cisco that Quinn was interested in fooling around with was the one he'd named Jeanette, she with the supercharged 383 LT1 stroker under her hood. The smartest move the woman in Burt's could make would be to get back in her car and get out of town.

"Have you got that picture yet?" he asked Kid, who had moved to the computer in the back of the shop.

"Running it through now, Captain."

Quinn let the rank slide, though he hadn't been a captain since a surface-to-air missile had taken him and his F-16 out over northern Iraq. Still, he had been a captain in the U.S. Air Force for a hell of a lot longer than he'd been a cripple holed up in Cisco.

Two weeks. *Shit*.

Dylan Hart, his boss at SDF, couldn't expect him to lie low forever. Quinn could only take so much sitting around listening to the wind blow through this nowhere town—Roper Jones was still out there, and Quinn needed to be out there, too. He needed to be back in the game.

He rolled his shoulder. It was healing. His leg half-worked. And he had a fucking vendetta with Roper Jones's name written all over it.

On the screen, the woman picked up a dusty pile of papers and looked them over, giving him a better view of her face. She was fine featured, with a dusting of freckles across her nose. She was pretty in a quirky way, not elegant, but cute, her eyebrows surprisingly dark in contrast with her hair. Her chin was delicately angled, but definitely set with determination. Her eyes were light, the color indiscernible on the screen. At odds with her all-American looks, her mouth was lush, exotically full, and covered with a smooth layer of plum-colored lipstick.

Okay. She was nice. Very nice.

The whole package was nice.

"Not a known felon," Kid said from the back of the shop.

Quinn absently nodded. He would have been damned surprised if the woman's picture had matched that of a known criminal, especially given the kind of wiseguys in Kid's current files.

"Try the official database," he said, knowing it was another long shot. Despite his niggling sense of familiarity, the chances of the woman in Burt's being part of an officially sanctioned U.S. government service were exceedingly damn low. And she sure as hell didn't belong to SDF, the very *unofficially* sanctioned group of Special Forces operators that he and Kid were part of. General Grant, the two-star who deployed them, would never hire a woman for fieldwork.

"Already on it," Kid confirmed.

Quinn kept his gaze glued to the woman. Where in the hell, he wondered, had he seen her? He didn't forget faces. He didn't dare, and he knew hers.

Or had known her.

"*Son of a bitch,*" Kid swore behind him,

showing more emotion in the one small phrase than he had in the whole two weeks they'd been camped out in the desert.

"You've got a match?"

"No, but it looks like we've got more company," Kid said, striding back toward the scope.

Quinn looked through the far window and saw what Kid had seen, a blue SUV coming off the top of a rise in the highway—and slowing down, way down.

"Two men, no visible weapons, but they don't look happy," Kid said from his position at the scope. Quinn watched him quickly scan the rest of the horizon and come back to the SUV. "They're checking out the woman's Ford . . . and . . . they're . . . well, hell. They're heading out of Cisco. What do you make of that?"

"A coincidence? Or maybe Cisco has just gotten real friggin' popular." Quinn limped back to the Camaro and picked up the Beretta 9mm he always kept close by.

"Maybe" was all Kid conceded as he checked the load on his rifle, a highly "accurized" sniper's M10.

Quinn and Kid weren't getting paid to take chances. Not today. *Keep your heads down and don't get your asses shot off* had been Dylan's orders. A couple of weeks ago, when his body had still been pretty messed up, Quinn had been willing to follow orders. But he was mobile now. His stitches were out, and he was ready to get back to the job of taking Roper Jones down. If the unhappy guys in the four-wheel drive were part of that job, great. He just had to get Little Miss Tourist out of the way.

Damn. In about five minutes, if she was an innocent civilian looking for ghost town junk, she was going to wish she'd driven right on by Burt's old place and Cisco. What he didn't like to think about was that niggling sense of familiarity and the possibility that what she was looking for was him—though God knew how a woman could have tracked him down in Cisco. Or why.

"Call Denver," he said to Kid. "Tell them we've got company. I'll get the woman."

"No," Kid insisted, quickly coming around the desk at the back of the shop. "I'll get her. You . . . uh, should be the one to call."

Quinn narrowed his gaze at the young-er man and was gratified to see him falter just a bit. It took a lot to make Kid Chaos falter.

"What I mean is, Dylan would rather hear the . . . uh, details of the operation from you . . . I'm sure." Kid didn't sound too damn sure to Quinn.

"Dylan's in Washington, D.C., and we don't have an operation yet," Quinn explained. "Skeeter's holding down the fort back at head-quarters."

"Well, see, there you have it." Kid kept moving toward the door, each step slower than the last, until he finally came to a complete stop under Quinn's unwavering gaze.

Quinn knew the distance between the barn and the gas station. A hundred yards. "I can handle it."

Kid didn't look convinced. "Maybe she's a decoy. Roper Jones is not going to give up, Quinn. Not until you're dead or Hawkins gets him."

"Roper Jones is not stumbling around in Burt's Gas Emporium. A woman is, and I'm pretty damn sure we better find out why."

With a reluctant nod, Kid finally agreed.

Quinn turned toward the door, slipping the Beretta under his shirt and into the waistband of his jeans. Hell. He wasn't making it easy for Kid to play bodyguard.

Bodyguard. Christ. He'd always been his own damn bodyguard, and done a damn good job of it—up until two weeks ago in those West Side rail yards.

The memory gave him an instant's pause.

Okay, he admitted. The Roper Jones heist had gone down bad, real bad, and Hawkins had literally had to scrape him off that friggin' back alley, but they'd gotten what they'd been after that night and he was healed now. He was ready to get back in the game. More than ready.

He slanted the computer screen a quick

glance as he passed by. Plum lipstick. Lavender shirt. Golden ponytail.

Hell. She didn't look like she was ready to get in the game. She didn't look like she'd ever even heard of the game. Ready or not, though, she was about to get her first taste of it.